ADVANCE PRAISE FOR BASEBALL DADS

"Sex, drugs, blackmail, and little-league baseball. Matthew S. Hiley takes readers on a dark, twisted, and hilarious journey into the perilous world of parenting with *Baseball Dads*. This motherfu**er is a homerun!"

—Brandon Christopher, author of *The Job Pirate*

"From *Casey at the Bat* to the *Bad News Bears* and *Bull Durham*, there's a long tradition of baseball, humor, and telling insight into the psyches and psychoses that fuel what many of us still consider the national pastime. With laughs and diamond-sharp observation on every page, Matthew Hiley's *Baseball Dads* is a worthy addition to the short list of great baseball tales."

—Chuck Thompson, former features editor for *Maxim* and author of *Better Off Without 'Em: A Northern Manifesto for Southern Secession*

"*Baseball Dads* is a story any parent who has survived little league baseball will find insightful and cathartic. Not to mention funny."

—Boyd Taylor, author of *The Hero of San Jacinto*

BASE
BALL
DADS

MATTHEW S. HILEY

BASE

BALL

Sex. Drugs. Murder. Children's baseball.

DADS

GREENLEAF
BOOK GROUP PRESS

Published by Greenleaf Book Group Press
Austin, Texas
www.gbgpress.com

Distributed by Greenleaf Book Group

For ordering information or special discounts for bulk purchases, please contact Greenleaf Book Group at PO Box 91869, Austin, TX 78709, 512.891.6100.

Design and composition by Greenleaf Book Group
Cover design by Greenleaf Book Group
Cover image credit: ©Shutterstock.com/Davydenko Yuliia

Publisher's Cataloging-in-Publication Data is available.

ISBN: 978-1-62634-203-3

Part of the Tree Neutral® program, which offsets the number of trees consumed in the production and printing of this book by taking proactive steps, such as planting trees in direct proportion to the number of trees used: www.treeneutral.com

TreeNeutral®

Printed in the United States of America on acid-free paper

15 16 17 18 19 20   10 9 8 7 6 5 4 3 2 1

First Edition

Other Edition(s):
eBook ISBN: 978-1-62634-204-0

*This book is dedicated to the men and women
who raise their children properly . . .*

*It is also dedicated to my lovely wife,
who puts up with my insanity on a daily basis,
and my children, for whom I will hoist
the black flag and slit throats any day . . .*

*Lastly, if you are a pretentious turd who
feigns outrage at the drop of a hat, please
take this book and plant it firmly in your anus.
I wrote this book about you, not for you,
so kindly be on your way . . .*

Let the adventure begin . . .

Every normal man must be tempted,
at times, to spit on his hands,
hoist the black flag,
and begin slitting throats.

H. L. MENCKEN

1.

"JESUS TAP-DANCING CHRIST, UMP! IS HE PAYING YOU ON THE SIDE? DID YOU FORGET YOUR ANTIPSYCHOTIC MEDS TODAY? MY BOY WAS SAFE, GODDAMMIT! GET YOUR GOD-DAMN VISION CHECKED!"

Russ Paisley was at the end of his tightly strung rope from horrible calls by the head umpire, Dave, at Jenny Field. Jenny Field was the swankiest little league ballpark in Fort Worth, Texas. If you lived in Fort Worth and belonged to high society, then your kids damn sure better have played baseball at Jenny Field if they didn't want the shit beat out of them in the cafeteria every day.

Dave the umpire was a familiar and imposing figure at the ballpark. He had thin, dirty-blond hair tucked under a black ball cap, stood about six feet four inches tall, and weighed in around 250 pounds. Tattoos covered his forearms, and a snarl was smeared across his pock-marked, unshaven face. Dave loved the power that he held over the snooty, upper-crust families while they were in his arena. He never hesitated to display that power.

Dave rushed to the fence where Russ was standing. Dust flew up behind him in the wind as he approached. He got to where their noses were so close that only a single chain link in the fence separated them. Dave stared down at Russ, who was only about five feet nine inches tall.

"I won't hesitate to throw your monkey-ass outta here, Russ," Dave growled down to him. "It's Friday night. Been a long week. Don't push me."

Russ held his gaze until Dave turned and walked back to home plate. Both of their faces were beet red. Russ had obviously not forgot-ten to take his daily coke bumps that day. He kicked the fence before returning to the outfield side of the dugout, where he and the rest of his crew watched the game. They were the *true* baseball dads on the team—the guys who never sat down, never went to take a leak, never went to the concession stand.

They stood there intensely, with their fingers tightly gripping the railing along the top of the chain-link fence. They drank from their water jugs, spat sunflower seeds, and bitched about how much better the team would be doing if they were coaching.

"Great," Russ muttered to the others. "Three goddamn outs again. This coach is a goddamn joke. And where's he gonna send my kid now? Right fucking field. And your kid, Dwayne? Left fucking field. This is absurd. Meanwhile, his kid is about six goddamn inches from being a full-blown retard, and he sticks him at shortstop."

Russ had no time for Dave the umpire, and even less for Coach Ricky Dale, with his permanent shit-eating, bleached-white grin and leathery tan skin. He'd taken control of the baseball operation at Jenny Field, calling most of the shots via major monetary donations. Many of the outfield signs were advertisements for Ricky Dale Furniture, his wildly successful string of inexpensive rent-to-own furniture stores.

Russ was about to blow a gasket as he watched the time expire on the game clock. They were headed toward yet another huge loss.

"Goddamn daddy baseball," he grunted.

Russ Paisley, a notoriously mouthy hedge fund manager, did business with the titans of Texas industry. He had made over $100 million in the previous year for putting together a national chain of storage facilities, inflating their values, and taking them public. He was on the board of directors at the local country club and was a deacon at the other major social club in town, the Westside Church of Jesus.

Also, he most likely snorted an eight ball of blow before lunch every day, and it was more than apparent in his constant enthusiasm.

Russ was thirty-nine years old, a little overweight, with hair covering every bit of his body except his head. He had attempted hair plugs a couple of years back but stopped after the front was finished because of the pain. He now slicked back the thin row of hair that traversed the front of his head in an unsuccessful effort to fool everyone.

Due to his inability to keep his penis in his pants, Russ had been married four times. His current wife, Jade, was a twenty-two-year-old former stripper whose penchant for cocaine use nearly exceeded his.

"I'll bet you that son of a bitch is a Democrat," Russ barked, referring to Coach Dale. "Who else would run a team like that? It's goddamn affirmative action."

"Um, excuse me, Russ," Tommy Johnson interjected. "If it were affirmative action, I'm pretty sure TJ wouldn't be sitting his happy ass on the bench right now. He *is* pretty much the only black kid on the west side of Fort Worth, you know."

"Gimme a fucking break, Tommy," Russ replied. "I'm talking about affirmative action for retards. I won't even begin to get into what little sense it makes to leave a black kid on the bench on a sports team full of white kids. Jesus Christ. Don't get me started."

Tommy shook his head. "I'm gonna give you a pass today because you've obviously lost your mind again," Tommy said.

Tommy Johnson, close to six feet tall with a medium build, thin beard, and bifocals, was *literally* the only black guy in town. He was a successful plastic surgeon who had moved to Texas from Beverly Hills to try and give his son a life that seemed somewhat normal, comparatively speaking. Tommy and his wife, Kelly, a gorgeous woman even though she was 90 percent nonbiodegradable, were secretly agnostic (and also possibly Democrats), but they attended the Westside Church of Jesus with all of the other upper crusters on the west side of Fort Worth. It had proven a great place to meet clients for his plastic surgery practice.

"Leave it to Russ to bring politics into a little league game," Steve jumped in. "My boy Jonathan has been on the bench more than anyone this season. He's also been last in the batting order for every single game. I'm not saying you guys don't have a reason to complain, but come on. Johnny's getting screwed more than any of your kids."

"Yeah, well," Russ chose his words carefully, "that's probably a little more *understandable* than the other situations."

Russ let his statement hang in the air for a bit before Steve responded.

"What the hell is that supposed to mean?" Steve asked.

"It's just that…" Russ stammered. "Well, come on, man. I don't wanna hurt your feelings, but let's face facts. You and your wife are goddamn bleeding-heart liberals. It's amazing Jonathan's stuck with it this long. He's just not that *good*, you know? Okay, fine. He fucking sucks. But let's just say I bet he'll be an amazing fashion designer, or some shit like that. What choice did you give him?"

"Fuck you," Steve replied flatly, in an almost unfazed manner.

"Whatever, dude," Russ said. "Your wife is a goddamn social worker. What did you expect?"

Steve Winwood was a high school principal who hated his name and the confusion it brought with it. He had been left with an enormous trust fund after graduating college and had always felt the need to do something positive with his life. He was in charge of the roughest high school in North Texas and was beaten to a pulp at least twice each semester. He never pressed charges, blaming society instead of the heathens who hospitalized him.

Steve stood about five feet seven inches tall, was thirty-five years old, and weighed in at a whopping 127 pounds. He had somewhat of a long brown white-man afro. He always attempted to dress hip in order to earn the respect of his students. But he always fell short. He was nervous by nature, as was his wife, Judith, who volunteered her time at battered women's shelters and animal rights organizations.

At the end of the line of baseball dads gripping the fence, Dwayne Devero stood quietly, taking it all in. Dwayne's son, Alex, was probably the most talented baseball player in the league. Alex had been dividing his time between left field and right field the entire season. Every other season he had played shortstop or first base. It killed Dwayne to see his son wasting his time in positions he hated to play.

Alex was a good sport, though. He never once complained. He had made it on base almost every time he'd been up to bat and was the only kid in the league to hit a ball over the outfield wall. He couldn't stand Coach Dale, though.

Coach Dale's inept son, Ace, played shortstop. The assistant coach, Pete, had a talentless son playing first base. Coach Dale's close friends had kids who ranged from decent to talentless at every infield position on the team of ten-year-olds. It was true "daddy baseball."

There were eleven kids on the team and nine positions. For every game all season long, the only boys who sat the bench were the sons of Russ, Tommy, Steve, and Dwayne.

Dwayne noticed Estelle, his wife, heading his direction as time expired on the game. He braced himself.

2.

"I guess you're not going to say anything again, are you, Dwayne?" Estelle Devero snapped at her husband. He knew it was coming. Estelle bitched about everything. "At least Russ has the balls to yell when things aren't going right. But you just stand there. It's so embarrassing. It's almost as embarrassing as that goddamn truck you have to park in the parking lot for all of the Westside parents to see. Do you have to remind everyone that you're a glorified lawn guy at every social function?"

"Jesus, Estelle," Dwayne snapped. "I own a goddamn landscaping company. I didn't have time to grab my car after a long day at work. I would've missed the game."

Estelle refused to acknowledge that Dwayne's "glorified lawn guy" business made her lifestyle possible. Dwayne's work ethic had taken him from having nothing to building a small empire. He had all of the major landscaping contracts in town, including Jenny Field. Lately, none of that mattered much because Estelle kept him strapped with debt. Dwayne struggled to make the tuition payments for Alex's private school. The membership dues to the country club, the Mercedes and Audi payments, the massive mortgage for the house in the affluent neighborhood, and the almost insurmountable credit card bills racked up by Estelle made every month a challenge.

"Whatever, Dwayne. I'm going to meet the girls at the club for drinks. Please have that truck gone first thing tomorrow. I'm having Bible study at the house, and the last thing I want is for the girls to see that awful thing parked out front."

Estelle turned and walked away in a huff. Dwayne looked at the other baseball dads, whose eyes were fixed firmly on Estelle's ass.

"Damn, bro," Russ said as he stared over the top of his sunglasses. "I'm *so gonna hit that* when you're not looking. With an ass like that, I bet the bitchy attitude is almost worth it."

"What the hell are you talking about? Your wife is still in high school," Steve blurted out.

Dwayne ignored them. He looked at the scoreboard as he waited for his son to come off the field. It read 14–1. That one run was from Alex, who'd had an inside-the-park homer in the third inning. Dwayne shook his head.

He wasn't raised to quit, though. It didn't matter that he could no longer stand his bitchy, superficial wife and her toned little yoga body. It didn't matter that she was probably sleeping around with any number of the rich guys she shook her bikini-clad ass for at the club. It didn't matter that his world seemed closer to crumbling to pieces every single day. It didn't matter. He'd keep working harder. The only thing he cared about was Alex. Alex was a good kid, through and through, and he wasn't going to let him down.

"Okay, fuckers, I'll see you on the golf course at 8:00 a.m.," Russ yelled to Dwayne, Tommy, and Steve as he walked toward his bright red Ferrari in the parking lot.

"Jesus, Russ—language, please," Tommy snapped.

"Oh, goddammit, I'm sorry."

The men all went their separate ways in the parking lot, consoling kids who had become unfortunately accustomed to losing. They all hated this part of this season—the quiet walk to the car and the offering of assurances that while the team may have lost, the boys individually had played well.

As Dwayne threw Alex's baseball bag into the bed of his truck, he saw Coach Dale, his assistant Pete, and a few of the other parents laughing and backslapping. The others were kissing Coach Dale's ass so that their kids could continue to play the good positions.

"We'll get 'em next time, Coach," Dwayne heard one of them say.

Dwayne and Alex were the last to leave the Jenny Field parking lot, with the exception of Dave, the head umpire, who was sitting in his old, rusted Honda smoking what appeared to be a very large joint. They were a couple of miles down the road when Dwayne passed

Russ's Ferrari headed back toward the ballpark. A few seconds later, Dwayne received a text from Russ.

"Jackson forgot his glove, C U in the morning, fucker."

When Russ pulled back into the parking lot, he didn't even notice the old Trans Am parked beside Dave's Honda. He left Jackson in the car with the beautiful Italian-tuned engine running and ran to the dugout.

After he grabbed the glove, Russ began to jog back toward the Ferrari. Suddenly, he noticed Dave and another rough-looking individual having what appeared to be a heated conversation by the dumpster at the far corner of the park. He crouched behind some bleachers to watch. The other man talking to Dave was holding a large baggie containing some kind of powdery substance.

"This is bullshit!" he heard the man yell at Dave, as he threw the baggie to the ground and poked Dave in the chest.

For the blink of an eye, the setting sun caught on a shiny object in Dave's hand. It seemed to disappear into the other man's stomach. The man slouched over and dropped to his knees.

A knife. The shiny object was a knife, Russ thought to himself. *Holy fuck.*

Then, Russ saw Dave grab the man's head and twist it. He wasn't going to stick around to see what happened next. Russ ran toward the parking lot, hopped in his Ferrari, and left a patch of rubber from the tires about a quarter of a mile long.

3.

Tommy, Dwayne, and Steve practiced their short game on the putting green next to the first hole at River Oaks Country Club as they awaited the habitually late Russ Paisley. As 8:30 a.m. approached, they saw Russ's Ferrari come sliding into the lot and pull diagonally across two parking spots.

"You know," Dwayne said to Steve and Tommy as he missed yet another putt, "I don't pray for much, but when I do, it usually has something to do with praying that someone keys his goddamn Ferrari for parking like a total jackass."

A golf cart with Russ's clubs placed in back met Russ at his car, and he sped toward the other three golfers. He bounced out of the cart and pulled his T-shirt off as he prepared to throw on a collared golf shirt.

"Jesus, man, that's just disgusting," Tommy remarked, referring to the quantity of hair on Russ's chest and back. "You're like one big 1978 bush walking around here. That shit just ain't cool these days."

"And if you can afford a Ferrari, I'll bet you can afford a treadmill," Steve added. "You're just, like, this jiggling mass of hair. Like black mold on Jell-O. It's just so awful, man."

Russ threw the golf shirt over his head and pulled it down as if he hadn't heard a thing. He pulled his glove out of his back pocket and slipped it over his left hand, wiping some white powdery residue from his nose. Russ didn't give a shit that the others could tell he'd just done a few lines.

"Guys, you're never gonna believe what happened last night," Russ said as they all approached the first tee box.

"Your wife got some new crayons and drew you a picture?" Steve replied.

"She made the JV gymnastics team?" Tommy popped off.

"She found a couple hundred bucks stashed in her ass from when she worked the VIP room at Dirty's Cabaret?" Dwayne jumped in.

All of the men looked over at Dwayne in stunned silence.

"My bad. Too far."

Russ cracked open a beer and chugged half of it as he glared at the others, mainly Dwayne. He lit up a cigarette.

"Are you guys done yet?"

"No."

"Nope."

"Not at all, dick."

"Fine," Russ stormed toward the tee box and placed his ball on a tee. "I'm going first."

Russ stepped up to his ball without taking a practice swing. He hovered over it, concentrating. He then reared back his club, swung as hard as he could, and sliced the ball over a large house in the neighborhood to the right. There was a crash, followed by a dog barking.

"WHAT THE FUCK?!" Russ yelled at the top of his lungs.

Russ was known for his short temper. This had a lot to do with why his friends gave him a huge ration of shit. He stormed off the tee box and back to his cart, where he sat behind the wheel with his arms crossed. The others could barely contain their laughter.

After the other three teed off, Dwayne offered an olive branch to Russ by pretending to be interested in what he had to say about the previous night. "So," Dwayne asked with mock sincerity, "are you gonna tell us what the hell happened last night?"

"I'll tell you guys on the green. I've gotta get my head straight. I can't lose another round of golf to this group of amateurs."

Russ hit the gas pedal on his golf cart and took off down the fairway. The other three watched in anticipation as he drove away, knowing that Tommy had unhooked the strap that held his golf bag onto the cart. As Russ made his first turn after fifty yards, his golf bag came crashing off the back, spilling clubs everywhere until it finally rolled to a stop.

Russ didn't look back at the others, who were doubled over in tears laughing. He punched his steering wheel twice, stood up, and gathered his clubs. After placing them back on the cart, he offered a middle finger to the guys before driving toward where his ball had gone out of bounds.

By the time the foursome reached the green, Russ had regained his composure. He managed to put together an amazing shot from far down the fairway, and was now going for a par. "Okay, guys, so what I was trying to tell you is . . ." He paused to line up his putt for a moment, leaning down toward the green and finding his line. "Last night, I saw Dave kill a guy at the ballpark."

Russ pulled back and took the shot, sending an almost impossible sixty-foot putt on its way toward the hole. The ball broke at just the right time, rode the lip of the hole, and fell in the back side.

"Fuck yeah!" Russ yelled as he threw his arms in the air. "Back door, bitches! Suck on that, Lawn Boy! Who's your daddy now, you friggin' liberal shitbag? What's up now, token black guy? Oh yeah! I'm back in this bitch!" Russ offered a few pelvic thrusts as he did his victory dance on the green.

Dwayne, Steve, and Tommy stood in silence, unable to comprehend what they had heard before the shot.

"What the hell is wrong with you guys? Jesus, gimme a high five or something! That was beautiful!" Russ said with disappointment.

"Dude," Dwayne said. "Did you say that you saw Dave kill somebody? As in Dave the umpire?"

"Yup. Stabbed him, then twisted that fucker's neck like a beer cap. It was crazy. Scared the shit outta me. He's lucky I didn't call the cops."

The guys stared at Russ while he nonchalantly pulled his ball from the hole, wiped the dirt and grass clippings from it, and lit a cigarette.

"And exactly why *didn't* you call the cops?" Dwayne asked.

"Are you guys gonna putt, or what? Jesus. You have seventeen more holes to hear the story. I gotta finish it now?" Russ snapped, secretly satisfied that he now had them all rattled and not into their golf games.

4.

Steve, Dwayne, Russ, and Tommy had not been lifelong friends. They weren't friends because they worked together, shared similar interests, or recognized any deep connection with one another. No, they were friends because their kids played baseball together. Their kids had all become friends, so the parents were forced to tolerate each other. That forced tolerance developed into a sort of baseball-dad clique through the seasons.

The relationship had evolved into an odd—but actual—friendship. The men began to hang out from time to time, going to sporting events, playing golf, and so on. They didn't know each other on anything other than a somewhat shallow basis, however. They were still getting to know each other. So, when Russ mentioned that he witnessed a murder and didn't think to call the police, it threw the other three for a pretty good loop. What kind of guy does that?

The foursome walked up to the second tee box with balls and drivers in hand. Not much had been said since Russ made his revelation. Russ cracked another beer, slammed it, and threw the can over his shoulder as he stared down the fairway, analyzing his next move.

"So, Russ," Dwayne said, trying to digest what they'd been told. "Why would you not call the police if you saw someone get murdered? That doesn't make any sense, man. This guy Dave is three feet from our kids several times a week. Help me understand this."

"Yeah, I'm having a little trouble with that too," Tommy added.

"Hang on." Russ placed his ball on the tee and stepped up to it. He checked his feet to make sure he was lined up properly. After no practice swing again, he pulled back his club and swung with all his might, sending the ball careening down the left side of the fairway and into a large pond. A small flock of ducks was immediately rattled into flight.

"FUUUUUCK! Fuck, fuck, fuck, fuck, FUCK!" he yelled. "This is such *bullshit*! FUCK this game!" Russ pounded at the ground with his driver, wiping the sweat off his forehead, still staring at the pond. "I need a new goddamn driver. This club sucks."

Dwayne, Tommy, and Steve wondered if Russ had any intention of finishing his story and answering their question about the police.

Russ turned and noticed them awaiting some kind of closure. "Oh, right. Why didn't I call the cops?" He paused for a moment. "Well, you know, my first thought was to get the hell out of there. Jackson was waiting in the car, for Christ's sake. Then when I got in the car I was gonna call, but I didn't want to startle Jackson. I figured I'd wait until I got home. Then I got home, and Jade had popped a little ecstasy. She'd gotten her nipples pierced and wanted to show them off, so you know how that goes, right?"

Russ looked at the guys for confirmation. He received none. "Okay, fine, never mind. Amazing, but whatever. After laying some pipe, I got into the vodka. So I got a little buzz, and I got to thinking . . . I don't know . . . maybe a guy like Dave is someone you want to have on your side, as opposed to someone you call the cops on. I know, this sounds crazy, but . . . I just started thinking that maybe a guy like Dave could help us with our baseball predicament. I mean, how much longer can we put up with this 'daddy-baseball' bullshit? Tell me that somewhere deep inside you that doesn't make some sense."

Again, Russ turned to them, searching for some level of reassurance. Again, he received none.

"No, man," Steve jumped in without any hesitation. "There's absolutely nowhere inside of me where that makes sense. I'm pretty sure I speak for all of us when I say that."

"What the fuck are you saying, man?" Tommy inquired in an almost sedated tone. "You want Dave to snap Coach Dale's neck? That can't possibly be what you're getting at."

Dwayne was at a loss for words. He stood back on his heels with his mouth agape. Finally, he cocked his head, waved his arm, and stepped up to take his shot. "He's fucking with us," Dwayne said with certainty. "Dave is an asshole, and he definitely hates anyone that makes more than ten bucks an hour, but come on. Russ is just fucking with us."

Dwayne took three perfect practice swings, stepped forward to his ball, and drove the ball hard left into a tree. It ricocheted off and then flew back toward the foursome. Steve dove to the ground to avoid taking one between the eyes. The ball came to rest about thirty yards behind the tee box, on the edge of the cart path.

"Stupid fucking game," Dwayne uttered under his breath as he walked off the tee box.

Tommy pulled a ball and tee from his pocket, set them in position, and took a few swings at the air to limber up. "You had me going for a minute, there, Russ," Tommy grinned as he pulled back and took his shot. He swung the club with every muscle in his body. The club hit the very top of the ball, causing it to rebound off the ground and pop straight up into the air about ten feet. The ball came down and landed about two inches from the tee.

"Mother*fucker*," he said softly.

After Steve sent his ball into the same pond that Russ's ball had ventured into, the men made their way back to the carts. Russ stopped and turned to them before they all took off.

"I'm not joking," he told them. "You're right. I probably should've called the cops. It's too late now, though. And I never once thought we should have Ricky Dale's neck broken. Jesus. Give me a little credit. I just thought we might entertain the idea of having someone put a scare into him. That's all. Bad idea, I know. I'll drop it."

The next few holes for the foursome went quietly. Russ's words lingered, especially with Dwayne. The thought of scaring, or even harming, someone who treats your kid badly might not be that uncommon. Everyone has thoughts like that, right? But acting on those thoughts . . . that was an entirely different matter.

Still, they were all thinking about it. A doctor, a money manager, a successful landscape artist, and a blue-blood high school principal—upstanding members of the community . . . they were the last people who would act on such thoughts. Trouble like this was typically reserved for trailer dwellers. Tornado bait did things like this, not guys like them. Not normally. But how much happier would they be if their sons were having a blast at baseball again?

The men finished the round of golf in just under five hours. Russ won with a score of 101. This killed the other three. Russ was a horrible winner.

5.

"Jesus, you guys are terrible," Russ said to the others as they walked into the clubhouse for lunch and drinks.

"Seriously, Russ?" Dwayne snapped back. "I just want you to know that you still suck at this game, and if the people who invented golf had known that your hairy ass would be playing it so poorly and embarrassingly, they probably never would have invented it."

The foursome took their seats at the clubhouse, ordered drinks, and examined menus. They pretended to be watching the baseball game that was playing on the large flat screen in the men's lounge, but their minds were preoccupied.

"So, Russ," Dwayne said. "Just for grins, I was wondering what your plan was. Dave hates you. How in the world did you think that you could get a guy like him on your side? Why would he do a favor for you that could land him in jail?"

Tommy and Steve looked at Russ. They had been thinking the same thing.

Russ finished his second vodka tonic since arriving back at the clubhouse. He had drunk a twelve pack of beers by himself on the golf course. He was feeling no pain as he thought about his answer. The white powder had returned to his nasal area. He leaned in so as not to be overheard. "Here's what I was thinking. Dave doesn't know that anyone saw him kill that guy. I was thinking that I could scare him anonymously . . . call him and disguise my voice or something. Just tell him that someone saw what he did, and if he'll scare Coach Dale into letting other kids play good positions, the cops will never be called. I won't be exact about which kids play which positions, I'll just be vague and see what happens."

Just then, the waiter appeared to take the men's food orders. It was obvious that the shaking, pimple-faced redheaded young man had heard of Russ before. All the waitstaff had, due to his well-known penchant for being an asshole. "Good afternoon, gentlemen," the waiter said apprehensively. "May I take your order?"

Russ glared. He just loved to fuck with people.

"May I take your order?" the waiter repeated.

"Yeah, my gay friend Steve here was wondering if the carpet matches the drapes," Russ spoke loudly while throwing a hand on Steve's shoulder.

"Pardon me, sir? I don't understand," the waiter responded.

"I said my gay friend Steve here wants to see your junk," Russ stated with a bit of a drunken slur. "He wants to bump mushrooms with you. You in?"

"No . . . sir . . . I'm, um, not exactly gay," the waiter replied, looking like he was on the verge of a nervous breakdown.

"You don't have to play with his balls or anything," Russ continued his assault. "You can just—"

"Jesus CHRIST, man!" Steve interrupted. "Have some class!"

"Sorry," Russ said to the waiter. "He's still coming to grips with his sexuality."

"What the hell is wrong with you, man?" Tommy asked. "I'll have a Reuben sandwich, please."

"He'll have the hotdog, obviously," Russ laughed as he nudged Steve.

Dwayne, Tommy, and Steve apologized for Russ's behavior. The poor, abused waiter hung his head, making his way back to the kitchen.

"Listen, guys," Tommy broke the silence. "I'm black, okay? And . . ."

"Wait a minute!" Russ jumped in. "Are you fucking serious? What kind of country club is this? We allow *black* people?! That's bullshit!"

Russ looked around for shared laughter and found none. He made a more serious face and turned back toward Tommy.

"As I was saying," Tommy continued, "black people who don't break the law, such as myself, have an unspoken code. If someone around us mentions breaking the law, we have to remove ourselves immediately from that group of people. Now, I'm not going to do that right now because I'd be sitting by myself in an all-but-me white country club. The last thing I need is to stand out any more than I do or have motherfuckers coming up to me asking for a sandwich like I work here, which happens every goddamn day. But I will say this, Russ: You need to proceed with caution."

Not a word was said again until the waiter brought their food. The waiter delicately placed everyone's order in front of them, praying to go unnoticed.

"You know, I'll rip your face off if you put pubes in my food, Ginger," Russ mumbled to the waiter. "It won't be hard to tell if they're yours."

"Sir, I would n-n-never—" the waiter stammered. "Of course you'd know, I mean . . . but I . . ."

"A-HA!" Russ yelled as he pointed at the waiter. "So the carpet DOES match the drapes! You have a bright red man muff! AAAAAAA-HAHAHAHA! That's awful! Your little pink guy down there dangling in a sea of red! Oh God, that's gross!"

A tear rolled down the waiter's cheek. The other men sat in total shock as Russ laughed and wheezed simultaneously. Russ didn't care. He smashed out his cigarette and tore into his sandwich.

"Jesus, you're not even human," Steve said.

The foursome ate like they hadn't had a meal in days. The thought of hiring Dave to scare Ricky Dale was still at the front of their thoughts as they finished the rest of their food.

Dwayne decided to play out the scenario a bit with the others.

"You really think you could make this thing work? Having Dave scare Coach Dale?" Dwayne asked.

"Of course I could," Russ replied with complete cockiness. "I've brought billionaires to their knees on four continents. I think I can get that jackass to shake things up on a baseball diamond."

Dwayne looked at Tommy and Steve. "I know this sounds crazy, guys, but it would sure as hell get Estelle off my back if Alex played a good position. And he's talking about remaining totally anonymous while just putting a little scare into a guy who is making our kids' lives miserable."

"Part of me wants to slap you right now for taking Russ seriously,"

Tommy said. "But another part of me wouldn't mind seeing my boy in the infield."

"I'm out," Steve threw in. "I'm totally out."

"Yeah, but your kid sucks, Steve," Russ offered. "No offense, of course, but he'd probably be riding the bench anyhow."

"Screw you, Russ." Steve tossed his napkin on the table. "I'm outta here. You guys are idiots if you let this hairy little Antichrist put something like this into action." Steve walked out the door without ever turning back to the others.

"What a nutless little twerp," Russ said. "We can do this, guys, and no one will ever know."

Dwayne and Tommy looked at each other, trying to read the other's expression in order to know how to proceed.

"I say we table the idea," Dwayne concluded, rising from his seat. "We can't make a decision as off-the-wall as this over a game of golf and a burger. I need to think about it."

6.

Dwayne drove around for a while before heading home. He needed to clear his head. The world was caving in on him. He had a loveless marriage to a coldhearted bitch, who had begun to make a regular habit of spending more than he could earn. She blamed her spending habits on his inability to earn enough to make her happy. He couldn't stand her friends, either. When they weren't shopping, they were sitting around at one of their houses or at the club, drinking and gossiping about people in the cruelest manner imaginable.

Alex was the only person who truly made Dwayne happy. If only his son could play a good position on the baseball team . . .

As Dwayne turned his truck onto his street, he couldn't help but notice the string of luxury vehicles parked in his driveway and in front of his house. "Goddammit," he said to himself. "Bible study."

Dwayne parked his truck down the street as Estelle had insisted and sparked up a half-smoked joint that had been resting in his ashtray. He took a few long pulls and then prepared himself, squirting his eyes with eye drops, popping gum in his mouth—and with a long sigh, he walked the block to his house.

He hoped that he might make it through the gaggle of women without being noticed, but when he opened the door and saw them all sitting around the massive dining room table, he knew that would not be possible. The ladies became uncomfortably quiet when he shut the door. He could tell that he had interrupted some juicy gossip. A dozen or so stretched faces turned in his direction to size him up.

Several unopened Bibles and empty wine bottles were strewn about. As he approached the table, Dwayne noticed the weekly Bible study fliers . . . the Gospel according to Matthew. He chuckled to himself.

"How goes it, ladies?" Dwayne asked insincerely, making his way to the kitchen.

"Just some good Christian fellowship," one of the ladies replied.

"Dwayne, honey," Estelle called out to the kitchen, "make sure you get paid from the Simpson account soon. Jacqueline was telling me that they paid their country club bill late. And if you hadn't noticed, they traded in their Mercedes S-class for a midlevel Lexus."

"Gotcha," Dwayne responded sarcastically as he rooted through the refrigerator for one of his favorite dark beers. "We probably shouldn't speak to them anymore until they can afford a proper luxury vehicle."

"You don't have to be an asshole, Dwayne," Estelle snapped back. "I just don't want us to get burned by people who don't have the good sense not to live beyond their means."

Dwayne rolled his eyes. He fantasized about telling all of the gossiping hens how much money *he* had in the bank as he drove golf balls at them from the living room. He'd love to see the wine glasses shattering everywhere, splashing hundred-dollar-a-bottle wine all over their thousand-dollar outfits. They'd dive to the floor, cursing him for his insubstantial income and known associations with a colored guy.

"By the way, ladies," he said instead, "I noticed that you're reading the Gospel according to Matthew. That's a great book. How far have you gotten?"

Dwayne peered his head around the corner to watch them search for an answer. They were dumbfounded.

"After the opening prayer, we got a little sidetracked," one of the fully stretched, prim-and-proper blue bloods responded. "We were just about to begin our studies."

"Oh, I see." Dwayne pounded the last drop of beer from his bottle into his mouth. "You should skip the first six chapters and cut right to chapter seven. It starts out, 'Judge not, that ye be not judged,' and gets considerably more interesting and applicable from there. Thank me later. I'll be in the other room watching the Rangers game with Alex."

Dwayne walked into the living room and sat down in his favorite chair. Alex was lying back with his legs up on the couch. He was doing the only thing he loved as much as playing baseball . . . watching it. The Texas Rangers were playing the New York Yankees in a much-anticipated afternoon game. Alex was glued to the television.

Dwayne grabbed the remote control, turning up the volume in an effort to drown out the cackling from the silicone, purple-toothed hens in the next room. He watched Alex's face as it hung on every play.

"Dad," Alex said as he looked toward Dwayne, "do you still think I'm good enough to play shortstop?"

"Yeah, I do." Dwayne could feel the self-consciousness settling into his son. "I think you're the best shortstop in the league."

"Thanks, Dad. I wish Coach Dale would give me a shot to prove myself. I feel like I'm letting you and Mom down."

Anger crept into Dwayne as he sat stoically staring at the screen. It began to nag and claw at him. What in the hell was Coach Dale thinking? Seriously! He had the option to *win games.* Instead he chose to crush the dreams of half of his team to overcome some deep insecurity he obviously harbored about fathering a kid who sucked at baseball. It wasn't fucking fair. He'd had enough.

"I'll be back in a minute, son," he said softly to Alex as he rose from his seat.

He walked back into the kitchen and grabbed another beer from the fridge. He popped the lid and quietly slipped out the back door. Leaning over the railing of his back porch, Dwayne surveyed the state of his lawn with a landscaper's eye. Every few feet along his eight-foot capped cedar fence, he noticed a baseball on the ground. An old aluminum bat lay propped up against a huge live oak. A tattered glove sat inches away. There were a few worn tracks shaped like a diamond in the grass where Alex and his friends had played backyard ball time and time again.

Dwayne couldn't take it anymore. He pulled his phone from his pocket and dialed. After a few rings, the line picked up with a loud commotion on the other end.

"This is . . . umm . . . *OH MY GOD THAT'S THE SPOT!*" Russ yelled as he dropped the phone to the floor.

Dwayne could hear Russ struggling to grab the phone as his young wife was obviously sexually assaulting him.

"This is . . . *OH GOD, BABY, DON'T TOUCH IT! IT'S SO SENSITIVE RIGHT NOW! DON'T EVEN LOOK AT IT! PLEASE! JESUS!*"

Dwayne was about to set the phone down, when an out-of-breath Russ managed to gain his composure.

"This is Russ Paisley," he said, panting and clearing his throat.

"Ummm, yeah, Russ . . . It's Dwayne. I was . . . uhhh . . . Is this a good time?"

"Yo! Dwayne! Thank Christ! I was hoping it wasn't the church calling again! Just getting a little wink-wink 'cardio' in, if you know what I mean. I swear, Jade's been so damn freaky since she got her nipples pierced, I think she's going to rip my d—"

"WHOAH! Hey, brother! That's a little too much info. Good for you, though. I just—"

"Dude, she's like a friggin' rabbit, 24/7, bro. Seriously. I can send you some pictures."

"No, no, no, man . . . That's just . . . Wait, okay, email them to my work email. But that's not why I called."

"Cool. I'm sending them now. Why did you call?"

Dwayne paused for a moment. He was getting cold feet. He had been so certain just moments before. His phone beeped. He looked at his phone. He had an email. He pushed the button quickly to glance at it.

"You get the email yet?" Russ barked.

"Yeah, I just . . . Jesus, is that a carrot?"

"She's been going through some weird vegetable fetish. Who am I to judge? I just let her go with it. Wait 'til you see the one with the—"

"Holy *shit!*"

"—large English cucumber."

"Yeah, man, I'm happy for you. I just . . . wow. Ummm . . . That thing we were talking about, with Dave . . ."

"Yeah? What about it?"

Dwayne paused again. Thinking it over one last time made him more angry and resolute.

"I'm in," Dwayne barked. "Let's do it."

"Cool. I'll get started."

"Nothing over the phone from this point forward though, okay?"

"Sure."

"And Russ . . ."

"Yeah?"

Dwayne took a deep breath. "Nobody gets hurt."

7.

"I know what you did, David," the heavily disguised voice said into the receiver.

Dave the umpire glanced down at his phone. The call was coming from a blocked number. He pushed his three large pit bulls off his nasty old mattress, which sat on the floor of his trailer, so that he could get a clear line of sight on his alarm clock. It was 3:21 a.m.

"Who the fuck is calling me at three in the morning? Is this a joke? Earl, this better not be you callin' from the pen again. I told you not to—"

"SHUT THE FUCK UP, LOSER!" the caller screamed. "I saw what you did at the baseball field, David. Would you like me to share what I saw with the police?"

"GODDAMMIT, WHO IS THIS?!" Dave sat up and rubbed his eyes to make sure he was awake. He was. He grabbed a half-burned joint from the ashtray and lit it.

"David, David, David. You've been a bad boy," the voice scolded. Russ was trying to sound like a cross between Hannibal Lector and the guy from the *Scream* movies.

"With your record," Russ continued, "I doubt that you'd like anyone to find out what you've done. You'd be locked up for good. You don't want that, do you?"

Dave jumped out of bed and walked to the window of his double-wide. He crinkled the mini blinds down, peering around the Movin' On Up trailer park for suspicious activity. He saw nothing.

"What do you want?" Dave asked.

Jade had begun to rustle from her slumber. Russ knew he had to get off the call quickly, before Jade grabbed the cocaine and wanted to have sex for the ninth time that evening. Russ had hoped to be making the phone call to Dave much earlier, but Jade just kept coming back for more. Now her hand slid up his thigh and into his new shimmery golden thong she'd just bought him.

"Ow, ow, ow, ow," Russ mumbled as he tried to grab Jade's hand before she latched on. "Not now, honey, just let me get off of this ph—"

POP!

She had pulled back the front of the thong, stretched it to full elasticity, and then released it, snapping Russ square in the twig and giggleberries.

"OH, JESUS!" Russ whispered loudly, with all of the breath gone from his lungs from the immense pain. "All I see is white! Oh God it hurts! You're such a twisted freak! Oh, why, why, WHY?!?!"

Dave listened to the commotion on the line. He was lost. "You talkin' to me, dipshit?" he asked the caller.

Russ flew out of bed and began jumping up and down. The pain was too much. He had to scream.

"NOOOOOOOOOOOOOOOOOOOOOOOO!!! NO, NO, NO, NOOOO!!!"

Russ stood on the white marble bedroom floor, doubled over in pain at the foot of his ornate eighteenth-century bed. He held the phone in one hand and pulled back the thong with the other to survey the damage. Aside from the agony and odd purplish coloring from overuse, everything appeared fine. He took a couple of deep breaths, walked toward the large picture window with his winky and a testicle protruding from the side of his thong, and jolted himself back into character

"Listen, Dave," he whispered menacingly. "You're going to do me a favor if you want to stay out of jail for the rest of your natural life."

"I'm listening," Dave replied. Dave was utterly bewildered by the early morning call. Normally, nothing scared him, but something wasn't right with the guy on the other end of the line. He knew he was dealing with a psychopath.

"Ricky Dale is a douche, Dave," Russ stated. "We both know this."

"Yeah. So?"

"He's playing too much daddy baseball these days, Dave, and some friends of mine and I have had enough."

Dave held the phone away from his head for a moment to glare at it, and then he placed it back to his ear and mouth. "Are you fucking kidding me?"

"Would you like to find out if I'm kidding you?"

"No, it's just . . . What the hell am I supposed to do? You want me to tell Ricky Dale how to coach his shitty baseball team?"

"I want you to make sure there's no more daddy baseball going on, Dave. That's all. I don't give a shit how you do it. It's simple. The good kids play the good spots, the shitty kids play the shitty spots. And no more good kids on the bench. This isn't the goddamned YMCA. We want to win. Who gives a shit about the kids that suck? Fucking Democrats! That's what's wrong with this goddamned society! Winners need to win! It's your job to make it happen!"

"But I just—"

"Goddammit, Dave! No excuses! It's your job to restore some goddamn order to the universe! I don't give a shit how! Scare him! Make it happen! Make it happen, or you go to jail!"

Russ clicked his phone off. He missed the days when phones had two parts to them, and you could slam them together to hang up with much more dramatic effect. But the days of the dramatic effect were no more. He knew the Democrats were behind this as well.

Dave sat back down on the end of his bed. His pit bulls were snoring again. He flipped on his old box television and hooked up his illegal cable box, turning the channel to a show about a guy who lived in the swamps of Louisiana and fished with his hands. He sparked up another joint and drifted off to sleep.

8.

Monday morning, Dwayne Devero stood over the stovetop frying bacon and eggs for Alex before he headed off to school. Alex was drinking his orange juice while watching *SportsCenter* on ESPN on the television near the kitchen table. He did this every Monday morning, catching up on all of the college and professional games he'd missed over the weekend.

Estelle came dragging into the kitchen as Dwayne set Alex's breakfast plate in front of him.

"I guess I have to make the coffee around here," Estelle mumbled as she filled the coffee machine with water and placed the filter with ground beans inside.

"Yeah," Dwayne replied. "It must be rough to have to go to the trouble of pouring water in that thing before a long day of spending money, drinking, and talking shit about people."

Dwayne was thankful that Alex stayed submerged in sports news so that he didn't hear the back-and-forth between his parents.

"You left the lawn truck parked out front again," Estelle sneered as she looked out over the kitchen sink into the driveway. "Jesus, Dwayne! You know how I feel about that!"

"Oh my God!" he snapped. "Now everyone in the neighborhood is going to find out I work for a living! Shit! Our cover is blown!"

"Okay, asshole," she said over her shoulder as she walked away. "I've got a yoga class in an hour. Bye."

Estelle offered an evil, yet quite sincere, middle finger to Dwayne as she walked back to the bedroom. This was what it had become.

"Comb your hair and brush your teeth when you're done, buddy, and I'll take you to school," Dwayne told Alex.

Dwayne set the frying pan in the sink. He squirted about a half a cup of dish soap into it, and let the hot water fill it up. As he turned the water off, he noticed his phone light blinking. He'd received a new text from Russ.

RUSS: The orange hyena is on the bike.

DWAYNE: What the fuck does that mean?

RUSS: I'm speaking in code, Lawn Boy!

Dwayne was getting impatient with Russ. It wasn't hard to do.

DWAYNE: Are you goddamn retarded?

RUSS: Dumbass! I'm just trying to say something without saying it!

DWAYNE: That doesn't make any sense! Are you coked up right now?

RUSS: Wtf does that have to do with anything??? LOL.

DWAYNE: Don't LOL me! I'm a grown-ass man! Are you 14 or something? Jesus! Just tell me!

RUSS: LMAO! You get so flustered! :)

DWAYNE: LMAO? Really? And did you just smiley-face me? What's wrong with you, man?! Jesus! Use your words! WHAT THE FUCK ARE YOU TALKING ABOUT?! SPELL IT OUT!!!

RUSS: Sorry. : (. . . Didn't mean to upset you. I made the call we talked about. It's happening. I'll see you at prac- tice tonight. After I nail your wife.

DWAYNE: Oh. Cool. See you tonight. Dick. You can have her. :)

The texting session over, Dwayne looked up from his phone to see that Alex had finished his breakfast, put his dishes in the dishwasher, combed his hair, and brushed his teeth.

"I'm ready!" Alex exclaimed as he headed for the truck, his back- pack on his shoulder.

What a good kid, Dwayne thought. He hoped he would never let such a perfect child down.

"Hey, Alex," he said softly. "Does it bother you that I drop you off for school in my work truck? I know lots of kids are riding in much cooler cars. It's just . . . if I head back to the office to get my car after work, that means I get to spend less time with you."

"I don't care, Dad," Alex responded. "It's just a car."

Dwayne smiled. He'd somehow managed to raise his kid pretty well so far. He handed Alex a few bucks for lunch as they approached the school drop-off, and gave him a little fist bump before he climbed out of the truck. "I'll be home around five to take you to practice, buddy. When you get home, do your homework first thing. I think things are about to get better for your baseball team. I can feel it."

9.

Ricky Dale arrived at Jenny Field an hour before practice to set up the bases and write up a game plan, as he always did. He illegally parked his classic silver 1961 Mercedes 300 SL convertible in the handicapped parking space nearest the entrance to the field.

An old black van, badly painted in a poor attempt to re-create the A-Team van, appeared out of nowhere. It came screeching up behind Coach Dale as he leaned deep inside his trunk to grab the team equipment bag. Coach Dale turned around to see the van's sliding side door fly open and thick marijuana smoke come pouring out.

Coach Dale stood paralyzed with fear as a large masked man dressed in a tattered red ski suit emerged from the smoke and sprang through the side door of the van wielding a large aluminum baseball bat. His red ski mask looked as though it were on sideways, and Dave was having a difficult time seeing through it. The scene looked straight out of a low-budget horror film.

"You're gonna stop playing daddy baseball out here, Ricky Dale," Dave demanded. He held the bat high, acting as if he might clobber the coach. "You're gonna play the good kids in the good spots, and the retards in the retard spots. Understand?"

The impeccably dressed and leathery tan Coach Dale leaned in to inspect the masked man. The lunatic with the bat reeked of cheap weed, cheap whiskey, and body odor. He knew that voice. He recognized it. He stared at the one bloodshot eye that had a line of sight through the mask. Then it clicked.

"Dave?" Coach Dale moved closer. "Is that you, Dave? What the fuck? Is this a joke?"

"I'm not Dave. I don't know anyone named Dave. I mean, I know a couple of guys named Dave . . . everybody knows a couple of guys named Dave . . . but not the Dave you're talking about."

"How do you know which Dave I'm talking about?"

Dave stood confused, and, using his one free eye, he glared with hatred at Coach Dale. He was way too high for a conversation. Plus, the hot Texas sun was beating down on him, and he was wearing a ski suit.

"I just . . . I don't know. But I'm not Dave, fucker. Now shut up and tell me you understand that it's time to play baseball the right way."

Coach Dale stared at Dave. He didn't like being pushed around. He was used to getting his way. He looked Dave up and down and assessed the situation.

"Dave, why the fuck are you wearing a ski suit? Seriously. That's just stupid. And furthermore, who in the fuck do you think you are? I run things around here. Do you want to get fired, Dave? How easy is it to find a job with your history? And by the way, you smell terrible, like old homeless balls."

Dave was getting more pissed by the minute. This little fake-tanned cocksucker was getting personal. And how did he know what homeless balls smelled like?

"I told you. I'm not Dave," he growled. "I came here to deliver a message, that's all. Nothing more, nothing less. You're going to play good kids in good positions. You're going to quit benching the talent on your team, and you're going to start benching the shitstains like your son. Tell me you understand, you rich prick, or things are going to get ugly."

"Oh, really?" Coach Dale snapped. "You white trash, Ramen-noo-dle-slurping, NASCAR-loving, trailer-park-living goddamn Neander-thal. Don't fucking tell me how to run things. You don't know shit about success. I own you, Dave. I fucking own you. And you just made a big mistake, jackass. I'm calling your parole officer. We're going to order up some drug tests. We'll see how you like getting your ass poked back in pr—"

TINK!

Dave had always loved the way an aluminum bat sounded when hit in the sweet spot.

Coach Dale never saw it coming. He managed to stay on his feet for a few moments after being struck. It was almost comical, Dave thought as he watched the coach grab at the air for balance.

Ricky Dale's head appeared somewhat caved in on one side. It had changed shape. It was lopsided. The coach gave a final half-pirouette, and collapsed to the ground. When Dave noticed a trickle of blood come out of Coach Dale's ear, he knew he'd swung the bat just a bit too hard. He looked around to make sure no one had seen the events that had just transpired. Once he realized he was safe, he lifted the body of Ricky Dale into his van and attempted to slide the door shut.

The door latch on the old cargo van had given him problems for months. He'd stolen the van several years back to transport large quantities of marijuana. He tried in vain multiple times to close it, but it wasn't working. The final time he slammed it, the latch went flying off behind him, and the door slid wide open again.

"Fuck it," Dave mumbled. He climbed over the lifeless body that was curled up inside the rear door, and hopped into the driver's seat. He fired up the engine, threw the van into drive, and disappeared as quickly as he had arrived.

"You shoulda listened to me, you dumb sonofabitch," Dave said to the deceased as he sped down Happy Trail Drive, away from the ballpark. "But no, you had to be your usual cocksucker self. You own me, huh? Yeah. Sure you do."

Without slowing, Dave took a hard left onto White Settlement Road. The tires screeched as they strained to keep the van upright. A couple of vehicles honked and swerved to miss him.

"Fuck!" Dave screamed. "That was a close one, eh, jackass?"

Dave looked into the rearview mirror for some reassurance from the corpse he'd been talking to. The corpse wasn't there. He whipped his body around quickly to see where Coach Dale's body had gone. He saw it for just a fleeting moment, as it rolled through the open side door of the van.

Dave immediately turned back to the rearview mirror, where he saw the body of Ricky Dale tumble three to four times before being struck in the feet by the vehicle behind him that had swerved to miss him. The impact sent Coach Dale spinning into the oncoming traffic lane, where he was smacked solid by the front bumper of a jacked-up four-wheel-drive truck. The bumper popped the coach's head off like a bottle cap, leaving it to bounce car to car like a hacky sack as his body was ground to mush.

"Holy shit," Dave chuckled. "That was fucking awesome."

Dave lit a roach, hit the gas, and headed home, where he parked the van behind his trailer. He covered it up quickly with old bed sheets and duct tape. He knew he had to come up with a plan. He'd have to think of it later, though. Right now he had to get to work. He took off his sweaty red ski suit, slapped some Old Spice aftershave on his cheeks, threw on his umpire/groundskeeper duds, grabbed the keys to his rusted old Honda, and headed back to Jenny Field.

10.

Dwayne was running behind. A local car dealership that his company had landscaped was having drainage issues. He and Alex were the last to arrive at Jenny Field for practice. The sun was shining and the sky was as blue as a monk's balls. It was a beautiful day for baseball.

But baseball wouldn't be happening today. The parking lot was total chaos. Police lights were flashing everywhere. Dwayne counted seven police cars and a crime scene van. His chest tightened. The Fort Worth Police Department had strung bright yellow police tape around half of the parking lot, including Ricky Dale's abandoned classic Mercedes.

Dwayne's palms became drenched with sweat as he pulled to the far side of the field where the other parents had parked. They were hugging each other and consoling their kids.

"What's going on, Dad?" Alex asked in a scared, hushed voice.

"I don't know. Let's find out."

They walked toward the crowd of parents. Alex ran over to his friends. Dwayne scanned the group for his. Over in the south field bleachers, about twenty yards away, sat Tommy and Steve. They looked like terrified statues, perched motionless with mouths wide open.

Dwayne didn't have to ask what happened. He knew. He sat down beside Tommy and Steve and dropped his head into his hands.

Just then, the door to the restroom across the park flew open, and an exuberant Russ Paisley burst through in a three-piece suit and sparkling diamond Rolex. He was playing air guitar and singing "Two Tickets to Paradise." He had white powder on his nose, top lip, and cheek, and went into an air-drum solo as he approached his friends. Russ leaned in for fist bumps. He received none.

"What the fuck is wrong with you guys?" Russ said with enthusiasm. "Our prayers were just answered!"

The guys stared at him while he rambled on.

"Don't be such pussies! Do you know what this means? We still have time to pull this season out! Playoffs, baby! That's what I'm talking about! And our kids will be shoo-ins for the All-Star team now! Except your kid, Steve, but that was never in the cards anyhow, right? Pull your tampons out, homos!"

Russ surveyed the scene proudly, with his hands on his hips.

"Russ," Dwayne grunted through his teeth. "You need to sit the fuck down, wipe the coke off your face, and act like a grieving friend right now. Are you trying to get us thrown in prison here, you fucking idiot?"

"Yeah, but—"

"But nothing, you hairy little freak," Dwayne continued. "You said no one gets hurt. No one. Gets. Hurt. That's what you said. They're putting up police tape everywhere. I don't even know what happened yet, but I'm pretty sure someone got hurt. By the looks of Tommy and Steve, I'm pretty sure someone got hurt. I'm pretty sure—"

"You don't know what happened?" Steve interrupted. "Oh, Jesus . . . I told you this was a bad idea. I told you. I can't believe you guys went ahead and did this. I thought we were talking in hypotheticals. How could you do this? I mean . . . Look at me, man. Do you know how *raped* I'm going to be in prison? I have no idea how the rape scale works, but I'm sure I'm going to be pretty fucking raped."

Dwayne looked at Steve, waiting to hear what had happened to Coach Dale, but Steve was a mess.

"What the fuck happened, Steve?" Dwayne wanted to know now.

"Just . . . imagine . . . " Steve struggled to get the words out as he spoke slowly, focusing on the ground. "Imagine the worst thing possible. Then multiply it by a hundred. Then remind yourself that Russ is involved." Steve's eyes welled up with tears, and he sunk his face into his hands again. "I'm so raped."

Tommy jumped in for Steve with a more concrete description of the event.

"They found his head about a 6-iron away from his body. Witnesses said Coach Dale got tossed out of a van that was hauling some serious ass a couple of blocks from here. Then he got hit by no less than fifteen cars, followed by a cement truck to seal the deal. He's pretty much a wallet, a tie clip, and a bowl of chili now, man. It's bad. We're so screwed. Especially me. I'm black. I'm calling Al Sharpton. I just want you motherfuckers to know. If the shit hits the fan, I'm calling Al."

"Holy shit," Dwayne said, looking back toward the Mercedes and police tape.

In the middle of the group of parents was Pete Rearden, Ricky Dale's assistant coach. Pete appeared to be quickly assuming the role of head coach.

Pete Rearden was the father of Eric Rearden, one of the worst players in the league. Because of Pete's propensity for ass-kissing and bitch work, Eric always batted near the top of the lineup and always played prominent infield positions. The baseball dads couldn't stand Pete.

Pete was thirty-eight years old and had been employed by Walmart since he was sixteen, working his way up through all of the low-level positions to be the manager of the largest Walmart in Fort Worth. He wasn't much to look at—short and pudgy, with nubby little arms and legs. He wore thick glasses and possessed the insecure-yet-overbearing personality of a rent-a-cop. Pete was obviously very much Hispanic, too, although no one ever cared enough about him to question why his name seemed so white. He appeared to not have a single athletic bone in his body, and that appeared to be genetic.

"Hey, guys," Pete said, approaching Dwayne and his friends. "I thought I'd come over here and let you know that the Tigers will continue to play ball this season. We'll all try and get together for practice this Thursday. That should give the kids a couple of days to come to grips with things. I'll step in and coach them the rest of the season. We've only got one more game in the regular season, and then the play-offs. Every team in this age group makes the playoffs. Hopefully we can win a game or two. Coach Dale would've wanted us to keep playing."

"Oh, really?" Russ remarked. "So, you and Ricky Dale had a contingency plan in case his head ever popped off while he was rolling down the road?"

"Russ!" Dwayne yelled. "Jesus!"

"What?" Russ continued. "Are we supposed to assume that Captain Walmart can get us a win in the playoffs? Who does he think he's kidding?"

Pete couldn't believe what he was hearing. No one could. Russ nonchalantly leaned over to pick up a baseball off the ground as Pete attempted to regain control of the conversation.

"Guys, I know this is hard. Coach Dale and I have put a lot of time and effort into this season. I've read books. I've watched videos. I feel confident that I can—"

"THINK FAST!" Russ called out to Pete as he whipped the baseball at his face.

The ball hit him square in the nose, which promptly began to bleed profusely. Pete stood in utter shock at what had just happened as blood began pouring down his face and onto his shirt.

"RUSS! WHAT THE FUCK?!" Tommy screamed. He rushed to Pete with a towel from his bag.

"SEE?" Russ yelled accusingly. "THIS GUY DOESN'T KNOW BASEBALL! A GUY WHO KNOWS BASEBALL WOULDA CAUGHT THAT!"

Tommy held the towel to Pete's face and tilted his head back. He offered a crude scowl to Russ. Dwayne and Steve stayed quiet, both too bewildered to speak.

Some of the other parents, upon seeing the commotion, began to walk toward the guys. As they got close, Dwayne motioned to them that everything was fine.

"I'm sorry, Pete," Dwayne said in a comforting tone. "I think everyone's emotions are running a little high right now."

Pete peeked awkwardly over the blood-soaked towel. He was sweaty and shaking. He seemed too afraid of Russ to speak.

"Hey, fellas," one of the moms from the team spoke up. "We were thinking that now might be a good time for us to join hands in prayer."

Dwayne braced himself for the inevitable.

"Seriously, lady?" Russ popped off. "What are you gonna pray for? Are you gonna pray for Ricky Dale to sprout a new head?"

"Oh my God," she replied, placing her hand over her mouth. "You monster!"

"Yeah, whatever," Russ said. "I'll see you guys at practice on Thursday. Try not to lose your head, Pete, you fucking Democrat." Russ patted Pete on the shoulder, brushing past the crowd of stunned parents to get Jackson and make his way to his Ferrari.

At the same time, Dave the umpire exited his old Honda. Russ caught a whiff of Old Spice and weed as they neared each other. He was surprised to see Dave returning to the scene of what was obviously his crime so soon after it had happened. But, Russ supposed, to *not* show up might draw attention.

Russ watched Dave's disposition. Dave seemed calm. They looked into each other's eyes. Time seemed to slow down, like an old western movie with wind blowing dust across the pavement and quiet desperation hanging in the air.

Russ grinned. Dave grinned back. It was just for a second, but it seemed like much longer. No one who mattered was nervous. That was all Russ cared about. Things were going to be just fine.

11.

Dwayne and Alex left the ballpark a short time after Dave the umpire arrived. The consoling tone being passed from one parent to the next had gone down the shitter once a coked-out Russ whipped a baseball at Pete's nose. The awkward situation thrust upon everyone caused a rather prompt disbanding of the crowd.

At home, Dwayne headed straight to the refrigerator for a beer. He slammed one quickly and then grabbed another, anxiously twisting the top off. Alex went to the living room and turned on ESPN. Neither had said much since leaving the ballpark.

Fresh out of the shower, wearing nothing but a towel on her head, Estelle walked into the kitchen. She brushed up against Dwayne, edging him out of the way so she could get into the fridge.

"I see you drove the truck home again," she said with disgust, reaching for her yogurt. The slight slur in her voice indicated that she'd been into the wine and Xanax.

"Yeah," Dwayne mumbled. He was distracted by her amazing, dripping-wet yoga ass. He wished his wife weren't such a raging, social-climbing snob and cheating whore, because she looked incredible naked.

"You know, babe," she leaned in close and whispered in his ear, "it's been a long time. Why don't we go in the bedroom and see if you can still make my toes curl up? I'll forget all about that dirty old truck out front for a few minutes."

Dwayne watched as Estelle walked slowly toward the bedroom. His eyes were fixed firmly on the slight jiggle of her tight butt until it disappeared around the corner. He pulled his shirt over his head and threw it on the dining room table as he sprinted through the house after her. He tripped over his pant legs as he quickly shed his clothes, almost falling over several times. He followed her into the bedroom and slammed the door behind him.

"I've been really bad, honey," she said in a playful tone as she slithered into bed, arched her back, and propped her rear-end up for him, looking back over her shoulder. "I think you need to punish me."

He wanted to tell her that he would love nothing more than to beat the shit out of her, but he knew that might hurt his chances of getting laid. He opted to just play along instead.

As Dwayne raised his arm in preparation to spank the bejeezus out of Estelle, his phone made a duck-quack noise, indicating that he had a new text. He lowered his arm and stared at his pants, where his phone was, as he contemplated his next move. *Screw it*, he thought, as he raised his arm again. It could wait.

His phone quacked again, distracting him from the task at hand.

"I swear to God, if you answer that," Estelle said coldly, "I'll be locking myself in here with my vibrator for the next hour."

"Hang on," Dwayne replied. He picked his pants up off the floor, opened the master bathroom door, and hurled them to the far end of the bathroom area. He closed the door behind himself and leapt over to the bed, where the spanking commenced immediately.

Within a matter of minutes, Estelle had him tied to the bed with her Pilates resistance bands. She rode him like Seabiscuit until his eyes rolled back into his head and they collapsed into a sweaty pile of lusty contempt. She climbed off, walked across the room and opened a window, and sparked up a joint.

Quack, quack.

Quack, quack.

The quacking of Dwayne's phone hadn't ceased for more than a few seconds. They had managed to drown out the annoying notification sound quite well, though, by banging the headboard against the wall and slapping each other. Now, it was becoming too much.

"Are you going to answer that fucking thing?" Estelle asked as she exhaled a large cloud of pot smoke.

Dwayne was still shaking from all of the physical exertion. He felt like he'd just climbed Everest.

Quack, quack.

"Goddammit," he said, dragging himself to the edge of the mattress. He swung his jittery legs off the bed, hobbled toward the bathroom, and swung the bathroom door open to retrieve his phone.

The baseball dads had apparently decided to address the Coach Dale situation in a group text and had been going at each other pretty good. There were twenty-seven texts.

STEVE: Guys, I think we need to talk about what happened today.

RUSS: Of course you do. Fag.

STEVE: Dammit, Russ, you took this way too far.

RUSS: Relax, you liberal pansy. We're gonna be fine. I've got this under control.

STEVE: Seriously? Under control? Dwayne? Tommy?

TOMMY: I'm black. I'm not involved. Don't talk to me.

STEVE: Dwayne? Hello? Is anyone else nervous here?

RUSS: Hey, turd, I said I've got this. Chill the fuck out.

STEVE: Whatever happened to nobody gets hurt, Russ?

RUSS: :)

STEVE: Seriously, Russ??? A smiley face?

RUSS: (o)(o)

STEVE: WTF, Russ??? Is that boobs? Are you psychotic?

RUSS: (v)

STEVE: WTF is that???

TOMMY: That's a vagina, Steve. You should try one sometime. They're outstanding. Sorry, the black guy is leaving again.

RUSS: :)

TOMMY: And that's a smiley face.

STEVE: Goddammit, Tommy! I know what that is! You guys are really goddamn funny! Does a prison sentence sound like a smiley-face situation to you? Grow up, guys!

TOMMY: : (

RUSS: LOL

STEVE: Not cool. I guess I need to learn how to make a shiv out of a toothbrush now or something.

TOMMY: Learn to hide it in your ass, too.

STEVE: GODDAMMIT, TOMMY!

RUSS: ROFLMAO

TOMMY: My bad.

STEVE: Where the hell is Dwayne???

Dwayne chuckled as he read through the texts before realizing that Steve was probably correct to be nervous about the situation. He decided to hop into the texting mix. Just as he pressed send, a response from Russ popped up.

RUSS: He's probably doing the indentured servitude thing with one of his Hispanic lawn guys . . . letting them tug on his Weedwacker . . . lol.

DWAYNE: Sorry, guys, I was tied up.

DWAYNE: GODDAMMIT, RUSS!

STEVE: So, what's up, Dwayne? Am I crazy, or do we have good reason to be shitting our pants right now?

RUSS: Fag.

STEVE: Fuck off.

DWAYNE: I think we should talk about this in person, as opposed to leaving a goddamn memoir for the cops to read. Tomorrow at noon. The club.

12.

Dwayne had become a touch uncomfortable with the erratic approach Russ had taken to the Coach Dale situation. He was too nonchalant. Everyone knows that the first people the cops interview after a murder are the ones who knew the victim. It wasn't as if what happened to Dale could be viewed as an accident. He had flown out of a van into traffic. No decent person owns a van. Vans are for murderers and pedophiles. And something about a person's head popping off makes cops want to try harder. Dwayne knew all of this.

The next day, on his way to the meeting at the club, he briefly turned down his street to make sure his lawn crew had planted the new batches of flowers that Estelle had asked for. He knew he'd never hear the end of it if "his Mexicans," as she referred to them, hadn't busted their asses to appease her.

When Dwayne pulled up in front of the house, the second thing he noticed was that all of the flowers had been planted to perfection, and his yard looked glorious, unquestionably placing him in contention for the coveted "Yard of the Month" sign. The first thing he noticed, however, troubled him.

Who the fuck owned the five-year-old burgundy Toyota Avalon parked in his driveway?

"Jesus Christ," he said to himself. "Who the fuck are you balling now, Estelle?"

He glanced over at the clock on his truck's radio: 11:58 a.m.

"Goddammit," he whispered.

He didn't have time to do what he had dreamed of for years—bust through his bedroom door and lay a baseball bat across the back of the head of a guy who was balls deep in his wife. He wanted to so badly, but he couldn't. He had to meet the guys. It was probably best. Being involved in one murder at a time was plenty.

He threw his truck into "drive" and sped toward the club. Steve's

Prius, Tommy's Benz, and Russ's Ferrari were already there. He parked inches away from Russ's door to piss him off.

Walking through the club's door, he heard two waiters arguing over who had to wait on Russ. One of the waiters was the redhead from a few days back, and the other a young Middle Eastern kid. Dwayne could tell the redhead had won the argument. He felt bad for the other kid.

Dwayne could plainly see that Steve was a bundle of nerves as he took his seat at the table and said his greetings to the guys. Tommy had sunglasses on, in a lame attempt to hide his identity.

Russ, as usual, was amped up, hammered, and partying balls. "Thanks for joining myself, Woody Allen, and Ray Charles today, Dwayne," he quipped in his usual smartass tone. "For fuck's sake, Tommy, you're the only goddamn black member of the club. You wanna blend in? Bleach your skin and trim a couple of inches off that damn python. If you're gonna wear glasses, go sit at the goddamn piano."

"Jesus Christ," Steve mumbled. "He never stops."

Russ glanced around the table, hoping that he was winning over the nervous crowd. Most people have this thing inside of them that tells them when they've fucked up; it's the same thing that might prompt most people to ask for forgiveness and attempt to make right whatever wrongs have been done. Russ didn't have that thing. He didn't have that thing at all.

The young Middle Eastern waiter approached the table. "Good afternoon, gentlemen," he began. "My name is—"

"Hang on there, Quick Stop," Russ interrupted. "Would you mind taking a step back and opening your jacket for me?"

"Here we go," Tommy muttered under his breath as he looked across the table to address Dwayne. "Am I obviously black? I know I am. How the fuck am I friends with this guy?"

"Your kids are friends, so you're forced friends, Tom," Dwayne replied. "It's like collateral damage but on a residential level, as opposed to actual damage from warfare."

"Gotcha. Thanks."

"No problem. I was just asking myself the same thing."

The waiter stepped back from the table, humiliated, and opened his jacket so that Russ could see.

"Are you pleased, sir?" the waiter asked, annoyed. "I have no bomb vest. I'm Catholic. My name is Ron."

"Ron?" Russ laughed. "Your fucking name is Ron? A goddamn jihadi named Ron? Oh, man. That's good stuff."

"Thank you, sir. I'm glad you like it. Would you like to hear about our specials today? The chef has prepared—"

"Listen, Ron," Russ cut in again. "It's not that I don't believe you, but I'm gonna need you to show me your shoes."

"Do you think I'm a potential shoe bomber, sir?"

"Potentially. Yes. It crossed my mind. Just keepin' it real, Ron."

Ron stood still and stared down at Russ. He was a short, thin Palestinian kid who looked no older than fifteen. He sounded like he'd grown up riding waves in California. He seemed mellow but ready to crack. He gripped his large round serving tray with both hands as he struggled to determine how to handle Russ.

Dwayne and the others knew that stepping in would accomplish nothing, so they simply sat and watched.

"If I allow you to inspect my shoes," Ron said, "can we then move on to discussing the menu and be done with the racial profiling?"

"Hey, 9/11, Ron. Never forget," Russ said righteously.

Steve buried his face in his hands and softly began to weep. Tommy and Dwayne admired the kid for showing some hint of a backbone.

"Gentlemen," Ron said after a long deliberate pause, "I apologize that you have to hear this, but your friend here can go fuck himself. I quit. This country-club servant bullshit ain't for me. I pray that your friend here is the only casualty in an act of domestic terror. Peace out."

Ron turned and threw his tray like a Frisbee at the redheaded waiter, who dove to avoid taking it in the teeth. He then tossed his apron and bowtie onto the floor and walked right out the door.

Tommy and Dwayne rose to their feet and applauded as they

watched him walk down the fairway of hole number one and off into the sunset.

Steve still had his head down. Russ was unfazed, as if nothing had happened at all.

"So who the fuck is gonna tell me about the specials?" Russ asked.

"Buffet, dick," Dwayne responded. "We're all having the buffet now."

Tommy, Steve, and Dwayne walked to the buffet area. Russ begrudgingly joined them. The men filled their plates with shrimp and salads, and returned to their table to accomplish what they'd all met up to do.

"Okay, guys, here's the plan," Russ began while chewing his food. A disgusting combination of ranch dressing and cocktail sauce dripped from his chin.

"Wait just a goddamn minute, you slimy piece of shit," Steve piped up to everyone's amazement. "You don't get to make the plans anymore! When you make the plans, people get thrown out of vans and die! Cops get involved! Someone else makes the plans this time."

Russ was pissed. He jumped up and put his finger right in Steve's face. "Fuck you, nerd!" he screamed through gritted teeth, "You don't get to tell me—"

"Russ!" Dwayne grabbed Russ's arm. "Jesus! You're causing a scene! He's right, okay?! You're not making the plans anymore. So sit down, shut the fuck up, and eat some more shrimp, okay? I already know what we need to do."

Russ saw the intensity in Dwayne's eyes. He could tell that Tommy and Steve were both aligned with Dwayne as well. He sat back down and crossed his arms across his chest in defeat.

Dwayne allowed the mood to calm for a moment before he spoke.

"Here's what we need to do: Nothing. Nothing at all. We don't say a word. We don't talk to anyone ever again about this. We were trying to do something good for our kids, and a force outside of our control took it to a level that we wouldn't have approved of. We can either live with that and shut the fuck up, or we can go to jail for a long time and miss out on seeing our kids grow up. It's that simple."

The guys ate in silence. They knew Dwayne was right. None of them wanted to do time.

"What about the cops?" Steve asked. "You know they're going to talk to us eventually."

"There's no doubt in my mind that the police will want to talk with at least some of the parents on the team," Dwayne continued, "but we don't know anything. We didn't see anything. We're as shocked as anyone."

"You know they're gonna talk to me," Tommy said, peering over his sunglasses. "You know the drill. The black guy gets smoked out first."

"Sweet Jesus, Tommy," Russ jumped in. "Stop telling us you're black. We know. We're obviously not racists. We have a black friend. We don't care."

"Not racist?" Tommy replied. "I wonder what Ron would have to say about that. Let's ask him. Oh, that's right, he skipped his happy brown ass on down the fairway."

"He was a terrorist, Tommy. For fuck's sake, be an American."

"Guys!" Dwayne said with a strain. "Please. Holy shit. Tommy, you're right. You'll probably be questioned. Just keep your answers short. Don't look guilty by offering up all kinds of information that doesn't matter. Don't go making shit up for no reason. That goes for all of us. We're shocked and saddened. It's a tragedy. That's it. There's nothing else to say. We don't need an elaborate plan. We don't know anything."

The men nodded in agreement. That *was* the best plan. Keep your fucking mouth shut. Act sad. No need to complicate things.

"Also," Dwayne kept going, "if anyone wants to talk about things, let's not leave a goddamn transcript of the conversation. No more texting about it. No talking over the phone about it. If anyone thinks our situation is being jeopardized, we need a code word to—"

"Code Red," Russ interjected enthusiastically, with the certainty of a five-star general laying out battle plans. He was attempting to gain some ground again with the group. He seemed 100 percent certain that his code word was a winner.

"No, dipshit," Dwayne replied. "Something inconspicuous, not something that sounds like we're under attack."

"Threat Level Orange," Steve jumped in.

Dwayne just looked at him. "Are you guys fucking retarded?"

"Captain Tiberious Lovebone," Tommy offered up with a big smile, quite proud of himself. "Or Chocolicious Lovebone."

Dwayne was beside himself.

"It's a nickname," Tommy explained.

Dwayne ran the palm of his hand across his forehead as he attempted to regain his composure.

"Chocolicious Lovebone?" Dwayne said to Tommy. "Really, Tom? How the fuck do you plan on inconspicuously using 'Chocolicious Lovebone' in a sentence?"

"I use it several times a day, Dwayne," he responded flatly. "If you don't like it, fine. Jesus. Don't be a dick."

Dwayne stared at Tommy.

"Okay," he said in an annoyed tone. "The code word will be 'briefcase.' Just say something about a briefcase, and then we'll all agree on a time to grab some food or a drink at the club. Does that sound good to you, fucking Chocolate Wonderbone, or whatever the fuck your nickname was?"

"'Briefcase' it is, Dwayne," Russ curtly replied, still halfway feeling snubbed as he stood up and tossed his napkin on the table. "I've gotta take a shit."

"Thanks, Russ," Steve said. "Always a beacon of class. 'Briefcase' is fine."

"Okay, then," Dwayne emphasized one more time for solidarity, "no one speaks of this via text, email, or phone call ever again."

In the parking lot, as Dwayne pulled himself into his truck, he noticed an envelope in the passenger's seat. Someone had slipped it through the window he'd left cracked open an inch or so. Dwayne opened the envelope and pulled out the contents—a stack of pictures of Estelle . . . naked, oiled up, very erotic . . . taken by someone else . . . in his own bedroom. He looked in all directions. Russ, Steve, and Tommy had left. He didn't recognize anyone else around. He had no idea who would've left the photos there. He was equal parts pissed and paranoid. Estelle slept around, that he knew, but she'd generally made a half-assed attempt to conceal it. But posing for pictures? Jesus. Not cool.

Dwayne tossed the envelope into the glove compartment and slammed it shut. He retrieved a half-smoked joint from his ashtray, lit it, and smoked it down to his fingers.

"What the *fuck*, Estelle?"

13.

Dwayne stayed at work late that night. He was trying to keep his mind off what was now an absolute certainty: His wife was a total whore.

His office complex, a few miles from his house, consisted of three small white stucco buildings and was located on the Trinity River. In addition, there was a rather large warehouse, which housed all of the lawn care equipment for jobs both large and small—mowers, tractors, hedge trimmers, wood chippers, bags of fertilizer, dirt, and mulch, and the trailers and trucks that transported them.

Dwayne's office wasn't in the small buildings. He preferred to be in the warehouse, above the dispatch office, where trucks and equipment were checked in and out. A large glass wall at the front gave him full view of everything that occurred there. This made him feel like he had his finger on the pulse of his business.

His office wasn't decorated to entertain or impress, either. A large but inexpensive desk sat in the center of the room, with multitudes of file cabinets scattered throughout. On his desk were several photos of Alex playing baseball and one photo of Estelle from their wedding day—before he knew what a raging whore she was. Also on his desk were the credit card bills Estelle had racked up. A mountain of them.

Dwayne had gotten into the habit of doing something that he wasn't particularly fond of: He had been paying the monthly minimums on several credit cards, not making a dent in the balances, while using two other credit cards to live off of. Business had been growing steadily but couldn't keep up with Estelle's expenses. He had recently renewed the lease on his work property, and the payments had doubled. He'd never imagined having a mortgage payment as high as he had. Alex's school was one of the most expensive in the state, and he'd almost depleted the fund he'd set up for college just trying to keep him there. The country club's monthly dues and Estelle's bar tab weren't helping, and neither was the payment on her new Mercedes.

She used to work. Now her job was spending money. It was all becoming too much for him.

Every time he spoke to Estelle about getting her spending under control, it fell on deaf ears. She turned things around on him, made it his fault. He was failing to provide for his family. He was a failure. Everyone else could do it. Why couldn't he?

Dwayne knew he couldn't pull off this balancing act for too much longer. It would all come crumbling down. Something had to change . . . soon.

He looked around his warehouse. What could he sell? Could he make it with less equipment? No, he couldn't. He had to find more business. He needed more income. He'd have to get on top of his existing accounts. He had let a few people slide. He couldn't do that anymore. He knew it might destroy a few people financially—some of them friends—but it was him or them now. It was time to call shit due.

He looked at a picture of Alex from his days in tee ball. He looked so much younger then. Dwayne didn't bust his ass for Estelle or her Mercedes. He didn't do it for himself, or his house in the ritzy part of town. He did it all for Alex. Everything was for him. Dwayne would find a way.

Dwayne locked up his office and turned off the lights. His work truck was parked next to his black Audi A8L. It was dusty. He hadn't driven it in days. He loved the Audi. It was a gorgeous vehicle, with every bell and whistle imaginable. It ran like a goddamn racecar. But the only reason he had bought it was to keep Estelle from bitching about the work truck.

"Fuck her," he said under his breath as he walked to the door of the truck. He climbed in and turned on the stereo. Ryan Bingham and The Dead Horses were playing. He cranked it up loud, singing along as he rolled a joint. Dwayne leaned back and enjoyed his doob as the soothing powers of the Mary Jane crept over him. The blanket of buzzed comfort began to smother the anxiety that had nearly pulled him to an early grave.

He would not tell anyone about the pictures of Estelle. He wouldn't even tell Estelle. He'd keep doing what he had done for the last few years: He'd keep his head down and keep busting his ass for Alex. And if things got to be too much, as they had a way of doing from time to time, he'd just roll another joint and turn up the music until it all passed.

And if that didn't fix things, then God help anyone who got in his way.

14.

Dwayne pulled the truck into his driveway just before 1:00 a.m. He had needed to drive around for a while, listen to music, and get his Zen going again. He dragged his tired ass toward the bedroom. The light from the television was shining from beneath the door. He opened the door and took a seat on the bed by his snoring wife. A bottle of Xanax sat beside an empty wine glass on the nightstand.

He looked into the bathroom. Two towels lay on the floor just outside the shower. He wondered what had happened to that girl he fell in love with so long ago. His marriage had reached a crossroads.

Before he climbed under the covers, he figured he should go check on Alex. He pushed himself up, groaning and tired, and headed to Alex's room. Dwayne stared at his sleeping son. Baseball cards and his perfectly broken-in baseball glove lay across his bed. It would break his heart, Dwayne thought to himself, if he and Alex ever had to be separated by a nasty divorce.

Dwayne knew he had to work things out with Estelle. She couldn't have done more to push him away, but he had to do it for his kid. He wouldn't let this lifestyle erected upon soulless money worship tear his family apart. He had to do whatever it took.

He knew that it was time to take the gloves off when it came to addressing those who were ripping his family to pieces. He would never again let all of this mounting bullshit interfere with a happy existence for Alex. He would destroy whatever got in his way.

Dwayne didn't know where life was about to take him, but that was okay. He was starting to feel good about things. And he knew that it was odd for him to be feeling good about things. His wife was fucking around. His business was losing profitability. His credit card bills were driving him into a sinkhole of insurmountable debt. But he suddenly felt up to the challenge, like the rage, the Zen, and the buzz had finally managed to coexist in his head.

Dwayne's alarm clock sounded at 6:00 a.m. He wasn't tired. He should've been. He knew this. He didn't care. He looked down in the direction of his feet, noticing a healthy morning boner obstructing his view. He immediately ripped his underwear off and threw them across the room before tearing back the sheets to reveal Estelle's perfect naked body.

Dwayne woke Estelle with a firm slap to the ass. He climbed on board and took care of business with an intense lovemaking session that lasted somewhere between two and three minutes.

He slapped her ass again, popped out of bed, got himself showered and shaved, and threw some bacon in the frying pan.

This motherfucker was ready for the world.

15.

Dwayne dropped Alex off at school and headed in to the office to finally get after his mounting "receivables" problem. People were going to pay. He kept thinking about the look on Estelle's face when he left for work. She hadn't looked at him like that for several years. It was hot. She was dumbfounded.

The texting chain from the guys started up midmorning.

TOMMY: You guys going to practice tonight?

DWAYNE: I sure am, Captain Chocolate Dick. Are you?

TOMMY: Yup. I've just gotta put some fake titties in a few ladies, then suck the fat outta half the women in town. But I'll be there.

RUSS: Jesus. Don't any of these broads exercise?

STEVE: Yeah, your wife does. Pole dancing has kept her pretty toned.

STEVE: Oh, SNAP!

TOMMY: Wait, what? What the fuck did you just say? Did you just say "Oh, SNAP"???

RUSS: Fucking nerd. LOL.

DWAYNE: Here we go again with the LOL shit.

TOMMY: :)

DWAYNE: So everyone is going tonight?

RUSS: I am. Tiberious is. I'm sure Steve is, because he's a fucking nerdy follower. So what are we going to do about Dipshit Pete, our new coach? He's a total fucking Democrat. I'm calling it right now. And that means more goddamn daddy baseball.

DWAYNE: I'll tell you this: I'm not putting up with it. I'm done with that bullshit. It's time to get this team playing baseball. I'll smack that fucker in the head if he benches Alex again.

STEVE: Hell yeah. I'm with you, Dwayne. Time to get Jonathan in the infield so we can win some games.

RUSS: Sorry Steve, but your dildo kid needs to walk away from sports entirely.

STEVE: WTF???

TOMMY: :(

DWAYNE: We need to take control of this team. If we get Alex, Jackson, and TJ in the infield and at the top of the batting order, we'll have a shot in the playoffs.

STEVE: And Jonathan. WTF, Dwayne?

RUSS: LOL.

DWAYNE: Of course. And Jonathan. I'll see you guys at the field.

TOMMY: Later.

STEVE: Later.

RUSS: TTYL.

DWAYNE: TTYL?

STEVE: Goddammit.

TOMMY: :p

DWAYNE: Seriously, Tommy, don't encourage him. What the fuck is TTYL? We're not a goddamn boy band.

RUSS: It stands for "talk to you later," you crotchety old fucks.

STEVE: Maybe if you didn't date 9-year-olds and mental midgets you'd assimilate some kind of actual vocabulary over time.

RUSS: Assimilate my dick, you liberal douche.

TOMMY: :|

Dwayne stared at his phone. He wanted to make sure that the texting conversation had ended. Thankfully, it had. He returned to working on his receivables. He couldn't believe how relaxed he'd allowed himself to become with several accounts. He spent the first half of his day making calls for payments. He had shifted into survival mode. It appeared to be working. He was able to gain commitments from more than half of his past-due accounts before lunchtime.

At just after 2:00 p.m., as Dwayne was nearing the end of his call list, he received a knock at his office door. The handle jiggled a few times before he remembered that he'd locked it. Dwayne stood, stretched his legs, and walked to the door.

He was stunned to see Estelle standing in the doorway, looking sultry and spectacular. She was wearing oversized sunglasses, a hint of red lipstick, and an old TCU ball cap over freshly showered, still wet hair. Her long, flowing, loose-fitting sundress allowed the light from behind her to cast a terribly sexy silhouette.

Estelle didn't say a word. She placed her index finger to the middle of Dwayne's chest and slowly pushed him backward to the front of his desk. She began to move her finger downward, following the buttons of his shirt, until her hand reached the top of his belt. She unfastened it and reached her hand inside.

"Do you remember," she said in a whisper as she leaned in close to his ear, "back before life got complicated? Back when we were just a couple of crazy kids?"

Dwayne couldn't speak. She had a solid grip on his johnson, and it was nearing the point where it couldn't get any firmer.

"All we ever wanted back then was to be happy, baby," Estelle continued. "And it was just sex, sex, sex . . . "

She ripped the belt out of the loops and whipped it across the desk like a dominatrix, which caused a *POP!* like a firecracker. Dwayne's pants fell to the floor.

Estelle took a step back and removed her hat and sunglasses before pulling her sundress over her head slowly and tossing it to a chair across the room. She turned away from Dwayne and walked to the glass wall overlooking the warehouse, wearing nothing but a yearning grin. She placed her hands up high on the window, arched her back, and assumed the position.

He hoped that none of his workers were in the warehouse to witness the show that was about to take place in the window of the boss's office.

"I don't know what's come over you, Dwayne," Estelle said. "But something's changed. And I like it. I want you to take me right fucking now."

God, she looked amazing, he thought. He tore his shirt off, popping every button in the process. He kicked his pants away from his feet and marched up behind Estelle, planting her face against the glass as he made love to her like he hadn't in years.

After several minutes, Estelle turned and pushed him backward to the desk. In one violent motion, she swept everything from the desk onto the floor, shoved Dwayne onto the desk, and climbed on top of him.

"Holy shit, Estelle," he grunted. "This is just like a porno! This is awesome!"

Estelle was screaming. She was really into it. Dwayne didn't know that sex like this actually existed. When they finished, he couldn't move a single muscle in his body. He had experienced one of those full-body orgasms that, up until then, he figured only people like Sting had. He lay flat on his back, completely naked atop his desk, as Estelle limped over to her sundress and pulled a joint and lighter from her pocket. She climbed back on top of him and lit the joint. They passed it back and forth a few times before anyone said a word.

"I know most guys don't like it when their wives show up unannounced at work," Dwayne said as he stared up at Estelle, who had begun to rock her hips ever so softly as she sat perched on top of him. "But feel free to do this anytime."

Estelle took a long pull from the joint as she constricted the muscles in her thighs. She looked back down at him with a seductive snarl on her perfect lips.

"You're a real fucking rock star when you want to be," she whispered.

"You haven't seen anything yet."

16.

For the rest of the afternoon, Dwayne couldn't shake the image of Estelle, how she slowly pulled her sundress up over her head, her sultry smile. She never wore underwear, and he was thankful for that gift. He'd stood at the window and watched her as she walked down the stairs and out the door. Something had stirred inside of him. He wanted things to work with her now. Perhaps they could. He had to find a way to convince her to reign in her spending or they would be having the best sex in the housing projects.

Dwayne looked at his watch. It was time for practice. First, he needed to stop by the house and throw on a different shirt. His office looked as though a tornado of porn had blown through it. A pornado, if you will. He left everything as it was, pulled his arm through the sleeves of his buttonless shirt, and flipped off the lights.

Dwayne grabbed what he needed from his work truck and hopped into the Audi. He popped on his Ray-Ban Wayfarers, pushed the ignition button, and let the engine purr for a few seconds before cranking up one of the best factory stereos ever placed inside a vehicle. Guns N' Roses, "Welcome to the Jungle." Perfect.

This was shaking out to be a kick-ass day. He wasn't thinking about his debts anymore. He had a Jedi level of focus, and the knob on his focus was now turning to baseball. He burst through his front door with his shirt torn open and wind-swept hair a mess, sunglasses still on to help mask being moderately high. A group of the neighborhood ladies were sitting around the dining room table with Estelle, knocking back bottles of wine and vodka. He'd obviously interrupted a heated session of talking shit.

Dwayne caught a few disapproving glances from the judgmental, gossiping bitches as he brushed past them. He glanced across the table at Estelle, who gave him a grin. He grinned back. God, she looked hot.

"What's going on with the torn shirt, Dwayne?" Tiffany Blaine, a trust-fund society snoot, snipped as he walked past the table. "Did you tear it mowing lawns, dear?"

"No, Tiff, I tore it mowing ass," he shot back. "You look great, by the way. The facelift looks amazing. And the collagen injections in your lips really add to the whole Picasso look. Bet you can't wait for the diet pills to kick in so you have the whole package."

Tiffany's surgically tightened face tightened even further. She had never been spoken to like that. Estelle turned away to hide her laughter. She was turned on to no end by the new Dwayne.

Moments later, Alex joined his father at the front door, bat bag in hand. The two of them walked out to the Audi, popped in, and tore off toward the field.

"You feeling okay, Dad?" Alex asked.

"Do I not look okay, buddy?" Dwayne replied.

"Actually, I don't think I've ever seen you with this much pep in your step. Just wanted to make sure things are okay."

"Things are great, buddy. Things are great."

Practice had already begun when Dwayne and Alex arrived. It was impossible to avoid the huddle of parents and nannies as Dwayne headed for the dugout. There was talk of how great a coach Ricky Dale had been, how they would miss him, what a big event the funeral would be the following day, and what a good thing it was that Pete Rearden had stepped in to fill his shoes as coach.

Pete had positioned Jackson at left field, with TJ and Jonathan both doubled up at right field. It was the same old shit. Nothing had changed.

Dwayne told Alex to put his bag in the dugout, grab his glove, and head to shortstop, where Ace, the son of the late Ricky Dale, was playing. "I'm making a change at shortstop," Dwayne said to the baseball dads. "Maybe you guys should make some changes too."

Pete, sporting two black eyes thanks to Russ, had been standing at home plate, hitting balls to the kids in the field. The only reason that left and right field were getting any action was because the infield couldn't catch a ball and make a play. Almost every ball hit to an infielder went between that infielder's legs and into the outfield.

When Alex walked to shortstop and stood beside Ace, Pete stopped hitting balls.

"Hey, Alex, glad you could make it," Pete yelled. "Try not to be late next time. Now head to left field with Jackson. You two can take turns."

"Stay right there, Alex," Dwayne called out. "Pete, Alex is playing shortstop now. Ace, go grab a spot in the outfield."

"But the outfield is already taken," Ace said to Dwayne.

"Yeah, I know, that sucks, but we're going to play this game to win now, and we can't do that with you at shortstop, so go double up at center."

Pete was furious. He didn't like his coaching being called into question.

"Now listen here, Dwayne, I'm the coach of this team, and—"

"And what? You want to lose? Is that what you want? Because that's what we've been doing while we waste talent on the bench, in the field, and in the lineup. This shit needs to stop."

"Well, if you don't like it, you can pack up and leave, Dwayne."

"I don't think so, Pete. And while we're making changes, I want Jonathan at third, TJ at second, and Jackson at first."

"My son plays first, Dwayne," Pete insisted.

"Whoop-dee-fuckin'-doo, Pete. Your son sucks at first. He also sucks at batting. He needs to be the goddamn caboose in our batting order."

"Fuck you, Dwayne, the positions stand as they did when Ricky Dale was coaching. If you don't like that, you can quit."

"Listen, man, I know it sucks to work at Walmart, but you made that decision on your own. Don't take your shitty life out on these kids. It's not helping anything. These kids deserve to win a game."

"Not everyone can afford a fancy house and fancy things, asshole, but that doesn't make you better than me. It's time for you to leave before I call the cops."

Dwayne wondered why Walmart Pete would know he had a fancy house but brushed it off. He knew he couldn't allow Pete to call the cops. Not after they'd just had the head coach killed. That wouldn't be smart. He looked over at Russ, Tommy, and Steve, who were in awe of the hostile takeover that had almost taken place.

Goddammit, Dwayne thought. The day had been going so well. He would have to lose this battle for the time being. He took a deep breath and exhaled.

"Go on out to left field, Alex," Dwayne shouted over to shortstop in defeat.

Alex slumped over and headed out to left. He was filled with disappointment and dragged his feet for the entire walk. It killed Dwayne. Dwayne had fire in his eyes as he marched back to where his friends were standing at the fence.

"Dude!" Steve sped over to Dwayne. "That was *awesome!*"

Dwayne was too pissed off to respond. He couldn't believe that miserable little Walmart nerd Pete didn't back down.

"What the hell has gotten into you, Dwayne?" Tommy asked.

"I'll tell you what got into me!" Dwayne snapped. "I thought we were all on the same page here, guys. Is it too much to ask for a little backup? I mean . . . Jesus, I was out there fighting for your kids too! Russ? What the fuck?! You can organize a hit and whip a baseball at a guy's face, but you can't get out there and fight for your son?"

"Take it easy there, asshole." Russ jumped in Dwayne's face. "Just because half the goddamn town is ballin' your wife doesn't give you the right to get shitty with me."

Dwayne grabbed Russ by the shirt and shoved him against the fence. He wanted to hit him. The fist was ready.

"*Fuck!*" Dwayne blurted out through gritted teeth. He let go of Russ and walked off past the bleachers, through the parking lot, and to his car. He climbed inside and sparked up a joint. He glanced to his right, at the old Honda parked next to his Audi. Dave the umpire was inside, smoking a joint of his own.

Dave started giggling at the idea of both of them smoking weed at the same time and motioned for Dwayne to roll his window down. "Hey, bro, you need any more weed?"

"No, Dave, I appreciate it though."

"Things not working out the way you'd hoped?"

"What the fuck does that mean?" Dwayne froze. He didn't want to give this jackass any indication that he'd been involved in the Ricky Dale situation.

Dave looked puzzled. He always looked puzzled, but even more so this time. "Oh. Never mind. I got some good weed back at the trailer if you ever wanna come smoke out or something."

"Sounds great, Dave. I'll put it on my calendar."

Dwayne rolled his window back up and tossed the joint on the ground as he exited his vehicle. He walked back into the ballpark, as batting practice had begun, and took a seat by his crew.

Pete was pitching the ball to the batters. He couldn't pitch a single ball into the strike zone. It frustrated Pete to no end that Dwayne, Russ, Tommy, and Steve were in the bleachers, watching . . . judging . . . harassing.

"I think they sell some good stuff for pitching practice at Target, Pete," Tommy yelled out to him.

"I mean, you could probably pick something up while you're greeting people at Walmart," Russ added. "But Walmart stuff sucks. Target is way better."

Pete was sweating. He was about to lose it. He continued to throw balls everywhere but where a kid could hit. The kids were swinging wildly, swatting the bats high and low, trying to make something connect.

"Wow," Tommy continued. "This is such a huge loss for Major League Baseball. I can't believe you never got signed. But Walmart sure scored. Damn, they are one lucky company to have you."

"Did you throw your arm out stacking tampons on the shelves? I hear that stacking tampons has ruined several otherwise potentially great athletes," Russ shouted.

"Guys, *PLEASE!*" Pete screamed. "I can't concentrate!"

Pete went through the first seven batters without throwing a strike. The catcher was sweating profusely from having to dive in every direction while attempting to catch the wild pitches.

"Hey, Pete, if your arm gets sore, I think they have sports cream on aisle seven," Russ yelled. "I'm sure you know where the sports cream is, being such a fucking athlete."

"*Jesus*, Russ," Dwayne said. "There are kids around."

Everyone was suddenly silent as Alex came out to bat. Dwayne almost didn't let him bat because he didn't want him to get in the habit of swinging at bad pitches. He was too pissed off to stop him, though.

The first pitch that Pete threw to Alex was high and inside. It wasn't intentionally high and inside, but that just happened to be where it went. And Alex loved the high and inside ball. He ripped into it with his gorgeous, natural swing . . . absolutely *crushed* it. It was a beautiful ball, sailing as sweet and deep as a ball can sail toward center field. It cleared the smiling, leathery face of Ricky Dale on the Ricky Dale's Furniture Store Official Scoreboard by a good ten feet.

Everyone in attendance stared at the face of Ricky Dale looking down upon them. Pete took his hat off as a gesture of respect. Ace dropped to the ground in tears. It was a touching moment.

"*FUCK YEAH, ALEX!*" Russ jumped to his feet. "WAY TO KNOCK THE *SHIT* OUTTA THAT BALL!!!"

Alex took off running around the bases, as you would in an important game with everything on the line. He raised his arms up in the air as he rounded third base and headed home. Jonathan, TJ, and Jackson all ran to home plate to tackle him.

The rest of the team had their arms around Ace, who sobbed uncontrollably.

"That's it for the day, people," Pete announced to the nannies, parents, and kids. "We'll practice again day after tomorrow, same time. I'm sure I'll see most of you at the funeral. Take care."

Pete set off solemnly toward the dugout.

"Thanks, Pete," Russ replied. "That was really cool of Walmart to supply your wardrobe, by the way."

Pete began to gather his things, as did the kids. He was angry and embarrassed at how the practice had gone, especially the heckling from Russ and Tommy. No one respected him. It was just like when he told his family he'd gotten a job at Walmart.

Alex ran up and hugged his dad. Dwayne's eyes teared up momentarily. Alex knew how much his dad wanted him to be happy, and he knew it upset him when he had to play left field again. Hitting the ball over the fence vindicated both of them.

Dwayne didn't have much to say to anyone as he walked out to his car with his son. He felt drained. Pete had taken the wind out of his sails. He told himself he would fight on, though. He wasn't going to give up. He liked who he was becoming. He had hope for his family, his business, his marriage . . .

He watched Pete with a simmering gaze as Pete exited the field juggling a large bucket of balls, a bat bag, and catcher's gear.

His jaw dropped as he watched Pete pop the trunk open on a five-year-old burgundy Toyota Avalon.

17.

Dwayne dropped Alex off at the house. He told him to let Estelle know he didn't get a chance to finish his work that day and had to head back to the warehouse. "She'll understand," he assured Alex with a smile.

Dwayne couldn't face Estelle right then. Things had been going too well. He needed to think about things. Technically, he thought to himself, she'd had sex with Pete *before* things were looking better between the two of them. So he might be able to give her a pass this time.

But Pete? Seriously? She had to fuck a guy who worked at Walmart? Jesus. He had known for a while that she'd slept around, but he didn't care then because he didn't even like her. Now, he thought, he might be falling back in love with her. And that Walmart thing really bugged him.

Dwayne needed to have a few stiff drinks and talk it over with a friend. He wasn't looking for advice. He wanted someone to shut up and listen. He definitely didn't feel like dealing with Russ, and Tommy was too woven into the social-climber scene to be trusted. Those two would never let him live it down if they knew Estelle had allowed a Walmart guy to throw a bone at her.

He dialed his phone.

"This is Steve."

"What's going on, bro?"

"Just looking at my teachers' progress reports and watching MSNBC. You?"

"Awww, man, I just need to have a few drinks and talk to somebody. I was gonna see if you wanted to join me."

"I would, but I—"

"Thanks, man. I'll see you at The Tavern in ten minutes."

Dwayne whipped the Audi into the run-down parking lot of The Tavern. It seemed a little bit out of place. He usually drove his truck there. The Tavern was a dilapidated old joint on the outskirts of the good part of town. Dwayne liked it, though. The people were real. You might actually get knifed if you ordered anything other than beer, tequila, or whiskey.

Dwayne waited until Steve pulled up. He arrived in his Prius and parked it between two heavy-duty GMC diesel trucks. Steve hopped out of his 50-MPG Democrat-hauler wearing gray corduroys and a tight white silk Sean John T-shirt.

"Holy Jesus," Dwayne said. "Are you trying to get us killed? What the hell is that shirt, man?"

"It's Sean John, by Puff Daddy, or P. Diddy, or Diddy. Why?"

"Didn't they at least sell them in your size?"

"It's formfitting. And it's a really nice shirt. I'll have you know that several kids at my school have been beat up for their Sean John clothes."

"That doesn't surprise me at all."

"No, I meant they got beat up in a good way."

"Of course. Hopefully, tonight you won't find out that there's really no difference between being beat up in a good way and being beat up in a bad way."

The two friends perched themselves atop a couple of barstools near the end of the bar. On the old square television hanging above a wall of cheap liquor, Dwayne was glad to see that the Rangers were up over the Angels 6–0.

"Two cold ones and two whiskeys, neat, please," Dwayne called out to the pregnant, acne-scarred bartender.

She poured the drinks and slid them in front of Dwayne and Steve. Steve recognized her from his high school a couple of years back. She'd been to his office several times. This was exactly where he told her she would end up if she didn't get her shit together. Steve's disapproving look was trumped by her look, which said *I'll fucking gut you like a fish.* He decided not to talk to her.

"So, what's going on, man?" Steve asked in his best school counselor tone.

Dwayne turned up the whiskey glass and slammed it, wincing and feeling the burn as he turned to answer. "Estelle is having an affair."

He tapped the counter for a refill.

"Oh, Jesus, Dwayne, I'm sorry," Steve replied. "Is it Russ?"

Dwayne shot a disgusted sideways glance at Steve.

"Russ?! Are you fucking kidding me? Why the fuck would it be Russ?"

The bartender set another whiskey down for Dwayne. He slammed it and tapped the bar for another, waiting for Steve to answer.

"I don't know, man. It's just the way he always talks about her to you. And Tommy. He mentions covering her ass in honey at least a half dozen times a day. He never talks about my wife that way."

"Steve, Judith has a terrible ass. It's huge. It's not proportionate at all to the rest of her body."

Dwayne looked at Steve. He'd gone too far. He could tell he'd hurt his feelings.

"I'm sorry, bro," Dwayne said consolingly. He threw an arm around Steve. "That wasn't cool. Judith's a sweet girl. I'm sure she's got great tits or something."

The two sat for several minutes in silence. The bartender continued to bring refills of whiskey and beer. Dwayne built up a healthy buzz.

"So anyhow," Dwayne broke the silence. "I asked you here because I needed to talk. I thought I turned over a new leaf today, bro, and it was really working for me. I got my shit together at work. Estelle stopped by the office and rode me like a mechanical bull. Things were going great, seemed like they might turn around. Then that Walmart bastard Pete fucked up the baseball practice."

"Yeah, he sure did. Same old shit."

"And he's the one that's fucking Estelle."

It was a hell of a bomb to drop. Steve was beside himself. He went into total shock. He picked up his whiskey and slammed it, tapping the bar afterward for another.

"I don't mean to rub salt in the wound here, Dwayne," Steve said. "But you know you can't make fun of Judith anymore. I mean, you know me, I'm not a big 'class warfare' kind of guy. But he fucking works at Walmart, man."

"I know. I know."

"That's gotta sting, Dwayne."

"It does."

"So what're you gonna do? You could probably get past it if it were a Men's Warehouse, or hell, even a Target. Target is pretty nice these days. I mean . . . Even Costco has stepped up their game. But Walmart? No, sir. They don't even *try*, man."

"I know. Even if it were Sears, or JC Penney, I mean . . . Christ, just give me something to work with, you know?"

"So what are you gonna do?"

Dwayne slammed another whiskey. He was good and drunk now.

"I don't think I could've said this last week, or hell, even yesterday. But I think I love her, man."

Steve hunched over the bar and stirred his whiskey with his finger while he pondered the situation. Was Walmart something they could get past? Would it eat at Dwayne for the rest of his life?

"I think you've gotta try, Dwayne. You've got Alex to think of here. You need to take control of the situation and fix it."

Dwayne rose to his feet. He could feel it again: that really good feeling about the way life was going. He knew he could get past this. It was worth a try.

"Thanks for being a friend, Steve." Dwayne extended his hand in gratitude.

Steve reached out and shook it, clasping his other hand on top for a more heartfelt gesture of support.

"And if you tell anyone about this," Dwayne pulled Steve in close, "I'll rip your fucking arms off and beat you to death with them."

Steve's smile dropped from his face. Dwayne turned and walked out the door.

Once he was in the Audi, Dwayne sparked up another joint. He turned the music up loud. It was Van Halen's "Hot for Teacher." He threw the car in reverse and punched the gas. He flew over the curb and into the middle of the road in a stunt-like reverse 180, popped the car down into drive, and sped toward home.

Only . . . he didn't go home. Dwayne drove past his street and headed to Walmart.

18.

There was a fire burning deep in Dwayne's soul. It was consuming him. It was that same level of emotion that had made him call every past-due customer. The same level of emotion that had pushed him to make love to his wife on top of his desk two more times than she had expected. It was that same level of emotion, only darker.

Dwayne parked in a quiet corner of the Walmart parking lot. From this spot, he had full visibility of the entrances and exits. It was a twenty-four-hour Walmart, he told himself, so he would have to be alert, watching every single vehicle.

He wasn't prepared for the midnight creatures of Walmart. It was mainly the meth-lab crowd: shirtless men and tube-topped women, all with mullets, carting around four- and five-year-old children, each wearing nothing but a diaper and drinking a coke. There were several "Dixie flag" bumper stickers on rusted vehicles with mismatched tires. It was a sight to behold. If they hung in there long enough, Dwayne thought, MTV might come along and give them a reality show, turning the process of evolution and the idea of celebrity completely on its head yet again.

He waited, lit a joint, and then waited more. His head began to fall every few moments from utter exhaustion. His eyes began to close. He managed to slap himself back to a state of alert several times before giving way to a whiskey- and weed-induced slumber.

A couple of hours later, a truck door slammed and jolted him to consciousness. He popped up, ready for action. It was 3:00 a.m.

Dwayne started his car and put it into drive. He still felt hammered. Just as he turned his vehicle's lights on, he noticed a five-year-old burgundy Toyota Avalon making its way into the lot.

Dwayne's heart raced. He was sweaty and mad, and had a crick in his neck. Neil Diamond's "America" played on the radio. Obviously, the station he had been listening to switched formats after he passed out. He turned it up anyway, inching the Audi to the end of the row of cars where the Avalon was parking.

No one was around. Dwayne watched Pete Rearden, showered and ready to kick ass for another day at Walmart, exit his Avalon and walk to the rear of it. He began to stack files of paperwork beneath his arms as he hunched himself over, digging around in the trunk.

The rage overtook Dwayne. He jammed his foot down on the gas pedal and proved the manufacturer's impressive zero-to-sixty claims to be spot-on. Pete turned to look at Dwayne at the last second, right before Dwayne nailed him head-on, sending him high into the night sky over the Audi with a full flip. Files of paper exploded into the air.

"Clean up on aisle four, motherfucker!" Dwayne screamed as Neil Diamond belted out the climax of the song with all his heart. He jacked the brakes hard and looked in the rearview mirror.

"Oh, shit," he whispered. He wasn't scared; he just hadn't planned anything out.

Dwayne threw the car in reverse and stopped just short of Pete. He got out of the vehicle and looked around. There was still no one. Pete was in bad shape. His legs were a mangled mess. He had propped himself up on his elbows and was trying to drag himself to safety. Blood was pouring from his nose and mouth. Dwayne had no idea how Pete was still conscious.

He popped the trunk on the Audi, impressed as the day he bought it at the ample trunk space. The salesman at the time had joked that there was room for three bodies back there. Dwayne needed room for only one.

He reached inside Alex's baseball bag and pulled out his $349 lucky tournament bat. He walked up behind Pete and took a full swing at his head, making that glorious *Tink!* sound that bats make when you put one over the fence.

Thankfully, Dwayne had spent a lot of time in his warehouse loading huge bags of dirt onto trucks. It was good training for loading a body into a trunk. It had always seemed so difficult in movies, he thought to himself, but this wasn't that bad at all. Dwayne threw the bat on top of Pete's lifeless body in the trunk, slammed it shut, and headed to the warehouse. Pete's spreadsheets and files flew up from the pavement in a horizontal tornado behind him as Dwayne hauled ass out of the parking lot.

He cranked up the radio again. It was more easy listening. He didn't mind. Dwayne was an easygoing kind of guy. He slapped his hands on the steering wheel to the percussion genius of Barry Manilow's "Copacabana." When he arrived at his office a few miles away, he was singing The Commodores' "Sail On" at the top of his lungs. God, those Commodores could sing.

He felt great.

19.

He pulled to one of the large warehouse doors around the back of the property, opened it up, drove the Audi in, and closed it again immediately. He then moved the car to the rear of the cavernous interior where the heavy equipment was housed. As he parked next to the hoist and leaf shredder, Dwayne heard soft thumps coming from the trunk. Pete wasn't quite dead yet.

Dwayne looked at his watch. It was 3:37 a.m. He was making good time. He knew that his work crews would start showing up around 6:30 a.m. He had enough time to make sure he did things right.

Dwayne grabbed some thick vinyl zip ties and opened the trunk.

"Dwayne," Pete sobbed. "Please . . . help me."

"I tried to help you earlier, Pete, but noooo, you wanted to run things your way. I mean, seriously, who puts a kid like Alex at left fucking field? And ninth batter? Please. That's just ridiculous."

Dwayne slipped the zip ties over Pete's ankles and around his wrists and tightened them as much as he could. He needed them on good. Pete didn't have the energy to struggle. He was in and out of consciousness. Dwayne reached over and slapped him on the cheek to make sure Pete could hear him.

"We're going deep into the playoffs, Pete. Deep. Hell, we may win it all. Our team has talent. And you could've been there for it, Pete. You could've been there."

He grabbed Pete's face and leaned in close, forcing Pete to look him in the eyes. "You could've been there. But you had to go and fuck my wife."

Pete's blackened, bloody eyes got huge. Dwayne shoved his face back down again and walked over to the hoist. The hoist was a gas-powered hybrid of a tractor and a crane, used to pick up crates, large bags, equipment, and so on. It had a large arm with a steel cable and hook that would pivot around and grab and move whatever needed to be grabbed and moved, up to 2,000 pounds.

Dwayne pushed the lifting lever forward. This lowered the hook into the car's trunk near Pete's feet. Enough slack was left in the line so that Dwayne could attach it to the zip ties, which he did, running the hook between Pete's ankles, positioning it squarely in place to lift the weight. Back on the hoist, Dwayne pulled back on the lever, lifting Pete slowly into the air, nearly eight feet off the ground.

Because his legs had been broken in several places, the process was excruciating for Pete. He didn't scream; he just cried until he lost consciousness. Blood and tears streamed steadily toward the ground, pooling together on the concrete floor. Dwayne lowered Pete a couple of feet and walked over to him. He gave him a hard slap to wake him up. They were face-to-face, with Pete dangling upside down.

"You made my son feel inadequate today, Pete, and that's just not cool. I want you to be awake for this."

Dwayne fired up the engine of the leaf shredder. He attached a large catch bag to the side, adjusted the setting to "fine," and then climbed aboard the hoist once again. Dwayne thought that Pete might be saying something, but the noise from the equipment drowned it out. Dwayne pivoted the hoist, bringing Pete above the opening of the shredder.

"Fucking Walmart, man," Dwayne said as he pushed the lever down. Pete's body went down, headfirst, into the shredder. He looked down toward the spinning blades, shaking wildly, as his head disappeared into the cylindrical opening atop the machine. His legs and body erupted into crazy, spasmodic motions as the noise from the machine indicated that the shredding had begun. The shaking stopped once the blades got to mid-chest.

Dwayne was impressed with how quickly he could damn near liquefy a human body. When only the feet were visible, he pulled the lever back, jumped down, and pulled the hook off. He dropped the bloody feet and ankles into the shredder and listened to the rest of Pete get blown against the back of the catch bag.

Next, Dwayne brought his truck into the warehouse and stationed it underneath the catch bag, then released the bag into the truck bed. He then picked up a residential-sized push-powered yard fertilizer and set it beside the bag of Pete.

Finally, he grabbed the power washer and blasted the equipment he'd used with full pressure, and then did the same to the inside of the trunk of his Audi. He walked in a circular motion around the equipment and the car, slowly pushing all traces of blood down the centrally located drain. He parked his Audi back outside, turned out the lights, pulled down the doors, and headed off to Jenny Field in the truck.

Once there, Dwayne dragged the bag over to the main field that the boys played on and left it in the dugout. He then grabbed the push-powered fertilizer, filled it up to the rim with red sludge formerly known as Pete, and walked back and forth across the baseball field until the machine cast out every tiny bit of him into the perfectly manicured grass. It took four trips back to the catch bag for refills to get all of Pete spread around.

After his final trip across the outfield, Dwayne looked up at the smiling face of Ricky Dale on the scoreboard advertisement. He shot a middle finger at him as he marched back to the dugout.

Dwayne loaded up his truck with the push-powered fertilizer and empty catch bag (which now weighed 180 pounds less), flipped on the main sprinkler for the fields, and drove down to the river behind Jenny Field.

Dwayne threw the fertilizer machine into the middle of the river behind the ballpark. He then found a large rock and placed it inside the catch bag before throwing it into the river as well.

He hopped back into his truck, sparked up a joint, and cranked up the music. Billy Idol was snarling his lip and singing "White Wedding." Dwayne couldn't help but snarl his lip and sing along.

Perhaps if he'd snarled his lip a bit less, he might have noticed Dave the umpire watching everything he'd done from the perch behind the scoreboard, where he'd passed out hours earlier after a two-day bender of crystal meth and bowling.

20.

Dwayne pulled into his driveway at 5:03 a.m. He wasn't going to sleep for more than forty-five minutes, and he knew it. He didn't care. He still had a crazy rush running through his body, and he was insanely high from the massive joint he'd just smoked.

He felt great.

He hoped to sneak into the house without making a sound, but the front door creaked when he opened it. Dwayne slithered through the living room and dining room and through his bedroom door in silence. He slipped into the bathroom and turned on the shower.

The nearly scalding water felt fantastic running over his head and down his back. He let the water run over him until the last bit of blood-tinged water had swirled down the drain. The shower door opened. The soap on his face kept Dwayne from opening his eyes, but he didn't need to. He knew who it was. He knew what she wanted. Two hands reached around his chest from behind and worked their way down. There was a light nibble at his earlobes as the hands reached their destination.

"Well, good morning, cowboy," Estelle whispered in his ear. "What were you up to last night? I missed you."

Dwayne hadn't heard that in years. It felt good. All of it felt good. "I was out there being a rock star, babe, just the way you like it." He picked her up, pushed her back against the shower wall, and made her toes and feet curl up. He then flung the shower door open and carried Estelle to the bathroom counter, where he finished the job.

When Dwayne was done, he made his way to the bed and flopped down, face first.

"Get some rest, baby," Estelle said. "Because I'm coming back for more later."

Dwayne sprung upright several hours later. He'd slept much longer than he'd wanted to. He felt something stuck to his ass. He reached back and grabbed it. It was a sticky note.

"I took Alex to school for you. See you at the funeral, rock star. —Estelle"

"Oh, shit!" he exclaimed as he looked at the clock. It was 11:36 a.m. The funeral had started at 11:00 a.m. He ran into the bathroom and grabbed his phone. He'd missed a shitload of text messages from the guys.

STEVE: Where the hell are you guys? Are you at the funeral? Anyone see Dwayne?

RUSS: We're sitting in the front row. Ran to the restroom. Grab a seat up there & we'll see you in a second. Haven't seen Dwayne.

There was a several-minute break from the texts, and then:

STEVE: Very funny, I just sat down in the front row & got asked to leave. Only family is allowed up there.

RUSS: LOL

TOMMY: :)

STEVE: Goddammit. Where are you guys?

RUSS: We're checking out the hot grieving nieces. Lobby.

STEVE: Bullshit! I was just in the lobby.

STEVE: Hello???

STEVE: Really funny, guys.

STEVE: Briefcase! Briefcase! Holy shit!

TOMMY: WTF?

RUSS: Is that the code word?

STEVE: Yes! Briefcase! Briefcase!

TOMMY: I think you're doing it wrong. Aren't you supposed to use it in a sentence?

RUSS: Yeah, but did we ever actually decide on "briefcase"? I was waaay hammered when we talked about it. What happened to Chocolate Lovebone?

TOMMY: Technically, it's Chocolicious Lovebone.

RUSS: That's right. Was "Chocolicious Lovebone" a no-go as a code word?

STEVE: Goddammit! BRIEFCASE! Where's Dwayne???

TOMMY: Not sure. What's up?

STEVE: Pete Rearden got abducted from Walmart last night.

RUSS: LOL

TOMMY: :)

STEVE: No, seriously!

RUSS: Whatever, dildo. It's disrespectful to be texting while they're trying to bury this asshole.

TOMMY: (*)

TOMMY: That was an asshole. I just made that up.

RUSS: Damn, you're good, Tommy.

TOMMY: : p

STEVE: Jesus Christ. Will you guys let Dwayne know I'm looking for him? If you see him tell him BRIEFCASE!

STEVE: Hello?

STEVE: HELLO??????

TOMMY: (*)

RUSS: LOL

STEVE: Goddammit.

Dwayne couldn't help but chuckle as he read the texts. The thing about Pete concerned him, but it wasn't fear. Dwayne wasn't sure if he could feel fear anymore.

He looked into the bathroom mirror. He couldn't understand what had happened to him.

Was he experiencing the world's first *positive* mental breakdown? His brain was no longer capable of dealing with the hypocrisy and the idiocy of the people he'd become embedded with over the last several years. On a very primal level, he felt like he might be the only person he knew who was willing to finally pull back the curtain and call it the way it was. Too many people spent their lives trying to break other people down. They stabbed them in the back. They talked shit. They destroyed people for sport. Why? Probably deep insecurity, Dwayne hypothesized. But he really didn't give a shit why it was. He didn't care. He wanted justice in a completely bullshit social setting. He wanted happiness among the kings and queens of unhappiness. He would bring a painful end to anyone who stood in the way of that.

Dwayne knew that these social forces had corrupted Estelle, but he was confident that he could make her see the light. He loved her. And he loved her ass. But he wouldn't allow Alex to be corrupted. It wouldn't happen.

Dwayne received a text from Estelle. "Alex is going to a friend's house after school. I'm having a prayer group at our house after the funeral."

Dwayne rolled his eyes. He had his work cut out for him with Estelle, but he was ready for it. He was ready for all of it. No one in the social circles that mattered ever *liked* Ricky Dale, but no one would dare miss a social event like a funeral for a really rich asshole. He figured that Walmart boy's funeral would be far less of a must-attend soirée. They'd never find the body, though, so it would be a while before the funeral invitations went out.

Dwayne sent out a text to the guys.

DWAYNE: Good job on keeping the code word inconspicuous. I'm taking the day off. Ricky Dale was a flaming cocksucker. I'm paying my respects today by drinking beer, smoking weed, and watching ESPN. We can meet up tomorrow for lunch.

STEVE: Briefcase! Did you hear about Pete Rearden? He got abducted at Walmart last night. Briefcase!

RUSS: That's hardly the first time something has been stolen from a Walmart.

TOMMY: LOL

STEVE: Damn. You guys are dicks!

DWAYNE: Yup. And this dick is gonna watch some TV and smoke a doob. Fuck Pete. See you guys tomorrow. Noon at the club.

STEVE: Dwayne . . . I just . . . briefcase. Briefcase, Dwayne. Briefcase.

DWAYNE: I caught that, Steve. I'm in mourning. We'll talk tomorrow.

Dwayne threw on a pair of old camouflage shorts and a T-shirt and slid his feet into his nicest flip-flops. He reached above his armoire for his rolling tray and bag of weed, and twisted up a few joints. A feeling of accomplishment from his previous day at the office, compounded with the awesome news that life from this point forward was his for the plucking, brought on a profound need for celebration via relaxation.

Alex wouldn't be home until later in the evening, so he figured he would tie on a pretty mean buzz. He walked out to his garage, grabbed an old Styrofoam ice chest, and filled it with beer and ice from the fridge. He slid the ice chest up close to his favorite recliner in the living room, within arm's reach. With a joint in his mouth and a beer in his hand, Dwayne pulled the recline lever on his favorite chair and hit the power button on the television's remote control.

21.

The air in the living room was thick with pot smoke in no time at all. The sun had begun to shine brightly into the living room, and the light cast interesting shapes in the clouds of smoke throughout the room. One particularly annoying beam of light had worked its way toward Dwayne's face, so he pulled his Wayfarers out and slid them on.

Dwayne indecisively flipped the channels back and forth between ESPN and National Geographic. NatGeo had an excellent African cat segment airing, and Dwayne didn't want to miss a single kill. The gazelle deaths were great, but the water buffalo takedowns were simply spectacular.

A pride of lions was enjoying a meal of kudu when the front door to Dwayne's house opened. Dwayne heard the multitude of footsteps from the finest Jimmy Choo and Prada heels. He then heard the chairs in the dining room slide in and out. The prayer group had arrived.

"Estelle, dear, what is that smell?" one of the ladies asked.

"Did a skunk die under your house?" another inquired.

Estelle knew exactly what the smell was. She was struggling with an explanation for the uppity women. Dwayne decided to help her out.

He popped the footrest down on the recliner and headed into the dining room. With his sunglasses on, he walked to where the ladies were seated, clasping a beer in one hand and holding the last inch of a smoldering doobie with the other. He leaned his back against the wall and began to rub it up and down slowly to take care of an itch before addressing the crowd.

"What's shakin', ladies?" he asked with a grin.

"Hello, dear," Estelle said, trying to conceal a grin of her own. "We're just—"

"Is that marijuana, Dwayne?" quizzed Janice Harper, wife of Pastor Jim from the Westside Church of Jesus.

"Why, yes it is," he responded. "It's some pretty good shit, too. I am *fuuuuucked up!*" Dwayne started giggling. He tried to stop but couldn't.

"Is this why you weren't at the funeral, Dwayne?" Tiffany Blaine asked. "You couldn't pay your respects to Ricky Dale because you'd rather abuse substances?"

"No, Tiff," Dwayne shot back. "I didn't go to the funeral because Ricky Dale was a douche. And on a very deep level, I just don't give a fuck." Dwayne took a long pull from the joint and blew a perfect smoke ring to the middle of the dining room table. The ladies watched it all the way, until it finally disappeared into the air.

"Pretty fuckin' sweet, eh, Janice?" Dwayne remarked to the pastor's wife. "You wanna hit this shit?"

Janice was appalled. He winked and blew her a kiss.

"Anyhow, ladies, I know you've got some praying to do." Dwayne headed to his throne in the living room. "I'll let you get back to it. If any of you wanna get high, I'll be watching the tube and twisting fatties in the next room."

Estelle hung somewhere between embarrassed and aroused as she heard Dwayne plunk down in the next room on his recliner. That noise was followed with the twisting *Fssst!* sound of a beer cap coming off a bottle, along with the sound of that cap being tossed, bouncing, and then rolling across the hardwood floor.

"Let me know when your friends leave, sweetie!" Dwayne called out to Estelle. "Daddy's feeling frisky!"

Estelle squirmed a bit, waiting for someone to change the subject. The prolonged awkward silence was broken by Brenda White, heiress to the White Oil fortune. "So, I'm going in to see Dr. Tom tomorrow," she proclaimed with her nose tilted upward as she sipped from her merlot. "He's got this new cutting edge diet injection I've been dying to try. I think it's rabbit semen."

"Oooh, I heard that's good," Tiffany replied.

"Dr. Tom has been giving me an iguana semen cream I've been rubbing on my face for the last several months," added Linda Honeycut, of Honeycut Land and Cattle fame. "It works fantastic."

"Amazing, Linda. Your skin looks great," said Janice. "I guess I never realized how powerful different semens were."

"You should see what it does for your teeth!" Dwayne yelled from the other room.

An uncomfortable silence fell over the group again. Estelle had been having a difficult time joining her friends in conversation. She couldn't quit thinking about Dwayne's new attitude. What had come over him? He'd never approved of the social climbers she ran with, but he'd always kept it to himself. He'd just kept his head down and worked. He had apparently decided to discard the silent approach and now offered a large middle finger to those he disapproved of. And it really turned her on.

"So did any of you hear about Pete Rearden?" Tiffany asked the ladies.

"Ewwww, the Walmart guy?" Janice responded.

"Yes, him," Tiffany said. "He got abducted from work early this morning."

Estelle's ears perked up.

"Oh, that poor dear, who's going to bring home the $1,800 per month to support his family now?" Linda smirked.

The ladies began to snicker. All except Estelle. She was snickering too, but she was faking it. The guy she'd been slumming it with behind Dwayne's back had gone missing early that morning . . . and Dwayne hadn't arrived home until almost five.

"Oh, great, let's just add them to the welfare pool now!" Janice said, with a hint of disgust at the idea of poor people. "I swear, the Democrats are going to sink this country."

"So what happened to him?" Estelle asked Tiffany before the political talk had a chance to gain momentum.

"They don't know. A friend of Ricky Dale's told me at the funeral. He made it to work in the wee hours of the morning but never made it inside the Walmart. His car was there with the trunk wide open, and his office papers were all over the place. No one saw a thing. He's just gone."

Estelle excused herself and walked into the kitchen, trying to wrap her head around what she'd just heard. She opened the medicine cabinet above the microwave and pulled out her Xanax. She popped three.

As soon as she left the room, Estelle could hear the ladies begin to whisper about Dwayne. These were her best friends, and yet she knew that they would turn on her in a heartbeat.

Estelle peeked into the living room where Dwayne was lounging in his recliner. She was amused as he pumped his fist in the air at the sight of an alligator snatching a baby deer from the bank of a river. Who was this guy? What had he been up to? Was she falling in love with her husband again, after years of shutting each other out? Was his "fuck these people" attitude contagious? Because she felt like she was catching it, too.

Dwayne looked back over the top of the recliner and saw Estelle standing in the kitchen, staring at him. He smiled at her.

"Hey, baby," he said.

"Hey," she said back.

"You wanna get high and watch Shark Week with me?"

"I'd love to."

Estelle walked into the dining room, where the elite ladies of Fort Worth were seated, with Dwayne following closely behind. She could tell she'd interrupted them talking about her. She'd been on the other side of that so many times.

"Sorry, girls, I'm going to have to cut this prayer group short," Estelle said as she shrugged her shoulders with a fake smile. "Dwayne and I haven't had a chance to spend much time together lately, so we thought we'd hang out a little and catch up."

Dwayne pinched Estelle's ass discreetly as the ladies looked at one another disapprovingly. They began to gather their things.

"You know, Dwayne, we'd love to have you join one of our Bible study groups one day," Janice sneered. "It might do you some good, judging by the path you're on."

In the past, Dwayne might have walked away. He might have made a crack before he walked away, but he normally would have let these women get away with their comments. That was how the social circles worked. Everyone feared the consequences of their rejection. The old Dwayne would have walked away. But this wasn't the old Dwayne.

"You know, Janice," Dwayne started in, "I'm pretty sure if Jesus were here today, he would want absolutely nothing to do with you and your group of hypocritical, backstabbing, social-climbing bitches. Have you ever even read the Bible? I'm not a particularly religious guy, but I've read it. Where does it talk about how you're supposed to be fake and shit on the little people? Where does it talk about how you're supposed to constantly sit in judgment with your friends and gossip? Where does it talk about showing off how much money you have, while criticizing those who don't have as much? Where does it cover getting fucking hammered on booze and pills all day, while talking about the lifestyles of others as if yours is superior? Where does it talk about raising your kids to be arrogant, superior, bigoted shits with no moral compass other than that guided by the almighty dollar? You want me to tell you where that is in the Bible? It's nowhere. If Jesus were here right now, he'd pimp-slap you. So thanks for the invite, Janice, but I'd rather not subject myself to the advice of you and your soul-corroding heathen friends."

Janice appeared as though she'd just been punched by Mike Tyson. She looked at Estelle. "Are you just going to stand there and let him get away with that?"

"Well," Estelle replied, as she subtly reached her arm behind herself and grabbed Dwayne's package. "It's like they say in the Bible. Women have to listen to their man, or they get stoned. Or something like that."

"Oh, she's gonna get stoned, alright," Dwayne grinned through his Ray-Bans. "So, without further ado, don't let the door hit ya where the Lord split ya, if you catch my drift."

The ladies were paralyzed. They had stepped into an alternate dimension where their shit actually *did* stink.

"Seriously," he continued. "Please, get the fuck out. I have to sacrifice some ass to the Lord."

Janice and her crew shuffled out the front door, slamming it behind them. Dwayne felt phenomenal. He had just said pretty much everything he'd ever wanted to say to them. It gave him a complete endorphin rush.

He spun Estelle around and kissed her passionately before she had an opportunity to say anything. He extended his arm across the dining room table and sent wine bottles, glasses, cheese, crackers, and place settings flying across the room and crashing into the wall. Dwayne was happy that he had listened to Estelle about buying the big, sturdy, expensive antique table. He reached his hands beneath her butt cheeks and lifted her up onto it, where they made love for the next two hours.

22.

That night, after Alex came home and finished his homework, Dwayne tucked him into bed with the feeling that the baseball team was going to be A-OK. He had concocted a plan, and he was ready to put it into place.

He would start with a group email to the parents of all team members. On the computer in his bedroom, Dwayne clicked the compose message tab, and began:

> Greetings, Team Parents—
>
> This is Dwayne Devero, Alex's dad. I know we're all heartbroken at the loss of Coach Dale. He will always be remembered as one of the finest furniture salesmen in the great state of Texas. I was told his funeral was an excellent tribute. Now I have learned that Coach Pete, who had nobly stepped in to fill Coach Dale's shoes, has gone missing. Our thoughts and prayers are with the Rearden family in this time of uncertainty. It is my belief that the best way to honor these two great men is to keep playing baseball. They would want it that way, I'm sure. I have decided, through much prayer and soul searching, to take over the position as head coach. I will be assisted by Russ Paisley, Dr. Tom Johnson, and Steve Winwood (no relation to the singer / songwriter). It is my personal goal to honor both our fallen coach and our coach who disappeared under questionable circumstances with a championship win. As you know, in this age bracket, every team makes the playoffs. It is my intention to win our final regular season game and go undefeated in the playoffs. It's a lofty goal, but mark my words, we will accomplish it. We will have practice tomorrow at the ballpark at 5:30 p.m., and we have a game the following day at 6:00 p.m. So let's get pumped up! GO TIGERS!
>
> —Dwayne Devero

Dwayne pushed send. He grinned. He felt good about things. He looked over at Estelle, who was sleeping. For the first time in ages, she'd fallen asleep from her body being thoroughly ravished by her husband, and not by taking a handful of pills washed down with Cabernet.

Quack. Quack. Quack.

Dwayne picked up his phone. The texting had begun.

STEVE: GO TIGERS??? Are you kidding me?

DWAYNE: Too much team spirit?

STEVE: They just put RD in the ground today! Was that necessary?

DWAYNE: If we want to turn this team around and dominate the playoffs, then we don't have time to act like a bunch of pussies, Steve.

STEVE: Jesus, Dwayne, they're 10 years old!

RUSS: I liked it. Way to take life by the balls.

TOMMY: Maybe a little harsh and poorly timed.

RUSS: Whatever, Tiberius. Go back to watching B.E.T.

TOMMY: What the fuck did you just say?

RUSS: My bad! I'm so fucked up right now! I just snorted ecstasy!

TOMMY: 0_o

STEVE: Nice job, Russ. I'm sure the other deacons in the church would be proud of you.

RUSS: This is awesome! Jade just surprised me! We're having a three-way now! I love you guys, by the way.

DWAYNE: Great. Guys, I'll need your help coaching. We can still kick ass this season. Are you all going to be at practice tomorrow?

TOMMY: Yup. Gotta stretch some faces, suck some fat, and sell some of the overflow from the sperm-donor clinic. Been telling people it's rabbit semen. LOL. But yeah, I'll be there.

STEVE: I'll be there! We need to talk!

RUSS: Oh shit, guys! Another dude just showed up! This just turned into a four-way! Not cool!

DWAYNE: Awesome, guys. I appreciate the help. We'll put these kids in the spots they belong in and adjust the batting order. I'm pumped.

RUSS: This guy's penis is HUGE! And it's totally shaved! Do people really shave their jim-jims now? Like . . . all the way? There's no hair! None! I want to look away, but I can't!

DWAYNE: Cool. I'll see you guys tomorrow.

STEVE: Great, Dwayne. See you there. Good luck with whatever the fuck a bald jim-jim is, Russ.

TOMMY: See you then, guys. Good luck getting ass-rammed on ecstasy, Russ.

STEVE: :)

DWAYNE: (*)

RUSS: Briefcase! Briefcase!

STEVE: LOL.

Dwayne turned the volume down on the television, pulled out a pen and paper, and began to write up the positions that the kids would need to play in order to be competitive. He felt excited for Alex and the other boys.

Pitching needed to be brought into the spotlight on the team. Dwayne knew that Ricky hadn't done near enough to develop pitchers. He knew he needed strength up the middle before anything, so he would put his best kids at second base, shortstop, pitcher, and catcher. The center fielder needed to be decent as well.

He figured he could stick the least talented turds at left and right field, and the heavyset kids at first and third base. The rotation on the bench from this point forward, he decided, would come from the shallow end of the talent pool . . . as it was supposed to.

A few of the parents from the team were going to be pissed off. There was no question about that. Some of the kids were about to have their feelings hurt. That was a lesson they needed to learn. But

Dwayne knew that at the end of the season, if they had championship trophies sitting beside their beds at night, pretty much all would be forgiven.

Dwayne finished writing out the player positions and set them on the dresser. He turned off the television, yanked his underwear off (having made the decision at that very instant to sleep nude for the rest of his life), and rolled over to spoon with Estelle. As he closed his eyes, he thought he heard the sound of an engine idling outside.

He jumped up and ran to the window, buck naked, where he saw what appeared to be an old van parked out front, staking out his house. The van had scraggly multicolored bedsheets duct-taped over the exterior, save for the front windows.

Dwayne could make out someone in the driver's seat wearing what looked like a ski suit from the early 1980s. He knew exactly who it was.

He grabbed a pillow to cover his balls and sprinted out the door and across the yard to confront Dave the umpire. Dave slid open the van's side door and emerged through a sheet with pot smoke pouring out behind him like he was in some crazy low-budget horror film. He was gripping the same bat that he'd used to split Ricky Dale's skull. The hard-hitting power chords of Megadeth filled the air as Dave the umpire raised his bat in the air.

"You want a piece of me, Lawn Boy?" Dave yelled. "I know what the fuck you've been up to!"

Dwayne charged him, raising his pillow to block a blow from the bat like a nude suburban gladiator. He tackled Dave back into the van with the force of a linebacker, tearing sheets off as they flew back through them. Dwayne unleashed a torrent of body blows to Dave's torso while holding the pillow over his face to silence his screams.

All that could be seen from the exterior of the van was Dave's snow boots kicking wildly at the air, while a bare ass popped in and out of the moonlight as its owner beat the shit out of Dave.

Finally, the kicking stopped. Dwayne managed to somehow refrain from killing Dave, but he did wrestle the bat from him. He held the bat across Dave's neck and leaned in closely to his face as he sat perched on his stomach.

"Do not fuck with me, Dave. I know what you did," he muttered coldly with just the right amount of snarl and psychotic eye twitch.

"Yeah, well I know what you did, too, Dwayne. The night Pete Rearden went missing, I watched you fertilize the baseball field with something that wasn't fertilizer. I think you were fertilizing it with Pete. So don't act like you're in charge here, bro."

Dwayne was confused. He didn't understand. He'd obviously forgotten to check his surroundings before he disposed of Pete's body. *Dammit*, he thought. *How could I have been so stupid?*

Dwayne knew he couldn't kill a guy in front of his house. Dave had already been parked for way too long. What Dwayne needed to do was to get Dave to leave. He would deal with him later.

He pushed the bat firmly down on Dave's trachea, put his lips up to Dave's ear, and said, "I'm gonna get off of you slowly now, Dave. Then I'm gonna back out through the side door. And then you're going to get up, get behind the wheel, put this shitbox in gear, and get the fuck out of here. I could end you right now, but we're going to go on about our lives like nothing ever happened. We each have something on the other, so we each need to shut the fuck up. But, I swear to God, Dave, if I ever see you near my house again, I will rip your goddamn head off and hit a motherfucking home run with it. Am I clear?"

"Whatever it takes to get your sack out of my belly button, man."

Dwayne backed slowly and deliberately out of the side of the van, and watched as Dave climbed up to the front, put the van in drive, and disappeared down the street.

He walked back inside, tossed the pillow back onto the couch, and climbed back into bed.

He would need to get this Dave thing under control soon, he thought to himself as he drifted off to sleep.

23.

Dwayne awoke the next day at 6:30 a.m. sharp, without the need for an alarm clock. He rolled over and gave Estelle a kiss on the earlobe, and she offered back a sleepy smile. That was all he needed to see.

"Hey, baby," she whispered with one eye barely open. "I got you a surprise yesterday. It's in that box on the dresser."

Dwayne found the box and took a seat on the edge of the bed to open it. His eyes went wide. It was the coolest gift he'd ever received. He jumped up excitedly, like a kid with a new bike on Christmas morning. He held Estelle's present up to his body to see if it would fit.

"Go ahead," she said. "Try it on."

"Is this what I think it is, babe?"

"If you think it's an authentic *Star Wars* Jedi bathrobe, complete with the Jedi logo and hood, designed stitch for stitch to what Obi-Wan Kenobi wore in the original *Star Wars* trilogy, then yes, it's what you think it is."

Dwayne slipped the robe over his shoulders, tied the front, and pulled the large brown hood up over his head. He ran to the bathroom to check himself out in the mirror.

"Oh, babe," he called out from the bathroom. "This is AWESOME! This totally encompasses how I feel lately! I feel like a fucking Jedi knight!"

"You *are* a Jedi knight, sweetie," she offered back in a sexy tone. "Now get in here and show me your lightsaber."

Estelle pulled the sheets off her body to reveal a Princess Leia metal bikini, just like Carrie Fisher had worn as a slave in *Return of the Jedi*.

"You . . . are . . . *awesome*," Dwayne said, stunned.

He leapt on top of her, slinging the robe across the room. She rolled him over and jumped on top of him.

"Oh yeah," Estelle growled into his ear. "The Force is strong with this one."

They were like college kids again. They couldn't keep their hands off each other. They had sex twice in the bed, and then one more time in the shower.

When they'd finished, Estelle slipped on her yoga outfit and went to the kitchen to make coffee. Neither of them could speak. They could only smile.

Dwayne decided that there was absolutely no way he could go to work. He needed to play hooky. He needed to play golf. He grabbed his phone and hopped on the text chain with the guys.

DWAYNE: I'm skipping work today. Let's play some golf. Who's in?

TOMMY: I'm in. I'll move some appointments around. I don't feel like working either. What time?

DWAYNE: Let's roll before it gets too hot. In about an hour? 8:30?

TOMMY: Sounds good. Russ? Little Stevie?

STEVE: I can't, guys. I'm supposed to have conferences with some at-risk youth groups today. Mainly gang members. One of them actually tried to kill me last semester.

Several minutes passed as Dwayne sipped his coffee and awaited further texts. Finally . . .

STEVE: Screw those kids. I'm in, too.

DWAYNE: Attaboy, Stevie! There's hope for you yet! Anyone hear from Russ?

TOMMY: Not since last night when he was staring at a massive shaved penis on ecstasy.

RUSS: I'm here. Dude. I have no idea what happened last night. That guy with the huge penis is literally lying beside me right now in bed. He has his arm around

me. No idea how many people are in my bed right
now. At least 7. This is some crazy shit, bro. I mean, I
love ecstasy and all, but this guy put his finger in my
ass last night! WTF???

TOMMY: Jesus.

DWAYNE: Wow. I got laid dressed like a Jedi this morning.
Estelle was dressed like Princess Leia. That was
pretty cool. But shit, Russ . . .

STEVE: Who *are* you people?

TOMMY: The metal bikini?

DWAYNE: Yup.

TOMMY: Sooo hot.

DWAYNE: Fuck yeah it was.

TOMMY: You da man.

DWAYNE: Fuck yeah I am.

TOMMY: And Russ got fingered.

DWAYNE: No shit. Not cool.

STEVE: (*)

RUSS: It wasn't that bad, actually.

TOMMY: Jesus.

DWAYNE: So, are you playing, or what, Russ?

RUSS: I'm in.

DWAYNE: Cool. See you guys there.

Dwayne was finishing his coffee when Estelle came up behind him and rested her head on his shoulder. He could tell something was on her mind.

"You okay, babe?"

"How long has it been since we asked each other if we were okay?" She squeezed him tightly.

"It's been too long," he replied.

They stood there, enjoying something that had been missing from their lives for years. Over time, the love they'd had for each other had been eroded and replaced by things . . . by stuff . . . stuff that had ultimately brought them zero joy and fulfillment. And when you took all of that away, when you broke it down and examined what it was that made them happiest, it was just the simple relationships. It was the wife, the husband, and the kid. That was it. It wasn't the house they lived in, the car they drove, the jewelry or the clothes that dangled from their bodies, the circles of mostly soulless people they had to swim among . . . It was just them.

"You know, babe," Estelle whispered with her eyes closed. "I've been pretty awful for a while. I know I have. And I just—"

"Nope," Dwayne cut her off. "We're not going there. That's a place we've left behind. It didn't serve us well. Let's just find our way back. We're doing a pretty good job of it lately."

"I know, Dwayne," she said, searching for the words. "But I was really bad. I don't want to hold anything back. You see . . . this guy Pete who went missing—"

"Estelle," he interrupted again, this time turning her around and locking eyes with her. "We're not going there. No one will get in the way of us, ever again."

Estelle could see it in his eyes. He didn't need to say anything else.

"I'm a motherfucking Jedi, now, sugar pie," he offered with a cocksure, steely gaze. "And this is how the motherfucking Jedi roll."

24.

Dwayne pulled into the River Oaks Country Club's golf course parking lot at just before 8:30 a.m., with "Little Wing" by Stevie Ray Vaughn blasting from the stereo. He parked his lawn truck beside Steve's hybrid-electric nerdmobile, where Steve sat tying his golf shoes. Tommy was already practicing his swing on the driving range, glad-handing and backslapping Westside Church of Jesus's Pastor Jim Harper. Dwayne approached the driving range to hit a few balls before their game. He could tell by the look he received from Pastor Jim that his wife, Janice, had informed him of their encounter.

"Well, hello there, Pastor Jim," Dwayne said with mock enthusiasm, extending his hand. "How are you this fine morning?"

"Doing well, Dwayne," Pastor Jim responded. "I was just talking to Dr. Tom about the plight of African-Americans in the inner-city areas, and how the Westside Church of Jesus is doing everything it can to utilize its resources to make a difference there."

"Aaaahh, yes, you're having a good old-fashioned white guilt conversation with the only black guy you know." Dwayne pulled a 3-wood from his golf bag. "I bet that's exactly the topic Tommy was looking to discuss while golfing. By the way, the new Porsche looks fantastic. How much did that set you back? Two hundred grand?"

Pastor Jim's face turned red.

"I'm sorry," Dwayne continued. "That was rude of me to change the subject. What were you saying about utilizing all of your resources to help the poor?"

Dwayne set a ball on the ground and stood behind it to analyze how he should approach his first practice shot. He stepped up, got in his stance, and took a solid swing.

Although he made very solid contact, the ball hooked hard left into the lunch-table area amidst the tennis courts, taking out the knee of a waiter carrying three Bloody Marys and a basket of breakfast tacos.

Dwayne immediately pointed at Pastor Jim as the waiter struggled back to his feet. Pastor Jim looked on in horror while Dwayne chuckled to himself.

Tommy and Steve couldn't believe the way Dwayne was talking to Pastor Jim. No one spoke to Pastor Jim that way. He was a local celebrity. A large portion of Tommy's plastic surgery business came from the Westside Church of Jesus. Pastor Jim and his wife, Janice, were a couple of his top clients. He tried to think of ways to distance himself from Dwayne.

Steve, an avowed atheist since college, stood in awe of Dwayne as a goofy grin swept across his face.

"Dwayne," the pastor said, attempting to regain composure. "I'm not sure what led you astray from my flock, son. Janice told me you've been using drugs. That's a dark path you're on."

Dwayne hit another ball. It went exactly where the previous ball had gone, but this time the waiter was prepared and held a serving tray up as a shield. The ball hit the tray at full speed, at which point the waiter dropped it and ran inside to seek shelter.

"Let me get this straight, Pastor," Dwayne said. "Your wife, who popped half a bottle of pain pills that were overprescribed from her recent face stretching, who was on antidepressants and antianxiety medication, who consumed two bottles of wine at lunch, told you that I smoked a joint—and you two are outraged by that?"

"Dwayne," the pastor's words turned vitriolic. "There's a pretty staunch difference between prescribed medication and illegal substances. Don't try and lump my wife in—"

"No, I'm not done yet," Dwayne cut in. "I'm tired of all of this bullshit outrage, Pastor. You and your wife . . . your flock . . . everything you represent . . . you know who probably feels justifiable outrage? God. That's who. You make several million dollars a year in tax-free income. You do this by passing judgment on others and offering your uneducated condemnation based on whatever fits your agenda. As a man of God, your agenda should be doing what Jesus said, things which align with taking care of the least among us, helping those who can't help themselves, being thankful for what you're given, and not denying some level of credibility to people just because they don't choose to aim for the fucking Fortune 500 list every year. If you were a missionary who'd built homes in third-world countries, then maybe I'd stop and lend an ear. But you're not. You're a pulpit hack who skates taxes, skimming from a pot which is supposed to feed the poor, praying to a God you don't represent . . . asking Him to give you more, more, more, so you can continue to fly high above everyone with your cape of hypocrisy. You make me sick, Pastor Jim. I know that at the end of the day, if you're outraged by me, then chances are I'm doing something right. Do you know why I know this, Pastor?"

Pastor Jim looked at Dwayne in disgust. He crossed his arms across his chest, refusing to give Dwayne the dignity of a response.

"I'll tell you why, Pastor," Dwayne said as he stuffed his 3-wood back into his golf bag and slung his bag across his shoulder. "Because I'm a motherfucking Jedi, and that's how I roll."

Dwayne walked off the driving range. Steve followed, offering up both hands for a double high five, which Dwayne gladly slapped. Pastor Jim ripped his golf glove off his hand, threw it on the ground, and stomped toward his Porsche.

"Pastor Jim, I—" Tommy called out to him, trying to calm him down. Pastor Jim slammed his door and sped away before he had a chance to finish his sentence. He almost had a head-on collision with Russ as he hauled ass out of the parking lot. Russ didn't recognize the pastor's new Porsche, so he flipped him off as he passed, further enraging the pastor.

25.

As usual, Russ pulled his Ferrari across two empty parking spaces beside Dwayne's truck. He appeared to be totally nude behind the wheel, except for his large Gucci sunglasses. His head dipped down toward the passenger seat, out of public view, as he blew through a few quick lines of coke.

Russ opened the door and pulled himself up, buck naked, for all the world to see. He shook his head wildly as the blow kicked in, and then managed to balance himself against the car door. His sweaty body hair glistened in the morning sun.

"Jesus," he said, standing in full glory beside his prized Ferrari. "What a night."

"Put some clothes on, man!" Steve shouted, looking away.

"God, I'm so sweaty," Russ mumbled almost incoherently, halfway to himself. "I was sliding all over the goddamned seat in the turns."

Russ turned and bent over into his car to grab his clothes, offering a hind view of his jiggling furry ass and marble bag.

"I really don't know what to say right now, Dwayne," Tommy offered in disgust. "You think Ernesto and some of your other lawn guys could get after that butt muff with a Weedwacker some day?"

"Hell, no," Dwayne replied. "They are a prideful bunch. It would totally throw them off their path to citizenship."

Dwayne pulled a toothpick from his pocket and placed it in his mouth, glancing sideways at Tommy a couple of times in amazement. They couldn't *not* watch.

"Didn't he get fingered in the ass last night, D?" Tommy asked Dwayne quietly. "Who the hell would put a finger in there, man?"

"I wouldn't go near that hairy ass without full HAZMAT gear, bro," Dwayne responded.

Russ finally slid on a pair of bright red bikini briefs, followed by tight white shorts and a golf shirt. He slipped his socks and shoes on and made his way over to the golf cart that had been brought around for him with his clubs attached to the back of it.

A twelve-pack of iced-down beer sat in the passenger seat of Russ's cart. He pulled out two beers, slammed them both, and then opened a third, which he took a sip from before placing it in the cup holder. He then took out a pack of smokes and lit one up.

"How are you still alive, Russ?" Steve asked, somewhere between sickened and impressed.

"Suck it, fuckface," he shot back. "Let's play some golf."

The baseball dads arrived at the first tee. They each grabbed a driver, put a sleeve of balls and a few tees in their pockets, and strategized their potential first shots.

"Got a little right-to-left wind here, kinda behind us though, so the ball should travel," Russ offered knowingly.

To designate who would hit first, Russ tossed a tee in the air in the middle of the foursome. The tee landed pointing at Steve, meaning Steve would hit first, followed clockwise around the circle by Tommy, Dwayne, and then Russ.

"Get us started, you fucking Obama-loving pansy," Russ said to Steve with fondness.

Steve placed his ball on a tee and squared up for his shot. He swung smoothly, made perfect contact, and hit a beautiful drive 275 yards down the middle of the fairway.

"Take that, buttfinger!" Steve said to Russ as he strutted off to the side.

Russ brushed him off and grimaced as Tommy stepped up to hit.

"Please fuck this one up, Tommy," Russ said. "We don't need another good black golfer. Please tell your people to leave us something besides hockey."

Tommy drove the ball low and hard up the right side of the fairway. It hooked back just enough to come to rest in the dead center, probably twenty yards past Steve's ball.

"Goddammit," Russ muttered.

Dwayne stepped up to hit as Tommy offered a fist bump to Steve while exiting the tee box. They were each quite impressed with their rare appearances in the fairway. Russ was agitated.

"Hey, Dwayne," Russ said just as Dwayne pulled into his back-swing. "I'll stop getting daily blowjobs from Estelle if you can outdrive Tommy."

Dwayne abandoned his backswing and lowered his driver. He turned to Russ and glared at him over his sunglasses. "Let's not go there today, Russ," he said. He turned back to his ball and reared back his driver once again.

"Oh, come on, Dwayne," Russ shot back. "Are you telling me you'll let Walmart Pete and half the town ball your wife, but I can't even make a blowjob joke?"

Dwayne dropped his club and whipped around in a lightning-fast MMA-style motion, grabbing Russ by the throat with his left hand and sweeping his legs out from under him. Russ landed with a thud, flat on his back, as Dwayne drove his head into the ground and dropped his knee into Russ's balls.

Russ's eyes became huge with terror. Dwayne leaned in, nose to nose. A single drop of sweat rolled across his face and down his nose, then dripped from an icy face of anger onto a bright red face of fear.

"We don't talk about my wife like that anymore, Russ. Understood?"

Given the fact that Dwayne was clutching his windpipe with full force, Russ nodded his head as best he could.

"Okay, then," Dwayne said with a half-psychotic smile, extending a hand to Russ. "Let's play some motherfuckin' golf!"

Dwayne picked up his club, lined up his shot, and drove the ball well past Tommy's. The ball came to a stop less than five yards from the green. He threw both arms into the air in celebration. He turned to face the guys to rub in the fact that he'd just hit the best drive that any of them had ever hit.

When Dwayne turned around, he noticed that the other three were still in complete shock, trying to digest his actions before the drive. This was no longer the Dwayne they knew. It was official. He had completely snapped.

Steve moved in closer, staring into Dwayne's eyes, trying to figure him out. He'd been witness to this growing disconnect more than they had. Something had changed that night at the bar.

Dwayne lowered his arms and cocked his head.

"Something wrong?" he asked.

"Yeah, Dwayne, it's just—" Steve tried to come up with the words. "You feelin' alright, brother?"

Dwayne looked at the three men. He could smell their fear, like a lion in the wilds of Africa. He offered a warm, predatory smile. It was eerie. "I'm feeling fucking fabulous!" he replied with gusto, in the manner of a motivational speaker pumping up a crowd. "Things have changed, and I'm changing them. I'm not waiting on the world to be fair anymore. I'm tipping the scales myself. I'm in love with my wife again. My son is playing shortstop again. I'm turning my business around. I have the balls of the future cupped firmly in my hands. *I'm a motherfucking superhuman antibullshit golf-ball-smashing maestro of life*, my friends. Fuck yeah, I'm alright."

The other three remained paralyzed. The fear they felt began to turn to awe and admiration. It wasn't unlike a young Clark Kent letting his friends in on a secret about himself. They couldn't help but believe him.

Russ pulled out a pack of smokes and produced a cigarette and a joint. He placed them both between his lips and lit them simultaneously.

Steve inched ever closer, inspecting Dwayne as if he were some sort of wax figure. Then their eyes met.

"Holy fuck," Steve spoke softly. "You killed Pete."

26.

Steve and Dwayne remained in some sort of mesmerizing staring contest that was taking place between two beings from opposite worlds. Tommy's mouth hung open as he recalled the events of the last few days. Russ, for once, was quiet. He took a long pull from his cigarette, exhaled, and then took a long pull from his joint.

All three friends knew that Estelle slept around. They'd heard rumors about countless men. They'd even heard rumors about Pete. They knew not to believe everything they heard though. But still . . .

Dwayne held Steve's stare, his eyes narrowing before he spoke. A sinister grin grew across his face.

"Yes, Steve. I killed Pete."

Dwayne walked over to Russ and grabbed the joint, taking a big hit. He passed the joint to Tommy, who also took a big hit. Tommy passed it to Steve. Steve took two big hits, then passed it back to Russ. The four of them passed the joint around in silence until it was gone. The idea of a vigilante murderer in their weekly golf game lingered heavily. It almost made it seem exciting, except that it was still technically golf.

"You can't just have sex with someone's wife, toss their kid in the outfield, and expect there to be zero consequences, guys," Dwayne said, breaking the silence. "We've all been allowing bullshit to happen in our lives that we shouldn't put up with. I'm tired of turning the other cheek. Would Han Solo allow that shit? Would Luke Skywalker? Would Obi-Wan? Well, fuck no, they wouldn't. We need to take a cue from people who *kick* ass, not people who *take it* in the ass."

They were all super high now, attempting to wrap their minds around things.

"Guys," Dwayne said in a faux-consoling tone. "Don't look at me like I've lost my mind. I haven't. I've found it. *Shift your paradigm.*"

Russ pushed his tee into the ground and placed his ball on it. Dwayne's new outlook on life was really beginning to make sense to him. It was so primitive and raw, yet streamlined and sensible. Russ gripped his club tightly with both hands and pulled into his backswing.

A voice called out from behind them. "If you guys are going to be this slow all day, I'd appreciate you letting us play through."

It was Royce Featherby III, the pompous thirty-five-year-old blue-blood trust-fund-baby billionaire owner of several multinational companies, most of which had ties to Middle East oil and war profiteering. There wasn't a golfer in Royce's foursome that wasn't wearing old-school golf knickers, argyle socks, a pastel shirt, and a visor.

"This is a gentleman's game, guys," Royce said snidely. "A gentleman would let us play through."

Russ remained frozen in his backswing. He looked over at Dwayne, who nodded with a smile.

Russ brought his club back down and walked purposefully toward Royce's pretentious waiting foursome. Three of the upper crusters were seated in golf carts. Only Royce was out of his cart, leaning against a large stone water fountain, offering a fake yawn as Russ approached.

Russ took a big pull from his joint and blew it right into Royce's thin, yacht-tanned face. "Do you have any idea who the fuck that is over there?" Russ asked, pointing to his friends.

"I don't know," Royce responded sarcastically. "Two golfers and a caddy?"

Royce's friends chuckled.

"Oh, it's like that, huh?" Tommy walked over to stand beside Russ, showing his support. Tommy knew he might be able to add a "crazy black guy" feel to the dispute, even though he'd never actually thrown a punch. He even tried to walk with a touch of gangster swagger, but he ended up just looking injured.

"I'll tell you who that is," Russ said as he pulled down his glasses to display his wild, bloodshot eyes. "That's the motherfucking Jedi

Alliance. And if you don't back the fuck up and happily play at whatever pace we deem proper, we will unleash The Force on your uppity asses until the angels of heaven scream and blood pours from your ears."

A look of horror swept over Royce and his friends' faces.

"And if you ever refer to me as a caddy again," Tommy added, "I'll jam every one of your custom-fitted golf clubs all the way up your asshole and stomp on your scrotum with my golf cleats until you scream that Billy Dee Williams is your daddy. Do I make myself clear?"

Royce was silent. His eyes had welled up with tears. He was considering peeing in his pants.

"*I asked you a question, boy!*" Tommy yelled.

"Yeah, I mean yes, sir. I mean—it's just that, I don't know who Billy Dee Williams is."

"Billy Dee?" Tommy shot back with disgust. "Lando motherfucking Calrissian? Are you fucking with me right now? Jesus! That's the most racist thing I've ever heard! Get the fuck off this golf course right now before I disembowel you with a ball repair tool, you arrogant little bastard!"

Royce began to slowly back away toward his cart. Tommy lunged at him, waving his driver while making lightsaber noises. Royce dove behind the wheel of the cart and sped away, his friends close behind him.

Russ lit another joint as he watched the foursome disappear into the parking lot. He turned to Tommy, and they exchanged a high five.

"There's a large part of me that wants to inform you guys that you've all gone completely insane," Steve said to the group. "But this *Star Wars* philosophy on life appears to be pretty effective. I mean, I was always more of a *Star Trek* guy, but shit. Not knowing who Lando Calrissian is? That's a whole new level of racism. That's tantamount to the Holocaust."

Dwayne stood back proudly, analyzing his ramshackle group of forced friends. They now appeared ready to embrace this new lifestyle. He hadn't stopped to think, much less care, what his friends' reactions might be to his new approach to the world. But he liked the idea of this not being a solo mission. He liked the idea of strength in numbers.

It was obvious that they were buying in, too. He could see that they'd been awakened, as he had, through the simple act of not taking shit.

"Gentlemen," he addressed his foursome, "I can't say that I have this endeavor we're embarking upon clearly mapped out. I take great joy, though, in seeing that you may come to know what I now know: We are in control. We deserve respect. We don't have to sit idly by if respect is not given. There is no real hierarchy. The caste system has no true control. We choose what rules do and do not apply. We ask for nothing that is not deserved. We are reintroducing ethics and natural law to a society that has tossed them aside, in favor of lives led by greed and pseudo spirituality."

Dwayne extended his arms out wide, his head tilted upward and eyes closed, like a rock star soaking in the glory from the stage.

"We're the new evolution of man," he continued. "We're the suburban Jedi."

Large grins overtook the faces of Dwayne's friends. He could see that their worldview had received a massive overhaul. The transformation had taken place. Even with Steve. They now looked at the world differently. They looked at it as Dwayne did.

"Get ready for where this will take you, guys," he said. "We're going to burn this motherfucker down, and build it back the right way."

27.

The newly formed Jedi Alliance continued on through eighteen holes of golf in the blistering Texas sun. Following four of the most spectacular tee shots ever made off the first tee box, the men were certain that this was to be a round of golf that would end with a record score. They had grand visions of a plaque being hung in the pro shop for all club members to envy.

Unfortunately, a superior attitude on life had no effect on the cruelest of sports. The tee shots on hole number one ended up being the only respectable shots made that day. However, that evil whore named golf, no matter how hard she tried, had been unsuccessful in stripping the crew of their newfound mental superiority.

The foursome stood in the parking lot after the game, drinking beer and passing joints. Dwayne hopped into his truck to slap on a pair of flip-flops. When he tossed his warm dank cleats over to the passenger seat floorboard, he noticed something that had not been there before. An envelope with photos peeking out. He rifled through them. It was more photos of Estelle. Just like last time, except far more explicit.

Estelle was in a seated position between two men who were standing. The men were only visible from the waist down. She was nude, while the men had on unfastened pants. Estelle had a firm grip on each less-than-soft penis. She'd probably been playing them like a circus seal on the horns.

"Jesus, Estelle," Dwayne said under his breath. He knew she'd slept around, but he'd always figured it was one at a time. He hadn't expected this. The rage began to grow.

Somehow he managed to remind himself that he was a Jedi now, and he put the beast back in the cage. In an extraordinary display of forgiveness, Dwayne decided to let it go. He loved his wife. She loved him. They were working it out. Those photos represented the former shell of her. She was different now. He knew it.

Dwayne took a long pull from a joint and let all of the anger go. This was how he rolled now. He returned to his crew, feeling fine.

In Dwayne's absence, five of the club's bag boys had joined Tommy, Russ, and Steve. The bag boys delivered and retrieved carts and loaded and unloaded golf bags. Each bag boy had been sent one at a time by the manager of the club to ask the men to extinguish their marijuana cigarettes because of complaints. But in the end, all five boys were swayed by The Force, joining the Jedi Alliance and smoking weed with the baseball dads.

Russ shared the group's ideas about the power of positive thinking, convincing the youthful Jedi apprentices that they could make it over the massive ravine that cut across the fourteenth fairway in a golf cart if they simply *believed* they could.

As Russ began his drive home, he glanced off in the distance at the fourteenth fairway. A lone cart barreled full-speed right up the middle. He noticed three of the bag boys sitting on the bench seat of the cart, with the other two hanging on to the back.

"*YOU GOTTA BELIEVE!*" Russ yelled, his body nearly halfway out the window of his Ferrari as he pumped his fist in the air with excitement.

The boys all looked back toward Russ and pumped their fists, yelling and whooping as the cart launched up the elevated edge of the ravine to make the seemingly impossible jump of a lifetime, equipped heavily with the power of positive thinking and an equally large lack of forethought. They quickly disappeared over the forty-foot drop-off.

Russ slowed and slid back in the cabin of his car. He watched as a tiny puff of smoke appeared above the ravine's edge. He pushed his sunglasses firmly onto the bridge of his nose, rolled up his window, and continued home.

His phone beeped from a text on the text chain. He glanced in his rearview mirror and noticed that Dwayne and the other guys were behind him, taking the same way home.

DWAYNE: For future reference, this whole using The Force thing is more of a lifestyle choice. I'm pretty sure it doesn't nullify the laws of physics.

RUSS: Duly noted.

STEVE: For the record, I was as curious to see if they could pull it off as anyone.

TOMMY: I hear ya, man. I was pulling for them.

DWAYNE: Me too. Oh well. Pretty cool way to go out, anyhow.

RUSS: Fuck yeah.

TOMMY: I'm digging this thing we're doing by the way, D. I suddenly feel like going home and making sweet love to my wife.

STEVE: Me too. I'm gonna rock that ass when I get home.

RUSS: That's disgusting, Steve. Don't tell us that shit.

STEVE: Screw you, Russ!

RUSS: Dude, your wife's nose is nothing short of massive, she has a mustache, and her ankles are bigger than my thighs. Have you really not noticed that? Tommy, can you fix that mangled train wreck?

TOMMY: I can dress it up a little for you, Steve. I can cut that shark fin off her face and laser that afro off her lip. Not sure about the ankles. Maybe camouflage socks or something. It still won't look good.

STEVE: What the HELL, guys? Jesus! Tommy, your wife is half plastic, and Russ, your wife has a first grade education!

RUSS: Yeah, but they're both hot, Steve. Huge difference. Your wife looks like John Belushi. But whatever, man. If that's what does it for you, that's cool. Just don't tell us about it. Keep that shit to yourself.

STEVE: Screw you guys. I love my wife.

RUSS: That's all that matters, bro. I'd probably hit her with a bat and light her on fire if I ever ran into her on a dark night, but that's just me. I'm glad you're happy.

DWAYNE: Okay, men. I'm pulling up to my house. I'm gonna have my way with Estelle and then get ready for baseball practice. We've got a game tomorrow, so we need to make it count today. See you there.

TOMMY: Cool. Gonna go get some.

RUSS: I'm gonna rock some booty too. See you there.

STEVE: And I don't care what you guys think. I'm gonna throw a rubber sheet on the bed, pour a gallon of oil on Judith and myself, and get all kinds of dirty.

RUSS: BLORF!

TOMMY: LOL.

DWAYNE: Jesus.

RUSS: Do us a favor and use kerosene instead of oil.

STEVE: Suck it. See you at practice.

DWAYNE: Later.

28.

All of the lights were dimmed at the Devero house. Candles were lit, and the sweet smell of lavender filled the air. Dwayne walked through the front door and immediately became aroused. He knew something, aside from his trouser snake, was up.

He repressed the memory of the photos. He vowed not to bring them up to Estelle. Forward, not backward.

On the entryway floor was a piece of paper. Estelle had scribbled, "Take all of your clothes off and meet me in the bathtub."

Dwayne stripped; threw a bottle of white wine, some fresh strawberries, whipped cream, and two glasses on a silver serving tray; and sprinted to the master bathroom. He was ready to head to pound town.

Estelle couldn't have looked more attractive. He was taken aback for a moment at her beauty as he turned the corner. He couldn't speak. He approached her slowly, ready to ravage her.

She held an unlit joint up to her voluptuous lips as she lay sprawled out beneath the clear water. She flicked the lighter. Her eyes looked stunning in the glow of the flame. Estelle took a long pull from the joint as Dwayne set the tray on the edge of the tub. She reached up with her free hand and grabbed his manhood, slowly massaging it as she stared deep into his eyes.

"What are you waiting on, Big Boy?" she whispered. "Why don't you climb in here and make me feel like a woman?"

Dwayne slid into the tub behind Estelle. He let his hand slide from beneath her breast to below her bellybutton, continuing downward. She placed her hand on top of his, guiding him, and began to moan as he kissed her neck and ear. She reached her other hand behind her, up his thigh, until she found what she was looking for.

After a couple of minutes, Dwayne couldn't take it any more. He had to have her. He lifted her up and spun her around, leaving them both standing in the tub facing one another. He leaned down and began to kiss her passionately, letting his hands glide over her lower back until they found her ass. He grabbed firmly and lifted her up, carrying her to the bathroom counter, where he placed her gently. Only then did he make his way down between her legs.

Estelle gripped Dwayne's hair until she almost pulled it out. She screamed as she climaxed, and he made his way back up. She forced herself forward off the counter, her body heaving in total ecstasy, and pushed him backward into the bedroom and onto the bed. She climbed on top of him and rode him, her hips grinding skillfully back and forth, harder and harder, until his whole body convulsed, and they collapsed together into complete and total full-body orgasms.

They lay atop the bed afterward, twitching and smiling from the euphoria that comes from those rare, once-in-a-decade, mind-bending orgasms. The combination of bath water and sweat had made their bodies slick, and Estelle slowly slid her mouth up to Dwayne's ear, offering a tiny nibble, followed by a giggle.

"Oh my God," she said quietly, all of her energy drained. "You fucking rock my world."

As he tried to catch his breath, Dwayne rolled Estelle onto her back and admired her body. She was perfect. He drew a line of kisses from her stomach to her lips.

Within seconds, they were full-on making out like a couple of college kids. It didn't take long before Dwayne was fully aroused again. He rolled her back over to where she was on top of him and sat up. He then stood with her in his arms and walked across the room and back into the bathroom. He pushed her up against the wall by the bathtub. Her feet didn't touch the ground at all for the next ten minutes as they went another round.

Estelle ran her fingernails down his back, and she gripped his ass and screamed until they were finished.

He walked them back over to the tub, stepped in, and lay down with Estelle on top. His legs fidgeted a few times from the muscle strain.

"I feel like I'm living in an awesome porno, you know? Like . . . a classy one," Dwayne said.

"I know, babe," Estelle replied. "I swear, I've never had orgasms like that. Holy *shit*, that was good."

"No shit," Dwayne sighed. "Maybe *porn* is the wrong word. Porn isn't really as good as this. It's like *mainstream* porn, like a Mickey Rourke movie that made it into theaters but got picketed by church groups or something, you know? Like . . . all of the other aspects of the movie are good too. It's not just the sex that's good. So it's not really porn. But at the same time, the sex is *outstanding*. Maybe like *9½ Weeks*, but also with a little bit of *The Notebook*, but so fucking badass that it's like *The Matrix* too."

He paused for a moment as he lit a joint again. Then it came to him.

"That's fucking *it*!" he exclaimed. "That's what this is like! It's like Neo banging it out with the chick from *The Notebook*!"

"And they're wearing *Star Wars* outfits," Estelle added.

"You're goddamn right, babe," Dwayne said with a smile. "You're goddamn right."

29

After his brief erotic escapade, Dwayne grabbed Alex from his friend's house and headed to practice at Jenny Field.

The other three newly appointed assistant coaches pulled up as Dwayne was unloading the baseball gear. They looked sexed-out and ragged. Russ was extra jumpy, Tommy was hunched over and limping, and Steve had what appeared to be a black eye with a chunk of hair missing from the front of his head, partially covered by a blood-soaked bandage.

"What happened to your face?" Dwayne asked Steve.

"No shit!" Tommy laughed.

"What are you laughing at, Tommy?" Steve snapped back. "Why the hell are you all bent over and limping, bro?"

"I've got my dick stuck to my leg with surgical tape," Tommy replied, wincing. "I took a boner pill. It hasn't worn off yet. I didn't want to coach baseball with a hard-on. Parents tend to frown on it. What's your excuse?"

"Well," Steve said, glancing toward the ground, knowing he was about to take a heaping helping of shit. "I was going to get all funky with Judith, but her bush has gotten out of control lately, like massive, so I felt like I had to bring it up before I went to town."

"So she fucking punched you and ripped your hair out?" Russ yelled. "Jesus!"

"No, no, it wasn't like that at all," Steve continued. "I don't know why I feel the need to justify myself to a guy who had a man's pinky in his ass twelve hours ago, but still . . . Judith was actually pretty cool with the bush conversation. I told her I wanted to shave it for her, you know? Get a little kinky."

Russ turned around, walked back toward the fence, and projectile-vomited for a few seconds. The other guys' eyes went wide. He walked back to the group, wiping his mouth on his T-shirt.

"Oh, fuck, Steve," Russ said, physically ill at the idea. "I'm sorry. Keep going."

"So, anyhow, I got my ball clippers out of my drawer and propped my little lady up on the bathroom counter and went to work. Unfortunately, on the first pass, the clippers snagged on her hair because it was so thick, and it yanked her bush a little, so she just kicked as a reflex. Her shin got me right on the cheekbone, and it knocked the clippers up right above my forehead and shaved a nice stripe. Took a little skin too."

Russ cocked his head, not really wanting to grasp or visualize what he'd just been told. A string of slobber hung from his bottom lip.

"So that's it?" Tommy asked. "You didn't get to hit it?"

"No, man, that's what's so awesome!" Steve said. "She was still *so* turned on, we just went at it! We—"

"Wait," Russ interrupted. "Are you fucking serious? That's like dirty Kentucky Internet shit there, man. You're telling me that I'm supposed to think a big-nosed chick with huge calves and half a bush getting it on with a skinny little dude with a blood-soaked stripe shaved out of the front of his head is awesome? Jesus. I'm fucking totally traumatized now."

"At least you can stand up straight, man," Tommy said. "If I try to stand up straight, I'll need a skin graft."

"Jesus, man, how much tape did that take?" Russ inquired. "I mean, you're black, so I'm assuming you have tape all the way down to your knee."

"Yup, no doubt. We can dance and shoot hoops, and our peckers look like elephant trunks. Some stereotypes are very real, my man. It took two full rolls of tape. By the way, I saw your pecker today at the golf course when you drove there naked. I can assure you I could've handled that with a Band-Aid."

"Yeah, well, I never claimed I'd hit the bottom of it," Russ smirked, then hocked a loogie. "But I'll knock the shit outta the sides."

The conversation was abruptly interrupted as the moms and dads who had been accustomed to kissing the previous coaches' asses, ensuring their children received primo positions on the team, came barreling over to greet the four baseball dads.

"God bless you men for stepping in during this time of need," one of the large-haired, insincere, fundamentalist, social-climbing moms said. "Would you like to join hands for a moment of prayer before we enter this new chapter with our baseball team?"

"No, not really," Russ replied.

"That's a no-go for me too, ma'am," Steve said with confidence.

"I'm pretty sure God doesn't care about baseball," Dwayne responded.

"Well, I just—" The lady was unsure how to continue.

"I'll say a little prayer for the boys tonight, ma'am," Tommy offered politely, so as not to jeopardize a future Botox opportunity.

Dwayne was ready to begin and asked the parents to take a seat on the bleachers. He'd made an honest effort to look the part of a baseball coach. He sported a light gray pair of bad "coach shorts" that were so skimpy his balls nearly dangled out of them and carried a very official-looking clipboard. He kept the black Wayfarers on at all times to mask how high he was. Good coaches, he convinced himself, were always high.

Once the parents were seated, Dwayne, with the Jedi Alliance supporting him, addressed the crowd.

"Hello, parents. Most of you are at least lightly acquainted with my assistants and myself. For those of you who are not, I'm Dwayne Devero. Behind me are Russ Paisley, Tommy Johnson, and Steve Winwood—no relation. I just wanted to sit you folks down for a moment and let you know a few things about the way we coach.

"You see, there are two main types of coaching in children's base-ball: There's 'playing to win,' and then there's 'daddy baseball.' Playing to win is just the way it sounds. You put players in positions and bat-ting lineup slots according to their level of talent in a way that is most likely to advance the team toward winning baseball games. Daddy baseball, on the other hand, takes talent completely out of the equa-tion. Daddy baseball is typically comprised of a group of ass-kissing parents who tickle the metaphorical ball sack of a head coach in order to ensure that their dipshit, talentless child plays a position far outside his respective wheelhouse. As most of you might have noticed from our horrific record this season, we've not been playing to win. We've been playing daddy baseball. And now, with the four of us coaching, we're simply not doing that anymore. I'm sure this news paints an awkward picture for most of you, seeing how I laid out this story and knowing what your role in it has been."

Dwayne scanned the crowd to see if the parents were smelling what he was cooking. Judging by the number of mouths hanging wide open, he knew they were.

Dwayne continued. "I know that this angers some of you. Lots of people don't like being told things that are true. And that's okay. I want you to know, from the bottom of my heart, that I don't give a shit. I know that sounds harsh, but on some level, isn't it refreshing? You may come to appreciate my candor. I hope you do. I'm like Obi-Wan and Neo, and I can give you multiple orgasms. I know that may not make sense right now, but that's how I roll. I'm taking over. The other guys . . . the old coaches . . . aren't here anymore."

"News flash: They're dead," Russ interrupted with a jolt. "Sorry, boss. Please continue."

"Thanks, Russ." Dwayne kept going. "That's right. They're dead. Or missing. Or whatever. They're not here, and I am. And I'm playing to win. We're going to be in the championship game, come hell or high water, because that's how I motherfucking roll up in this bitch. Oh, and one last thing. Some coaches *love* getting input from parents about who should play where, batting order, game strategy, and so on. And that's great. I'm just *not one of those coaches*. If you feel like you have some good insight on what might help us win, or if you think you might have a helpful suggestion, I want you to do me a favor, okay? I want you to make a fist, clinch it up really tightly, and then punch yourself in the face as hard as you can. Then, I want you to take that same fist and stick it up your ass. If you still feel like offering sugges-tions or advice after that, then you either didn't punch yourself in the face hard enough, or you didn't stick your fist far enough up your ass. Any questions?"

The parents looked at each other in dismay. No one spoke.

"Cool," he said. "We'll see you back here at 7:00 p.m. I've got a team to coach. Take care." Dwayne turned and marched toward the field with his clipboard in hand. The other three coaches scurried behind him. The crowd in the bleachers slowly dissipated after a few moments, as the parents made their way to their vehicles and left in almost PTSD-like shock.

Dwayne had the boys form two lines, facing each other, so that they could get warmed up throwing the ball back and forth.

"I think that went well," Dwayne said to the other coaches confidently, while staring intently at the warm-up exercise. "I expect you all to be dressed like coaches at every game and practice from this point forward, by the way. No one will take you seriously without small shorts and a clipboard. Fucking step up your game, men."

30.

The practice began to take shape after a half-hour or so. Dwayne and the baseball dads started to notice what Dwayne had suspected all along: Some of these kids weren't half bad. They just needed to play positions according to their talents and be given a bit of direction. The two worst kids on the team ended up being the spawn of the deceased, Ace Dale and Eric Rearden. Still, Dwayne thought there might be hope for the team.

Dwayne noticed that T-Bone Sprinkle, the head coach of the team Dwayne's team would play next, had come to do some not-so-secret scouting.

T-Bone was a short, bald, goateed, burly little animal of a man. He owned a prominent commercial real estate investment agency and was an obnoxious asshole, through and through. He had a reputation for arguing with every umpire and every coach on damn near every play, and he verbally abused every child on his team.

But T-Bone Sprinkle won. A lot. Every season, he would finish in a top spot. The Yankees, his team this season, had won all but two games. After those two losses, he made every player on his team run bases until they vomited, and then he went home, got drunk, and beat his son and his wife. His team won because of one simple factor. Fear.

"Oh, man, you dipshits sure have your work cut out for you, huh?" T-Bone yelled out to Dwayne from the other side of the infield fence.

Dwayne didn't acknowledge him. He continued running an infield drill with Steve while Tommy and Russ ran the outfield drill.

"What a bunch of retards!" T-Bone continued, still unable to shake Dwayne. "I swear to God, if I looked up and saw those boys on my team, I'd drive into the woods and put a shotgun in my mouth!"

Tommy and Russ looked to Dwayne. He remained unfazed. They were impressed. They hadn't reached that level of Jedi meditation yet. They were fast becoming ready to kill.

T-Bone was irritated that he couldn't rattle Dwayne. He'd have to step up his game. He moved along the fence, closer to where Dwayne was running his drill—directly behind home plate.

"Jesus, you guys are awful," T-Bone said, now less than ten feet from Dwayne. "I'm gonna take a victory tomorrow, and then I'll go have my way with your wife for a little while. If she gets home late tomorrow, don't worry. I'll take good care of her."

Dwayne paused. He lowered the bat he'd been using to hit grounders, and stared down at the ground for a moment.

"Oooh, that got you, didn't it?" T-Bone taunted. "I guess I found your weak spot. I'll remember that. You know, if Alex is free tomorrow after he loses, he's welcome to hold my beer while I make your little lady squeal. He's gotta be good for something."

Dwayne tapped the bat on home plate two times, and then smiled as he lifted up the bat to inspect it. A wave of fear swept over Steve. He knew what Dwayne had become capable of. He was afraid that T-Bone was about to find out.

Dwayne looked out at Tommy and Russ. They hadn't been able to hear the last barbs from T-Bone, but they could tell something was up. Dwayne motioned for Russ to head over.

"Steve, take over for me," Dwayne said. "Hit some grounders to shortstop and third. Have them work on the double play. I'll be back in a few."

T-Bone puffed up his chest. He had a feeling he was about to be in a fight. That made him happy. He didn't lose fights.

Russ and Dwayne walked off the field together, not saying a word. They headed toward T-Bone. A small flash of concern hit T-Bone when he saw the look on Dwayne's face.

"Parking lot. Now," Dwayne told T-Bone. "I'm not doing this in front of the kids."

"Jesus, Lawn Boy, relax." T-Bone attempted to maintain his badass demeanor, masking a growing fear. "I'm just trying to rattle you. You don't want to do this. I'll fucking rip you to pieces."

Out of nowhere, Dave the umpire appeared. He had been watching the confrontation unfold from the scoring box above the concession stand. And while Dave and Dwayne had had their differences lately, and he and Russ had often been at odds, there was no parent or coach at Jenny Field that belittled and talked down to the umpires more than Coach T-Bone Sprinkle.

"You fellas want to borrow the scoring box for a few minutes to settle your differences?" Dave asked, looking at Dwayne with a sinister grin.

Dwayne grinned back. Russ watched the manner in which the two of them looked at each other and figured there was something larger between them that he was unaware of. Dwayne and Dave certainly had developed some history. Maybe this was some form of reckoning, Russ figured.

Or maybe Dave had become a Jedi, too.

"The scoring box is probably a good idea," T-Bone responded in a shitty tone. "You don't want Dwayne to leave on a stretcher."

Dave held open the door to the scoring box. The four men made their way up the stairs above the concession stand, and the three coaches sat at a small conference table by the scoring window where the pitch count was kept and the scoreboard machine was operated. It was a small, dark, cheaply decorated room, with an old ceiling fan spinning and squealing overhead above brown shag carpet.

Dwayne and T-Bone stared at each other across the flimsy off-white conference table in silence as Russ looked on in anticipation. He was anxious to see what the new and psychotically improved Dwayne would do next. Dave dug around in the lost-and-found closet behind T-Bone. The sunlight tore through the mini blinds into the dankness of the room, and a horizontal fraction of light caught Dwayne across the eyes in a perfectly evil way.

"So, what was it that T-Bone said that has you so upset, Dwayne?" Dave the umpire asked from the closet.

"Fuck you, Dave, this doesn't concern you," T-Bone replied. "If we want to know what uneducated dumbasses think about things, we'll ask one of Lawn Boy's coworkers."

Dwayne smiled at T-Bone. He didn't say a word. He didn't break eye contact at all, even when Dave appeared behind T-Bone clutching a confiscated big-barrel bat that was illegal during regular season little league play.

"Hey, dickstain," Dave said to T-Bone.

T-Bone turned around just in time to see the bat coming full speed at his face. He took a solid hit right in the teeth and dropped unconscious onto the dirty floor.

"Jesus, Dave, you've got a great swing," Russ offered. "Fucking fantastic form."

"Thanks, man," Dave replied, throwing the bat up over his shoulder, where he let it rest. "I was All State in high school, then I got a full ride in college. I had over a .500 average for three years."

Dave fondly relished the good old days before his eyebrows turned downward and his attention was brought back to a twitching and contorted T-Bone Sprinkle. "Then I went to prison."

Dave picked the bat back up off his shoulder and swung down as hard as he could at T-Bone's skull, which cracked open like a coconut. Blood splattered out onto Russ and Dwayne's faces and across the surface of the old conference table. It shot through the mini blinds and dripped down the window of the booth.

T-Bone's body fidgeted a few times again. It was probably just nerves, but Dave wanted to make sure, so he hit him in the face with the bat three more times at full strength. Each time Dave swung the bat, bits of blood would stream from it, catching in the scattered sunlight like confetti reflecting off a disco ball in a dark dance club.

Dave stood heaving over the lifeless body. He had so much blood on his face that he had to wipe it away from his eyes so he could see. He kicked a couple of skull fragments and an eyeball that had popped out with his weathered work boots, then chuckled to himself. Blood began to pool all around in the old shag carpet. He tossed the bat onto the floor.

"So I'm guessing we're all cool now, huh?" Dave the umpire asked Dwayne and Russ.

"Yup," Russ answered. "I think we're okeydokey."

"Yeah, I'd say we're cool, Dave," Dwayne said. "And by the way, if you're ever free when we're practicing, I'd love it if you could head on over and show the team that swing. No bullshit. It really is outstanding."

"That'd be great." Dave was genuinely flattered. "So, ummm, we've got a dead body here now, so that might be something we should address."

"Yup. No doubt about it," Russ said back, lighting a joint and passing it to Dave.

Dave took a toke, then tilted his head, raised his eyebrows, and gave Russ a thumbs-up.

"Can you keep this building secure until about 11:00 p.m. tonight?" Dwayne asked.

"Sure, man," Dave replied. "I'm pretty sure I'm the only one that has a key to it, but I'll throw a padlock on the door anyhow."

"You got shovels here?"

"Yup."

"Power washer?"

"Yup."

"When our practice is over, I think you'll need to redo the pitcher's mound. You think you could dig out the existing one? Maybe go six feet deep or so? It should be pretty soft. It's mostly red dirt and sand."

"No prob, Dwayne."

"Russ and I are going to run to the restroom and wash any residual blood splatter and brain matter off our faces and clothes, and then we're going to go finish our practice strong. We need a win tomorrow. The three of us will meet back here at 11:00 p.m. tonight. Sound good?"

Dave the umpire and Russ nodded in agreement.

"By the way, Dwayne," Dave said. "I just wanted to let you know that I think it's great what you're doing here, bro. Too many douchebags have been fucking up our game. This is *baseball*, for God's sake.

I'm glad we're taking it back, man. Win or lose, you're going to show these kids the way the game is supposed to be played. That's awesome."

"Thanks," Dwayne replied softly. "That's all I'm trying to do."

Russ and Dwayne headed to the restroom and then down to the field while Dave locked up.

Steve became concerned when Russ and Dwayne resumed their positions on the field. It did not go unnoticed by him that *four* men had entered the scoring box and three had returned.

Dwayne smiled at Steve. "Well, let's hope T-Bone had a better backup coach than Ricky Dale." Dwayne gripped his bat and continued the infield drill. "Two to one, then fire it home!" he yelled to the infielders.

"Oh Jesus, Dwayne," Steve said. "I think you need a vacation."

"Fuck that, hombre," Dwayne shot back. "Why should life be so difficult and full of bullshit that we need a break from it? Life is my vacation now."

Steve had become a bit nervous about the course his friendship with the other three had taken.

"You know, Dwayne, I saw *Star Wars*," he said. "I mean, it's been a while, but I don't remember any of them being serial killers. You've killed three people now, Dwayne. I'm not sure what the minimum requirement is to be considered a serial killer, but—"

"One, Stevie," Dwayne interrupted. "I've technically only killed one. Dave killed the other two. But still, I get your point. And as far as the Jedi go . . . they were damn near wiped out by the conclusion of Episode VI, just one left standing. Imagine how far they could've gone if they'd adopted some of *my* core values. I'm telling you, they would've prospered."

Dwayne called all of the players in and put them into actual positions according to their talents, the way it should have been done all season. He began calling in kids to bat, one by one, to help establish his batting order. He was beginning to feel good about the team's potential. They looked as though they might be real contenders.

He continued this until 7:00 p.m., when it was time for practice to be over. When practice ended, not a single parent so much as exited their vehicle. They simply let the kids come out to them in the parking lot.

There was no backslapping. No ass-kissing. Nothing. They just gathered their kids and left.

"Good," Dwayne said to himself. "They were listening."

31

DWAYNE: Practice went well tonight.

STEVE: Dude, seriously? You killed a guy in the scoring booth with a little league bat.

DWAYNE: That bat had been banned by little league because of the barrel size, Steve. So technically, you're wrong.

RUSS: LOL.

TOMMY: Lalalalalala. Black guy knows nothing.

DWAYNE: We're gonna kill that team tomorrow in the game.

STEVE: WHAT???

DWAYNE: Sorry. Poor choice of words.

RUSS: Unless they fuck with us.

STEVE: JESUS!!!

TOMMY: I guess we should feel confident about the calls from the home plate umpire tomorrow.

DWAYNE: Correct, Tiberius. I've never been this comfortable with the potential for favoritism. Dave the umpire has joined the Jedi Alliance.

STEVE: Really raising the bar on Jedi, eh?

DWAYNE: Jedi don't believe in class warfare, Steve. The Force does not discriminate.

RUSS: Hell, Steve, look at Tommy. He's three shades darker than midnight. His driver's license is a picture of a pair of hovering eyeballs. You wanna start being a bigot, you'll have to deal with him too.

TOMMY: Yeah. What the fuck, Steve?!

DWAYNE: Racist.

RUSS: How do you sleep at night?

STEVE: What the HELL? Don't throw this back on me! I'm just saying Dave is a fucking moron! I deal with inner-city kids and gang members every day at work!

TOMMY: So someone mentions race, and you go straight to gang affiliation? That's just wrong, man.

DWAYNE: How do they let someone who hates black people run an inner-city school?

STEVE: Goddammit.

TOMMY: Anyone else getting laid tonight? I'm gonna go drive it home with my boo Kelly.

RUSS: Your boo? Seriously? Who the fuck are you, Ice Cube?

TOMMY: Whatevs, bro, I'm about to go get some. Gonna be ass-tastic.

STEVE: No doubt. Me too.

RUSS: LOL, Steve. Pretty sure our definitions of getting some are different.

STEVE: Yeah, mine doesn't involve waking up with a shaved penis on my chin and a dude's finger in my ass.

TOMMY: BURN!

RUSS: WTF? Burn??? Are you 8 years old? And fuck off, Steve, at least my wife's calves are smaller than the goddamn Manhattan subway tunnels!

STEVE: Yeah, well, your asshole isn't.

TOMMY: OOOOH, SNAP! BURN!

RUSS: Jesus, this is like texting with a retarded boy band.

DWAYNE: Alright, fellow Jedi warriors, gotta go eat dinner with the family. Russ, I'll see you at 11:00 p.m. Tommy and Steve, see you tomorrow at the game. Tap that ass like the Rebel Alliance tonight, boys!

Dwayne had been texting from the living room while watching ESPN with Alex. Estelle was putting the final touches on vegetarian enchiladas, a recipe she'd gotten from her fitness club. A story came on the television about more Major League Baseball players being suspended for steroid use. One of the players was Alex's favorite, and he was pretty crushed.

"Why do those guys do steroids, Dad?" he asked. "They already have it made. They get to play baseball for a living. What more could they want?"

"Wow, bud," Dwayne answered. "That's probably the best comment I've heard about the subject. I think what it comes down to is that they only love themselves. You've got to love the game if you want to be great. They're just trying to cheat their way into the record books. If you love something bigger than yourself, you wouldn't do that. They don't deserve to have the honor of walking out onto a baseball field."

"I agree," Alex said. "I wish they knew how lucky they were."

"Well, if it makes you feel better," Dwayne added, "their balls have most likely shriveled up into tiny little beans, and they'll most likely go to jail at some point for flying into a coke-induced rage and locking a prostitute into a motel closet after their home is foreclosed upon and the IRS seizes all of their remaining assets that haven't been pawned on eBay for OxyContin . . . followed soon after by several stints in rehab and early organ failure. Karma is an unforgiving bitch."

This particular information was hard for Alex to process.

"Oh Jesus, Alex," Dwayne said with mild concern. "My bad. But it's good that you learn these things early."

Alex returned to watching *SportsCenter*, not sure what his dad had meant. Dwayne could tell it had flown over Alex's head, so he didn't feel the need to do any sort of damage control.

Dwayne had thoroughly enjoyed watching Alex play ball that afternoon. The kid was gifted. The team had come together in support of something bigger—the joy of playing baseball the way it was supposed to be played: turning the body just right to make the double play, keeping a foot on the base while stretching out as far as possible to make a catch and beat the runner, fully extending the body in a dive toward a ball that was uncatchable, and catching it.

Dwayne hadn't seen that for a while. It was beautiful.

"Dad, today was awesome," Alex said.

And that was all Dwayne needed to hear.

32.

After dinner, Dwayne retired to the back porch for a doobie and a glass of whiskey. Estelle had taken Alex upstairs to help him study for a math test before tucking him into bed. She hadn't done that for a long time.

Dwayne felt warm all over, and not just from the whiskey. Alex deserved a lot of love and attention, and he was finally getting it. Not many kids showed such respect for others or cared so much about doing the right thing. Alex paid attention in school, never let his friends down, and showed compassion. He was the kind of kid every parent wanted.

Alex was going to get the notice he deserved in baseball, too. Dwayne couldn't wait to get out on the field with the boys and allow them to properly compete in the greatest game ever played. He was excited for the boys. He wanted them to have a strong sense of accomplishment and achievement.

He took a long pull from his joint and slowly exhaled. There was hardly any wind at all, and the smoke lingered delicately in front of him, slowly changing shapes in the moonlight.

A rattling commotion by the trash cans jarred him from his dance with inner peace. Unsure of what he would find, Dwayne set down his whiskey and grabbed a baseball bat that was lying in the yard.

There had been a significant raccoon problem in the neighborhood due to the location of several dumpsters behind the high-end apartment complex around the corner. Roving bands of black-eyed rodents scurried through yards and over fences at night. They knocked over trash cans, tore up trash bags, and ate the outdoor dog and cat food. Aside from arrogant fundamentalist trust-fund babies, they were the most damaging things Fort Worth had ever seen.

Dwayne snuck to the side of his garage and found an overturned trash can with garbage scattered all around. Perched atop the toppled container sat the most massive raccoon in the state of Texas. It wasn't afraid of Dwayne at all. The raccoon simply sat and ate, as if at any moment it would reach out its paw and shake Dwayne's hand.

The quality of the weed Dwayne had been smoking played no small part in Dwayne's fascination with the critter. He leaned in closely, watching the coon strip every bit of meat off last week's KFC. Dwayne giggled when the raccoon tossed a bone over his shoulder. He felt like they were bonding. Perhaps it was a Jedi thing, he thought. He was still holding the joint, so he took a massive hit from it and blew the smoke at the rodent's face. It just shook its head quickly, glanced up at Dwayne, and tore into another piece of chicken. Dwayne could've sworn the raccoon smiled.

He glanced down at his watch. It was time to head to the ballpark. He used the bat to push himself up from the squatting position he'd been in and tried to maintain balance. He stood tall and pointed at the fence at the far side of his yard. Dwayne spread his feet shoulder width apart, bent his knees slightly, shifted his weight to his back leg, and lifted the bat into the "loaded up" position, just as he had taught the kids at practice. Then, he turned with his hips, exploding forward with a step, and offered up a beautiful level swing that caught the raccoon right in the teeth.

The raccoon did approximately twenty backflips in the air, spraying blood out in every direction as it spun, and hit the far fence with a loud thud. Dwayne was mildly disappointed that the raccoon didn't make it over the fence, but he also knew to never be upset with a solid line drive.

Dwayne's phone let out a quack. Russ had started a group text with Dwayne and Dave the umpire.

RUSS: You guys ready to take out the trash?
DWAYNE: Yup. Headed to the field in a second. Just killed a coon. It was awesome.
RUSS: You killed Tommy???

DWAYNE: No, you fucking racist! I killed a raccoon! It was in my garbage.

RUSS: Fucking twisted, bro.

DAVE: I nevr text befor. Cool.

RUSS: Are you fucking kidding me? What, were you too busy winning spelling bees?

DAVE: Fuck off. Your an asshole.

RUSS: *You're.

DAVE: You're an asshole. I dug a hole. Its hot out their.

RUSS: *It's, *there.

DAVE: I'm gonna whip you're hairy ass, Russ.

DWAYNE: You guys ready, or what? Let's do this.

RUSS: Yeah, I just . . . fuck . . . he did it again. Do I not call that out? Jesus, that kills me. The concept is so fuck-ing simple.

DAVE: I'm a umpire n ex con. Dont need to spell. Suck my umpire balls, Russ.

RUSS: Thank you for your honesty. Let's move on.

DAVE: Your welcome.

RUSS: Goddammit.

DWAYNE: See you guys in a few.

It bothered Dwayne that Russ was wound so tight. He wished Russ would smoke more weed and snort less blow. He didn't know if Russ was cut out for the Jedi life. Russ didn't have enough Kenny Rogers in him. He couldn't discern when it was time to hold 'em, fold 'em, walk away, or run. But Dwayne and Russ were in this together now. And Dave, too. That was the way it was.

Dwayne walked into his kitchen and grabbed some paper towels. He was by the sink wiping raccoon blood off the baseball bat when Estelle walked up behind him and gently wrapped her arms around him. He set the bloody paper towel and the bat on the dark granite countertop and placed his hands on hers. They intertwined their fingers and took in the warmth of the moment.

"Gotta run for a bit, baby," he said. "Daddy's gotta handle some business."

"No problem, sweetie," she whispered as she nibbled his earlobe. "Take your time. I've got a new costume I want you to see."

"Wait, what?" Dwayne said, ready to abandon the guys and sensually tackle his wife on the kitchen floor.

"Nope, I'll be waiting," she replied.

"Come on, gorgeous! Can I at least get a hint?"

Estelle turned and walked toward the bedroom, dropping her robe on the floor as she walked away, revealing her perfectly sculpted ass.

"Meow," she purred, walking through the door to their room and closing it behind her.

Dwayne grabbed his keys and hauled ass out the front door.

33.

Dwayne arrived at the ballpark at precisely 11:00 p.m. He noticed Russ's Ferrari parked off in the corner of the lot, obscured by foliage. Parked beside it was an old dirt-track motorcycle with an expired, dangling license plate. Dwayne could only assume that this belonged to Dave the umpire. Dwayne pulled his truck beside them.

Dave and Russ were sitting inside the Ferrari having a clambake. The windows were up, and you could barely see either of them because of the thickness of the smoke. Both of them were wiping tears from their eyes, apparently from several minutes of intense laughter.

Dwayne walked to the front of Russ's car and held his hands in the air, as if to ask if they ever intended to get out of the vehicle. This just made Dave and Russ laugh harder. Dwayne frowned and headed toward the field.

Just as Dave the umpire had been instructed to do, he had dug a hole about six feet deep at the pitcher's mound. Dwayne peered over into it. Dave may not have been good for much, but he could sure dig a mighty fine hole. He headed over toward the scoring booth to assess the carnage.

Dave and Russ came stumbling up. They were slurring, wobbly, and high, yet full of energy.

"You've gotta try the coke, D-dog," Dave said to Dwayne. "This shit is intense, bro."

"That's okay, man," he replied. "You go ahead and snort my portion. More for you."

Dave gave a smile and a nod, as if he'd somehow just come out ahead on doing lines of Russ's coke.

"Okay, bros, I finished digging early and had some time to kill, so I power-washed the scoring booth," Dave said proudly. He pulled the padlock from the stairwell door to show them.

The door swung open and came to a quick stop on the side of T-Bone Sprinkle's very dead head. T-Bone's body lay twisted at the bottom of the narrow stairs, hard in the grips of rigor mortis, with one leg sticking straight up in the air.

"Yeah, I didn't feel like carrying him down the steps, so, you know . . ." Dave said sheepishly. "Fucker got down quick, though. He's hard as a rock, too. Check out that leg, man. That's fuckin' funny. I don't care who you are."

Dwayne eased around the corpse of T-Bone Sprinkle, looking down at him as he passed. His head was caved in above the nose, and he was missing an eye. Portions of his skull pierced through his scalp. His hands were bent upward at the wrist, his fingers outstretched like he was about to play the piano. He didn't look good.

Not a good way to go, he thought. T-Bone deserved it, though. He deserved to be whacked in the face and sacrificed to the baseball gods, with a pitcher's-mound burial. It was fitting.

Dwayne continued up into the scoring booth. He couldn't help but be impressed. The room was immaculate. There wasn't a drop of blood anywhere in sight. The carpet was still wet from the power washer, but everything else was perfect.

"What about T-Bone's car? What did he drive?" Dwayne yelled down the stairs to Dave.

"He lived a couple of miles from here," Dave responded. "T-Bone walked a few miles every day. This is where he turned around to go back. He always came in and fucked with people before heading back. So no worries there. The cops will probably think he got jumped walking by the river. We're cool."

"Okay then," Dwayne asserted. "Let's drag this sack of shit to the hole. Russ, assume the lookout position."

"Aye aye, Captain." Russ moved toward the front entrance. He edged back into the shadow of a large redbrick column so as not to be seen in the moonlight.

The stadium lights were off, so Dave the umpire and Dwayne were able to drag T-Bone's body through the fence and across the third base line in the comfort of darkness. It proved to be an awkward endeavor due to the rigor mortis.

They realized that T-Bone's leg sticking up would make it impossible to get the body into the hole. It wouldn't fit. Dave struggled to push the leg down. Dwayne took a few turns as well. It wouldn't budge. Even hitting the leg full swing with a shovel proved futile. It just wasn't going down.

"Any ideas?" Dwayne asked the umpire.

"I've got a chainsaw."

"Too loud."

"I've got a hacksaw."

"Perfect."

Dwayne sat on the ground to catch his breath while Dave went to get the hacksaw. Dwayne loved being on the baseball field. Even if it was to bury a body, there was no place he would rather be. The bright green of the field was so striking in the moonlight. He hadn't ever seen the field this green. His lawn crew had done an amazing job since they'd gotten the contract, he thought to himself. He wondered if Pete Rearden's ground-up body had some kind of positive effect, producing the vibrant color of the grass. He would keep that in mind for the future.

When Dave the umpire made it back to the mound, he took a seat Indian-style beside T-Bone's leg and got to work. Without hesitation, Dave sawed his way across the upper thigh. Blood came pouring out.

Dave had no problems getting through the flesh, but the bone proved more of an issue. After getting halfway through the femur, he paused for a break. The intensity of the coke had worn off. He wiped the sweat from his forehead, streaking blood across it and into his hair.

"Here, man, take a break," Dwayne said. "I'll finish."

Several minutes later, Dwayne was able to finish the amputation. He had no idea it would be that difficult. He tossed the leg off to the side and looked at his hands, arms, and shirt. They were drenched in deep red blood. Dwayne wiped his hands on his pants and pulled a joint from his pocket, needing a break before the final stretch.

"Be back in a minute, bro," Dave growled. "I'm gonna get a beer and check on that hairy little bastard, Russ. Plus, the acid he gave me earlier kicked in a few minutes ago."

"Jesus," Dwayne replied. He didn't know they'd dipped into the hardcore hallucinogens. They might need to hurry before things got out of hand.

Because of Russ and Dave's increasingly altered states, Dwayne knew he should keep working to get the dead asshole under some dirt. He positioned himself on the ground perpendicular to the body, with his feet pressed firmly against T-Bone's hip. He pushed as hard as he could with his legs, inching the corpse slowly toward the edge of the hole. After a couple of minutes struggling to make progress, the one-legged body dropped headfirst into the freshly dug pit, landing awkwardly on its flattened head. Dwayne fell backward, relieved and exhausted but pleased with his progress.

Behind him, Dwayne heard Russ and Dave the umpire come giggling and running down the third base line toward home plate. Dwayne popped up and rolled over to check out what the commotion was about. He was decently startled at what he saw.

Russ rounded home plate in a full sprint and headed toward first base, completely naked with his arms waving in the air as he laughingly screamed. Dave was close behind, giving chase, swinging T-Bone's severed leg above his head.

Dwayne sat in the middle of the infield, at the pitcher's mound, and watched in silence as they ran all the way around the bases several times. Russ's small and ridiculously hairy package flopped side to side as he reached his full stride.

Russ grabbed an old baseball that was resting against the backstop, and then ran out beside Dwayne. Russ and Dave must have been on the same page because Dave stepped into the batter's box and loaded up, holding T-Bone's leg by the ankle like a baseball bat, with his arms cocked back in a perfect stance. Russ held the ball to his chest. He checked his left shoulder, looking for a runner at first. He went into the windup and sent a perfect screaming fastball right toward home.

Dave made perfect contact with the ball just above T-Bone's kneecap, and drove the ball into right field. After a brief moment of enjoying the hallucinatory effects of watching a ball fly through the air in the moonlight, Dave the umpire took off for first base.

Instinct took over with Dwayne. He jumped up and took off toward the ball while Russ ran to cover home. Dave was rounding third as Dwayne snatched the ball off the ground, spun, and whipped the ball to Russ. It was an immaculate throw.

Russ stood with one foot on each side of the third base line, just in from of home plate. He nabbed the ball from the air right above his head and swung his arm downward to tag out the runner. But Dave had already begun his feet-first slide precisely between Russ's legs. All at the exact same moment, Russ tagged Dave's shoulder with the ball, Dave's foot touched home base, and Dave's face went right into Russ's hairy, sweaty balls.

"Safe!" Dave yelled with such determination that he didn't notice the penis resting against his cheek.

"Are you fucking kidding me, Dave?!" Russ screamed. "I tagged you way before your foot hit the bag! There's no goddamn way you're safe! Another bad call from Dave the umpire!"

Dave started to yell something, and then suddenly became very aware that any time he moved his head ever so slightly, Russ's penis touched his face. He hadn't taken into account that there was an actual, live scrotum literally *right there*.

An awkward silence filled the baseball field. Russ slowly backed away from Dave's face, and the three men began to quietly walk toward the freshly dug grave at the pitcher's mound. Dave grabbed T-Bone's leg and brought it with them.

"She's no Louisville Slugger," Dave said firmly, tossing T-Bone's leg into the hole, "but she came through when I needed her."

The three of them took turns shoveling dirt onto the body. When they finished, Dave and Dwayne artfully rounded the top of the pitcher's mound to sheer perfection and placed the rectangular white plate on top.

Russ was laying down on his back, still totally nude, in the darkness of center field.

"Well, that should just about do it, men," Dwayne said loudly enough to stir Russ from his psychedelic state. "I'm sure I don't need to mention that we tell no one about this, we were never here tonight, and we haven't seen T-Bone recently."

Dave the umpire nodded. Dwayne looked over to Russ, who was walking toward them. Russ gave a thumbs-up as his balls flopped side to side.

"Okeydokey, then, boys," Dwayne announced. "I've seen just about enough penis this fine evening. Therefore, I'm going to go home and try to see a vagina. You boys have fun."

Dwayne walked to his truck, looking in all directions to make sure he wasn't seen. He pulled himself up into the front seat, groaning from the soreness of his increased activity the previous few days. He backed out from behind the trees and glanced back toward the field. He could barely make out the shapes of a naked little chunky man being chased full speed around the bases by a much larger clothed man.

"Jesus," Dwayne whispered to himself.

He picked up his phone before departing and sent a quick text to Estelle. It said simply, "On my way."

Dwayne turned up the radio. "Across 110th Street," by Bobby Womack, was playing. He cranked it up loud and sparked a joint.

A second later, his phone quacked. Estelle had replied to his text.

"I want you to wear me out like you've never done before. I want you to make me hurt."

He popped the vehicle into drive, slid the truck sideways exiting the parking lot, and headed home.

34.

Dwayne enjoyed coming home now. He never knew what to expect from Estelle. He only knew that good things awaited him.

These days, their marriage was so different. He used to dread walking through the door. In the past, at any given point in time, there would have been Bible study, prayer group, party planning, or whatever kind of socialite gossip circle activities that you could think of. He had to be careful about which vehicle he drove home and what he was wearing. And he'd had no desire to see or speak to his wife. But that wasn't the case anymore. Now, he couldn't wait to see her.

Estelle lay nude on her stomach atop the blankets on the bed, facing away from the entrance to the room. She was looking back over her shoulder at Dwayne playfully. She knew this was her best angle, with her gorgeous ass on display.

Two large boxes with big red bows rested at the end of the bed.

"Oh, baby," Estelle whispered in a sultry tone to Dwayne. "That's a lot of blood. We need to get you cleaned up."

She rolled off the bed and grabbed Dwayne by the belt buckle, leading him into the bathroom. She stood behind him as they both faced the mirror. Dwayne was surprised by the amount of blood he had on his arms and shirt.

"Rough day, sweetie?"

"Oh, you know how it is, babe," he replied. "Little league can be a bitch sometimes."

Estelle walked around in front of him and pulled his shirt up over his head. He couldn't stop staring at her ass in the mirror. He loved the way it jiggled when she moved. She motioned toward his shoes, which he promptly kicked off using his feet to pry the backs down. She undid his belt buckle and slowly pulled his pants down, never losing eye contact. Jesus she was awesome, he thought to himself.

Dwayne was led to the shower, being pulled by his johnson. He didn't have to do a thing while he was in there. Estelle lathered up every inch of his body for several heavenly minutes. She spent more time on some areas than others. He enjoyed it that she seemed to like his body as much as he liked hers. He wasn't conceited, but he knew he'd held up well over the years. He was strong as hell, had a low body-fat percentage, and a pretty decent-sized package.

"Now, you take a few minutes to rinse off while I get your surprise ready," Estelle said as she stepped out of the shower to dry off.

Dwayne let the piping-hot water run down his face and body. He could feel the soap sliding down his torso and legs. He watched as it circled down the drain. Tinges of orange from the dirt and red from the blood became less and less visible. The ridiculously expensive showerhead was worth every penny, he thought. He turned the water off and began to pat himself dry. Although he was well beyond tired, he knew he smelled amazing, and he was very much looking forward to terrorizing some booty. Dwayne walked through the steam from the shower and emerged on the other side in the bedroom, like a naked hero walking through artillery smoke in battle.

"Open the box and put your costume on," a voice called out from the closet.

The two boxes were no longer side by side. One now sat empty on the floor. Dwayne lifted the lid to the remaining box and found an official movie-quality Batman costume inside. "This is so fucking sweet," he said, admiring the craftsmanship. "I may wear this to work tomorrow."

It took several minutes for Dwayne to get the bodysuit, codpiece, gadget belt, boots, gloves, cape, and mask on. Once the costume was all in its proper place, he walked back into the bathroom to check himself out.

"Oh, fuck yeah," he said to himself, putting his hands on his hips.

"If you'll look at your yellow gadget belt, you'll notice I added two pairs of handcuffs," Estelle softly stated with a sexy snarl as she emerged from the closet, where she'd been hiding.

Estelle looked stunning in a black leather skin-tight Catwoman costume. He loved the sound her footsteps made in her high heel boots as she walked across the hardwood floors. She was absolutely the sexiest and most ravishing woman he'd ever seen.

"You wanna handcuff me to the bedrails and fight some crime in my pants, big fella?" she whispered softly in his ear. "I've been a really bad kitty."

Dwayne spun Estelle around and pinned her to the wall, kissing her passionately. He reached around behind her and picked her up under her butt cheeks. She wrapped her legs tightly around him, thrusting her pelvis hard on his codpiece. He spun, walking toward the bed. When he got a few feet away, he reached his hands under her arms, lifting her in the air above him, where he held her for a moment as they stared at each other. "Punish me," she said.

He threw her onto the bed, assuming the role of a sex-crazed crime fighter, reaching to his side to grab his handcuffs as if he'd done it a thousand times before. He forcefully cuffed her wrists out wide across the wrought-iron headboard.

Estelle was writhing on the bed in anticipation as Dwayne slowly pulled the zipper down on her leather pants. He peeled them down slowly to her knees and then paused.

"Holy shaved vagina, Catwoman!" Dwayne exclaimed, admiring her freshly manicured nether regions.

"Don't stop! Take me now!" Estelle yelled back at him.

Dwayne unzipped each of Estelle's long boots and flung them across the room, sending them crashing into the walls. He pulled her pants the rest of the way off, tossing those as well, and placed her feet on his shoulders. He kissed down her ankles, down her calves, and then down her inner thighs, until he made it to his favorite place. Estelle squeezed her legs together hard as Dwayne put a lifetime of knowledge he had concerning technique into his efforts. Estelle's toes were curled under completely as she kicked at the air.

"Oh God!" she yelled. "Fuck me like a Democrat, Batman!"

While it may have taken Dwayne several minutes to put the costume on, it took him less than ten seconds to get almost the entire thing off upon hearing Estelle's command. He decided to keep the mask on to keep things interesting.

"Unhook me now so I can grab your ass, Batman," Estelle demanded.

"No," he responded in his gruff Batman voice. "I don't think you've learned your lesson yet." Dwayne picked Estelle up by the waist as she held onto the rails she was cuffed to behind her head. He edged his body up closely and went in for the attack, shaking and slamming the headboard against the wall, giving Estelle two consecutive eye-popping orgasms.

Estelle pulled hard with her arms while moaning loudly in ecstasy, causing the rails the handcuffs were latched onto to pop out of place, freeing her hands. She thrust her body forward, now sitting in Dwayne's lap facing him, and ripped the top of her costume off.

The two of them rolled over in a wild motion, leaving Dwayne on top with Estelle underneath. She gripped one of his butt cheeks with one hand while clawing her fingernails across his back with the other. "Finish the job, Batman," she said forcefully as she gripped his ass as hard as she could. "Fight that fucking crime."

Estelle couldn't keep up the act any more. She started to giggle after thinking about what she'd said. They both began to laugh until Estelle snorted, something she did rarely that Dwayne found irresistible.

"Let's smoke a joint," she said.

"God, I fucking love you," he replied.

35.

Dwayne popped out of bed the next morning at 5:00 a.m. sharp. He'd had maybe two hours of sleep. He didn't care. His bike had been calling his name lately, and he wanted to get a twenty-mile ride in before the sun came up. This was going to be a big day, and he knew he had to start it off kicking ass.

The big game was at 6:00 p.m. that evening. Dwayne had taken a little time away from work the previous couple of days, and he needed to get to the office and muscle some more past-due accounts. At some point, possibly two or three times, he would need to make sweet love to Catwoman as well.

As he was walking out of the bedroom after throwing on a pair of wind shorts, Dwayne noticed a hole in the wall from where he'd thrown one of his Batman boots across the room. He chuckled all the way to the kitchen, where he filled up his water bottles for the ride.

After topping his bicycle tires off with air, Dwayne popped in his earbud headphones and cranked up the Original Motion Picture Soundtrack for *Eddie and the Cruisers* on his iPod. He headed down the driveway and off into the darkness of the early morning. He decided to hop on the bike trail that ran parallel to the Trinity River and take it by the ballpark to make sure everything was cool after burying the rival coach under the pitcher's mound.

When Dwayne arrived near the parking lot, he noticed that Russ's car and Dave the umpire's motorcycle were still parked behind the trees. It didn't take him long to find the guys. Dave was passed out, face down and snoring, on the top row of the bleachers near the entrance. One of his arms and one of his legs hung over the back side. He was about a half an inch from falling off.

Russ was passed out also, on the third baseline by home plate. He was lying face up, still totally nude, and covered in mud. He was completely stretched out with one hand touching the base, as if he'd slid headfirst into home and then fallen asleep. His other hand was firmly cupping his unfortunately sized genitals. Dwayne pulled out his phone and took a picture, as was customary in the modern age, and then decided to wake them up so they'd be gone before sunrise.

"Dave!" Dwayne yelled up to the bleachers.

Dave popped his head up quickly, startled. He went to prop himself up with his arm, misjudged the width of the bench he was on, and disappeared over the back side. Dwayne couldn't see him fall the ten or so feet, but he heard him land.

"Oh, Jesus, what happened? Where the fuck am I?" Dwayne heard from behind the bleachers.

Dwayne was happy that Dave the umpire had survived the fall. He had a busy day ahead. There wasn't time to dig another hole. He turned to where Russ was lying.

"Russ! Wake the fuck up!" Dwayne shouted from behind the backstop.

Russ took his hand off his package, arched his back, and extended both arms out behind him in a yawn. He had contracted a bad case of "morning wood," and his little buddy stood up straight as Russ rubbed his eyes, rolled over, and pulled himself to his feet.

With a full erection, he stood up facing Dwayne.

"What's up, bro?" Russ said to Dwayne as he stretched again.

"Dude, I've seen your penis way too much in the last twenty-four hours," Dwayne stated.

"Pretty nice, huh?" Russ replied proudly. "I mean, sure, it's not that big, but the shape of it is phenomenal. It's straight as an arrow. No bend at all. And my man muff is top-notch too. Not right now, of course, because it's full of dirt and debris, but it's normally really shiny and soft, not all bristly like we've come to expect from thick pubes. I even have special conditioner for it."

"Sweet Jesus, just put it away," Dwayne said, turning away.

"No way, bro. I drive my Ferrari naked all the time. It rules. Sometimes I'll wear a shirt so people think I have clothes on, but really it's just a shirt. A lot of the time, when I'm leaving work, I'll just whip my pants off real quick. I've probably talked to you a thousand times through my window with no pants on, and you didn't have a clue. Don't be so judgmental."

"I'm not listening anymore," Dwayne said dismissively.

"I love the feel of perforated leather on my bare ass," Russ continued, oblivious to the fact that no one was paying attention. "Plus, it's easier when I see somebody cruising around with an Obama bumper sticker. I just raise my ass right up to the window."

Just then, Dave came crawling around from behind the bleachers on his hands and knees, groaning with every bit of movement. "Dudes," he struggled to speak, grabbing on to a bleacher rail beside him and pulling himself up. "I wouldn't go back there. I just hurled all over the place, and . . . OH MY GOD, WHAT THE HELL IS WRONG WITH YOUR PENIS, RUSS? OH JESUS! MY EYES! IS THAT THING ERECT? WHAT HAPPENED TO IT?"

"What do you mean, Dave?" Russ asked, brushing dirt out of his chest hair.

"WHY IS IT SO SMALL?" Dave screamed, pointing at it with both hands.

"Don't pay attention to the size, just look at how perfect it is. It's a masterpiece," Russ stated proudly.

"WHY DON'T YOU EVER WEAR PANTS, RUSS? WHAT THE FUCK IS WRONG WITH YOU?" Dave yelled again.

Russ put his hands on his hips and glared at Dave.

"I'm not going through this again, Dave," Russ said, turning and grabbing his car keys. "Fuck you guys. Fuck both of you. Right in the earhole. I'm a sex stallion. And a Jedi knight. I don't need to hear this shit. I'm outta here."

"See you at the game, bro," Dwayne said as Russ stormed off. "The game is at 6:00 p.m., so we'll warm up and throw some batting practice starting at 5:00 p.m."

Russ held up his middle finger as he walked away. Dwayne hopped back on his bike to finish his ride before he took Alex to school. He'd been at the ballpark long enough, and the sky was just beginning to get a bit lighter.

"I'll see you tonight, Dave," he said as he popped his earbuds back in.

"Later, Dwayne."

Dwayne finally sat down at his desk after a quickie with Estelle and dropping Alex off at school. In front of him was a list of his biggest past-due accounts, those that hadn't been responsive to friendly payment reminders.

It was time for a stepped-up approach. Dwayne lit a doob and called the first delinquent customer.

"Eric Schimmy, please," he said to the receptionist who answered the phone. "This is his doctor."

Eric Schimmy had been an extremely successful Fort Worth real estate agent before the economic bubble in the market burst. He had purchased several dozen commercial and residential properties just weeks before the shit hit the fan and was financially devastated as a result.

As a favor, Dwayne had helped keep Schimmy's lawns in shape until he could unload the real estate at a huge loss. Eventually, Schimmy turned it around and found success again. Dwayne was now handling more than thirty properties for Eric.

The whispers on the street were that Schimmy had been offered several million dollars for his agency, and the deal would be closing any day. The whispers also said he'd decided to quit paying his bills a few months back and would walk away from the deal, screwing many folks out of what they were owed. He hadn't been taking or returning calls, and that left Dwayne having to pretend he was his doctor.

"What's up, Doc?" the voice on the other end of the line said.

"Sorry, Eric," Dwayne offered, void of emotion. "It's not your doctor. It's Dwayne. You haven't returned our calls. You're five months behind on your payments. You owe me $137,000."

"Dwayne!" Schimmy said, having been caught completely off guard. "How's it going, man? Hey, I heard my boy is playing your boy tonight at the ballpark! That was really good of you to take over coaching after Ricky Dale and the Walmart guy died."

"That's great, Eric," Dwayne replied. "I'm sure it'll be a great game. And thanks for the kind words. You're going to love Alex's pitching. He's got a great fastball. Hey, I've got an idea . . . How about you bring me all of the money you owe me *right now*, and I'll tell Alex not to bean your kid in the fucking head with a baseball tonight? Sound good?"

"Yeah, Dwayne, I just—"

"You just nothing, dick. I helped you when you needed help, and just like so many motherfuckers on this side of town, you don't know how to do the right thing. You just fuck people. And that's fine. The only problem is that I dropped out of the game. I'm a freedom fighter now. So bring me my money right now, or I'll cut your fucking limbs off and give your boy a concussion tonight. Sound good?"

"Jesus, Dwayne, I—"

"Great talking to you too, Eric. Drop off $137,000 with my secretary before noon. See you at the ballpark. Take care."

Up next was Jimmy Watts. Jimmy Watts had made over a hundred million dollars as CEO of National Bank. He was a king in the arena of predatory loans and risking his customers' investments. He almost single-handedly took down the entire bank and ruined the lives of many thousands of people around the world in doing so. A government bailout saved the bank, and he stepped down from his CEO position with a fifty-million-dollar severance package.

After banking, he took a brief foray into lobbying for Republican interests, such as deregulation of the banking industry. But that bored him. So he decided to get into the fast-food business and opened Awesomeburger.

He spent nearly twenty million dollars, all from naïve investors, getting forty-five stores opened around North Texas. He made the front page of newspapers and investment magazines, posing with his prize purebred teacup poodles, bragging about his new enterprise in the fast-food world. Dwayne won the bidding war for the landscaping contract at all of them.

The only problem with Awesomeburger was that the burgers

tasted like ass, and the project failed miserably. All of the investors lost their shirts, and Jimmy gave himself a big bonus before filing for bankruptcy protection.

This pissed Dwayne off more than most past-due accounts. He hated that white-collar criminals were never held accountable. The company hired by Watts to build the buildings and the advertising agency that launched Awesomeburger in the media both went out of business because they had never been paid. He owed Dwayne a very sizable chunk as well. And he had the money to pay all of them. He just didn't.

Dwayne picked up the phone and called his office.

"James W. Watts Enterprises," the young receptionist answered. "How may I direct your call?"

"Yes, this is Mr. Watts's girlfriend's gynecologist," Dwayne said. "I'm calling with some results."

"But Mr. Watts is marr— . . . umm . . . please hold."

A few moments passed. The religious praise music being played while he was on hold nearly made a vein pop in Dwayne's head.

"This is James Watts. Who the hell is this?" the angry man on the line demanded.

"This is one of the thousands of people you fucked over in the last few years, Jimmy. The only difference between the others and myself is that I'm not going to take it. My name is Dwayne Devero. You owe my landscaping company $182,000 for several months of work we did at your Awesomeburger restaurants. I need that check by noon today."

"Sorry, Dwayne. Awesomeburger is under bankruptcy protection by the courts. I'm sure you'll get a portion of your money someday. So I guess you—"

"You missed the part where I said I'm not going to take it," Dwayne interrupted. "You see, you've got tons of money and tons of power. That's great. Good for you. And that may intimidate a shitload of people, but—"

"Who the fuck do you think you're talking to, jackass? Do you know who—"

"Don't fucking interrupt me, Jimmy. I'm talking now. Yes, I know who you are. Your bank account is a lot bigger than mine. You know many more powerful people. Again, good for you. But I'm a lot bigger than you, and I carry a baseball bat. If I don't have my money by noon today, I'm going to find all of your cute little fucking teacup poodles and beat the fuck out of them. I will pound them into the ground, brother, and I will enjoy the shit out of it. Those are the stupidest looking dogs on the fucking planet. When I'm done with them, I'm going to find you, break your legs in several places, and knock all of your teeth out."

"Listen, Dwayne, maybe we got off on the wrong foot."

"Have it here by noon, Jim. And have a blessed day."

Dwayne's heart was racing. He loved being able to speak to people the way they deserved to be spoken to. He was convinced that he had cracked the code to the universe with his new outlook on life. There was no more dancing around shit.

On the corner of his desk, he kept a baby wipes dispenser to remove dirt and sweat from his hands and face. Dwayne loved baby wipes. Noticing that he had worked up a sweat while making calls, he pulled two from the dispenser. The first one came out fine. The second one, however, didn't attach to the first one like it was supposed to. In a perfect world, each wipe, when pulled out, was supposed to pull the next wipe up through the chute. This lack of perfection pissed him off. No one cared anymore. No one took pride in their work.

He turned over the dispenser and found the customer service phone number and called them.

"Customer service. This is Lisa. How may I help you?" said the polite female with a Southern drawl.

"Hi. My name is Dwayne Devero. I just pulled a baby wipe from my dispenser, and it didn't pull the next one up. Now I'm going to have to dig through that little hole with the ends of my fingers and try to pull one out, with the hope that it remains attached to the one that follows it. But you know what always happens? I either tear off a small piece of the next one and pull out a tiny piece, or I end up pulling four or five out, and the last of those four or five ends up not being connected. It's remarkably frustrating. Why can't they just get it right?"

"I'm so sorry, sir, I—"

"Get your shit together, Lisa."

Dwayne set the phone back on the receiver again. As soon as he set it down, his secretary called. Apparently Eric Schimmy had just dropped off a check clearing the $137,000 balance of what he owed, and Jimmy Watts's secretary had called to get directions to bring a check for $182,000 over. Dwayne could now pay off all of his credit card debt and still have plenty of working capital in the company. He breathed a sigh of relief.

All of a sudden, life was working out. Dwayne was hopeful that the baseball game that night would go as smoothly. With the big accounts in order, it was time to get to work on the lineup and field positions. Dwayne would've gotten right on the baseball work, too, but Estelle showed up wearing pretty much nothing.

They destroyed his office for the second time in a week, making passionate, crazy love on every desk, window, chair, phone, one-year-old-but-now-obsolete computer, and file cabinet in the room.

Aside from sex, Estelle had another reason for stopping by. She tried to break it to Dwayne gently, because she knew what his feelings would be to this news.

"Like three months ago, I agreed to sponsor a table at the 'Helping Hands for the Homeless' event downtown," Estelle said apologetically. "We both know it's just another bullshit event, babe, but I bought a table for eight. It's one of those silent auction things for blue bloods and social climbers. It's tomorrow night. I'm really sorry. I totally forgot. Things have been so good between us, I forgot about the life I'd been living before, which is a good thing. I really feel like we need to go, though. We're on the sponsorship list. But you don't have to suffer alone. I called your buddies' wives."

"Fuck," Dwayne muttered. "Well, babe, you gave your word, so we'll honor it."

He loathed these situations. The crowd that would be in attendance had a lack of sincerity for helping others. It was such a dishonest gesture. But because he loved Estelle again, Dwayne tried to put a positive spin on it. "At least we can tie on a good buzz together and laugh at people. Hell, it may even be fun."

Dwayne sat down once again to prepare his baseball strategy. Game time was just hours away. And then his phone quacked.

RUSS: WHAT THE FUCK DID YOU GET US INTO, DWAYNE? A FUCKING FUNDRAISER??? NOT COOL, BRO.

TOMMY: No shit! Kelly just called me! I mean, really Dwayne? Do you know how uncomfortable it is being black at an event like that? Do you know how many drink orders I'll be taking, or how many cars I'll be asked to park?

RUSS: Here goes Tommy with the race card again.

TOMMY: Really, Russ? How many people there have gotten back-room lap dances from Jade in the last couple of years, huh? Maybe a tug job too? Isn't that uncomfortable for you?

RUSS: I'm typically way too high to care.

STEVE: We'll be there, Dwayne. Thanks for the invitation. We don't usually get invited to these things.

RUSS: That's because your wife looks like a silverback gorilla in an evening gown, and you voted for Obama.

TOMMY: LOL.

STEVE: What the hell, man?

DWAYNE: Sorry, guys. I didn't know about it until a few minutes ago. But we're Jedi now. We'll be fine.

STEVE: I'm not sure it's a good idea for the Jedi Alliance to show up. We need to be low key. I don't want the bodies to stack up any more than they already have.

RUSS: That reminds me. I'm bringing a gun and a shovel.

STEVE: Goddammit, Russ, don't joke about that.

RUSS: Joke?

TOMMY: Ah, screw it, I'm in, D. I've sucked fat out of half those asses anyway. Probably be good for business.

RUSS: I'll be there, but I'm taking a bunch of acid first. And I'm bringing a ton of blow.

DWAYNE: Great, so everyone is in. If anything, it will be interesting, and I bet it will ensure that none of us get invited to fundraisers anymore. See you at the game tonight.

TOMMY: Later.

STEVE: Peace.

RUSS: Suck it, homos.

36.

Dwayne pulled up to the ballpark ready to play baseball. His assistant coaches were already there, which made him proud. To make things even better, Alex had never been so excited to play.

Russ, Tommy, and Steve were already at the batting cages. They sported tiny coaching shorts, tube socks pulled halfway up their calves, team-color athletic shirts, aviator sunglasses, and whistles. Russ and Tommy were working the batting cages, and Steve was working on throwing technique. Dwayne smiled when he saw them. They had become a full-blown coaching unit overnight.

Every member of the team had a "game day" look on his face. Dwayne hadn't seen that before. Even the kids who sucked appeared ready to give it their all. The parents kept their distance. Just the way Dwayne liked it.

The team listened when they were told about loading up, making a level swing, coming down on the ball, timing the swing right, stepping out of the batter's box to throw the pitcher off his pace, and trusting their own abilities. A few even learned how to read the pitch by the way the pitcher held the ball in his glove and entered the windup. It was a thing of beauty. They were pounding the hell out of the ball in the cage.

Before they were set to take the field, the coaches went through a quick refresher course on fielding the ball.

"Keep your body in front of it," Tommy said. "No side-arm catches. Don't let anything by you."

"And outfielders," Steve added, "make sure you hit your cutoff man on a deep ball."

"Don't forget to point your front shoulder where you're throwing the ball," Russ jumped in, with a cigarette dangling from his bottom lip. "Take that extra split second to make a good throw. That's what keeps a single from being a triple."

Dwayne looked at his coaches and nodded approvingly before stepping in front of the kids. He felt like General Patton addressing his soldiers.

"Take a knee, kids," Dwayne commanded. He walked back and forth a couple of times, looking each player in the eye. He wanted their undivided attention.

"Today, we get the honor of playing America's sport. Many people take this honor for granted. Many people dishonor the baseball gods by doing it wrong. That is not what champions do. And make no mistake, team, *we are champions*. We've been doing it wrong for too long, though. But I shit you not, guys, if you'll put your trust in me and play this game in a way that honors it, we will claim a victory here today.

"Are we outmatched? If you'd asked me a week ago, I would've said yes. But not today. No way. Not up in here. We can put the wood on the ball every bit as well as these guys. Probably better. We can make defensive plays every bit as well as these guys. Probably better. Know this, team. *Believe this*. Today, the gods of baseball will shine favorably on our team.

"If the pitcher throws a strike and you miss, spit on home plate and smile at him. If the first baseman talks smack to you when you're on his base, laugh at him and tell him you're going to beat his ass today. If someone is blocking the base you're running to, lower your shoulder and mow their ass down. Forget our record. Forget their record. Just get out there and own them. We came to kick ass today, gang, and I will accept nothing less than that. Do I make myself clear?"

"Yes, sir!" the team responded.

"I can't hear you!" Dwayne yelled back. *"I ASKED IF I MADE MYSELF CLEAR!"*

"YES, SIR!" they screamed in unison.

"Good! Now go get some water and get ready to whip some ass!"

Dwayne headed toward home plate. The umpire was waiting for the coaches to have the coin toss that decided who was Home Team and who was Visitor. The assistant coach for the opposing team, Ed Snyder, walked out to greet them, looking disheveled.

Ed Snyder owned a very shady home-warranty company and was known throughout the baseball community to be as much of a hothead and asshole as his missing predecessor, the late T-Bone Sprinkle.

"Hello, guys," Ed offered to Dave the umpire and Dwayne. "I've got an issue here. T-Bone hasn't made it yet. I have no clue where he is. His wife said he goes on a bender every couple of months, so I'm assuming he's hammered in a bar somewhere. Problem is, he's got all of the team notes, lineup, and so on, and I was wondering if—"

"You wanna postpone the game?" Dave interrupted.

"Well, yeah, if I—"

"Go fuck yourself," Dave replied. "Suck it up, buttercup. Dwayne's head coach, Ricky, got pancaked on the road and his head flew off. Ricky's assistant coach, Pete, got abducted at a Walmart. Do you see Dwayne bitching? Nope. It's time to play ball. Heads or tails, Ed?"

"Whatever, dick. My boys could beat this sorry-ass team with no coaches. Heads."

Dave flipped the coin, and heads it was.

"We'll take home," Ed snarled as he walked away without shaking Dwayne's hand.

Dave the umpire and Dwayne shook hands, though. Not shaking hands was like spitting in the eye of the baseball gods. You just weren't supposed to do that.

Dave offered Dwayne a wink through his umpire mask.

"I'm not asking for any favors today, Dave," he said. "Just make good calls like you usually do."

Dwayne had the boys circle around and put their arms in before they kicked off the game.

"Tigers kill, on three," Dwayne said. "Alex, start it off."

"One, two, three," Alex yelled.

"TIGERS KILL!" they screamed.

The Yankees were startled. They looked out from their dugout at the opposing team. Just seconds before, they assumed they'd have no trouble winning in a huge way. But something seemed different with the Tigers now.

"Grab your bats, boys," Dwayne called out to his team. "And make your mommas proud!"

"PLAY BALL!" Dave the umpire called out after the catcher practiced his throwdown to second base.

On the throwdown, the ball hit the ground a few feet before making it to second base. Dwayne took a mental note that the catcher might not have the arm strength to pick off runners and then gave instructions to his assistant coaches.

"Tommy, you run the lineup. Steve, you get the players in the positions I've assigned. Russ, you're my first-base coach. I'll be at third. Let's be aggressive with the baserunning, Russ. Steal on passed balls. If we have a runner at first and third, and second is empty, send your first-base runner on the first pitch. If they take the bait and try for the pick-off, we'll score with the runner at third. Let's get 'em rattled early, men. Oh, also, Russ . . . I see that they've got Jake Schimmy playing first base. Torture him. His dad is a tool. We had a few words earlier today."

Russ nodded.

Dwayne stepped out of the visitor dugout to third base, and Russ ran over to first.

"Jackson, you're up," Tommy yelled over to the boys. "After that, it's TJ, then Jonathan, then Alex at cleanup. Bats and helmets, boys. Let's make some noise!"

Jackson Paisley made his way out of the dugout and approached the batter's box. He looked over to his dad, Russ, at first base and gave a sinister grin.

Russ leaned over and whispered in Jake Schimmy's ear.

"My boy is about to knock the piss out of that ball. If you get in his way while he's rounding first, I'll hit you so hard in the kidney you'll be shitting blood for a month."

He patted the terrified boy on the back and slid back into coaching position.

Jackson made perfect contact with the first pitch. He hit a line drive just over the shortstop's head, deep into left field. Jake Schimmy stepped out of Jackson's way as he ran to second, where he was held to a double.

Russ leaned over to the first baseman again as TJ approached the plate.

"Good move, getting out of the way. You may not be as dumb as you look. And you look pretty fucking dumb. I hope to God you grow out of that. Anyhow, you see this next kid? He's black, so automatically there's something inside you that's scared, right? Well, just so you know, his dad just got out of prison. He's in the dugout now. He used to be in a gang. Probably still is. He's a fucking psychopath. I just thought you should know."

Jake wiped a couple of tears from his eyes and then assumed the baseball ready position.

The pitcher threw a changeup as his first pitch. The ball dropped right at the plate. It was a good pitch, but it wasn't good enough to get TJ swinging. Dave gave the signal for 1–0.

The next pitch was an outside curve. TJ loved the curve. He connected with the ball and sent it to right field for a solid single. Jackson advanced to third. Steve's son, Jonathan, stepped up to the plate.

Jake Schimmy had a tough time concentrating on the batter. He was scared of being close to TJ. He thought that at any moment, TJ's crazed father would come out of the dugout and run a knife across his throat.

Jonathan hit a slow-rolling single off a first-pitch fastball. It happened to roll to just the right spot, between shortstop and third. By the time the kid got to the ball, he couldn't make a play at first without allowing the runner at third to score. He had no option but to hold onto the ball and watch the batter run safely to first.

The bases were now loaded. Alex came out of the dugout. He stared down the pitcher all the way to the box. All of a sudden, the crowd in the bleachers came alive. The parents of the Tigers were going wild. They'd never started a game like this. Dwayne could hear Estelle over all of the others, cheering wildly for Alex to get a good hit.

"Bounce that fucking ball off the pitcher's forehead, Alex!" Russ called out from first base.

Russ winked at Jake Schimmy. "Your dad is a douche," Russ said.

The pitcher sent a blistering fastball by Alex first. He didn't even flinch.

"STRIKE!"

The crowd got louder. Dwayne was loving it. He knew exactly what Alex was doing. He was going to shatter the pitcher's confidence for the rest of the season.

The pitcher whipped his second pitch out, a screaming curveball that pulled right back over the corner of the plate at the last second. Alex never took his eyes off the pitcher. His bat still rested on his shoulder.

"STRIKE TWO!"

The pitcher stepped off the mound and walked around it, glaring at Alex. Alex spat on the plate and smiled at him. The pitcher walked back onto the mound, trying to figure out what pitch to throw.

Alex raised his bat off his shoulder, and the bleachers went silent. The pitcher went into a huge windup, bringing the ball from way back to throw the fastest fastball he'd ever thrown across the inside corner.

Dwayne heard the unmistakable *crack* that a bat makes when it devastates a ball. Alex, along with everyone on the field and in the dugouts and bleachers, watched in silence as the ball sailed deep into center field and disappeared over the wall.

Alex lowered his bat as the crowd erupted, and then he ran, offering high fives to Russ and his dad as he cleared the bases. The entire team dogpiled him when he crossed home plate.

No one had ever scored more than three runs in an entire game on T-Bone's team. The Tigers went on to score seven in the first inning. The final score of the game ended up at 21–2. It was a historic, old-school ass whipping that ended with Alex and TJ dumping a cooler full of water over Dwayne's head.

Eric Schimmy came walking by a few minutes later, consoling his crying son, attempting to avoid being noticed by Dwayne when they passed by the Tigers.

"Later, asshats!" Russ called out to father and son Schimmy.

As was the custom, parents and kids gathered together in the out-field. And even though the sucky kids hadn't played good positions, none were upset.

"Take a knee, team," Dwayne shouted.

The four men in tiny coach's shorts and whistles stood side by side with their arms crossed. The crowd waited for Dwayne to speak.

"Kids," Dwayne began, "I promised you that if you did the things we trained you to do, you would whip some ass today."

"Coach Dwayne," one of the parents interrupted. "I'm not sure it's appropriate to use the word ass in front of the kids."

Dwayne was visibly irritated at the interruption.

Russ stepped in. "Did Coach Dale ever use the word ass?"

"No, I don't believe he did," the parent replied.

"And how did that work out for you?" Russ asked.

"Well, we didn't win, but—"

"So shut the fuck up."

The parents all gasped. The kids tried to stay focused on Dwayne, positive that they hadn't just heard what they thought they'd heard.

"Yeah, umm, Russ," Steve stepped in. "I'm okay with some light cursing, like ass, but I'm not sure I'm okay with fuck."

"Really?" Russ asked, genuinely confused. "Why the fuck not? Because I'm a fucking deacon? Or because there are kids three feet away?"

"Fuck is a more offensive word than ass, Russ," Tommy interjected. "I personally think you shouldn't say fuck as a deacon, and I *know* you shouldn't say fuck three feet away from kids."

"Yeah, but you just said fuck three times in a row," Russ replied. "Why is it okay for you to say it, but not me? Is it a black thing? Can only black people say it? Is it like the N word?"

"Oh, Jesus," Steve said. "Can we just get back to talking about the game we just won? Please?"

"As I was saying," Dwayne continued, "if you put your heart into this, if you'll play hard, and play smart, we will win the championship. You kids did awesome today. I'd like to congratulate you all on earning that win. You came together as a team. And coaches, great job out there. It was so fluid. So perfect. And how about those fans, huh? Parents, you did great. I love it that not a single one of you offered me your opinions before the game. It warms my heart that you know how much I don't care what you think. Thanks for keeping the energy level high throughout the whole game. Let's give ourselves a round of applause."

Dwayne raised his hands in the air and clapped loudly. The kids and assistant coaches followed. The parents joined in after looking back and forth at each other awkwardly.

Dwayne threw his arm out so the team would stack their hands. "Okay! Bring it in, boys! Lead us off, Alex! Tigers kill, on three!"

"One, two, three . . ."

"TIGERS KILL!"

37.

Dwayne jolted upright in his bed in a cold sweat. It was the middle of the night. His side of the bed was soaked. A thousand things rushed through his mind.

He hadn't been thinking right. He hadn't been paying attention. What the hell was going on? Whatever happened to that cop who was looking for Ricky Dale's attackers? Could they trace it back to him? Would Dave roll over on him under pressure?

And what about Pete Rearden? Jesus Christ, he never checked for cameras in the parking lot. And there was no way Steve could hold his own in an interrogation. More importantly, half the fucking town knew about Estelle slumming it with Walmart Pete. *Motive.* Goddammit. He had *motive.* Shit.

And what the fuck was he thinking using his own office building as a kill site for Pete? His DNA *had to be* all over the place. In his trunk. On his equipment. Shit.

Not to mention, had anyone else seen T-Bone at the ballpark? Shit, only a dozen kids. Shit, shit, shit. Did anyone see them enter the score-keeper's office? Could anyone see into the office when they bashed in T-Bone's skull? Did anyone see them cut his leg off and bury him under the pitcher's mound? Shit, shit, shit.

He was smarter than this. What the fuck happened? *What the fuck had he been thinking?* He'd watched enough detective shows on TV to know that they wouldn't need to dig too deep. Jesus. What was going on?

Was he waking up from a complete psychotic break from reality? Was he putting Alex at risk? What would Alex do if his father were in *prison* for the rest of his life? What else was he capable of? Shit!

Had he made so many stupid mistakes that prison was inevitable? Was it possible that he might actually *belong* in prison?

Dwayne put his face in the palm of his hands. His heart was racing.

He reached over to the nightstand beside his bed, grabbed a half-smoked joint, and lit it. He took a drink of water, walked into the bathroom, and turned on the light.

In the mirror, Dwayne stared deep into his own eyes.

"Who the fuck are you?" he asked himself.

He thought about the people who had died in the previous few days. He thought about the condescending assholes he had stood up to. He thought about those arrogant, hypocritical, soulless insults to humanity. He'd put them in their places.

There was no doubt that what he was doing and who he had become might be considered unconventional. But taking a step back from the way the world viewed society and taking a look at how evolution and the cosmos really worked . . . wasn't he ultimately doing it *right*? Wasn't it possible that everyone else was *wrong*?

Was it possible that for most of his life he had been living in a break from reality, and the true reality—the primal, real, violent, natural, but ultimately *honest* way—wasn't it possible that *this* was the way it was meant to be?

Regardless of lives lost and the risk of collateral damage, wasn't this way the *only* way to have a civilization with any shred of social justice?

That's when it came back to him. "I know who the fuck you are," Dwayne said to himself.

He leaned in close to the mirror. "You're a motherfucking Jedi."

38.

Alex came blasting through the bedroom door the next morning at 7:03. He dove into the bed between his mom and dad, laughing. His parents took turns tickling him.

"WAAAHOOOOOO!" he yelled. "I can't believe we won yesterday! Finally! That was so awesome!"

"*You* were awesome, buddy," Estelle said proudly. "You were crushing the ball! And your pitching totally killed those guys!"

"Thank you *so much* for coaching, Dad!" Alex beamed. "You're so much better than Coach Dale and Coach Rearden. I hope it's okay to say that. I know they died and all. Or at least Coach Dale did."

Estelle looked over at Dwayne.

"I'm pretty sure Coach Rearden is dead too," she said. "What do you think, Dwayne?"

"Yeah, he may not have been a very good coach, son," Dwayne smiled. "But he makes a hell of a fertilizer."

Alex looked confused, and then moved on to the next subject.

"Hey, Dad, you think we can go to the batting cages today?"

"Sure thing, little man. Go watch TV while your mom and I get ready, and then I'll cook up some bacon and eggs."

Alex jumped off the end of the bed and took off toward the living room, swinging the bedroom door shut behind him.

Estelle rolled over on her side, facing Dwayne, and ran her hand up his leg slowly until it reached its destination. She gripped him tightly. "Well, hello there, fella," she whispered in his ear. "You sure feel happy to see me."

"I need to brush my teeth real quick, babe," he said. "And then I'm gonna lay the smack down on that ass."

"Oooh," she grinned. "I love when you talk hip-hop."

Dwayne ripped his underwear off as quickly as he could without tearing his skin, and hustled into the bathroom. Estelle joined him and passed a toothbrush covered in toothpaste back over her shoulder with one hand as she brushed away with her other. Dwayne moved in close behind her, and she closed her eyes.

Within seconds, both toothbrushes hit the floor. Estelle planted both hands firmly on the mirror in front of her and pushed herself back into Dwayne over and over again. Dwayne spun her around and picked her up, hobbling around as he walked, and the two of them crashed through the master bedroom closet door.

Dwayne pushed Estelle up against the side of the closet where his suits and dress shirts hung. She swung one arm behind her, searching for something to balance herself on while she held on to Dwayne with the other arm. She grabbed the railing his clothes were hanging on as he thrust himself against her. The entire rack of suits and shirts came crashing to the floor.

Dwayne bent over and set her down on the pile of freshly fallen clothing, where they spent the next twenty minutes rolling around on the floor, ripping clothes from hangers, tossing shoes out of the way, and completely destroying their closet in the throes of passion.

When they were finished, Dwayne helped Estelle to her feet. They laughed at the damage they'd done. Dwayne loved watching Estelle laugh, especially when she was naked, with her hair pointing in a thousand directions.

One hour after Alex had left, Estelle and Dwayne emerged from the bedroom, fresh and ready to go.

"Holy cow, what took so long?" Alex called from the living room.

"Sorry, son, I had to give something to your mom. Three times, actually."

Alex could tell there was an inside joke. He turned back to the television to watch sports bloopers. Dwayne figured he might have two more years left of being able to say shit like that to Alex before he figured out that it was code for driving wood.

Dwayne got the bacon and eggs started. Estelle started the coffee and sat down with her iPad to read the local news.

"Oh, shit," she said. "Honey, you may want to take a look at this."

On the front of the local news website was an article entitled "Missing Coaches at Jenny Field."

The article opened with the details of Ricky Dale's abduction—his body flying out of an old van that was driven by a man or woman in a snowsuit. It didn't pull any punches when discussing the condition of the body, and the distance between it and the head.

Police believed they were looking for at least two people . . . the driver and the person who pushed Ricky Dale out of the van. The cops said they had no leads in the case, but were very actively investigating, especially in light of the fact that two more coaches went missing after Ricky's demise.

Pete Rearden, the article stated, had disappeared from the parking lot of the Walmart where he had worked for several years. The surveillance system set up in the parking lot at the Walmart had not been set to record, a flaw that went unnoticed until the incident. Again, police had no leads, but were actively investigating.

Thomas "T-Bone" Sprinkle had not been seen since Thursday afternoon. A quote from his wife stated, "He's probably drunk and got robbed by whores." Police took this into consideration, but were still expressing concern.

The only common denominator between the three men was their connection to Jenny Field. Police said this could be a coincidence, but they would be following up.

Dwayne's phone quacked.

"Sweetie, I think I need to take this," Dwayne said, kissing Estelle on the forehead. "Don't worry, babe, everything is fine. Can you finish up with the bacon and eggs?"

"Sure thing, honeybuns," she replied.

Dwayne walked out to his back porch and took a seat on a lawn chair. He pulled his phone out of his pocket.

STEVE: Holy SHIT. Check the *Fort Worth News* website.
DWAYNE: Already did. Stay calm. Dave, time to ditch the van and burn it.

RUSS: Oh my God. There's a dude in my bed again.

DAVE: I don't have intrneet. Whut happnd?

RUSS: Oh Jesus, this guy looks like he's 80 years old! WTF?

DAVE: Don't unnerstand.

RUSS: NAKED OLD LADY! NAKED OLD LADY! Oh, thank God, it's a naked old lady.

DWAYNE: Dave, drop whatever you're doing, put your motorcycle in your van, take the van a long way away in the middle of nowhere, pour gasoline all over it, light it, and haul ass on your motorcycle. Now.

RUSS: Holy shit. This old lady has really short hair. I totally thought she was a dude. Must wear a wig or something. I had to pull the covers back to see what I was working with.

TOMMY: Damn. It's in the news, Dave. Cops are investigating. Looking for your van. Don't forget to take your license plates off before you burn it, but for God's sake, get off your ass and go burn it.

STEVE: I don't think we should be texting about all this.

DWAYNE: Right. No more texting. Erase these messages.

RUSS: Wow. This old lady is a deep sleeper.

DWAYNE: Okay, Jedi Alliance, we're cool, okay? Just remember that. No one has seen anything. Everyone play dumb if anyone asks questions.

STEVE: Oh God. Are we going to prison???

RUSS: HA! I totally just slapped this old lady, and she's still snoozing away! What a dumbass!

DWAYNE: Relax, Steve. They have no leads. You don't know anything, okay?

DAVE: I'm leeving now. I'll tekst you guys when its dun.

TOMMY: No shit, Stevie. Don't lose your shit. We're going to be fine.

RUSS: HOLY FUCK. SHE'S DEAD.

DWAYNE: Thanks, Dave. Talk to you later. Take the back roads.

DWAYNE: Wait, what?

TOMMY: What's Russ talking about?

STEVE: GODDAMMIT! AGAIN!

RUSS: Dave? You still there? I need you to grab something from my house before you torch the van.

TOMMY: Oh Jesus.

STEVE: WHY IS THERE A DEAD OLD LADY IN YOUR BED, RUSS???

RUSS: I'm not sure, you fucking Democrat. Maybe she did too much blow. Maybe it was the ecstasy, or the acid. Could've been anything. Congenital heart disease. Scurvy. I don't know what kind of shit old people get. Whatever it was, she went out rockin'. Better than *Matlock*, I fucking promise.

DWAYNE: Dave, stop by Russ's house please.

DAVE: On my way, boss.

DWAYNE: We'll talk tonight, guys. I'm probably renting a limo, so get ready to party.

RUSS: Always.

TOMMY: See you then.

STEVE: That's FOUR now, guys.

DAVE: LLO.

DAVE: Sorry. OL.

DAVE: Goddammit. I meen LOL.

DAVE: Bye.

39.

Dwayne spent the day doing the things he loved. He hit the batting cages with Alex and Estelle for a couple of hours, then shared a great lunch at Alex's favorite hibachi grill, followed by a full family race around the go-kart track. Other families seemed to stare at them, hoping to someday reach that level of happiness.

In between events, Dwayne coordinated the disposal of a body, the torching of a vehicle used in a homicide, and the rental of a limousine for the fundraiser that evening. In a twisted way, Dwayne almost *wanted* to go to the gala now. He knew, somewhere deep inside, that the smart thing to do would be to lie low and not draw attention.

But a Jedi Alliance was hard to hide.

That evening, ready for the gala fundraiser, Estelle looked like a goddess in her formfitting peach-colored Oscar de la Renta dress and diamond-drop necklace. Her ass popped out immaculately with every step she took.

"Oh my God, babe," Dwayne said. "How did I ever get so lucky?"

Estelle blushed. "You don't look too shabby yourself. I'm glad everything fits."

Dwayne didn't dress up often. Estelle had purchased an insanely expensive outfit for him at Neiman's, which he now wore. He had never heard of any of the fine Italian brands he was sporting.

The limousine arrived shortly after the babysitter. Dwayne had spent an hour prerolling thirty joints for the evening. He had five bottles of his favorite Scotch, three bottles of champagne, and a case of his favorite Cabernet.

"You think this will be enough, babe?" he asked Estelle as she climbed into the limo.

"Better to have too much than not enough, sweetie," she replied.

"God, I love you," he said back, touching her cheek.

The driver shut the door behind them and hopped in the front. He revved up the engine and took off down the road.

"Yo, driver," Dwayne called out to the front of the vehicle as they headed to Tommy's house. "What's your name, bro?"

The driver lowered the window that separated the passengers from himself. So far, the driver hadn't attempted small talk. No bullshit. Dwayne liked him.

He was an extremely short Asian kid dressed in a black suit, white shirt, and black driving hat. He wore black driving gloves to complete the look. He appeared to take his job seriously. Dwayne figured he was maybe twenty years old.

"Name's Uzi, sir," the kid said.

"Cool name," Dwayne replied. "Where you from? What got you into this line of work?"

"I'm from LA, sir," Uzi spoke into the rearview mirror as he drove. Dwayne thought he could see a neck tattoo creeping above Uzi's collar.

"I built street racers out there since I was fourteen. Got pretty heavy into the underground racing scene. Always loved to drive. I needed to get out of town and lay low for a while. I headed to Texas. Figured this was at least a job I could do and stay behind the wheel."

"That's badass, man," Dwayne said. "Pretty big change in performance levels between a street racer and a limo, though, I'd assume."

Uzi smiled confidently. "It's always the driver, sir. It's rarely the car. You'd shit a brick if I showed you what I can do with this thing. Oh, dammit. Pardon my language, sir."

Dwayne definitely liked this kid. "I'm looking forward to it," he said to Uzi. "And don't worry about the language. I'm guessing the group you're driving tonight is going to be a lot different than the groups you normally drive. We're going to get along just fine. I'll go ahead and warn you about Russ, though. He'll be the short, fat, hairy guy with the stripper wife. I'm going to tip you really well at the end of the evening . . . but I'll tip you a lot more if you don't take any shit from him."

"Understood, sir."

"I'm not sir. I'm Dwayne, and it's good to meet you, Uzi. Please excuse all of the drugs in your limo tonight. We'll pass the joints your way too. And don't roll that window divider up. You're one of us now."

Uzi nodded.

They arrived at Tommy's house. Tommy and Kelly Johnson came through their front door looking like the epitome of American success. Tommy was dressed in a slender-cut black Prada suit, a thin black Tom Ford tie, and Gucci shoes. Kelly looked stunning in a dark blue low-cut Vera Wang dress that was cut high up the side to show off her gorgeous legs. Her Jimmy Choo heels made her calves look carved from stone.

Uzi held open the limo door for the dashing pair. Dwayne and Estelle poured a glass of wine for Kelly and a tall Scotch for Tommy.

The two couples managed to knock back a couple of drinks on the way to Russ's house. They knew they'd need to be loosened up to deal with him. They had no idea what to expect from Jade. She was half their age, had lived in a trailer her whole life until her marriage to Russ, and had been an exotic dancer since she was fifteen years old.

Russ had always been a loose cannon. He had simply become looser since the Alliance formed. It concerned Dwayne. He'd have to keep an eye on him.

The limo pulled up to Russ's monstrosity of a home. Parked out front were Russ's red Ferrari, Jade's bright yellow lifted Jeep, and a fifteen-year-old tan Buick. The front door opened, and out walked Russ and Jade. Russ wore a bright blue custom-made three-piece velvet suit, a light grey silk shirt, and a silver tie. He tied the outfit together with light blue patent leather shoes. Jade was wearing an almost uncomfortably tight, tiny, sheer white dress. Her nipple rings and bright red thong were visible through it from across the yard.

"Oh, sweet baby Jesus," Kelly said under her breath.

"Well? What do you think?" Russ asked. "Jade picked it out. She wanted me to dress young."

"Great choice, Jade," Dwayne said, offering a thumbs-up. "He looks amazing."

"Pardon me, sir," Uzi jumped in. "For the record, I'm young, and young people don't dress like that . . . unless they're in the NFL, maybe."

Russ glared at Uzi. "Who the fuck invited the Chinese midget?" Russ asked.

"I'm Korean, for the record. Name's Uzi. What's yours? DJ Jazzy Russ? MC Velvet?"

Russ looked at Tommy and Dwayne, who were doing everything they could to keep a straight face. Dwayne handed a joint to Uzi.

"Jesus, guys," Russ said. "I *really* fucking like this kid. Jade, get your sweet ass in the limo. Uzi, spark that joint up and let's get this party started."

Jade flashed her underwear to everyone in the vehicle several times while getting comfortable. She finally settled in next to Kelly. "I've never been with a black woman before," she whispered in Kelly's ear.

Kelly wasn't sure that she'd heard Jade correctly and smiled politely.

"Hey, Russ, what's up with the Buick in your driveway?" Dwayne inquired.

"That belonged to Rosie, the sweet old freak that spent the night last night, God rest her soul," he said back.

"Oh my *God*, you guys," Jade jumped into the conversation. "You should've *seen* the stuff she did with Russ! I mean, she was *really* old, but she was *really* limber too! She could put her good leg all the way behind her head!"

Estelle and Kelly looked confused. Tommy looked nauseous.

"Did anyone else know she spent the night at your place?" Dwayne asked.

"No way, bro," Russ said. "Jade picked her up at the drug store. She followed Jade home. That old broad was just looking for a party. She even let Jade wax her."

"It was crazy!" Jade laughed. "She was so *stretchy*!"

"That's awesome, Jade," Dwayne said flatly. "What about the car, Russ?"

"Dave's coming back for it."

"Cool."

Russ pulled a pill bottle out and dumped a few pills in his hand. "Anybody want some really pure ecstasy?"

Russ popped one in his mouth, and then set one in Jade's hand. Everyone else passed, except for Uzi, who reached his arm to the back. Russ dropped a pill in his hand.

Dwayne handed Russ a glass of Scotch and Estelle handed Jade a glass of red wine. Jade politely accepted the wine, and made a request to stop and get beer on the way. Uzi had gotten the joint going strong. He passed it back through the window to Tommy, who gladly toked away before passing it to the others. Russ dug around in his jacket pocket again, and this time he pulled out a small mirror, a straw, and tiny ziplock bag full of coke. He dumped the coke on the mirror, carved out a few lines, snorted two of them, and passed it to Jade. Jade blew two lines also.

"WOOOOOHOOOOO!" she yelled. "Who's next?"

Dwayne, Estelle, Tommy, and Kelly all passed. Uzi reached his arm back again. She placed the mirror and straw in his hand. Five loud "snorts" came echoing from the front of the limo, and then he passed the blow back to Jade.

"Okay, dudes, we're at the other guy's house now," Uzi called out from the front.

He pulled into Steve's driveway and threw the limo in park. Dwayne had texted them to be ready when they left Russ's house, so the front door opened immediately upon their arrival.

Steve stepped out, trying way too hard to be a hipster. He wore a tight, fitted dark brown pinstripe suit with tapered pants that drew attention to how underweight he actually was. A skinny argyle tie, square spectacles on his humongous beak, and platform shoes finished off the outfit. He looked like an ad exec for NPR.

Judith followed in an unfortunately formfitting floral dress. Her legs had never looked so large. She was trying something new with a short hairdo and had it spiked out in all directions.

"Christ," Russ mumbled to the others. "It looks like a goddamn wildebeest got tangled in the drapes and electrocuted. Holy balls, that's hideous."

"Come on, Russ," Jade said. "Not everyone can look as delicious as Kelly." Jade placed her hand on Kelly's thigh and winked at her while licking her lips.

Kelly looked across to Tommy. The expression in her eyes was a plea for help.

Tommy mouthed the words "I'm in" back to Kelly. He held up three fingers and nodded his head. Kelly frowned back at him.

Uzi opened the limo door for Steve and Judith. Judith froze when a thick cloud of pot smoke came billowing out.

"Is that pot smoke, guys?" she called disapprovingly into the limo.

"Yup!" Russ answered. "But if pot's not your thing, I've got blow, acid, and ecstasy. So slide that welfare-recipient-loving social worker ass of yours on in here, Judith. Let's party."

Judith reluctantly climbed in.

"Well, we're all here now," Russ said. "Let's get the champagne flowing!"

Russ poured the bubbly into two glasses. No one noticed when he dropped an ecstasy pill into each glass. "Steve and Judith," Russ announced, "you two are first with the champagne."

Glasses were filled for the rest of the passengers, and of course, the driver. All nine raised their champagne flutes and clinked them together.

"Champagne for my real friends," Dwayne toasted, his glasses still held high. "And real pain for my sham friends."

40.

Dwayne asked Uzi to make a few laps around downtown Fort Worth before dropping the crew off at the "Helping Hands for the Homeless" benefit, which was being held in the ballroom of the historic Grand Marquis hotel. He wanted to make sure they had killed at least two of the bottles of Scotch and ten or so joints.

Everyone in the vehicle had become high as fuck, whether they actually smoked the joints or not. Judith and Steve had begun to seem exceedingly friendly due to the ecstasy they were unaware they'd consumed. Russ managed to pop two hits of acid while no one was looking. Uzi had the stereo volume all the way up.

The Jedi Alliance arrived at the benefit easily an hour after it had kicked off. The limo hopped halfway up the curb as Uzi screeched it to a halt by the valet stand. The valets dove out of the way so as not to be killed. Jade stood halfway out of the sunroof with her arms raised high, banging her head to Guns N' Roses, with pot smoke pouring out around her like special effects from a heavy metal video. When the valets opened the limo door, Judith, who had been leaning against it, fell out backward, doing a back somersault onto the sidewalk. And no one was laughing about it harder than Judith. She was snorting, in tears, wheezing, just laying on her back and flashing her large underwear in the middle of the sidewalk. Everyone finally came stumbling out after her, trying to catch their breath, still laughing hysterically.

Dwayne held Estelle back as the other six entered the hotel. He pulled her in closely, and they put their arms around each other like the true lovebirds they'd become.

"Are you ready for this, babe?" he asked her with genuine concern.

"Ready for what, hot stuff?" she replied.

"Well, we both know what's coming here. We both know who most of these people are deep down. We've been playing on their side of the field for a while. It's all changed now, though. You know how these women turn on people. You know they'll be talking. That's what shitty, rotten souls do. They sit around and talk. They'll be friendly. They'll say hi. They'll chat for a while. But when you walk away—"

"I know, sweetie. Happiness drives them crazy. The idea that I don't care if they approve of me really eats at them. I'm not one of them anymore. And I've never been happier. Ever. I'm your Princess Leia. I'm your Catwoman. I'm in love. I wear it as a badge of honor that I no longer fit in with those catty, unhappy bitches."

Estelle gave Dwayne a big squeeze.

"Okay, babe, I just wanted to make sure. And so you know, Batman is going to fight a ton of crime in your panties tonight."

"That sounds fun, babe, but I'm not wearing any panties."

She leaned up and gave Dwayne a quick nibble on his bottom lip, offered a sexy glance into his eyes, and walked off toward the door. Dwayne followed close behind, slightly aroused, with the full knowledge that at some point during the fundraiser he'd be pushing her into a secluded space somewhere and ravaging her.

Estelle and Dwayne joined the rest of the group at the bar. Jade had ordered everyone a round of buttery nipple shots. Before they navigated the crowd toward their table, Jade made sure to hand a shot personally to Kelly. "Do you like buttery nipples, Kelly?" Jade asked. "Because I have some butter back at my place."

The buffet was top-notch. The most respected chefs from South Africa, Italy, and Chile had been flown in on private planes to prepare rare cuisine from around the world. The dishes being served, the fundraiser's website bragged, averaged over $1,000 per plate, while the wine being offered cost $500 per glass, and the brandy hung in at around $350 per shot.

Next to the buffet was an elaborate water bar. The water was 100 percent unfiltered, made from melted ice taken from the summit of Mount Everest. An elite team of native Himalayan Sherpas had made several trips up to gather the ice using specially designed containment packs. They carried it down in small portions to the base camp, where they were met by hikers who would transport the delicacy to a jet in town. The Sherpas who actually gathered the ice were serving as water bartenders, explaining the process through interpreters.

The entire Mount Everest water operation took more than two years and cost $3.6 million. Russ and Dwayne stopped for a glass on the way to their table, and both agreed on the taste. It tasted exactly like water.

On their table, bidding badges were positioned between every second plate. These would be used during the after-dinner auction, which boasted expensive jewelry, exotic pets, fine purses, and luxurious vacations. All would be bid upon to raise money for the homeless.

The table, sponsored by Dwayne's landscaping company, couldn't have been better placed to ensure an exciting evening. Pastor Jim Harper and his wife, Janice, sat at the table behind Dwayne, which was sponsored by the Westside Church of Jesus. The table to the left was sponsored by Honeycut Land and Cattle, where Estelle's Bible-study partner Linda Honeycut was seated. To the right was Ed Snyder, the replacement coach for the late T-Bone Sprinkle. Eric Schimmy, who was now thankfully current on his landscaping bill, was a guest at Ed Snyder's table. White Oil, owned by Brenda White's family, had sponsored the table across from Dwayne. Brenda had been another of Estelle's fellow biblical scholars.

And at yet another nearby table sat Holly Dale, the widow of Ricky Dale. His furniture stores had purchased a sponsorship table before Ricky met his violent end, and Holly had come with friends to honor him. Pete Rearden's wife, Selena, was in attendance with Holly. Their guests wore black armbands in remembrance of the fallen.

A variety of other social climbers and baseball coaches could be seen mingling throughout the room, greeting each other while dripping with faux sincerity. Dwayne and Estelle knew they were in for a big night.

In fact, it appeared that all four couples were in for a big night— with Steve and Judith being no exception. The ecstasy that Russ slipped them had apparently kicked in big time. They excused themselves from the table shortly after sitting down and made their way to the dance floor, getting down like they'd never gotten down before. Their intense, energetic disco fever was interrupted periodically by passionate make-out sessions. One session became so lascivious that while Steve grabbed two fists full of ass, Judith jammed her hand down the front of Steve's pants. They disappeared a short time later for a half an hour. When they returned, Judith had grass stains on her back and Steve was missing a shoe.

Dwayne sensed that the members of his table were setting off alarms in the heads of the other social circles. He could see them turning away conspicuously when he looked their way, obviously deep into gossip about his wife, his friends, and himself.

After dinner, Russ, Dwayne, and Tommy excused themselves from their seats to stretch their legs, smoke a joint or two, and sample some dessert. The three of them were shitfaced. Russ appeared less hammered due to the startling amount of cocaine and LSD in his system. Steve didn't join them. He and Judith continued to have the time of their lives.

The three Jedi headed to the back of the ballroom, to the parking garage door. It seemed the parking garage was the best place to smoke some buds. On the way, they passed Ed Snyder and a couple of other baseball coaches.

"I can't fucking believe I lost to those guys and their fucking retarded kids," Ed whined to Chip Conner and Reese Pepper, fellow baseball coaches.

Dwayne and the guys slowed down. He looked at Russ and Tommy in a way that said, "We'll pretend we didn't hear that," and continued walking.

"I feel bad for their kids," Chip Conner added. "I wouldn't mind getting some ass from their wives, though."

"From what I understand, that would be pretty easy," Reese Pepper cracked.

The Jedi Alliance were very familiar with Chip Conner and Reese Pepper. They had coached at Jenny Field for years. Chip had been a very competitive coach. His teams typically did well. He was a big guy, maybe six foot two, with an athletic build and a blond flattop haircut. He also had a mustache. Dwayne hated mustaches.

Reese, unlike Chip, was very much a daddy baseball coach. He was a smaller guy, about five foot nine, and carried around about fifty extra pounds. Reese had a manicured goatee. Dwayne hated goatees.

Like Ed Snyder, both Chip Conner and Reese Pepper were obnoxious jackasses. And both were set to play Dwayne's team the following week in the playoffs.

Dwayne, Russ, and Tommy all stopped walking once the comments had been made about their wives. The three of them turned and approached Ed, Chip, and Reese.

"Hey, Russ," Dwayne said, stepping close to Chip. "I read this article recently called 'The Three Ps of Mustaches.' It basically said that 100 percent of guys with mustaches were either policemen, porn stars, or pedophiles. Which category do you think our buddy Chip here falls into?"

Russ didn't answer. He was silent for a few moments. Finally, Tommy swatted Russ on the shoulder.

"What? Oh, fuck, man. I'm sorry," Russ finally answered. "I'm tripping my balls off right now. I don't understand anything you're saying. Just tell me when to hit one of them."

"He's gotta be a pedophile, Dwayne," Tommy stepped in. "He's not a cop. He owns pawnshops or something, I can't remember. It's some line of work where stupid people find success."

"Yeah, I kinda figured him for a pedophile too, Doc," Dwayne replied, getting an inch from Chip's nose.

"I guess he could be a porn star though, Dwayne," Tommy said while moving closer to Reese. "If it's gay porn you're talking about. I bet he loves getting it on with his little buddy Reese."

Russ followed Dwayne and Tommy's lead and inched closer to Ed Snyder.

"I can't fucking understand anything right now, guys," Russ said. "It's all garbled, like the teachers in the Charlie Brown cartoons. And my arms feel a lot longer for some reason. And my clothes are melting.

And my shoes keep yelling at me. Fuck, I miss my cat. Jesus. Please let me know when to hit this guy."

Chip and Dwayne sized each other up. The others waited to see what would happen with them to determine what course of action to take next.

"You need to think long and hard about what you do next, Dwayne," Chip snarled. "I'm about to fuck you up."

Dwayne smiled. "I think it might be time to take this conversation out to the parking garage, fellas," Dwayne said. "Tommy, Russ . . . you ready to take out the trash?"

"Hell, yeah," Tommy replied.

"Al-Qaeda and motherfucking cheeseburgers," Russ growled. "They're fucking up my Wi-Fi."

"You're goddamn right they are, Russ," Tommy said. "Let's fucking do this."

41.

Estelle and Kelly had been trying (somewhat in vain) to have a conversation with Jade. She fascinated them. They wondered if she might be some variety of genius. Her spiritual and sexual freedom, her quick vault from poverty to wealth, and her uncanny ability to entirely block out what social circles deemed acceptable appeared to imply that she might be an intellectual force to be reckoned with.

"Gum is so stupid," Jade commented to Estelle and Kelly while staring at the overhead lighting. "It just doesn't make any sense. Why put all the effort into chewing it if you can't swallow it?"

Other times, though, Estelle and Kelly were just shocked that Jade had managed to survive for as long as she had.

"Hello, ladies, are we interrupting anything?" Janice Harper, the pastor's wife, asked as she took the empty seat next to Jade, with a glass of wine in hand.

Tiffany Blaine and Linda Honeycut took two other vacant seats at the table. The three of them looked as though they had been mixing the pain medication from their facelifts with their antianxiety meds and a sizable quantity of alcohol.

"It's so wonderful for Jesus to give us such an amazing opportunity to help the homeless," Janice remarked.

"Praise Jesus," Tiffany threw in righteously.

"Yup. That was pretty awesome of Jesus," Estelle said. "You know what would've been more awesome? Not making them homeless."

Janice attempted a fake smile, but her Botox proved to be a worthy opponent. Jade slid her chair closer to Janice and rested her head on the shoulder of the preacher's wife. She gently placed her hand on Janice's thigh. "You smell fucking amazing," Jade whispered in her ear. "You wanna get out of here for a few minutes?"

"How's Dwayne doing, dear?" Tiffany jumped in, adding to what seemed like a coordinated gossip-research mission. "Is he still dabbling in drugs?"

"We'd be willing to hold an intervention at the church if you'd like, Estelle," Janice added. "Your home is not a good environment to raise a child in right now."

"We just want what's best for you and your family," Linda consolingly continued. "His behavior has been erratic. The way he spoke to us was awful. There's no need to talk so distastefully to a group of women studying and trying to live the words of Jesus."

Estelle and Kelly sat staring at the women, unsure of where to begin. Jade was content rubbing Janice's leg, humming.

"What do you think, Estelle?" Janice asked.

Estelle picked up Dwayne's half-full glass of Scotch and pounded it. She wiped a drop from her lower lip with her arm and stood up so that all of the women at the table could hear her. She was shitfaced, and she decided to get a few things off her chest.

"What do I think?" She was ready to let them know. "Here's what I think: I think that what upsets you the most is that someone actually said that stuff to your face. You're totally incapable of saying things to people's faces. You've spent your entire lives operating behind people's backs. And don't tell me that I don't know what I'm talking about. Until recently, I was right there with you.

"You are the self-appointed dictators of local high society. You decide who makes the cut and who is to be humiliated for not reaching your bullshit standards. You justify all of your condemnation by quoting Jesus, as if Jesus would actually approve of anything about you. Your prayer groups are just wine-filled judgment groups attended by hate-filled women. Again, I know firsthand, because I was right there with you.

"As for my home not being a good environment to raise a child in, well, I love my family. We were lost for a while, but we're good now. My son is pitching, playing shortstop, and hitting home runs on a team my husband is coaching. My husband puts his son and his wife above everything. He makes sure he spends *real time* with us every day. And at least a couple of times a day, my husband makes love to me in ways that are so deeply satisfying, you'll never understand. We do it dressed as *Star Wars* characters. We do it dressed as superheroes. We do it on every surface in our home and office that's big enough to set my ass on. We break shit when we make love. And it's good.

"I know how your home lives are. They're unhappy. But you take pills so that you don't care that you're unhappy, and you point your fingers at others so they don't look at your unhappiness. It's the simple psychology of bullies.

"You've attached your happiness to the number of diamonds you have, the cars you drive, how big your house is, what publications your name shows up in . . . This is how you measure your life. There's no kindness or willingness to reach out and help. Your smile is a mask. I think that *your* homes are not good environments to raise a child in.

"But I've rambled on for too long here, ladies. So allow me to summarize things: You are sad, fake, pathetic, insecure, insincere, arrogant, materialistic, out-of-touch, hypocritical, self-serving, gossiping, backstabbing bitches, and the world would be a better place if Jesus poured gasoline on you and lit you on fire. Any questions?"

Estelle slammed the rest of her wine and looked around. The area surrounding her table had become quiet. Kelly's jaw hung wide open. Others in the crowd had stopped to listen in. Linda, Tiffany, and Janice were humiliated, their stretched faces bright red.

"Wow," Jade said to the three horrified socialites, "Jesus *totally* hates you people."

Janice Harper stormed across the ballroom. Linda Honeycut crossed her arms, giving Estelle the ultimate stink eye. And Tiffany Blaine was too combative to go down without a fight. She decided to fire back.

"Maybe I'd take you more seriously if you weren't fucking half the town, Estelle," she snapped. "I hardly think someone who's humping the manager at Walmart has any room to cast aspersions at me."

"And thanks for standing up for us, Kelly," Linda added, slurring her speech heavily. "I thought we had a bond after I told you I sponsored that black baby in Africa. Fucking Obama! So much for Fort Worth diversity!"

Kelly was both offended and confused by Linda's accusation.

"Tiff, Linda, I think it's time you two gathered your things and left my table," Estelle stated firmly.

"Right," Tiffany responded. "You probably need to go screw a waiter or something. Maybe I'll go find Dwayne and see if he'd like a blowjob from someone with some class. It's probably been a while."

Estelle walked around the table and stopped in front of Tiffany. She leaned over, getting in her face. "Or maybe we should just step into the parking garage for a few minutes."

42.

Linda, Tiffany, Estelle, and Kelly marched through the ballroom toward the parking garage. They moved with purpose, knocking people in the crowd to the side. It was go time. They were ready for a fight.

Jade started to follow behind, but when the band cranked into "Superstitious" by Stevie Wonder, she redirected to the dance floor, where she and Judith began grinding on both sides of Steve.

When the ladies came bursting through the parking garage door, they were startled to see six guys already squared off and ready to battle.

"What the *fuck*?!" Tiffany shouted.

Dwayne and Chip Conner were circling each other, their fists up in the middle of the drive, like boxers in a heavyweight fight. The other men were nose to nose, talking shit.

The ladies all stepped into the garage, joining the action, tossing their heels off and assuming the ready position. Estelle gave a "come on" motion to Tiffany.

"Well, I guess the whores are here," Chip smirked. "Hey, Estelle, you wanna bring that hot little yoga ass over here and get a taste of a real man?"

And that was all it took.

Dwayne threw a swift right cross at Chip. Chip stumbled back a few steps, and then drove a hard uppercut at Dwayne's jaw before throwing him into a headlock.

Tommy took a massive shot to the cheek and then delivered one right back to Reese, which caused Reese to go down on all fours. Tommy began kicking him in the chest and face until Reese no longer moved.

Russ ripped his shirt off and cast it aside. He secured his tie around his forehead and let out a crazy battle cry. He lunged toward Ed, seizing him by the balls and squeezing with all his might. He then rammed his knee repeatedly into Ed's crotch, followed by several elbow shots to his nose. Ed never had a chance.

Tiffany sprinted toward Estelle with her fingernails out front. Estelle stepped to the side to dodge her while picking up a "SLOW" traffic sign, which was attached to a metal pole. Estelle spun around with lightning speed and swung the sign, catching Tiffany square in the face and sending her back on her ass with a substantial gash in her forehead.

"GREAT FUCKING *SWING*, HONEY!" Dwayne yelled, even though Chip still had him in a headlock and he was receiving punch after punch to the face.

"THANKS, SWEETIE!" she shouted back. "I LEARNED FROM THE BEST!"

Kelly was next to enter the brawl. "Gimme that motherfuckin' sign, Estelle," Kelly growled, blocking Linda Honeycut from the door. "This little bitch is trying to get away. I'm gonna go all Serena Williams on her ass."

Estelle tossed Kelly the sign. Linda charged her, but it was no use. Kelly had been winning tennis championships since she was a child, and it showed. Backhand, forehand, backhand, forehand . . . And down Linda went, out cold.

Blood dripped steadily from the "SLOW" sign as Kelly breathed heavily, standing over the unconscious body of Linda Honeycut.

Chip Conner became distracted briefly by Kelly's beatdown of Linda. Dwayne reached up over Chip's shoulder and grabbed firmly. Dwayne shifted his weight, positioned his leg, then flipped Chip over in front of him, the hard cement ground knocking the wind out of Chip's lungs. Dwayne kicked Chip in the side of the head with all his might.

The fights between the others had come to a standstill, with the guests of Dwayne and Estelle, as well as Estelle herself, emerging victorious. None of them had faced an opponent like Dwayne, though. This was an epic battle between two large, strong, severely intoxicated men. The others stood back and watched. Occasionally, Russ or

Tommy would try to jump in, but Dwayne would wave them off, even though he was taking a beating. He wanted Chip all to himself. No one talked to his wife that way and got away with it. Not anymore.

He was fighting for her honor. It was a Jedi thing.

The two of them rolled around on the pavement, trading blows. Blood dripped from both their faces onto their torn shirts. After several minutes of struggle, Chip regained the high-ground position and sat on Dwayne's chest, delivering shot after shot to his face. His eyes had almost swollen shut.

"You had enough yet, Lawn Boy?" Chip said with an angry snarl, his arm cocked back ready to finish him. "I told you I was gonna fuck you up. That's exactly what I did. Now I'm gonna go take that pretty little wife of yours and—"

Dwayne whipped his arm up before Chip could finish his sentence and jammed his index and middle fingers into Chip's eye socket. As Chip shrieked in agony, swinging wildly and pulling back, Dwayne shot upward and pushed his thumb in as well.

He clutched Chip's eyeball and ripped it from his head. He held it up for Chip to see, then hurled it as far as he could off to the side. Blood came squirting and pouring from Chip's face, and Dwayne flipped around behind him and put him in a headlock. He lifted Chip up onto his feet by his neck and ran forward with him, driving his head through the side window of a parked Cadillac.

Chip slid down to his knees, broken glass cutting into his throat as he tried to hold himself upright.

Dwayne reached over Chip, through the window and into the Caddy, and felt around for the lever that popped the trunk open. He found it, pulled it, and walked to the rear of the vehicle, where he retrieved the tire iron used to change flat tires.

He walked up behind Chip, wielding the tire iron. Chip turned around just in time to see Dwayne raise it up high.

"Please, Dwayne, I—" Chip started to say, but it was too late.

Dwayne swung the tire iron mightily, caving in Chip's skull, sending chunks of his face in all directions.

When Dwayne finished, he turned to face the others. His chest was heaving. His face was drenched with blood. His shirt hung open, almost all the way off on one side. He staggered, limping, gripping the bloody tire iron tightly.

He walked to where each of the other downed socialites lay and swung brutally at each of their heads, one by one, until he felt certain they were all dead.

The tire iron clanked to the ground as he swayed over the last of them. He fished around in his pocket and pulled out a joint. He felt around his other pockets, searching for something to light it with.

Estelle stepped forward with a lighter and held it with her hand blocking the flame from the wind so that Dwayne could light his doob. She picked up the tire iron, walked over to the garage door, and slid it through the handle so that no one from the ballroom could enter the parking garage.

Everyone else stood in stunned silence, watching Dwayne. He walked, wobbling the whole way, over to where his coat had been thrown and picked it up. He reached inside and pulled out his phone, punching in a few numbers. "Uzi?" he said. "It's Dwayne. How many bodies can you fit in that trunk?"

"Six, sir," Uzi replied.

"Okay then, I've got five. Meet me in the parking garage around back. Pronto. Your tip just got bigger."

43.

The limo sounded like a freight train when it headed down the parking garage drive. The tires were like nails on a chalkboard. Uzi stopped the vehicle abruptly, the front bumper just inches from Dwayne's knees. Dwayne didn't budge; he just looked at Uzi through the windshield, giving him a subtle nod with his chin.

Uzi opened the limo's trunk. Tommy, Russ, and Dwayne jumped into action, carrying the five bodies to the trunk and stacking them inside. After Chip Conner, Ed Snyder, Reese Pepper, Linda Honeycut, and Tiffany Blaine were packed into the trunk, Uzi instructed everyone to get into the passenger cabin.

"Hang on," Dwayne said to Uzi as the others climbed aboard.

He ran over and picked up Chip's eyeball, then grabbed the tire iron that was securing the door handles. He threw them both in the trunk and closed it. Uzi hit the gas as soon as Dwayne dove in.

"Inside the cabinet under the bar area, you'll find paper towels, water bottles, and a couple of trash bags," Uzi spoke into the rearview mirror. "Get yourselves cleaned up, and put the towels in the trash bags when you're done."

Estelle sat on Dwayne's lap, and Uzi found a dark place to park. She dabbed Dwayne's swollen face with wet towels, wiping away the blood and putting pressure on his cuts.

"My hero," she whispered.

Dwayne was the only living passenger with multiple injuries. Estelle removed what was left of his shirt and threw it into the trash bag. Tommy's eye had a small cut and was swollen. He had a fair amount of blood on his shoe from kicking Reese, but otherwise he looked decent. Russ was shirtless and sporting a necktie around his forehead. He had put on sunglasses when he got in the limo, and now looked like a hairy, overweight Rambo.

Estelle and Kelly had only a small amount of blood spatter on their clothing. They had barely broken a sweat.

"We've gotta go back for Steve and Judith," Dwayne stated to his fellow soldiers.

"And Jade," Russ added.

"Kelly and I need to go back to the ballroom to get our purses," Estelle said. "But you and Russ don't even have shirts. That's the kind of thing people notice, sweetie."

"I've got a couple of T-shirts up here," Uzi said. "I'm not saying they won't be tight, but if you throw your jackets over them maybe no one will notice. I mean, they'll think you dress pretty stupid, but that's probably nothing new for you, Russ."

Russ grabbed a bottle of Scotch and took several pulls from it, then passed it to Kelly, who did the same. The bottle continued to make rotations until it was empty.

"Fried catfish and chewing tobacco, man," Russ mumbled.

"That's what I'm talking about, Russ," Tommy replied.

"I mean, Simon and fucking Garfunkel, bro," Russ continued. "Fucking Garfunkel. On the grassy knoll. Like a bridge over Dealey Plaza."

"He was the shooter, no doubt," Dwayne added in a consoling tone. "Glad the acid is working out for you, man. Now . . . let's get out there and *finish* this fucking party."

Uzi tossed a couple of T-shirts into the back of the limo. Russ put on the lime green one that had the word "KRUNK!" in bold black letters. His hairy stomach hung out the bottom. Dwayne chose the bright blue shirt with a picture of a DJ and turntables on it that said "Back That Ass Up!" The T-shirt was so tight it nearly strangled him. They both looked only slightly more presentable once they put their jackets on.

"Let's roll!" Dwayne called out to Uzi.

For the second time that night, the limo came blazing full-speed to the valet stand and popped the curb. The battle-hardened crew exited the vehicle and made their return to the ballroom.

Dwayne and Estelle led the pack. They walked like they owned the place, almost strutting. When they reached the entrance, Estelle held Dwayne's tattered hand and kissed his bruised cheek. She placed Russ's gold aviator sunglasses over Dwayne's swollen eyes.

"We need to be quick here," Tommy instructed. "Let's not draw any unnecessary attention to ourselves. We'll just grab—oh, Jesus—"

Tommy's advice was interrupted by a commotion that came from the dance floor.

The band was playing Def Leppard's "Pour Some Sugar on Me." Steve was swinging his pants over his head, leaving his sagging tighty-whiteys exposed, while Jade emptied a bottle of champagne all over him. Judith stood behind him, slapping his wet ass to the beat. Jade's dress was completely drenched and extremely transparent. A large circle of guests had formed around the three of them, clapping, both entertained and appalled.

Russ sprinted to the dance floor, sliding up to them on his knees while playing air guitar. The crowd went wild.

"I think we're going to need a Plan B," Kelly said to Tommy. "I'm not sure, but I think we've attracted attention."

Pastor Jim came rushing to Dwayne's table in a huff. His wife, Janice, was in tow.

"I can't believe what I'm seeing, Dwayne," the pastor condescendingly stated. "You can clearly see that young woman's breasts. And Mr. Winwood's underwear has fallen off twice now. This has gone on long enough. They are your guests, and you need to get them out of here."

"Are you kidding me?" Dwayne shot back. "This place *sucked* before we got here."

"So you're not going to do anything about this?" the pastor continued.

"Hell no, man. We fuckin' *rule!*" Dwayne grinned.

The pastor and his wife took off to the front desk. Seconds later, two security guards approached Russ, Steve, Jade, and Judith on the dance floor. Russ appeared to give them some difficulty at first, and then acquiesced to their requests and allowed the guards to escort them all back to Dwayne's table.

After the guards left, Russ leaned over to Dwayne and Tommy and opened his jacket. "Check it out, man. I got his Taser gun when he wasn't looking."

Dwayne and Tommy nodded their heads, impressed.

With the dinner and dessert plates cleared away, it was time for the main event—it was time for the auction to begin. The band faded their song and then played a short fanfare, a cue for the chairman of "Helping Hands for the Homeless" to take the stage. The chairman read from a long list, intending to recognize and thank every socialite on the large gala committee.

"This is a good time for us to leave," Tommy said.

The Jedi Alliance and their wives began to gather their things. They slammed their drinks and stood to leave, when one of the exotic animals up for auction caught Russ's eye.

"How much for the Wookie?" Russ shouted, interrupting the chairman's speech.

Everyone in attendance was silent, staring at the short fat guy in the "KRUNK" T-shirt with his belly hanging out.

"I'm sorry, sir, we haven't begun the auction."

"The Wookie," Russ shouted again. "I'm leaving, and the Wookie is coming with me. How much?"

The chairman looked over at the auction items.

"Are you referring to the orangutan, sir?"

"Orangutan, Wookie, what-the-fuck-ever, man. I gotta roll. How much?"

The chairman shrugged, looking around, hoping someone would step in. No one did.

"Fine. Fifty thousand dollars for the Wookie. Anyone else?" Russ yelled, holding a bidder badge in the air as a challenge to the other guests in the room.

No one budged.

"SOLD! To the guy who kicks so much ass he has his own Wookie!" Russ said loudly, pulling out his checkbook and stroking a check for the full amount.

Russ stumbled between the ballroom tables and struggled as he climbed up onto the stage. He licked the back of the check and slapped it onto the chairman's forehead, where it stuck.

Russ jumped back off the stage and walked over to the orangutan cage. Everyone in the ballroom let out a collective gasp when Russ opened it and reached his hand inside. The orangutan accepted Russ's hand, and the two hairy friends walked through the crowd to the front door, where the baseball dads and their ladies waited.

As they neared the waiting limo outside, Russ leaned over to the orangutan.

"Hey, check this out," he whispered. Russ pulled out the Taser gun and showed it to the orangutan. The orangutan reached over and grabbed it, pointed it in front of him, and pulled the trigger. The prongs carrying thousands of volts of electricity shot out instantly, hitting Judith right between the shoulder blades. She dropped to the ground, convulsing. The orangutan began squealing with what Russ could only assume was laughter, causing Russ to laugh with him.

"Jesus Christ, Russ!" Steve yelled. "Not cool!"

Russ pointed at the orangutan and smiled, absolving himself of any responsibility. Steve and Dwayne frowned at Russ, walked to both sides of Judith, picked her up, and tossed her into the limo. The Jedi Alliance, now complete with their Wookie, finally made their escape.

"To Jenny Field, Uzi," Dwayne ordered.

44.

Uzi drove carefully for the first time that evening. Judith had been so hammered from hard liquor and ecstasy that, when she regained consciousness, she had no idea she'd even been shot with a Taser. Everyone was laughing their asses off watching Russ try to teach the orangutan how to smoke weed. Dwayne removed his sunglasses to wipe a tear from his eye, exposing his severely battered eyes.

"Jesus, Dwayne, what happened to you?" Steve asked.

"Oh, don't worry about it, bro," Dwayne replied. He'd forgotten that Steve and Judith were unaware of the slaughter that had taken place in the parking garage. Dwayne suddenly thought that it would be a good idea if Steve and Judith were dropped off at their house before heading to the ballpark. He didn't know how Judith would react, and Steve had almost cracked a couple of times already.

A look of concern swept over Steve's face. He was starting to get the idea that he was missing something. Something seemed wrong. "And what happened to *your* face, Tommy?" There was panic in Steve's voice. "Why did you guys change clothes?"

"Here you go, buddy," Russ said to Steve, holding a pill bottle out. "Have a little more ecstasy."

"What do you mean, *more* ecstasy?"

"Oh, nothing, just a figure of—"

Before Russ could finish his sentence, the orangutan snatched the pill bottle from Russ and dumped the remaining tablets into his prominent ape mouth. He tossed the bottle out the sunroof, then looked at Russ and smiled.

"Oh, fuck," Russ said.

"Did that monkey just take ecstasy, Russ?" Steve demanded.

"It's a Wookie, Steve," Russ replied.

"Did that Wookie just take ecstasy, Russ?"

"Yes."

"How much?"

"A lot."

"Is he going to die?"

"I think we have to start considering that possibility."

"Oh, Jesus."

"I know," Russ said. "I was really starting to like him."

Steve was sweating and frantic, about to fully lose his shit.

And then it got worse.

WHAM! WHAM! WHAM!

"Oh God! Where the fuck am I? Somebody please let me out of here!"

The unexpected noise coming from the trunk gave everyone a jolt, especially the orangutan, which shot straight up and flew out of the sunroof. All passengers turned at once to look out the rear window, where they saw the orangutan do several somersaults in the road behind them, jump up, and look around, then haul ass over the guardrail and into the woods.

"How fast are we going, Uzi?" Russ called out to the front.

"Seventy-one."

"Jesus, that little guy is tough," Tommy remarked.

"Yeah, he's in for a rough night, though," Dwayne surmised.

"Be strong, kid," Russ said solemnly.

Steve pulled himself close to Dwayne. "Do you want to tell me what the hell is going on?"

"No, not really. I'd prefer we just dropped you and Judith off."

"Who's screaming in the trunk, Dwayne?" Steve demanded.

"I can't answer that, Steve."

"Why not, goddammit?"

"Because I'm not sure."

"Why aren't you sure?"

"Because there are five possibilities."

"What do you mean? How could there be . . ."

Steve stopped quizzing Dwayne and slid back in his seat. He didn't want to hear anymore. Judith was still giggling, rubbing the felt ceiling, oblivious. The screaming from the trunk hadn't fazed her.

"Oh God! Help! I'm bleeding! Get me out of here!"

"Uzi, please turn up the music. Loud," Steve hollered. "And please drop Judith and I off ASAP."

"Relax, brother, everything is fine," Dwayne slurred.

"This shit's gone too far, man," Steve replied to his friend and hero. Steve suddenly felt stone-cold sober and wondered how he had become seduced by both Dwayne and the Jedi outlook. He felt betrayed by both. "This was just supposed to be about baseball."

"It still is, man. It still is."

45.

Uzi dropped Steve and Judith off and took Kelly, Jade, and Estelle home as well. Jade managed to convince Kelly that she couldn't be alone, so Kelly allowed her to stay at her place until the guys finished up at Jenny Field.

Dwayne took control. He told Russ to text Dave so that Dave could meet them at the ballpark.

RUSS: Meet me at Jenny Field ASAP.

DAVE: Why?

RUSS: I'll tell you when you get there.

DAVE: You'll tell me whut?

RUSS: Just go to the fucking field, retard.

DAVE: I'm wastd.

RUSS: Me too. Tripping, rolling, high, drunk. Bring shovels. Got a chainsaw?

DAVE: Why you nede a chainsaw?

RUSS: Do you have one?

DAVE: A chainsaw?

RUSS: Yes. Fuck. A fucking chainsaw. Do you have one?

DAVE: Yep.

RUSS: Great. Bring it too.

DAVE: And shovels?

RUSS: A chainsaw and shovels. Yes. Bring them. Holy fucking fuck. I feel so much dumber now than I felt a few minutes ago. No more questions. See you there.

Russ put his phone back in his pocket and glared at Dwayne and Tommy. "That was way tougher than it needed to be," he stated. Moments later, the gang arrived at the ballpark.

"Pull around to the side, Uzi," Dwayne instructed. "Try and park behind the trees. Stay in the shadows as much as possible. Russ, hand me that Taser you lifted from the guard. Somebody is still thumping around in the trunk."

Uzi pulled the limo along the side of Jenny Field, behind a section of trees and bushes. He turned the lights off so that they might remain undetectable to any passersby. Then he popped the trunk.

Dwayne hopped out quickly, before the others.

"Oh, thank God! Someone's coming to save me! I'm hurt bad! I need a—"

The next sound Russ and Tommy heard was the *TZZZZZZT!* from the Taser, followed by a *Tink! Tink! Tink!* from the tire iron.

"I'm pretty sure that did the trick, boys," Dwayne called out. "I believe Tiffany Blaine has finally shut the hell up."

Seconds later, Dave the umpire came blazing into the parking lot on his motorcycle. He wore only boxer shorts, a tank top, and flip-flops. A large burlap bag holding shovels and a bulging chainsaw hung across his back.

Dave spied Uzi right away and began sizing him up. "Who's the fuckin' Chinaman?"

"Relax, Dave, he's with us," Dwayne assured him. "He's cool."

"Dude, do you have a boner?" Uzi asked him. Dave looked down. He hadn't noticed it, but he did, in fact, have an erection. "Yeah, well, you try getting a 75 MPH breeze whistling on your junk, with a blown suspension," Dave said without an ounce of shame.

Dave pulled the bag off his back and set it on the ground. Russ took the opportunity to hold a small vial up to his nose and snort. He then passed it to Uzi. Uzi snorted, then passed it to Dave. Dave snorted. His eyes teared up. He slapped himself, then looked over at Dwayne.

"So what's up tonight, boss?" Dave asked Dwayne.

Dwayne motioned for Dave to take a peek inside the trunk. He did.

"You guys fuckin' party, boss," Dave said with admiration. "I'm gonna go grab a wheelbarrow. The softest dirt is at the bases on the infield. We'll use the chainsaw to get their arms and legs off so the holes don't have to be as big."

"Cool," Dwayne replied. "Line 'em up on the bottom row of the bleachers, and we'll figure out what bases these fuckers are playing tonight."

In no time at all, Dave and Uzi loaded the bodies onto the wheelbarrow and dropped them off, one by one, at the bleachers as Dwayne instructed.

Dwayne stood at home plate, looking out over the field. He held a baseball bat in one hand and a chainsaw in the other. He envisioned the playoffs, fantasized about the championship win. He imagined the roar of the crowd as Alex struck out batter after batter, hitting line drives into the outfield wall, maybe even sending one or two balls over the wall.

It was close now. It was so close. The people who had gotten in his way in life and in the game he loved were now being buried on the field where he would bring Alex the glory he'd been due. They were the sacrificial lambs being offered up to the baseball gods. They were the fecal matter in the fertilizer that would fly from the cleats of those who honored the baseball gods as they rounded the bases.

"Dwayne?" Dave called out, bringing him back to earth. "You ready to get started, boss?"

Dwayne looked through the chain-link fence at the backstop behind home plate. The bloody bodies of Chip Conner, Reese Pepper, Ed Snyder, Tiffany Blaine, and Linda Honeycut sat upright on the bottom row of the bleachers, as if they were some jacked-up cheering section from the afterlife.

Tommy and Russ walked up to the top row of seating, above and behind the corpses. They lit a joint and watched as Dwayne made his way off the field and over to the stands. Dave and Uzi walked out onto the field to dig holes beneath first, second, and third base. Dwayne rested the bat on his shoulder. His other arm hung limp, with his hand gripping the chainsaw. He was ready to address his blank-eyed, lifeless, hemorrhaging audience.

"Hello, you arrogant fucks," Dwayne announced. "Glad you could join me here tonight."

He paced back and forth, selecting each word as if he were an executioner condemning prisoners to death. Tommy and Russ sat transfixed. They hung on Dwayne's every word.

"You had the option in your lives not to become the pieces of shit that you became," he preached. "And yet you became those pieces of shit anyway. You spent your lives sitting in judgment of others. Your social circles were just fucked up neighborhood torture chambers. And you had the gall to bring baseball into it. You are nothing more than bullying little cockroaches and whores."

Dwayne paused and beamed at each dead socialite. He smiled with a wild psychotic look in his eyes. He took a deep breath, and then resumed his lecture.

"And I am here today to notify you that your sentences have been handed down from the baseball gods . . . to be carried out by me, the grand Jedi master ninja motherfucker with the chainsaw and the bat."

Dwayne lifted the bat from his shoulder and swung it down with all his might upon the already disfigured head of Chip Conner. Blood splattered up on Dwayne's face. Chip's head caved in. Blood poured from his ears.

"PAY ATTENTION, YOU FUCKS!" he screamed.

Dwayne was breathing heavily. There was nothing at all hidden about his rage. It had come fully to the surface, and there was no squashing the festering, pent-up fury now. The eruption was an all-out explosion. He tossed the bat to the side and pulled the cord on the chainsaw. The chainsaw came rumbling to life. It was roaring, hungry for blood. Dwayne lifted it over his head.

"Chip Conner, Reese Pepper, and Ed Snyder. You disrespected my wife. You disrespected me. And you disrespected the purity of America's game. I hereby sentence you to be decapitated and dismembered, and spend eternity rotting beneath the bases of Jenny Field. I would put your heads on spikes at the entrance to the field if I thought I could get away with it. But justice will be served regardless. May God have mercy on your vacant souls."

Dwayne placed the chainsaw at the base of Chip Conner's neck.

Blood sprayed in all directions as the rotating blades worked their way through skin, spine, and ligaments. Within seconds, the chainsaw emerged on the other side, and Chip Conner's head rolled off his shoulders, bounced off the bench seat, and came to rest inches from Dwayne's feet.

The same fate fell upon Reese and Ed. Dwayne's clothing was soaked entirely through with blood. It dripped down his arms, trickled onto the chainsaw, and was launched into the dank evening air from the spinning chain.

He approached Tiffany Blaine and Linda Honeycut, again raising the loud, violent piece of machinery over his head.

"Linda and Tiffany . . . You and your minions made my home life almost unlivable for years. You tainted the spirit of my beautiful wife for too long. But you can't have her. She's back in my arms. Gone are the days when you could look down upon those with less. Gone are the days when you could spend your days stabbing people in the back with your incessant vile gossip. Gone are the days when you could cast judgments while cloaked beneath the banner of God. You are contemptible, repugnant, noxious stains on this earth, and I am the motherfucking industrial-strength cleaner that's here to wipe you up. I hereby sentence you to decapitation and dismemberment, to spend eternity being talked about while unable to respond as you decompose beneath the bases of Jenny Field."

Dwayne dug the chainsaw first into Tiffany's neck, and then into Linda's. The first four rows of the bleachers were bright red. On the ground, surrounding Dwayne's feet, lay the heads of the elite members of Fort Worth society.

Dwayne then carved up the bodies like five large Thanksgiving turkeys. When he had finally finished, he was left wading through a pile of arms, legs, heads, and torsos behind the backstop of his favorite field.

Russ and Tommy watched in silent wonder as Dwayne turned off the chainsaw and wiped the blood from his eyes.

"That was fucking crazy, bro," Tommy muttered. "You okay, Dwayne?"

Dwayne looked around, wild-eyed, with a half smile on his face. He was trembling. His ears were still ringing from the roar of the chainsaw.

"Dwayne? You good?" Tommy asked again.

Dwayne flashed a huge grin. "Get the wheelbarrow, boys. Let's load 'em up."

46.

Dwayne was the last member of the Jedi Alliance to be dropped home that night. Russ wrote Uzi a check for a tip: $10,000. He wrote another for Dave—$5,000 just to keep his shit together. They had earned every penny. Dave and Uzi had busted their asses. They had dug holes, buried bodies, and gotten the field back in shape for the playoffs.

The bases looked nothing short of fantastic. First, second, and third were impeccable. Everything was level, and the softened up dirt would cause fewer injuries when the kids slid into base. Dwayne felt as though he'd provided a service to the baseball players of Jenny Field.

And that was before anyone took into consideration how great the pitcher's mound now sat, or how green the grass in the outfield had been growing. Seven bodies being sacrificed to the baseball gods at the field might have been just what the ballpark needed.

Dwayne walked through the door to his home, dripping wet from having blood, dirt, and bone fragments hosed off him. His phone quacked.

RUSS: Has anyone seen Jade?

STEVE: Jesus. Tell me you didn't off her too.

DAVE: Cant txt n ride modorsicle.

DWAYNE: We dropped her off with Kelly, remember?

DAVE: Feeld looks good.

STEVE: Please take me off of this text chain.

DWAYNE: Field looks great, Dave. Can't wait to play on it.

STEVE: Please take me off of this text chain.

RUSS: Oh yeah. Man, I was out of it. Tommy? Is Jade at your house?

TOMMY: :)

RUSS: Oh lord.

STEVE: LOL.

RUSS: Don't do this to me, Tommy. I have a tiny penis. You're black. Not cool, bro.

DWAYNE: I can vouch for him, T. It's tiny.

RUSS: Proportionally exceptional though, asshole. But still. Tom?

DAVE: Can I come ovr, Tom?

TOMMY: Hell no.

RUSS: Don't do it, Tom.

DAVE: Feeld looks good, guys.

STEVE: Please, God, take me off this text chain.

RUSS: Shut the fuck up, Dave.

TOMMY: Later, homies. Girls are in the shower.

DAVE: Hit it for me, Tom.

RUSS: SHUT THE FUCK UP, DAVE!

DWAYNE: Later.

RUSS: Tom?

Dwayne shut his phone off. He smelled jasmine and eucalyptus when he walked through the bedroom door.

"I figured you could use a good aromatherapy bath, honeybuns," Estelle said sweetly. "It'll help soothe your muscles. Now let's get you out of those pants."

Estelle unlatched his belt and unbuttoned his pants, then helped him climb into the tub. It was exactly what Dwayne needed. He relaxed and leaned his head back. The love of his life pulled her tiny nightgown over her head and lowered herself into the tub on top of him. She grabbed a sponge and tenderly began to wash her husband's entire body as she straddled him.

Dwayne and Estelle couldn't help but become aroused. Everything that one of them did turned the other on. An unquenchable, tantalizing sexual chemistry had developed between them.

They made love twice in the bathtub, until Dwayne's neck could no longer take the awkward positioning. Not to mention, he almost drowned a couple of times when his head slid under the surface of the water. They moved from there onto the bed, where Estelle insisted on doing all of the work while Dwayne lay back and enjoyed the view. The two of them made love until it was no longer physically possible to continue.

It was love and lust, admiration and desire, domination and submissiveness, blood and sweat . . . all rolled into one. Rooted firmly at its foundation was love—love of each other, love of family, and love of baseball.

47.

"Wake up, my hairy little sex machine," Jade announced as she came through her front door Sunday morning. "It's time to go to church!"

The slamming of the front door caused Russ to jolt upright. He looked around, trying to figure out where he was. It was dark. There were sheets and towels stacked beside him. He realized he'd passed out in the linen closet.

When Russ opened the closet door and crawled out, the bright morning light blinded him. Jade giggled when she saw him roll out and collapse onto his back, shielding his eyes.

"Oh, my little snuggles, you pass out in the funniest places," she offered adoringly.

"Sweet Jesus, Jade, I had to hide from a tribe of pygmies last night," he explained. "They chased me everywhere! I think I beat one to death in the kitchen. It jumped out of the fridge when I went to put the milk back. I had to put a dagger through its heart."

Jade glanced into the kitchen. In the middle of the floor sat a pummeled raw chicken with a large butcher knife sticking up from it. All of the cabinet doors were open. A broken bowl of cereal lay spilled across the floor beside an empty gallon of milk.

"Aww, baby, I'm glad you're okay," she soothed. "It's time to get ready for church, okay? Jackson is getting dropped off from his sleepover any minute."

Russ pulled himself up and balanced against the wall.

"Are you just now getting home?"

"Yes, I spent the night with Kelly and Tommy, sweetie pie, and now I need to go ask Jesus for a little forgiveness."

Jade walked into her bedroom and stripped her clothes off. Russ heard the shower turn on as he tried to process what Jade had just said. He flung his underwear across the room and joined Jade in the shower so that he could interrogate her concerning the previous night's activities.

"Why the hell do you need to talk to Jesus, Jade?" Russ demanded. "Did you see Tommy naked? Just answer me that."

Jade looked down at Russ's package briefly and winced.

"Don't worry about it, sweetie," she said with pity. "It was a lot like any other crazy night in *our* bedroom."

"Yeah, except it wasn't *our* bedroom, and *I* wasn't there!"

"You're so cute, honey," she said in a baby voice as she softly grabbed his manhood. "I wuv my furry widdle fella!"

"Goddammit," he muttered as he stepped out of the shower and toweled off.

Tommy, Kelly, and TJ had saved seats for Russ's family at the West-side Church of Jesus. Russ glanced accusingly at Tommy as they took their seats. Kelly had a mildly uncomfortable look on her face as she hugged Jade, who took the seat right beside her. Tommy just grinned.

Pastor Jim Harper asked everyone to bow their heads, hold hands, and join him in prayer. When he asked for God to forgive everyone of their sins, Russ felt Jade squeeze his hand a bit tighter. He looked over at Tommy, who was standing with his eyes closed while smiling. He watched Jade's hand release Kelly's, and then find its way down the small of Kelly's back and onto her ass, where she gave a gentle squeeze.

The pastor asked God to watch over those who had gone missing in recent weeks, including a group that had disappeared the previous evening.

"I'm not sure what your plan is for these people, Lord, but I know it must be something amazing. With the exception of the guy who worked at Walmart, these people had valuable lives. Please offer comfort to us as we try to understand your plan. In Jesus' name, Amen."

Russ and Tommy slid down in their seats. Pastor Jim then launched into his sermon for the day: "Jesus Was a Capitalist." When church finally ended, Russ and the other deacons went to greet Pastor Jim, to congratulate him on another fine sermon.

"Just wait until you hear next week's sermon," the pastor boasted.

"It's titled 'Science: The Tool of Lucifer.' It's a big part of my campaign to get creationism back in public schools. Should be amazing."

Once the deacons began to depart, Pastor Jim pulled Russ to the side. "Russ, I'm concerned for you," he counseled. "You've been running around with a known drug abuser, Dwayne Devero. And your actions at the fundraiser last night were jaw dropping."

"Sometimes, the sheep strays from the herd, Pastor," Russ said, placing his hand on the pastor's shoulder. "And sometimes the sheep has an orgy with the herd. Hell, sometimes the sheep takes ecstasy and snorts cocaine and then gratifies himself watching other sheep mount his wife. Sheep can get crazy, Pastor Jim. They can lose their fucking shit. But as long as they have a good shepherd, they can usually take a shower with a crab-lice comb and be forgiven. Am I right?"

Pastor Jim mustered a half smile, unsure of what to say. Russ leaned in and slapped him on the butt.

"Good stuff, Pastor. You're the man. How's that Porsche running? It's gorgeous."

"It's running great, Russ. The Germans have a proud history."

"Indeed they do, Pastor."

48.

Monday morning, Dwayne rolled out of bed ready to swing at whatever pitch life threw him. The Tigers' first playoff game was that evening, and no one was more excited than Alex. The championship game would be two weeks away, and he knew he'd be in it. He was proud of his dad for bringing honor back to the game. Anyone who watched them knew that they were fast becoming the team to beat. They were no longer a joke.

Lately, Estelle appeared able to sense when Dwayne would wake up. Even if she'd been sleeping deeply, something would nudge her brain and pull her from her slumber. She was glad for it. She loved their playful nature in the mornings. Estelle rubbed her eyes and grinned at Dwayne from the bed as she lay there watching him turn the shower on and throw a towel over the shower door. He offered her a fully nude, goofy, "come-hither" raised eyebrow when he noticed her watching him. She instantly threw the covers off and sprinted in to join him.

With most couples, the quality of the sex might have declined at this stage . . . or they might have started to pass on it altogether. But for Estelle and Dwayne, sex just kept getting better and better, the desire stronger and stronger.

After their morning shower session, Estelle headed to the kitchen to make breakfast for Alex while Dwayne got ready for work.

"Honey, turn on channel eight, please," she called from the kitchen.

Dwayne was just in time to catch a reporter interviewing Detective Loffland. He turned the volume up.

"So, Detective, do you have any leads in the case? That's seven missing people now from the upscale Westside area of Fort Worth, and one confirmed murder on top of that."

"Yes, we've got a few leads right now that we're working on. We need as much help from the public on this as possible, though. Late last night, we

located an old burned van that could possibly fit the description of the van used in the kidnapping and murder of Ricky Dale. The charred remains of a body were found inside. Our team of forensic specialists are combing it for evidence as we speak."

"Do you have any suspects or persons of interest?"

"Not just yet, but we're pretty sure we're dealing with professionals here. We're looking into the backgrounds of all who went missing and looking for a common thread that ties it all together."

"Any luck so far? From what I understand, these are some very wealthy and powerful people that have gone missing."

"Not all of them were rich and powerful. One of them worked at Walmart."

Quack. Quack. Quack.

"Walmart? Jesus, that's awful."

"Indeed it is. As if life hadn't been cruel enough for the poor guy, he had to go and get abducted by sociopaths."

"That's inhumane. They could've at least taken someone from a Super Target. But Walmart? These people must be twisted. That's just uncalled for."

"Salt on the wound, without question."

.   .   .

Dwayne looked at his texts. It was just as he thought. Steve was freaking out.

STEVE: BRIEFCASE! BRIEFCASE!

DAVE: I dont unnerstand wht that meens.

STEVE: Turn on your TV, numbnuts! They found your van!

DAVE: Waz their a breefcase in it?

RUSS: Dave, please go into the "settings" section of your phone, click on "texting," and then hit "spellcheck on." Please do this before I go slam my goddamn head in the door.

STEVE: I told you guys you'd gone too far!

DAVE: Wheres sittings?

RUSS: Settings! Fuck!

DWAYNE: Calm down, Steve. We're fine.

TOMMY: Dave, did you get the license plates and VIN numbers off the van? Is there any way to trace it back to you?

STEVE: Dave?

DWAYNE: Dave?

TOMMY: Dave?

RUSS: You know we have to kill Dave now, right?

DAVE: I cant figur out settings thing, Russ.

STEVE: No more killing!

DAVE: Wait whut?

STEVE: No more killing! I'm serious!

DWAYNE: Did you burn the van, Dave? Is it untraceable? The cops found it. And the old lady.

DAVE: Done, bro. Both totally crispy. No worries.

DWAYNE: See there, Steve? We're cool. You guys excited about the game tonight?

STEVE: Oh, you mean the game on the field where you just buried a half dozen people? That game?

DWAYNE: Yup. You pumped?

TOMMY: I'm pumped.

RUSS: Well fuck yeah, Captain. We're gonna destroy them.

DAVE: Im pimped.

TOMMY: ?

RUSS: Idiot.

DAVE: Fcuk you.

RUSS: This is killing me. Please stop inviting Dave on these text chains.

STEVE: And me.

DWAYNE: Okay. Game at 6. See you at the cages at 5. Playing Reese Pepper's daddy baseball team. It'll be a bloodbath.

STEVE: I'm assuming Reese won't be there, due to being dead.

DWAYNE: He'll be under 2nd base if you need him.

TOMMY: LOL.

Dwayne walked into the kitchen after he finished getting dressed for a day of ass kicking at work. He gave Estelle a big kiss and a smile.

"Is everything okay, babe?" she whispered in his ear.

"No worries, hon," he replied. He slapped her on the ass and walked over to the table where Alex was seated.

"Time to go brush your teeth, buddy," Dwayne said, punching Alex softly on the shoulder. "I'll meet you out front at the truck."

Alex stood up and hugged his dad, then headed off to finish getting ready. Dwayne shoved a piece of toast in his mouth, then grabbed his bag and headed out the door to his truck.

When Dwayne opened his truck, he saw another envelope resting on his seat. He didn't like these envelopes. He was quite certain that he would kill whoever had been leaving them.

This time, the anonymous person had left a message written in black marker. "Your whole life is a lie . . . quit while you're ahead."

Dwayne opened up the envelope. It was more of the same—photos of Estelle posing nude, doing things he wished he'd never seen. The men's faces were always cut off, unidentifiable. But this time, Dwayne caught a new detail . . . something he hadn't seen before. These photos had dates on them. They were barely two months old.

Blind rage flooded over him. Dwayne understood that the photos were taken before his reconciliation with Estelle but still . . . these dates were so close. He gripped the side of the door tightly as he remained standing beside his truck.

Then he noticed something else.

One of the naked guys in the background appeared to be black. Or was it the lighting? He couldn't tell. Logically, Dwayne knew the guy could've been anyone. Unless he was black, that is. He knew only one black guy.

Dwayne told himself that there was absolutely no way that Tommy would ever do such a thing to him. He decided not to think about anyone in the picture, especially Estelle. Things were different now. He pulled himself together and slid the envelope into his pocket just as Alex came through the door.

49

Dwayne sat in his office, trying not to think about the latest batch of photos. Who was leaving them? What did they want? How much did they know? Whoever it was obviously knew too much.

He peeked inside the envelope again and then threw it in the garbage can. There was a baseball game to prepare for. Those pictures were taken in a previous life, before he had been anointed into the Jedi Alliance. They didn't reflect the world as it now stood.

The office phone buzzed, shaking him out of Estelle's photo shoot at the orgy. Dwayne's secretary was on the line.

"Dwayne," she said in her nasal tone, "there's a Detective Loffland with the Fort Worth Police Department here to talk to you."

"Send him up."

Dwayne supposed he should've been nervous, especially considering the fact that he had two black eyes from the fundraiser fight. He knew that most people in his situation would be freaking out. But Dwayne was cool as a cucumber.

A few seconds later, there was a knock at his office door.

"Come in!" he shouted.

The office door opened, and in walked Detective Loffland. Dwayne thought he looked smaller on television. The detective wasn't tall; he was just built like a brick shithouse. He stood about 5 feet 11 inches tall and probably weighed 230 pounds. He was solid muscle. His head was shaved bald and shiny, and he had a short white goatee. He couldn't have been more than forty years old.

The two men shook hands, and Dwayne offered the detective a seat.

"I'm sure you know why I'm here, Mr. Devero," Detective Loffland said firmly.

"Lots of people going missing in my neck of the woods," Dwayne responded. "I'm glad you're on top of it."

Dwayne figured that the detective was probably a pretty good dude, based on the way he carried himself. He didn't appear to throw his power around.

"You mind if I ask what happened to your face, Mr. Devero?"

"Not at all, sir. I've had issues with my sinuses since I was a kid. Dr. Tom Johnson fixed it for me a few days ago. He had to break the bone in my nose to access my sinus cavity. It caused bruising under my eyes and made me look like I was dating an R&B singer."

The detective nodded approvingly at Dwayne's answer. Dwayne smiled back, satisfied that he'd created such a believable bullshit story on the fly.

"What was your relationship with the deceased, Mr. Ricky Dale?" the detective asked.

"He coached my son's baseball team."

"And Pete Rearden?"

"He stepped in to coach after Ricky Dale died."

"Were you friends with them outside of baseball?"

"No, sir. They were . . . ummm . . . Can I speak freely, sir?"

Detective Loffland smiled. "Please do. I've had enough of these pretentious douchebags trying to fake sincerity about all of this shit."

Yup. Dwayne definitely liked this guy.

"They were cocksuckers, sir. I couldn't stand them. The same goes for all of the missing people. They were shitty human beings. I can't begin to imagine how long the list must be of people that would like to see them dead."

"But *you* didn't want to see them dead, right?"

"It wouldn't be my first choice, Detective, but I can honestly say I haven't lost any sleep over it."

Dwayne was happy with his answer. It wasn't technically a lie. His first choice would have been that they not be assholes to begin with.

"Mr. Devero, I've had a few people tell me that you've been acting odd lately. Do you care to comment on that?"

"Sure, I'll comment on that. I've stood up to parents recently who don't respect the game of baseball. They want to have an 'everybody is a winner' mentality, and play 'daddy baseball.' I think it's important to teach kids how to play the game. I think it's important that they want to win. There are plenty of entitled little pussies out there, Detective. This town is full of them. I think we should raise our kids to actually accomplish things, and I started teaching that lesson on the baseball diamond when the coaching spots were vacated. Somebody had to step in. I did. But I did it my way, not the loser way."

The detective nodded his head. He liked Dwayne. He couldn't stand all of the entitled little pussies in town either. He could tell right away that Dwayne had earned every penny he had. He admired that.

"Oh, also," Dwayne continued, "I recently had some heated phone calls with some past-due accounts here at work. These were guys who had plenty of money, and they were looking for loopholes to get out of paying me for work I had completed. They fuck people over all the time, if I may speak bluntly. I simply held them accountable. They inherited most of their money and screwed people over for more. I earned mine."

Detective Loffland chuckled. "What about your buddies, Mr. Devero? What about Russ Paisley, Dr. Tommy Johnson, and Steve Winwood? That's a great name, by the way. But tell me about your friends, please."

"Well, to be honest, we can be a bit rowdy when we drink. We've been known to party, sir. Especially Russ. He's a lunatic. But we're good guys, Detective. You'll see that when you speak to them. We just like to have a good time."

Again, Dwayne felt good about his answer. He didn't say that they didn't murder people. It wasn't necessary. He simply told it like it was, with no bullshit. The detective obviously appreciated the approach.

"I don't think I'll need to talk to your buddies," the detective said as he rose to his feet. "Between you and me, those fuckers that got killed and went missing probably got what was coming to them. I'm just glad I got to interview someone who seems sincere. And I'd like to thank you for not raising pussies. Nobody should be allowed to fuck with baseball."

"Amen, Detective."

"You take care of yourself, Mr. Devero. And if you see anything suspicious, please give me a call."

The two men shook hands again by the door. It was a good, solid, tight-gripping handshake that only honest men give.

50.

The entire team showed up on time for batting practice and warm-ups that afternoon before the game. All of the coaches were at least fifteen minutes early. They were ready to play ball.

Jade had gotten shirts made for the coaches. She felt it was important for them to match perfectly. The shirts were slim cut and made to fit snug. They were bright orange, with "Tigers" written in black and silver sequins.

"Wow, Jade, you really went out of your way," Dwayne said as Jade handed out the shirts.

"Really amazing craftsmanship, Jade," Tommy stated, looking awkwardly at the others.

"Thanks, sweetie," she replied with a wink to Tommy. "The people who used to make my outfits at the Cabaret made them. They have the best sequins. They never fall off and wind up stuck in your vagina or anything."

Jade waited for the men to put on their shirts. They looked back at her with blank faces.

"Come on, guys, the game's about to start. Put them on!"

Steve glanced sideways at the others. Dwayne shrugged and pulled his shirt off. Tommy, Russ, and Steve followed suit.

Russ struggled to pull his shirt over his furry gut. He was frustrated with the slender cut. He was even more frustrated by the extra attention Jade had been giving to Tommy.

Steve pulled his shirt on and tucked it into his tiny gray coach's shorts. He seemed pleased with it and smiled at the others through his dorky spectacles. Dwayne could not have cared less. He was far too focused on winning. All that mattered to him was that they matched. He pulled the shirt on and sparked up a small joint, then passed it to the others.

While Tommy was pulling his sparkly new shirt over his head, Jade reached over and pinched his nipple and grinned. He grinned back, knowing full well that it was driving Russ insane.

She then turned and walked back toward the stands, glancing back at Tommy a couple of times along the way.

"Are you going to tell me what in God's name happened after the fundraiser?" Russ demanded. "Why the fuck is she calling you *sweetie*? And why did she just tweak your goddamn nipple?"

Tommy just smiled and walked toward the dugout with Dwayne and Steve.

"Keep her off that soul pole, Tommy!" Russ yelled as they walked away. "Not cool at all!"

Dave the umpire was behind home plate watching Alex warm up, pitching with Russ's son, Jackson, at catcher. He called for the head coaches to come meet him by the backstop to discuss the rules for the playoffs.

Gray Smith trudged out of the opposing team's dugout to shake Dwayne's hand.

"Sorry, guys," he apologized. "Reese went missing. You probably heard. Jesus, I don't know what's going on around here lately. Anyhow, I'm filling in."

Gray was a spineless nerd. He was tall and skinny with bright red hair, freckles, and fair skin. He had no business coaching baseball. He had most likely never even *held* a baseball. When they shook, Dwayne gripped Gray's hand extra firmly, and gave him a look that said *I own you*. Gray looked nervous as hell.

"Okay, men," Dave the umpire said. "Playoffs rules are a bit different. We go six innings, no matter how long it takes. No time limit, and no run limit. Dwayne, you're the home team. Gray, you guys bat first, so get your sticks and let's roll. Play ball!"

Dwayne patted his assistant coaches on the back. "This is what it's all about, guys," he said. "This is what all of the hard work has been for. Let's have smart coaching today. It's fucking playoffs time."

Gray Smith assumed his position as first-base coach for his batters. He stood roughly fifteen feet from Dwayne's dugout.

"Good luck today, guys," Gray nervously offered.

"Fuck you, Ginger," Russ said back. "We're about to rape your dreams. Eat a dick."

Gray looked startled and turned away. Steve hung his head and put his hand over his face.

"Russ, why do you have to be such an asshole?" Steve snapped. "He was just being friendly."

"Kiss my ass, you Obama-loving liberal." Russ stated flatly to Steve while still staring at Gray. "Get your game face on."

"We're going to dance all over these guys," Tommy threw in. "Just like Jade on my big brown ding-a-ling."

Russ scowled at Tommy and shoved a fistful of sunflower seeds in his mouth. Steve smiled.

Just as Dwayne predicted, the game turned into a blowout. The late Reese Pepper's team was massacred, just another example of what happens when daddy baseball meets a winning strategy.

Alex pitched for the first three innings, before Dwayne pulled him so that he would be available to pitch the following game. As long as a pitcher stayed under thirty pitches, they could pitch back-to-back games. This was done so as not to do any long-term damage to kids' arms.

He struck out six batters in the first three innings, and the other three got a small piece of his curveball, just as he intended, and were thrown out at first base. Tommy's son, TJ, pitched the fourth and fifth innings, and Russ's son, Jackson, came in to close in the sixth. They each pitched exceptionally well.

The only thing that rivaled the talent at the pitcher's mound was the batting. The boys brought the wood and exposed the major weaknesses in putting talentless kids in field positions that require talent.

Alex hit two balls over the fence. Jackson and TJ each had inside-the-park home runs. Steve's son, Jonathan, got his first-ever triple off a well-placed bunt and infield errors. Even Ricky Dale's and Pete Rearden's sons managed to score. It was every bit the victory Dwayne had predicted.

The final score was 27–0.

The losing team slumped into the consoling arms of their parents. Dwayne called for his team to meet him in the outfield and take a knee. They crowded around him in excitement, slapping each other's backs, reveling in the win. Moms and dads lined up behind them, proud.

Dwayne stood to address his team. His three assistants lined up beside him, arms crossed, sunglasses on, looking not too dissimilar from horribly dressed secret service agents.

"Well, Tigers, we did it again," Dwayne stated firmly to the kids.

Cheers erupted. Dwayne allowed them to hoot and holler for a moment before raising his hand for silence.

"I want you to know that I don't feel like I've done my job as a coach," he continued, "unless the kids on the other team cry themselves to sleep after meeting you."

The parents looked moderately dismayed. The kids broke into another round of wild cheers.

"You have destroyed their dinner . . . their evening . . . their week . . . their month. You have forced them to question what they are capable of in life. You have chewed up their spirits and spat them back in their faces. You have snuffed out the light of joy in their young lives with your fielding and beat their souls into oblivion with your bats. And for this, I commend you."

The team hung on Dwayne's every word. He had fast become their hero. The parents, on the other hand, were distressed.

Holly Dale, wife of the late Ricky Dale and mother of Ace, raised her hand sheepishly. "Coach Dwayne," she said. "I think I speak for all of the parents when I say that . . . while we're all happy with winning a couple of games, I'm not sure that we're sending the right message with this kind of talk. I mean—"

Holly Dale was interrupted by the shrill sound of Russ's coaching whistle. Russ blew until there was no more breath left in his lungs.

Holly looked around, hoping for backup from other parents so that she wouldn't be left to confront this lunatic alone. When she received none, she tried again.

"I just—"

Russ immediately blew the whistle again as loudly as he could, cutting Holly off before she could get started. She became agitated and turned directly to face Russ.

"I don't know who you think you are, but—"

Russ blew the whistle again with everything he had, stepping toward her and coming less than a foot from her face before his lungs finally gave out. He pulled his sunglasses off and stared angrily at her with his beady, bloodshot eyes.

Under the bright lights of the ballpark, a tense, strained silence blanketed the parents. No one moved. Russ cocked an eyebrow and snarled his lip around the whistle. Holly, now overcome with fear, stepped back among the parents.

"Thank you, Russ," Dwayne said. "Now, I know we've come a long way in the last couple of weeks, but let's not start hiring hookers and buying blow just yet. We still have our toughest games ahead. We have to remain focused if we want to make it to the championship. I know that many of you have been told by your parents that winning isn't everything, but that's what losers always say. That's why we keep score. That's why we practice. We play to win. End of story. We've won a couple of battles now, team. We have a few more left to win. And then, we will win the war. Stay salty. Stay gritty. Our next game is in two days. They're a good team. And I want to win."

"You're trained killers now, guys," Russ jumped in. "I want them pissing blood when it's over."

The kids jumped up and screamed. A couple of dads nodded in agreement, offering a refreshing (albeit mild) level of approval.

"Bring it in, team!" Tommy yelled. "Tigers kill . . . on three!"

The kids threw their hands together in a circle. "One, two, three. TIGERS KILL!" they shouted before heading off the fields with their parents.

Coach Dwayne and his assistants sent their boys home with their moms and ex-stripper stepmom. Dwayne wanted to burn a couple of joints in celebration.

He joined Russ, Tommy, Steve, and Dave the umpire in center field beneath the well-lit scoreboard after everyone had left, and sparked up. With the exception of Steve, the men seemed satisfied with the way the playoffs were shaking out.

"Great job out there today, Dwayne," Dave said, taking a hit from a joint and looking up at the score. "Those boys are taking your direction well. You might just win the whole damned thing."

"Goddamn right we will," Russ reported. "We're gonna turn this motherfucker on its head."

"And the field looks outstanding, Dwayne," Tommy added.

"I think I saw a patch of dead grass behind first base," Steve stated with agitated disgust. "Maybe we should murder a family and bury them there to get it blooming again."

Steve turned and marched off the field toward the dugout. He grabbed his son's baseball gear, headed out to the parking lot, and left.

"Fucking Democrat," Russ groaned, watching as Steve's Prius pulled out. "Maybe we should bury him there."

As Steve left Jenny Field, he noticed an unmarked police car parked in the corner of the lot. Inside the car sat Detective Loffland, silently watching the men who gathered at center field.

He picked up his phone and hopped on the text chain.

STEVE: Guys, there's a cop watching you in the parking lot!

All of the coaches and Dave received the text at about the same time. They pulled their phones from their pockets and read the text, then attempted to steal an inconspicuous glance at the parked cruiser.

"We're fine, guys," Dwayne whispered in counsel to the others. "The detective was cool. He's probably been checking everyone out. Let's get our gear and head out."

The coaches made their way to the dugout while Dave the umpire headed to the scoring box to shut the lights and scoreboard off. Dwayne texted Steve back.

DWAYNE: Thanks for the heads-up, Steve. We're fine. Relax.

RUSS: Your wife has fat legs.

STEVE: You're an asshole, Russ!

DAVE: She isn that ovrwate. Her hair sux tho. i'd still hav sex wiht her.

STEVE: You guys are idiots! We're screwed! They're totally onto us! This isn't the time for jokes!

TOMMY: I'm gonna see if Jade wants a chocolate Popsicle tonight. Maybe Kelly & I can do the Oreo thing again.

RUSS: WTF, Tom??? That's not cool! I'm standing right beside you!

STEVE: Have fun in prison.

DWAYNE: Relax, little buddy. The Jedi Alliance will overcome, and the gods of the ballpark will look favorably upon us.

STEVE: You've lost your mind.

RUSS: Fuck you.

STEVE: Fuck you!

DAVE: Fcuk you to.

DAVE: Damit.

DAVE: Dammit.

DAVE: Fuck oyu.

DAVE: Shit.

DAVE: Fck you.

RUSS: You done yet, retard?

DAVE: Fuck ou.

RUSS: Jesus. Someone take his phone away.

DAVE: Fuck you.

51.

Dwayne Devero couldn't remember a single week that had gone as well as the first week of playoffs. Sure, the police were visiting his office and watching him coach, but still . . . All of his accounts were paying on time. Several paid early. And Estelle continued to amaze him at home (and at the office) with her perky, playful attitude and untethered sexual energy.

The next two games the Tigers played that week both ended up being incredible. Both had been close, but the boys never gave up. They pulled off solid wins each time.

The Tigers continued to grow as a team. Under Dwayne's reign, kids who had never shown an ounce of ability were stepping up and delivering. Outfielders were hitting their cutoffs. Players were backing up plays. They were keeping the ball in front of them, letting nothing get past. The batting lineup began to deliver from top to bottom. Quality base hits were coming out of kids who had never made contact. They had confidence for the first time ever.

But Steve Winwood was losing it. He had become an increasingly paranoid nervous wreck. The other coaches could hardly stand to talk to him.

Detective Loffland had been to every playoff game thus far—gathering intelligence and trying to find anything that would help him solve the recent disappearances and murders of the local elite. This drove Steve absolutely nuts. He was certain the detective would storm onto the field at any time and throw them all in cuffs.

That didn't happen, though. And because it continued *not* to happen, Russ Paisley became more and more emboldened. He had increased his cocaine and LSD intake considerably. He bragged about waking up naked with a female midget wrestling team, a support group of blind sex addicts, and his favorite, a tribe of Native Americans who filled him with peyote, painted him blue, and pierced his nose.

Dr. Tommy Johnson, however, appeared to not notice Russ and Steve's journey toward opposite ends of the spectrum. He and Kelly had been inviting Jade over nearly every night after Russ passed out. Dr. Tom experimented constantly with the latest and greatest boner pills to the point that he was getting maybe an hour or two of sleep per night. Jedi sex had taken over his life.

Dwayne carefully watched each of them as they evolved. None of them appeared to be handling their newfound powers the way he had hoped. Balance was something that Dwayne felt must exist in the life of the urban caped crusader ninja grandmaster Jedi. There had to be joy. There had to be justice. There had to be true love. There had to be a life worth getting bloody and fighting for. There had to be a code. And there had to be the willpower to abide by that code.

And above all . . . there had to be baseball.

As they entered the final week of the playoffs, Dwayne felt that he should gather the crew for a round of golf to discuss how the Jedi Alliance should proceed.

DWAYNE: Golf anyone?

TOMMY: I've had an erection for three days straight. If that doesn't bother you, I'm in. I probably won't even need clubs.

STEVE: It won't do me any good to fight you. I might as well just agree to it. I think we need to talk about the cops too. I can't sleep. I know they're watching.

RUSS: Holy FUCKBALLS, man! What fucking time is it? OH JESUS! I think I'm in a tree house or something! I took SO MUCH acid last night! I think I fucked a squirrel!

DWAYNE: Okay then. 8:30 at the club.

RUSS: SHIT! I'm painted blue again! The Indians are back!

TOMMY: Native Americans, Russ. Show some respect.

Russ climbed down from the tree house and attempted to get his bearings. He gathered that he was two blocks away from his house.

He sprinted all the way home, bright blue and totally nude, clutching his phone in his hand as he ran. The morning jogging group from the neighborhood seemed almost disappointed that he outpaced them when he passed them rounding the corner to his street. He arrived at his home to find that a teepee had been constructed in his front yard, and Jade's Jeep was missing. He hopped back on the text chain.

RUSS: Has anyone see Jade?

TOMMY: *ahem*

RUSS: WTF, TOMMY?! I swear to God I'm cracking a fucking 3-wood over your head today! I don't care what Jade does with Kelly, but if you get up in there I'm TOTALLY having sex with your wife!

TOMMY: Good one, Russ. You're a quivering little fatbody with hair plugs and a tiny penis. She'd laugh herself unconscious.

RUSS: Well then, I have roofies.

STEVE: Jesus. Hello, Mr. Date Rape.

TOMMY: Fine, bro. I'll send her home after we get out of the shower.

RUSS: Wow. It's on, man. It's on like Donkey Kong.

DWAYNE: Great. I'll see you guys at 8:30.

Estelle had been up for several minutes. She had been acting odd the night before, but then she whipped out handcuffs and flavored body paint and Dwayne forgot about it. But now he was curious.

He walked into the bathroom (nude, as always), and found Estelle (also nude) leaning back against the sink and clutching what looked like a strange thermometer in her hand. She looked up at Dwayne, terrified.

"What's going on, babe?" he asked.

She struggled to tell him. Her eyes filled with tears.

"It's just that . . . honey, I'm always on time, and . . . so I was barely even late, but I had to check, and . . . and now things are so

great between us, and I don't want to ruin it . . . but . . . well, here."
She handed Dwayne the odd thermometer. He noticed two identical
thermometers next to the sink. This one had a blue plus on it.

It took Dwayne longer than it should have to realize what was going
on, but then it hit him. And after it hit him, he did some quick mental
math to make sure *he* was the guy who should be happy. According to
his math, he was that guy.

"Babe . . . are you . . . pregnant?"

Estelle smiled at Dwayne nervously as tears poured down her
cheeks. She nodded.

"*Wooooo-hoooo!*" he yelled, throwing his hands up in the air. Dwayne
picked her up and squeezed her, then spun her around, dancing all
over the bedroom and bathroom.

"Oh, babe, this is awesome!" he said. "I love my life!" He set Estelle
back down and looked her in the eyes. She was humbled by his joy,
feeling undeserving. Her whole body shook.

"Thank you, Dwayne," she cried. "I love my life too. I'm not proud
of the road we took to get here, but at least we're here, and I'm so
thankful. I love you, babe."

"I love you too. And our little Jedi."

52.

Dwayne, Steve, and Tommy showed up early for golf. They each wanted time to hit a bucket of balls on the driving range and get warmed up before the game. As was the norm, Russ screeched into the parking lot at the last minute. Thankfully, however, he was already wearing his golf shirt this time.

"Well, there's a first," Steve said smugly to the others. "At least we don't have to watch him change cl—"

Russ stepped out of his Ferrari completely nude from the waist down. Russ looked over at the others and held his arms straight out to his sides, smiling proudly.

"SEE?!" he yelled over to them. "You had no idea I didn't have any pants on, did you? I told you nobody could tell!"

The guys turned back to the driving range, doing their best to ignore Russ. A golf attendant pulled his cart up for him with his clubs already on it, avoiding looking in Russ's direction as much as possible. Russ grabbed his 3-wood and headed up to the range. Thankfully, no other club members were present.

"Man, this breeze feels fucking *great*!" Russ said just loud enough for the others to hear him.

They wouldn't look. They didn't want to give him the satisfaction of watching him tee up and hit balls at the range with his lower half fully exposed.

"Hey, Steve," Russ called out. "Does my swing look off to you? I'm kinda slicing them right now."

"Goddammit," Steve muttered. "Can we just *please* go play this game? And can you put your damn pants on, Russ?"

"Agreed," Dwayne said. "Let's go play some golf, men. I don't think I've ever hit better than just now. Every damn ball went three hundred yards up the middle. Let's do this."

"I've gotta say," Tommy added, "I'm feelin' it too. My God, I'm absolutely *crushing* the ball."

"Me too," Steve enthusiastically threw in. Dwayne's infectious gusto was hard for Steve to resist. He thought he might need to give the Jedi life another try. "Let's roll!"

The three of them headed to the number one tee box. Russ went back to his car and put on his shorts and shoes, meeting them a few minutes later. He marched past them without saying a word, placed his ball on a tee, and took his shot. The ball sailed perfectly up the middle of the fairway, coming to a rest just short of the green. Russ offered a karate-chop high kick in celebration.

"Suck it, douchebags," he said, holding his middle finger up to the baseball dads.

He then walked straight back to his cart without a word. The others watched him pass in disgust. The little bastard never practiced yet almost always won.

When the others stepped over to the box and took turns teeing off, Russ dropped two tablets of LSD into Tommy's water bottle.

Dwayne teed up his ball with precision, took a beautiful practice swing, then stepped up and hit. His ball sliced hard right into a huge oak tree, which it ricocheted off, cutting back across the fairway and landing in a duck pond. "Stupid fucking game," Dwayne whispered to himself.

Dwayne picked up his tee and stuck it in his pocket as Tommy assumed his stance. Tommy stared down the fairway, visualizing his shot. He spaced his feet out properly, pulled his club back, and swung mightily.

Tommy's ball sliced hard right as well, except his didn't have a tree to stop it from crossing the street and going through the large second-story picture window of a gorgeous nineteenth-century Victorian home. The entire ten-foot window shattered and came crashing down onto the sidewalk beneath it. They stood and watched, waiting for someone to come out screaming. Apparently no one was home.

"Jesus," Steve said. "You fucked that place up."

"Yup," Dwayne added. "Hurry up and hit, Steve. Let's get the fuck outta here."

Steve hurriedly set his ball down, lined up, and swung. He topped the ball, sending it about five feet past the ladies' tee box, narrowly avoiding "Arkansas Rules," which states that if your ball doesn't pass the ladies' tees, you must complete the hole you are on with your pants around your ankles. While not an actual PGA-sanctioned rule, "Arkansas Rules" was adhered to at most country clubs.

Russ laughed at the guys as he sped away down the fairway toward his ball.

"Wait for it," Tommy said, as he and the other two stood and watched.

At the first slight bump Russ hit, his golf bag came crashing off his cart, spilling all over the fairway.

Russ looked back at the other three. They all held up their middle fingers.

After about forty-five minutes of play, Russ was destroying the others with his score. He was on track to hit in the low 70s, while Dwayne, Tommy, and Steve were each pacing 110 plus. And that was before the LSD kicked in with Tommy on hole number five.

Dwayne had just begun to ease his way into the conversation he'd been hoping to have with the guys about "the code" of the suburban Jedi. The guys needed to understand. It had been difficult because Steve wouldn't quit interrupting with his concerns about the police. Dwayne wasn't worried about that. He liked Detective Loffland, and he felt as though they'd been careful enough to get away with what they'd done thus far. But he wasn't sure if they'd be able to continue to get away with things if Tommy and Russ didn't follow the code.

Dwayne had barely gotten into what the code of the suburban Jedi must entail when Tommy started to behave erratically. Russ was the only one who knew that Tommy was on acid. Even Tommy didn't know.

Hole five was a tricky par three. It took a perfect wedge with a touch of backspin to get the ball over a large pond and then stop on the green at the other side. Russ had that perfect wedge. None of the others came close. The other three guys sent multiple balls into the water.

The four guys hopped into their four carts after multiple attempts. While three of them headed to the green, Tommy drove straight into the pond. The entire cart went underwater, with Tommy behind the wheel.

Dwayne was preparing to rip his shoes off and go on a rescue mission, when Tommy's head popped above the surface. "Got 'em!" he yelled, holding up two golf balls. "I didn't see yours though, guys. You want me to just leave them?"

Steve and Dwayne looked at each other, confused. Russ fell to the ground laughing.

"We're good, Tom," Steve shouted back to him.

Tommy went back under for another minute or so. It was both impressive and concerning. The others stood by, watching, waiting to see what could possibly happen next. Tommy finally came up for air again. "I can't get my golf cart to move," he called out. "I'm wondering if the battery went dead. You guys have any jumper cables?"

"Sorry, Tom," Dwayne replied. "Why don't you just grab your clubs and hop on with Steve?"

Steve scowled at Dwayne. Tommy went under again.

Dwayne looked at Russ. "How much did you give him?"

"Two."

"How long is it gonna last?"

"Eight to ten hours."

"Strong?"

"The strongest."

Moments later, Tommy emerged from the other side of the pond and walked onto the green, dripping wet, his golf bag over his shoulder. He made his way to Steve's cart, strapped his bag on, and grabbed his putter.

"Well, okay then," Dwayne said.

Tommy approached his golf ball on the green and meticulously lined up his putt. His ball lay roughly fifteen feet from the hole. He took his shot. The ball rolled about six inches. He stepped up again and hit. It made it another three to four inches. This continued for the entire fifteen feet.

Walking back to the carts, Dwayne asked the others what score they got on the hole so that he could fill out the scorecard.

"I got a nine," Dwayne told them.

"Birdie, bitches!" Russ bragged.

"I got a nine also, D," Steve added.

Tommy paused to count his shots. He was pointing at each spot his ball went to, then calculating the sum of them in his mind.

"I got a twenty-seven," he said.

Tommy then looked over at Russ, who had turned almost blue from holding in his chuckles. He looked at Dwayne, who offered a sympathetic smile. He turned his attention to Steve, sitting beside him, who was still clutching his putter and looking scared shitless of Tom.

"Hang on just a second," Tommy continued. "So, I just drove a golf cart into the pond to find the two balls I hit into it. I putted the ball over twenty times. I've seen at least a half dozen birds flying backward in the last minute, and I'm pretty sure there's a panda in that tree over there playing Metallica on a saxophone. Sooooo . . . I'm guessing I should say thanks for the LSD, Russ."

Russ burst out laughing. He laughed so hard he started wheezing.

"I was hoping to have a serious conversation about keeping our shit together and following a code," Dwayne stated. "But I guess that talk will have to happen later. Just try and hold it together at the game tonight, guys. We're getting close to winning this thing, and Steve is right about one thing. The cops are watching."

The rest of the round of golf went as rounds of golf with the baseball dads typically went, with the exception of Tommy. Dwayne, Russ, and Steve each achieved varying levels of inebriation, as usual. Tommy was an overachiever, though. He rode on the roof of the cart for the entire back nine with his legs dangling over the front windshield.

Russ won the golf game with a 72. Dwayne got a 113, and Steve got a 115. Tommy finished with a 121, but he didn't play the last seven holes.

"Russ, you get the honor of dropping Tommy off at his house, since you dosed him," Dwayne said at the end of the game. "Tell Kelly to get some food in him and keep him in front of a television. Maybe throw on some cartoons. Nothing with clowns."

Dwayne left the country club mildly disappointed. Russ and Tommy had begun to take the Jedi lifestyle out of context, and it was bothering him. They had little desire to use their powers for justice. They just wanted to use them for self-gratification. It was a recipe for disaster. And as much as Dwayne knew that he currently had a great relationship operating above suspicion with the police, he was no longer certain of what the future held for the Jedi Alliance.

Steve, while overboard in his paranoia, may have been onto something. Dwayne felt like he wouldn't be doing right by his family if he didn't at least prepare for the possibility that the world could come crashing down around them. He had an amazing family and a baby on the way. For the first time since becoming a grandmaster caped crusader Jedi ninja, Dwayne was scared. He had forgotten what it was like to have uncertainty. He needed a way to quell it.

What Dwayne needed was a backup plan, just in case the proverbial shit hit the fan. He had to plan an escape. Just in case.

To make matters worse, there was yet another envelope sitting on Dwayne's seat when he opened the door to his truck. On it was written, "How long until they know what you're up to?" He didn't even open the envelope this time; he just threw it in the glove box.

Yup, he needed a plan. He wouldn't allow his chest to tighten up, even though it wanted to. He had to win the championship. He had to stay focused. He slapped himself hard across the face. "Get your fucking head in the game, Dwayne!" he yelled into the mirror. "Don't fucking lose it now! You're *close*, man! You're *close*!"

Instead of heading straight home, Dwayne made sure he wasn't being followed and then made his way to the local RV dealership. He scoured the lot with an obnoxious, brown-toothed salesman, who wore a tan polyester suit straight out of the early '80s, until they came upon the most badass RV Dwayne had ever seen.

Dwayne used his ninja powers to grind the salesman down to an amazing deal and, after two hours of haggling, signed the paperwork. Dwayne let him know that either he or his assistant would return within a couple of days to pick the RV up.

He called Uzi as soon as he got back in his truck.

"Wass crack-a-lackin', boss man?" Uzi asked.

"You want to make some more cheddar, my man?"

"Always, Big D. Whatchoo got?"

"I need your email address. I'm going to send you passport photos of my wife, my son, and myself. I need new identities, a new credit profile, and new credit cards, brother."

"I got your back, homie. Anything I need to be aware of?"

"Not yet. I just live by a code, man. I see that code in you too, bro. I hope you stick with it. The other guys aren't quite cutting it. I need to be prepared, man. And this stays between us."

"No worries. How quick you need 'em?"

"A couple of days."

"Coolio, bro. My email is twerknasty@gmail.com."

"Nice."

"Thanks."

"I'll leave a wad of cash in my mailbox tonight. Take care."

"Peace."

Dwayne's phone quacked immediately after hanging up with Uzi. He glanced down at it. It was the text chain again.

TOMMY: hsgdybkwhsk&&&88%%#@$

STEVE: Nice job, Russ.

RUSS: LOL.

TOMMY: monkeeeeeeeeeey

DWAYNE: Okay, guys, be at the field at 5. We're playing the
          Mariners tonight. That's Pastor Harper's team. They're
          going to be our toughest opponents. We're the only two

undefeated teams in the playoffs. We'll probably be
seeing them in the championship game. Let's do this.

STEVE: No prob. I'd love to win the championship before my
life sentence.

RUSS: Technically, I think this would be a death penalty
case, Steve.

STEVE: Oh, right. Let's win it all before our lethal injections
then, okay?

RUSS: And Tommy, just so you know, I'm totally drilling Kelly
tonight.

TOMMY: ffffffffffuuuhhhyyyyyyyyyooooooo

DWAYNE: See you there. Don't fuck this up, guys.

RUSS: Later.

STEVE: Whatever.

TOMMY: %

53.

The day had gone downhill for Dwayne since he received the amazing news about Estelle being pregnant. He felt his Jedi-ninja powers evolving. The urge to protect his family at all costs had never been so prominent.

Estelle ran to the front door and leapt into his arms. "I missed you, babe," she said. "How much time do we have?"

"Enough." He smiled back at her.

He carried her into the bedroom, where he set her down slowly as they kissed. They peeled each other's clothes off and stumbled toward the shower. The two of them were more in love than ever. Something about the pregnancy had elevated things to an incomprehensible level.

"You're amazing, my little Catwoman," he said.

"You're not too bad either, my big strong Batman," she said, returning the compliment. "You still doing okay, sweetie?"

"I'll be fine, babe. We both will. It's not always rainbows and butterflies in the life of a ninja though, you know? I forget that sometimes."

"You're still okay with *us* though, right?"

"You know it, babe. I'm excited as hell about our little bun in the oven. It gives me perspective. It makes me more aware of what's going on around me. I'm still a badass motherfucking ninja Jedi warrior, it's just that now I'm a badass motherfucking ninja Jedi warrior with an eye on the future. Gotta adapt, sugartits."

"Good. You've just been so confident lately, honeyballs . . . And then today, something looked . . . *different*."

"I'm still confident, muffinbutt. Totally. I think I may have misjudged some people, though. That's all. I'm taking a few steps to make sure that if our ninja lifestyle is misunderstood by the long arm of the law, we'll still be fine. It's the evolution of the warrior."

"Are you sure everything is okay?"

"I'm positive. Do me a favor though, babe. Think about something. If we had to drop everything and leave town tomorrow, what would you bring with us? Whatever that is, I want you to get it together."

"But . . . why?"

"Just in case."

54.

Dwayne and Alex arrived at Jenny Field at 4:58 p.m. Both of them were excited for the challenge that lay ahead. They knew that Pastor Harper's team, the Mariners, would put up a fight. The Mariners played dirty, hard, real baseball. It was going to be fun.

Steve, Russ, and Tommy pulled into the parking lot with their boys just as Dwayne and Alex were about to grab the baseball gear from the back of Dwayne's truck. Everyone was in uniform. That gave Dwayne a small level of comfort.

The boys all high-fived each other, then pulled the two buckets of balls and catcher's equipment from the truck bed and headed to the batting cages.

Russ pulled an enormous joint from his pack of cigarettes and sparked it up, then passed it around. In between hits, Russ snuck his little cocaine contraption from his pocket and snorted away. He reeked of beer and liquor, and could barely piece a sentence together.

Tommy wasn't faring much better. He hadn't said a word since he arrived. He merely stood and nodded when Dwayne reviewed strategies with them. He pushed his sunglasses up every few minutes and had developed something of a nervous twitch.

Steve was constantly looking over his shoulder. He couldn't shake the crazy feeling that he was being watched. And as it turned out, he was right. Dwayne spotted Detective Loffland's unmarked car hidden around the side of the ballpark.

Dwayne decided to stop by and say hello to the detective. As Dwayne approached his vehicle, Detective Loffland opened up his door and stepped out.

"You're a hell of a coach, Mr. Devero," he said. "I've been impressed. Not so much with your dazzly little coach's shirts, but still."

"Thanks, Detective!" Dwayne replied. "You should come grab a seat in the bleachers tonight. It's gonna be a good game."

"I would, but I've been working this case day and night. At some point I'm hoping to see something bigger than possession of marijuana. I kinda need to stay behind the scenes."

Dwayne grinned. He could tell Detective Loffland was one of those cops that could care less about weed violations. "I hear ya, Detective. That's a good thing, too. We all need ways of coping with assholes. And by the way, speaking of assholes, I'm playing the King of Assholes tonight, Pastor Jim Harper."

"Man, that guy is a douche. Beat the shit out of him for me. Good luck!"

"Thanks. Let me know if I can help at all with the case."

The two shook hands and slapped shoulders. Dwayne headed over to the cages while the detective attempted to resume his "hidden" position.

After batting practice was completed, Dwayne called the team and coaches together for a pump-up meeting and asked the boys to take a knee. "This is the team to beat, men," he began. "And it's time for me to let you know something: You've played great so far in the playoffs. But that won't be enough tonight. Tonight, I need you to play better. You've hit well so far in the playoffs, also. But tonight, I need you to hit better."

Dwayne paced back and forth in front of the team. They were listening intently. They were focused. There were no smiles, only snarls.

"You *can* claim a victory here tonight, men," he continued. "But it won't be given to you. You'll have to latch on to it with both hands and *rip it away* from the Mariners. And make no mistake about it, they will play dirty, and we will not. They will be loose with the rules. We will not be. They will cheat. We will not. We will unite as a team once again, we will shut them down defensively, and we will explode while in the batter's box. Every inning, we will kill. Every inning, we will destroy. Every inning, we will make the Mariners rue the day someone handed them a baseball bat and told them they could do something with it."

Dwayne paused. He looked each boy in the eye.

"And once our six innings have come to an end, we will emerge victorious."

The boys erupted in excitement. Russ, Steve, and Tommy felt as though they'd just been privy to one of the greatest speeches in the history of sports.

"Bring it in, boys! Tigers kill, on three!"

"One . . . two . . . three . . . TIGERS KILL!!!"

Dwayne headed to the mound to shake hands with Dave the umpire and Pastor Jim before the game. Dave went through the rules, as was customary, and they flipped a coin to determine who would be "home" and who would be "visitor." Pastor Jim won the coin toss and elected to be the "home" team.

"Okay, men, shake hands, and then let's play some baseball," Dave said.

The two reached out their hands and shook as the crowd began to cheer. Pastor Jim leaned over to Dwayne to attempt to rattle him. "I've always admired your wife, Dwayne," he said. "I bet she'd be a great missionary. She's had an incredible amount of practice in the missionary position."

That struck a nerve. Dwayne squeezed Pastor Jim's hand as tightly as he could, almost bringing him to his knees. The aggressive gesture didn't go unnoticed by the crowd. A few boos could be heard from the stands.

"Listen here, you hypocritical pedophile," Dwayne said through gritted teeth. "If you ever mention my wife again, I will sodomize you with a baseball bat until blood pours from your ears. Am I clear on that?"

Pastor Jim nodded. Dwayne released his hand, leaving the pastor to rub his fingers and assess for damage.

"Now, go pray for mercy, douchebag," Dwayne added, giving a mockingly playful punch to the pastor's shoulder. "I'm about to unleash the hounds of Hell on you."

Dwayne turned and walked back to his dugout. He was pissed.

And he wasn't the only one. Pastor Jim was rather upset as well. These two men absolutely hated each other. The battle was set to begin.

Russ's son, Jackson, was the lead-off batter for the Tigers. Russ scurried to serve as first-base coach, beside the Mariners' dugout.

"I hope you know that you're attaching yourself to a sinking ship by being friends with Dwayne," Pastor Jim called over to Russ.

Russ was doing everything he could not to respond. He was ready to explode into a violent cocaine-and-alcohol rage. Unfortunately, Russ was a deacon in the church, and the church had been his prime source of business investors. Because of this, Pastor Jim was pretty much the only person Russ had never blown up on.

Still, Russ wasn't about to let it go. He moved close to the kid on first and whispered, "Hey, has Pastor Jim ever asked you to find your happy place while he tickled your privates?"

The boy just shook his head as a look of fear overcame him.

"Good to hear, son. Good luck today."

Pastor Jim's son, Noah, was pitching. Noah went to work on Jackson, throwing everything in his bag of tricks. Jackson swung at a beautiful curveball and an extremely slow changeup. He missed both. Noah finished Jackson off with an incredible fastball that painted the outside corner.

Defeated and humiliated, Jackson dragged back to the dugout with his head down. TJ took the plate next. It was the same story. Great pitching had neutralized another great batter. Noah struck TJ out in four pitches. Now it was up to Steve's son, Jonathan, to keep the inning alive before Alex could get a shot at batting cleanup.

Jonathan took Noah to a full count, with three balls and two strikes. Noah decided to send a message to the Tigers with his next pitch. He figured it was time to get inside their heads. He threw a screaming fastball right at Jonathan's head. Jonathan managed to turn just enough so that the ball merely grazed his cheek, but it was enough to draw blood. It was also enough to throw him off balance, and he fell backward to the ground.

The crowd went silent. Dave the umpire looked at Dwayne. Dwayne looked at Pastor Jim. Pastor Jim smiled.

It was on.

Jonathan rose to his feet, and Dave directed him to jog out to first base. He wiped away the blood as he ran. The crowd clapped for Jonathan, happy that he wasn't going to the emergency room.

Steve grabbed Alex's shoulder before he headed to the plate.

"Blood for blood, Alex," Steve grunted, obviously pissed off. Alex had no idea what Steve meant. He just nodded and headed out to bat.

Noah Harper and Alex Devero had a bit of history. They were thought to be the best players in their age group. The locals had enjoyed watching the two face off as they grew up. With the recent tension between their fathers, the boys' rivalry had deepened. It was unspoken but highly visible.

Noah started with a curveball that ventured to the outside, trying to get Alex swinging. It didn't work. Noah figured he needed to wake Alex up with his next pitch, so he threw one right at him. Alex dove out of the way, and the ball barely missed him.

Alex hopped to his feet and dusted himself off. He was unfazed. This drove Noah crazy. He tried once more to rattle Alex, sending another speeding ball toward his head. This one was even closer, but Alex dodged it.

The next pitch, however, was perfect. It had to be, and Alex knew that. Noah had already thrown three balls. He had to throw strikes now. His fourth pitch was fast, low, and right up the middle. Alex waited on it to travel back as far as he could. He cracked it masterfully, sending the ball sailing down the first baseline. It cleared the fence by probably a greater margin than any ball had ever cleared it before.

Two-run homer. Boom. The tone had been set. Alex could not be shaken. He glanced across to Dwayne as he rounded third base. Alex wasn't smiling like most kids would have been. There was something far more fierce there. Something deeper. It was the glare of a young badass grandmaster ninja Jedi warrior.

Noah managed to pull himself together for the next kid, Ace Dale.

Ace never even swung the bat. He committed one of the worst crimes you can commit at the plate . . . he watched three perfect up-the-middle throws in a row and struck out.

The Mariners came out with their guns blazing. Alex managed to strike the first two batters out, but the third got a small piece of the ball. A fielding error allowed him to make it to first. But then, when Noah took the plate, the tide shifted.

Noah made excellent contact with Alex's fastball and hit a screamer over the center fielder's head to the outfield wall. Eric Rearden, the late Pete Rearden's son, was playing center field. He made a great throw to his cutoff man at second base. The cutoff was able to pivot perfectly because of the freshly manicured dirt, and he whipped the ball to Jackson at home plate.

Noah came in for the slide at home just as Jackson caught the ball. Noah raised his leg at the last second, sending his spikes into Jackson's shin. Jackson fell over hard, and the ball rolled out of his glove as he hit the ground in agony. The dirty move allowed the Mariners to tie the Tigers and caused Jackson to have to sit out for the remainder of the game with a sore and shredded leg.

The game remained tied at 2–2 until the sixth and final inning. It was a game of "small ball"—very few hits, and exceptional defense.

The final run of the game was scored by TJ, who managed to hit a solid double and was knocked in by a line-drive triple from Alex. The Mariners managed to get a couple of players on base at the bottom of the sixth, but TJ's turn at pitching ultimately proved effective, and the Tigers squeaked by with a score of 3–2.

At the end of the game, the Mariners and the Tigers crossed to the middle of the field to shake hands and offer the obligatory "good game" to one another. When it came time for Noah to shake Jackson's hand, he dropped his shoulder and knocked Jackson back a few steps. Alex lunged forward and grabbed Noah's "shaking hand," whipping him around into a half nelson while twisting his fingers back. Alex demanded that Noah apologize to Jackson for spiking him and pushing him while in line.

"Hey there, Alex!" Pastor Jim called out. "You stop that right now! Dwayne, don't you think you should say something here?!"

The ruckus caused the parents to hurry onto the field, mortified.

"Yes, Pastor, I do," Dwayne replied. "Alex, if you twist his fingers while you're pushing them back, he'll probably apologize more quickly."

Alex did as his father advised, and Noah dropped to his knees. The group of parents gasped.

Pastor Jim darted toward the boys, but Dwayne stepped in front of him, clutching the front of the pastor's shirt with both hands. "Don't even think about it, Jim," Dwayne growled. "Your boy played dirty. Now he's gonna apologize."

"Come on, Dad, you fucking pussy!" Noah screamed in pain. "Hit that fucking low-rent yard guy and get this asshole off of me!"

The pastor and his wife were shocked and embarrassed. The other parents pulled their kids away from the melee and attempted to cover their ears, protecting them from further profanity. Dave the umpire chuckled.

None of this deterred Alex. He twisted Noah's fingers harder. Any more, and bones would break.

"DAAAAAD! DAAAAD!" Noah yelled. "Fuck! Fine! Okay! I'm sorry! I'm sorry!"

Alex let go of Noah's hand, and Dwayne released Pastor Jim's shirt. Jedi-ninja warrior father and son returned to the dugout. The rest of the Tigers followed. The Mariners stayed, crumpled in defeat, in the middle of the field.

Dwayne asked the boys to take a seat on the bench.

"Normally, we'd be out in the field for our postgame talk," he said, turning and pointing to where the other team was still attempting to figure out what the hell had just happened. "But today, there's too much trash on the field. So we'll do it here."

Dwayne glared out at Pastor Jim from the dugout. Pastor Jim was glaring back. Dwayne shot him a quick middle finger. The pastor scowled.

"You did good today, team," Dwayne continued. "We lost a key player early on, and you banded together and carried the weight. Alex, I'm proud of you for standing up for Jackson. That's what soldiers do in the game of baseball. That's called honor. That's called brotherhood."

"They whipped out their peckers and tried to piss all over you boys," Russ interrupted, slurring horribly. "And you pulled out a goddamn umbrella and blocked that shit! Ain't nobody gonna piss on these boys! Am I right?!"

Russ threw a hand up and looked around for a high five. Tommy finally gave him one out of pity. Dwayne analyzed the level at which the Tigers parents were offended and decided that they should have been used to it by now.

"There's a code that we can live by as we grow, men," Dwayne said to the boys, and he hoped his fellow coaches would realize that he was speaking to them as well. "It's a choice we make to follow this code. I can see you beginning to grasp it. I'm glad to see that. It's a ninja code. It's a Jedi code. It's a superhero code. And let me tell you . . . it works. And you are beginning to exemplify that code. The code is pretty simple: Don't take shit from anyone, and don't give shit to anyone who doesn't deserve it. Play the game of life and the game of baseball with honor."

It was silent in the dugout. The boys let Dwayne's words permeate their brains.

"Here's the thing, boys," Dwayne continued. "Let this sink in: The playoffs are double elimination, and—"

"That's different than double penetration, in case you were wondering," Russ added. He raised his arm up in search of a high five again, but this time he found no takers.

"Jesus Christ, Russ, maybe you should just tell some abortion jokes," Steve offered in disgust.

"That's it! I can't do this anymore!" Holly Dale yelled. "Ace, get your bag! I'm reporting these coaches to the league! We're leaving!"

"Be quiet, Mom!" Ace snapped back. "Coach Dwayne is speaking."

Russ put the whistle in his mouth, but Tommy ripped it out before he could blow.

Dwayne reached his hand out to Ace for a fist bump. He was beginning to like the kid.

"Like I was saying, the playoffs are double elimination. There's only one more game before the championship. That means that whether we win or lose our next game, we will be playing in the championship game this Saturday. I don't expect to lose our next game. The team we just played will most likely be the one we play on Saturday. And they will play harder next time. They will play dirtier next time. But if you continue to follow the code, we will destroy them. There will be blood . . . and blood makes the grass grow."

Dwayne could see the intense excitement growing inside them.

"NOW BRING IT IN, TIGERS! TIGERS KILL, ON THREE!"

Dwayne screamed with a fire in his eyes.

"ONE . . . TWO . . . THREE . . . TIGERS KILL!!!"

On their way to the parking lot, after everyone had gathered their things, Russ handed Tommy and Kelly each a bottle of ice-cold water. "There ya go, Tom," Russ said. "That's a little apology gift from me for slipping you acid on the golf course this morning."

"That's sweet, Russ," Kelly replied. Tommy was still about 80 percent unable to speak.

Russ failed to mention to Tommy and Kelly that he had dosed each of their water bottles with roofies.

55.

After dinner that night, Dwayne walked Alex upstairs to his bedroom and tucked him into bed. He told his son how proud he was for standing up to Noah. Alex told his dad how much fun he'd been having since he took over the team. He begged his dad to coach every year.

"I'll do it, son," Dwayne told him. "I promise."

Estelle didn't need to do much to coax Dwayne into the shower that night. She merely stripped off her clothes slowly and silently, staring at Dwayne the whole time, and glanced back over her shoulder at him as she walked away into the master bathroom. There was something about her—that glow that came from being pregnant, perhaps; it made him forget about how tired he was, and how concerned he was that their world might come crashing down.

Estelle finally passed out cold after making love to Dwayne three times. Dwayne couldn't sleep. He climbed out of bed, making sure not to wake his sleeping beauty, and made his way into his closet. He pulled down the large box containing his Batman outfit and put the costume on.

The large bat went to the kitchen and grabbed a six-pack of beer. He then walked to the medicine cabinet and reached up to the back corner until his hands found his stash of weed. Dwayne then took great care in meticulously rolling a perfect joint.

He crept outside into his garage and found his ladder and, making as little noise as possible, placed it up against the side of his house. Purposefully, he climbed up onto the roof, to the highest point, and looked out around the neighborhood. He understood the symbolism of how profound and noble a silhouette he was probably casting against the large Texas moon. The wind blowing through his cape humbled him.

Dwayne looked all around in every direction, drinking his beer and sparking up his joint. He could smell the humidity forming in the air and hear the growing rustle of the leaves in the trees. He watched the wind carry the pot smoke a few houses away before it finally broke apart into nothing. The clouds offered a gentle rumble. There was a flash of light off in the distance.

A storm was coming.

56.

The next morning, as the sun came piping through Tommy's bedroom window, a shrill shriek pierced the early solitude. Kelly sat up on her side of the bed, gasping. Tommy leapt up, thinking someone must have been dead for her to make such a sound.

"WHAT THE FUCK, TOM?!" she yelled.

Laying totally nude on top of the covers between a totally nude Kelly and Tommy Johnson was Russ Paisley. He was smiling, face up, with his hands clasped behind his head.

"WHAT THE FUCK, RUSS?!" Tommy screamed.

"Oh, come on now, you two," Russ bragged as he sparked up a cigarette. "Don't go pulling that walk of shame stuff with me! You couldn't get enough of my raw sexuality last night!"

"Sweet JESUS, Russ! What did you do?!" Tommy barked.

"What did I do? Hell, what *didn't* I do?" Russ laughed. "You guys wanna go again? My little fella is waking up!"

Kelly shot a glance down toward Russ's not-so-flaccid yet tiny penis and began to dry heave. She got up and sprinted toward the bathroom, where she could be heard seconds later emptying her stomach into the toilet.

"Jesus, Russ! What the hell is wrong with you? This is *so* wrong! I don't remember anything! Goddammit, *what did you do* to us?" Tommy frantically prodded.

"I got even, bitch! That's what I did! Doesn't feel so good now, does it? I was the cream filling in a sexy chocolate cookie last night! And *oh my God*, Kelly is amazing!"

"You son of a bitch!"

Kelly came wobbling out of the bathroom. Russ jumped up on the end of the bed and began bouncing to twirl his microscopic manhood around beneath his flabby mass of a hairy stomach. "You know you loved it, Kelly," Russ goaded with a wanton snarl. "You motorboated my belly button last night when things got kinky."

Kelly raced back to the toilet and began to throw up again. Tommy hurled a pillow at Russ's face, causing him to lose his balance and fall backward off the bed.

"You crossed the line, Russ! You had nonconsensual sex with *my wife*, bro!"

"Not *just* your wife, Tom!"

Tommy's jaw dropped open. He clasped his hand over his mouth.

"That's it, I'm getting my gun!" Tommy yelled as he bolted out of his bed and headed for the closet.

Russ took off running, grabbing his clothes along the way. Tommy wasn't far behind. He burst through the front door, nude and brandishing a pistol, as Russ's Ferrari rumbled to life and peeled out sideways down the street.

Tommy moseyed slowly back toward his front door, paying little attention to the elderly couple next door shaking their heads in disappointment as they walked their Shih Tzu.

Tommy could hear his phone beeping on his nightstand, alerting him to a text message, when he strolled back into house. Russ had started the text chain back up.

RUSS: I bet your neighbors are happy they let a black guy move in. Way to go against the stereotype, waving a gun around naked in your yard. Maybe you should blast some rap music and drink some purple soda.

TOMMY: YOU WENT TOO FAR, RUSS!

STEVE: Oh lord, what did he do now?

TOMMY: He had sex with my wife!

RUSS: I got all up in Tommy too.

STEVE: Didn't you have sex with Russ's wife, Tom?

TOMMY: Stay out of this, Steve!

STEVE: You guys texted me, dick.

RUSS: Exactly! You had sex with my wife!

TOMMY: Yeah, but she WANTED IT! Kelly didn't want it!

RUSS: That's not what she said last night!

STEVE: Kinda splitting hairs here, aren't we Tom?

RUSS: You wanted it too, Tiberius.

STEVE: You're gay now, Tom?

TOMMY: No! I'm not gay!

RUSS: You were last night.

STEVE: That makes you gay too, Russ.

RUSS: Shut the fuck up, Steve! It was revenge!

STEVE: It was gay revenge.

RUSS: Shut the fuck up, Steve! Stop texting!

STEVE: Dude, YOU texted ME. You obviously just hopped back on a previous text chain instead of messaging Tommy directly!

DAVE: Uou had sex wiht Tomy, Russ?

RUSS: Oh Jesus. Why the fuck are you texting, Dave?

TOMMY: I'm going to kill you, you hairy little bastard!

DAVE: Do I nede to dog anuther hole?

DAVE: Dg.

DAVE: Dig. Shit.

DAVE: Dog. Haha. That's funy.

RUSS: We're even now, Tom!

STEVE: Except for the gay part.

TOMMY: How do you sleep at night, Russ?

RUSS: On a really soft pillow, you black bastard!

DAVE: Whut kind of pllow you use? I nede a new one.

STEVE: Great convo, guys. Thanks for including me. I'm going to go huff some paint and try to forget this.

DAVE: I huff gas.

STEVE: Thanks, Dave. You're always an intellectual power-house. See you guys at the game tomorrow.

Dwayne didn't respond to the text thread this time. He simply sat back and watched. It pained him to see how out of control Russ and

Tommy had become. Having sex with each other's wives was far out-side the code. Their behavior was a bitter disappointment.

After showering up with Estelle and having a heaping helping of morning nookie, Dwayne made breakfast for the family and took Alex to school. He drove to his office and parked beside his Audi.

Dwayne's fingers gripped his steering wheel tightly. He suddenly felt the urge to skip work, get high, and drive fast. He kept telling him-self that regardless of the mounting pressure, *he* had to remain a Jedi.

He hopped out of his truck and walked to the back, grabbing his baseball gear out of the bed of his truck and throwing it in the trunk of the Audi. He then hopped into the Audi and hauled ass home.

The Audi squealed to a stop in front of Dwayne's house. Dwayne went inside and put the Batman costume on again, and then rolled a behemoth joint. He hopped back in the Audi, sparked up the joint, and turned up Metallica's cover of the Queen song "Stone Cold Crazy."

Dwayne pulled onto Interstate 30, headed east, and put the pedal to the floor.

57

The Audi reached 150 MPH with ease. Dwayne loved the intensity and adrenaline of driving at breakneck speeds in traffic. It often involved utilization of the road's shoulder, which could prove tricky if debris had gathered there. He cracked the sunroof and blew pot smoke out of the opening. He was weaving wildly in and out of traffic like a maniacal professional.

After a few short miles, Dwayne blew right through a speed trap that had been set up on an overpass. He was clocked by police at 161 MPH. Naturally, they decided to try to pull him over. It started with one motorcycle cop and one cop in a sedan. Once they realized there was a possibility that Dwayne wasn't pulling over anytime soon, the number of police joining the chase began to increase.

It wasn't that Dwayne didn't realize there was a growing party of law enforcement personnel pursuing his beautiful black luxury vehicle on that fine morning; he just didn't care. Since when were badass grandmaster caped crusader Jedi-ninja motherfuckers held to the same rules as the common folk?

No less than a dozen cruisers were on his tail as he neared the edge of Fort Worth and entered Arlington. The Arlington Police Department was already well aware of Dwayne's impending journey through their city and had ten officers join in the chase as soon as he crossed into their territory. Twenty-three police vehicles were behind Dwayne when he passed the Dallas Cowboys Stadium.

"Bring Aikman back, Jerry!" Dwayne yelled out of his window as he went screaming past the large sports dome, home of his favorite NFL team.

Dwayne messed with his MP3 player until he got to Pink Floyd: *The Wall*.

He sung loudly at the top of his lungs about all of humanity merely being bricks in the wall.

Several times, whenever Dwayne's speed dipped to 120 MPH, the police would pull up beside him and instruct Dwayne to pull over. He would simply take a hit from his joint and wave. The police didn't know how to proceed. They'd never pursued a pot-smoking Batman at racetrack speeds before. No precedent had been set.

By the time Dwayne made it to Dallas, there were thirty-one cop cars and eleven motorcycles hot on his tail. In his peripheral vision, he saw that three helicopters monitored the chase from above. Never having been a big fan of the city of Dallas, Dwayne decided to head back to Fort Worth.

Dwayne, thirty-one police cars, and eleven police motorcycles all put on their right-hand blinkers and took the next exit. A dozen Dallas Police Department cruisers had already been en route to join the chase and were soon intermingled among the other police vehicles, all traveling at over 130 MPH.

On the other end of the Dallas–Fort Worth metroplex, Estelle was returning home from her morning yoga class. She had been having a nice relaxing morning of exercise and green tea.

Estelle slipped out of her sweaty clothes and out of habit flipped on the bedroom television. A breaking news flash came across the screen. A man dressed as Batman was leading a high-speed police chase from Fort Worth to Dallas and was now heading back to Fort Worth again. Estelle immediately jumped over and turned up the volume.

"We're in the KJTX traffic chopper here, Gretchen, following a Batman impersonator who appears to be yelling angrily out the window at the Dallas Cowboys Stadium. Like many of us, he appears to have some pretty disparaging words about the owner, Jerry Jones."

"Thanks, Todd. Now, you said he was a Batman impersonator. In order for someone to be an impersonator, doesn't the person who they are impersonating actually have to be real? Are you implying that Batman is actually real? Is that the story here?"

"Jesus, Gretchen, are you being serious?"

"Just trying to be grammatically correct here, Todd."

"Oh, I see, you're like one of those freakin' grammar Nazis on the Internet, huh? Well, let me tell you what you can—"

Estelle hit the television's mute button. She nervously dialed Dwayne on her cell phone. He answered after one ring.

"Hello, sugarbuns! What's shakin'?" Dwayne said. "Hey, I've been thinking about the baby . . . If it's a boy, can we call him Skywalker? How cool would that be?!" Dwayne was speaking fast. The adrenaline was coursing through his veins.

"Honeyballs, how fast are you driving right now?" Estelle asked, hoping against hope that somehow it wasn't Dwayne on the television.

"One hundred fifty-eight, cupcake titties, why?"

Estelle wanted to be more upset than she was, but she couldn't. "Just making sure that it's you I'm watching on TV, pulling an OJ."

Dwayne laughed, hit his joint, and turned the stereo down so that he could hear Estelle better. "That's awesome, babe. Great reference. So you can see me right now?"

"Yes."

"Sweet! Keep watching!"

Estelle watched as Dwayne leaned out of the driver's window of the Audi, pointed toward the closest news helicopter, and waved.

"You see that, baby? I'm waving at you!"

"I see, honey. I'm waving at the television right now." A single tear of joy trickled down Estelle's face. She loved him *so* much.

"Awww, you're so cute," Dwayne said.

"Dwayne, you have like fifty cop cars behind you. Don't you think you should slow down and maybe consider pulling over? You have a baby on the way! I don't want anything to happen to you!"

"I know, boogerbottom. I just wanted to go for a drive and listen to some music. It's not like I wanted all those cops to follow me."

"That's okay, butterweenie, I understand. Pull over now, before something happens, okay?"

"Okay, babynipples, I will. I love you."

"I love you too."

Estelle watched the television intently. After a few seconds, the Audi began to slow down, and several police cruisers pulled in front of it. He was instructed via megaphone to shut off his engine and step outside his vehicle. As the news helicopters circled the scene, Fort Worth's skyline could be seen in the background.

Estelle's phone rang again. It was Dwayne.

"Hey, cookienookie, I was just thinking. Can you go ahead and head down to the police station? I may need you to bail me out."

"I'm leaving now, babe."

Millions of television viewers watched the scene unfold on what had quickly become a national news story. There wasn't anyone in the entire country who didn't think Dwayne was at least a *little* bit of a badass as he stepped out from his $120,000 luxury car in full Batman regalia.

Dozens of officers approached Dwayne as he stood with his hands above the back of his Batman mask.

As the police closed in on him, Dwayne's phone quacked.

"Hang on, guys," Dwayne said to the cops. "I just got a text."

He methodically pulled his phone from his pocket with two fingers, making sure the police didn't think he was reaching for a gun. He looked at his phone. It was the text chain again.

RUSS: Are you guys watching the news? Some fucking guy dressed like Batman just led the cops on a chase from Fort Worth to Dallas and back!

STEVE: No shit! I'm watching it now! This is awesome!

DWAYNE: Can't text right now. Getting arrested.

TOMMY: Are you kidding me? Are you watching this? The guy is texting while the cops are yelling at him!

DAVE: Tv doesn't werk.

RUSS: This guy has balls! We've gotta meet this guy!

"Drop the phone!" one of the cops yelled at Dwayne. "Now!" Dwayne's phone quacked again.

"Hang on, sir," Dwayne said. "I apologize. I know it's rude to respond right now, but it's rude not to respond also. I'm in a real bind here. Just gimme a second."

STEVE: Oh man, this guy is so screwed!

RUSS: Look! He's reading his texts again! This guy is my hero!

TOMMY: Did you see him yelling at Cowboys Stadium? Oh man, that was priceless! I wonder what he said!

DWAYNE: I said Jerry needs to step back and actually let someone coach, and he needs to invest in a badass defensive coordinator and a young backup quarterback. Now, seriously, I can't text right now. It's pissing the bacon off.

STEVE: Wait . . . Dwayne?

RUSS: Whoa.

TOMMY: Holy shit.

DAVE: Stop texting. Tryin to poo.

Dwayne handed his phone to one of the cops. "Thanks," he said, offering a thumbs-up. "You guys were great today."

Dwayne was promptly tackled, Tasered, and handcuffed.

58.

Detective Loffland greeted Dwayne in one of the interrogation rooms a couple of hours after he was stuffed into the back of a police car. Dwayne was still handcuffed and wearing everything but the mask and gloves from his Batman costume. He sat at a small metal table, rubbing the black ink on his hands—hands that had just been fingerprinted.

The detective took the seat across from Dwayne. The overhead light was reflecting brightly off Loffland's bald head. Dwayne pretended to be blinded by it momentarily in an attempt to elicit a laugh. It didn't work.

"Hello, Dwayne," Detective Loffland said without a hint of a smile.

"Hello, Detective," Dwayne replied.

"Dwayne, do you understand why you're here right now?"

"Was it for criticizing Jerry Jones?" Dwayne queried sarcastically. "Because I was just saying what everyone else is thinking!"

Detective Loffland stared at Dwayne. He didn't look amused. Dwayne was beginning to wonder if his rapport with the detective was dwindling.

"Dwayne, you just had forty-three police cars and eleven police motorcycles chasing you from city to city. You were reaching speeds in excess of one hundred and sixty MPH while smoking dope and wearing a superhero costume."

The detective paused, waiting for Dwayne to defend himself. He didn't.

"Here's the thing, Dwayne. I like you, okay? You seem like a good dude. But you embarrassed the city today, and you put the lives of my men at risk. Don't you have anything to say for yourself?"

Dwayne took his time before answering. He knew he had to do this right. He figured there was a distinct possibility that his midmorning drive might have drawn too much unnecessary attention to himself, and he worried that the detective might be onto him.

"I apologize for putting the officers' lives in danger," Dwayne began.

"I also apologize if I made the city look bad. That wasn't my intention. I've just been dealing with a lot of assholes lately, sir. I wanted to blow off some steam. So, I hopped on the highway, hit the gas pedal hard, and sparked up a joint."

"In a Batman costume."

"Yes."

"Does that strike you as . . . odd, Dwayne?"

"No, sir. I love Batman."

"Well, I love Spider-Man, but you don't see me throwing on goddamn red and blue tights and jumping rooftop to rooftop. Sweet Jesus, Dwayne."

"I understand, sir. Probably a bad call."

"Yeah. Probably."

The detective leaned back in his chair and exhaled. He placed his hands on his forehead, and slid them all the way over the top of his head. Then he did something Dwayne didn't expect.

Detective Loffland giggled.

He immediately tried to conceal it and act tough again, but the giggles kept coming back. It was a really high-pitched, funny giggle too. It was like an Anderson Cooper giggle. When he'd try to trap it in his mouth, it would find its way out his nose.

Detective Loffland finally gave in to it. His face turned bright red. He doubled over and just kept giggling.

And it was contagious, too. Soon Dwayne began to giggle. Two more officers came in to find out what was going on, and they started giggling. Before long, there were ten cops, one detective, and Batman, all in a tiny interrogation room laughing their ever-loving asses off.

"I told you he's a good sumbitch, boys!" Detective Loffland said to the others. "Oh, man . . . This is one for the record books!"

One of the cops unhooked Dwayne's handcuffs. Another handed him a cup of coffee and a breakfast muffin.

Estelle walked in a few moments later, quietly watching Dwayne and the officers joke about the police chase. She couldn't believe it.

Dwayne looked over at Estelle and winked.

"He's such a *badass*!" she said to herself.

"Oh, brother," one of the officers exclaimed. "You know Jerry Jones is gonna be catching some shit about you for a while!"

"Yeah, man!" another shouted out. "Thank you for saying it!"

"Even Batman hates Jerry!" a third officer yelled.

After a round of backslapping, Detective Loffland held up a hand to calm the room.

"Okay, okay, okay," he said. "Now Dwayne, I'm gonna have to write you a couple of tickets. I can let the weed thing slide, and I'll throw out what I can, but this still ain't gonna be cheap, buddy."

"I understand," Dwayne replied. "You guys have been very cool. It's refreshing to meet good people. I meet way too many assholes."

"Well, it was a nice diversion from trying to find some crazy band of serial killers," the detective said, holding Dwayne's gaze. "And for that, we thank you. So why don't you and your lovely wife go sign the release papers, and the other officers and I will get back to the business of catching killers."

"Yes, sir," Dwayne said, standing up. He gave yet another firm handshake to the detective. He then shook hands with the other officers. He felt like a celebrity.

Several officers made cracks when Dwayne walked out the door.

"Keep it real, Batman!"

"Watch out for the Joker!"

"Be watching the sky for the Bat-Signal! We may need you!"

Dwayne and Estelle headed home after spending another hour filling out legal paperwork. Dwayne burst out in giggle fits several times on his drive home. The two of them had barely made it through their front door before Estelle slammed Dwayne against the entryway wall.

"I don't think I've ever wanted you more," she said as she ripped her top off.

Estelle handed Dwayne his mask and instructed him to put it on. She then began to unhook his bright yellow official Batman utility belt and pull his rubber pants down.

"Give it to me, Batman," she growled. "Give it to me now."

59

The baseball game the following evening went exactly as Dwayne expected, with the Tigers easily clutching a victory. The outcome of the game, however, was the only thing that had gone according to plan.

The entire country had become fascinated with Dwayne. Media vans and reporters camped out in his front yard, following his every move. Their local little league baseball game inadvertently became a nationally televised event. There were easily a thousand people in attendance. Everyone wanted to know who this rebellious outlaw Batman guy was.

Overnight, Dwayne had captured the hearts and minds of Americans. He was a regular dad who loved coaching baseball, and he'd had enough of the bullshit. He'd decided to take a stand against it. His attitude resonated with the average working-class Joe. Several fans wore Batman masks to show their support.

After the game, the crowd roared for the Tigers as they shook their opponents' hands. Dwayne somehow managed to keep his team focused for the postgame speech, which wasn't easy. Camera flashes illuminated the ballpark from all angles. Dwayne needed to pump his boys up for the next game and make sure their eyes remained on the prize.

"No one took you seriously, men," Dwayne addressed the team. "No one took you seriously as athletes. No one took you seriously as baseball players. No one took you seriously as soldiers. No one took you seriously as fighters. And I know how you feel."

Dwayne paced before them. He stole glances at each boy, as was his custom. He wanted every player engaged in what was being said.

"No one took me seriously either. No one took me seriously about doing what was right if we wanted this team to win. No one took me seriously when I said this team was fierce, and had the talent to win it all. No one took me seriously. No one. But I want to ask you . . ."

Dwayne turned and pointed to the scoreboard, displaying a score of 17–2. Cameras flashed wildly from beyond the fences.

"Do you think they take us seriously now?"

"YES, SIR!" they all screamed in unison, throwing their arms in the air.

"Do they know you're athletes now?"

"YES, SIR!"

"Do they know you're fighters now?"

"YES, SIR!"

"Do they know you're soldiers now?"

"YES, SIR!"

"You're goddamn right they do," he said proudly. "It was a mistake to underestimate us, men. It was a huge mistake. And it was a mistake the Mariners won't make again. They're going to come out swinging on Saturday, men. And have no doubt about one thing: This will be the toughest game you've ever played. They'll play ugly. They'll play dirty. They'll play hard. But it won't matter, because we're going to do what the Tigers do . . . *and what is it that the Tigers do?*"

"TIGERS KILL!"

"*What do they do?*"

"TIGERS KILL!"

"*One more time, everybody in, on three.*"

"One, two, three . . . TIGERS KILL!!!"

The players walked toward the dugout and grabbed their bags. The media flooded the field and surrounded the boys and their parents, especially Coach Dwayne and his assistants. All of the parents who had once been critical of Dwayne now gave high praise, as if they'd supported his coaching style all along. Everyone was now Dwayne's best friend.

Dwayne managed to pay absolutely zero attention to the reporters' endless barrage of questions. All he could think of was the championship. Reporters trailed Dwayne and his family on all sides to the parking lot. Dwayne made sure to hold Estelle's hand and kept his other arm around Alex. He tucked the two of them into Estelle's car and kissed Estelle through her window.

"I'll be home shortly, babe," he said with a wink. "My assistant coaches and I need to strategize."

Dwayne scanned the crowd for his crew as Estelle and Alex drove off. Russ, Tommy, and Steve all began to make their way toward him. He continued to ignore the press as a litany of queries was hurled his way.

The four coaches all high-fived each other as they came together at the rear of Dwayne's Audi. He opened the trunk and the guys all reached into a cooler, pulling out ice-cold cans of beer and popping them open. Russ dug around in his pocket for a moment, then whipped out a massive joint and proceeded to light it.

A reporter interrupted. "Excuse me, sir," he queried Russ. "I'm Ed Zarecky, with the KFWI News Team. Can I get your name?"

Russ ignored the interruption and took a long pull from the joint, sucking until his face turned red and his eyes crossed.

"That's Russ Paisley," Tommy responded to the reporter with a big smile. "He's a money manager, financial advisor, and godless rapist heathen. He's also a deacon at the Westside Church of Jesus. Can I get an amen?"

The reporter's eyes went wide at the revelation. He looked around at his fellow journalists to see if they'd gotten the scoop as well.

Russ didn't necessarily appreciate Tommy totally outing him, but Russ also figured it was an understandable form of revenge, given the previous evening's roofies and unauthorized sex. He coughed out two lungs full of smoke and passed the joint to Tommy.

Tommy didn't hesitate at all. He reflexively grabbed the joint and proceeded to take a monster hit, chuckling to himself as Russ slammed his beer.

"And that's Dr. Tommy Johnson," Russ wheezed before crushing his beer can on his forehead. "He's probably the top plastic surgeon in all of North Texas. He belongs to the Westside Church of Jesus, too. Oh, and he's also possibly both an atheist and a Democrat."

The reporter cocked his head, attempting to grasp the situation. He wanted to get the scoop on Dwayne, as did all of the other reporters circled around them, but they were quickly finding out that all four baseball dads were fascinating character studies. And Dwayne's silence made it impossible *not* to listen to the other guys.

"Okay, so—hang on just a minute," the reporter interjected. "You guys are prominent members of the Fort Worth business scene, right? And you're active members of your church, and you're baseball coaches. Yet here you are slamming beers and smoking . . . ummm, what exactly is that you're smoking?"

"Well, Ed, what we've got here is a hybrid mix of Hindu Kush and Purple Haze," Russ said proudly. "It's got a deep, floral aroma with hints of mocha. And it will jump up and kick you in the sack if you're not careful."

Russ smiled and offered a thumbs-up to the camera, then reached his arm into the cooler and fished out another beer.

"But how do you explain your actions to your clients? How do you explain yourselves to your congregation?" Zarecky probed.

"We don't explain shit, Ed," Russ replied. "We just fucking rock, bro." He slammed his second beer and again crushed the can on his forehead before letting out a deep, bellowing belch.

Steve couldn't believe the speed at which their lives continued to spiral out of control. At a time when it would be wise to hide for being accessories to mass murder, here they were . . . slamming beers and smoking weed in front of the national media.

Tommy passed the joint to Steve. Steve scowled at him and grabbed the joint out of irritation. He begrudgingly took a long pull from it before passing it to Dwayne.

The journalists were perplexed. They elbowed each other, pushing and shoving, fighting for the best camera angle, but at the same time, they were unable to think of questions. They were just letting it all play out in front of them.

"So, the championship baseball game is in a couple of days," Ed Zarecky attempted to recap the situation, hoping this would lead to some comprehensible answers. "The whole country is transfixed by your baseball team. You guys suffered some serious blows late in the regular season, with the untimely abduction and death of your original coaching staff. You four stepped up and assumed the responsibility. Your team fought back from last place. And here you are in the big game. You're like that story of the little train making its way up the hill, never giving up."

"We're like a train all right, Ed," Russ opined, leaning back against the Audi in a faux-philosophical pose. "We're like a freight train . . . a freight train packed full of fuck you, and we're about to pull into the station and deliver our payload."

Steve glared at Dwayne. Why wouldn't he step in and stop the insanity? Steve knew it was a terrible idea for Russ to be the self-appointed national media spokesman for the baseball dads. But Dwayne simply stood back and watched.

"From what I understand, there's a good little friendly rivalry between your team and the team you'll be playing," Summer Pruett, one of the few female reporters, belted out. "And the coach of the other team is the pastor at your church. Do you have anything you'd like to say to the other team?"

"Yeah, as a matter of fact, I do," Russ said. "I'd like to tell the other team that while they're away from their homes, I'm gonna be breaking into their bedrooms and farting on both sides of their pillows. And not just on them, but *in* them. Deep, deep inside them, so that every time they drop their heads onto them, a big whiff of my ass is gonna come whooshing out."

"Do you, ummm . . ." the reporter stammered, attempting to digest the answer. "Do you think that will affect your standing in the church?"

"Nope."

"Okay, then." The reporter sheepishly stepped back into the crowd. She had no further questions.

"Mr. Devero," a reporter beckoned from the masses. "You've been pretty silent since your arrest in the Batman costume. Yet somehow, in your silence, the whole country has rallied around you. Are you a rebel? Are you an outlaw? Everyone in America is dying to know."

Dwayne took in the media spectacle surrounding him. He cracked open the top of his beer and sipped, then stepped forward to speak. The camera flashes went crazy.

"Am I a rebel? Am I an outlaw?" Dwayne began. "I've never looked at myself that way. I'm a father. I'm a husband. I'm a baseball coach."

He looked out to the baseball field and admired it. The lights were still on. It looked so green and perfect.

"I'm just a guy who's trying to do it right, you know?" he continued. "There are so many people out there doing it wrong . . . and we just get used to it . . . and we sit back and take it. But we don't have to. That's the biggest lie we've all been told . . . that we have to take it."

Dwayne paused, reflecting on the day's game. He loved that his boys had stepped up and delivered yet again. "We don't have to let assholes push us around. Not in our personal lives, not in business, and certainly not in fucking baseball."

Dwayne shut the trunk of his car, walked over to driver's side, and climbed in. The crowd of reporters moved with him.

"Is there anything you'd like to say to Pastor Jim and the Mariners team, Dwayne?" a voice called out with the hope of one last comment.

Dwayne smiled, extended his arm through the Audi window, and held out a big middle finger. Cheers erupted from the media. Dwayne revved up his engine, dropped it into drive, and sped off into the night.

60.

Saturday could not have come soon enough. The day of the big game had arrived.

Dwayne knew that this would be no ordinary day. No, in fact, this was the kind of day he would use to measure all future life events. There was nothing inside him that would allow any part of this day to be ordinary. He had to start it strong in order to finish it strong.

Yesterday, he had labored, creating varying lineups and field positions in the most strategic manner imaginable. He'd studied each opposing batter and made notes of which pitches to throw at them. Dwayne couldn't possibly have been more prepared.

Now, he needed to relax. He needed to get out in the early morning air and go for a run to get his mind right. But this couldn't be just any run. This run had to be different. It had to be the best run ever.

Dwayne crept into his bedroom. There, on the dresser, he saw it laid out in all its glory. He sat on the edge of his bed and slowly climbed into his Batman costume. Yet instead of wearing his official Batman boots, he slipped on his favorite gray New Balance running shoes.

After pulling on his black cape and fastening his yellow utility belt, Dwayne made his way to the front door, swinging it open quickly for dramatic effect. The hundreds of media personnel camped out in his front yard sprang to life. Cameras flashed from every direction. Cheers and applause crashed through the neighborhood as Batman jogged down the sidewalk and out into the street.

There must have been five hundred journalists and camera operators jogging alongside Dwayne. As they passed down the street, house lights came on, doors opened, and husbands and children came rushing out to join the jogging crowd.

Dwayne tried in vain to think of a building with lots of stairs that he could run up in order to make the scene even more Rocky-esque, but he couldn't come up with one. So, he just ran. He ran past the

Westside Church of Jesus, which elicited a few jeers. He led the grow-ing parade down the old redbrick section of Camp Bowie Boulevard and over to the River Oaks Country Club. The caddies and golf cart attendants preparing for the day dropped what they were doing and followed the masses down the first three fairways.

Dwayne finally led them across a busy intersection on White Settle-ment Road, and headed toward the ballpark. Traffic was at a standstill as thousands of people came running by out of nowhere, following the charismatic grandmaster ninja in a Batman costume. Drivers every-where were abandoning their vehicles and joining in on what was fast becoming the most exciting run in American history.

Dwayne didn't dare lead the runners onto the baseball field. He didn't want to trample what he considered sacred ground. Instead, he retrieved an American flag resting in a flagpole holder at the entrance gate and waved it wildly above his head. The crowd went nuts. They loved him.

Media helicopters circled overhead, capturing the spectacle for the entire nation. Dwayne led his devoted followers on three laps around the ballpark before returning the flag to its holder. He then headed back toward his home.

With hands outstretched over his head, pumping his fists, a now exhausted Dwayne spoke to the crowd from his front yard.

"What do Tigers do?" he shouted out.

"TIGERS KILL!" they screamed their reply.

"I said . . . *What do Tigers do?*" he yelled again.

"TIGERS KILL!" they roared back.

"That's right! *Now let's go play some baseball!*"

The noise from Dwayne's fans was deafening as he disappeared behind his door. He walked back into his bedroom, sweating and ready for a shower. Estelle was rustling a bit, just waking up, and rubbing her eyes.

"Hey, sugarbottom, where did you go?" a sleepy Estelle whispered to Dwayne as he peeled of his costume.

"Oh, I went for a little run. Nothing big. You wanna hop in the shower with me?"

"You know I do."

"Batman needs a little ass this morning."

"Ooooh, baby, Catwoman will gladly give it to him."

"I love you."

"I love you too."

61.

Dwayne, Alex, and Estelle pulled into Jenny Field an hour before game time in the now-famous black Audi. Dave the umpire had reserved four parking spaces near the entrance for the baseball dads and one additional space for Uzi, who had begged the guys to let him attend.

No spaces had been reserved for Pastor Jim. Dwayne saw the angry pastor making his way through the media spectacle with his son, Noah. Pastor Jim had not been a fan of the way the media had painted him. Both his hometown and his country had turned against him. They cheered for a man whom Pastor Jim deemed nothing short of psychotic.

Every costume shop in the country had sold out of Batman masks. One glance at the fans attending the Jenny Field Little League Baseball Championship game left little doubt as to why. Every other person Dwayne saw was wearing one. Many were homemade, and more than a few were created from cardboard beer cases.

Crowds of this size had typically been seen only at major sporting events such as the World Series or the Super Bowl. Tailgaters were strewn about everywhere. Grills were blazing. Kegs were flowing. Breasts painted with tiger stripes were on display.

Dwayne wanted to make sure that on this day, more than any other, he and his fellow coaches looked official. He was thrilled when Tommy surprised the baseball dads with new orange-and-black tiger-striped shirts, which they tucked into their tiny gray coaching shorts. They pulled their matching tube socks up to their knees, positioned their visors, placed their aviator sunglasses atop their noses, and hung whistles from their necks. Dwayne held his clipboard close, satisfied.

Detective Loffland and five other officers greeted Dwayne and his crew as they walked through the entrance. Steve's, Tommy's, and Russ's buttholes all puckered up as the cops surrounded them.

"What's up, Big D?" the detective said with a smile, raising his hand up for a high five.

Dwayne slapped his hand, and then the hands of the other officers who had each raised theirs.

"I thought you guys might like a little protection to keep these damn reporters from getting in your face," Detective Loffland offered. "And I was hoping you might hook a buddy up with some primo seats."

"Shit, Detective," Dwayne grinned. "You guys can chill in the dugout with the boys if you want! You can't get better seats than that!"

"Hell, yeah!" the other cops exclaimed.

Russ and Tommy introduced themselves. Dwayne's magnetic personality never ceased to amaze them. Steve could only manage an uneasy smile.

"You got any weed, bro?" one of the cops asked Russ.

"Yup," Russ replied.

"Spark that shit up, man. Let's get our swerve on!"

Russ and Tommy escorted a few of the police behind the batting cages to smoke a few joints and drink a few beers while Detective Loffland helped Dwayne and Steve warm up the batters. Detective Loffland shared a flask filled with perfectly aged Scotch among the three of them. By the time the team finished warming up, they had all achieved full inebriation.

And then it was game time. Dave the umpire walked out onto the field with a megaphone. He called upon the head coaches to meet him at home plate for the coin toss. The crowd of thousands cheered Dwayne and booed Pastor Jim as they entered from opposing sides of the field and made their way to Dave.

"Gentlemen," Dave grumbled. "You know the rules. We're going six innings. Seventy-five pitch maximum per player and loose bases. Dwayne, you've got the honors. Call it in the air."

Dave flipped the coin up above the men's ball caps.

"Heads," Dwayne said.

The coin came down and landed with tails facing up.

"Sorry, D," Dave the umpire uttered.

Pastor Jim offered an asshole's smile at the two of them. "We'll take 'home,' you pricks," he said.

Dwayne extended his hand to shake. Pastor Jim glanced down at Dwayne's hand and grinned, then turned and walked back to his dugout.

The fans booed and shouted at the pastor for the snub.

"Oh, shit, Dwayne," Dave the umpire said, pulling down his umpire mask. "It's *on*, bro."

62.

The Mariners warmed up on the field, looking angry and ready. Pastor Jim barked orders at his team while hitting balls to them from beside home plate. Noah was on the pitcher's mound, throwing hard and fast. He glared over at the Tigers' bench after every pitch, wanting to make sure that the Tigers knew what he was capable of.

But the Tigers weren't watching . . . and that pissed Noah off. Dwayne wouldn't allow the Mariners the satisfaction. He wouldn't allow his boys to be intimidated and made sure that all eyes were on him as he rallied them around their cause.

"Tigers," he spoke, "we have but one single mission today. That mission is the complete and total devastation of the Mariners baseball organization."

Cameras flashed around the Tigers' dugout as Dwayne's voice permeated the souls of all who heard him. He had his team, his assistant coaches, the police, the parents, and the hundreds that surrounded them completely mesmerized.

"Now, here's the thing, soldiers," he continued. "Lots of times in these situations, you'll hear coaches say fluffy little things like, 'no matter what happens today, you're all winners.' But I'm here to tell you . . . that's total bullshit. I'll be pissed off if we lose today. You should be too. We came here to win, and I expect nothing less of you."

The kids nodded. The cops nodded. Everyone nodded. It just made sense.

"You should count on a war out here today, men. If they draw blood, we will draw tears of pain and loss. If they throw a punch, we will sever a limb, and allow them to make do with a bloody stump. We must do nothing short of crushing the skulls that create the thoughts that they can win, so that bone fragments pierce their brains, rendering them incapable of ever having such deeply absurd thoughts again. I want you angry at their ridiculous assumption that they have enough talent to share a field with you. I want you to make a raw meal of their ability to ever experience pleasure again. I want you to destroy them."

A fire burned in Dwayne's eyes as he delivered his speech, and the fury he spouted was contagious. The team was rabid and snarling. They were ready to annihilate the Mariners. Dwayne had the boys right where he wanted them.

Dwayne paced. He let the words he had just spoken hang in the air for a few minutes so that the boys could fully digest them. When the time was right, he drew them back in for the finish.

"Now, one more time for the record books, troops," Dwayne screamed. "Pull this one from deep down. Let the whole world hear you. *WHAT DO TIGERS DO?*"

Their young voices rose up at once, "TIGERS KILL!!!"

The world did hear them, or at least those in the stands did, and the intoxicating cheer invited thousands of fans to echo the boys. "TIGERS KILL!!! TIGERS KILL!!! TIGERS KILL!!!"

Every Mariner on the field jolted, stopped what they were doing, and looked over at the Tigers. A wave of fear swept over Pastor Jim as the crowd ignited into a wildfire of screaming cheers.

Behind the backstop, a large banner was unraveled that read, "FEAR THE BAT." Another banner opened up next to it, with a ten-foot-tall illustration of Batman wielding a baseball bat. News cameramen dashed out onto the field to get a shot of the banners and were swiftly yelled back off the field by Pastor Jim.

Dave the umpire squirted a splash of whiskey through his mask, then turned to Dwayne and nodded. It was time. "PLAY BALL!" he announced loudly.

The police sharing the Tigers' dugout patted the coaches on the back as they broke into their third case of beer. Russ grinned back over his shoulder at them as he walked out. He had what most would consider to be a difficult assignment. He was the first-base coach. He would be standing just feet away from Pastor Jim's dugout.

Russ took a quick bump of cocaine and strutted across the field, lighting a cigarette on the way. With the police on his side, he felt invincible. He took his place beside the first baseman.

Dwayne stepped out next to take his spot beside third base. The crowd erupted, blowing air horns, cheering, and whistling. Several women flashed their breasts as they chanted his name. "Dwayne! Dwayne! Dwayne!"

Jackson Paisley and TJ Johnson emerged from the dugout, swinging their bats. After a few swings, Jackson approached the plate.

"Hey, Noah," Russ called out from first base. "You hit my kid with a pitch and I'll gut you with a rusty knife, you satanic little bastard!"

Noah didn't acknowledge Russ. He refused to let him get inside his head.

Pastor Jim couldn't believe what he'd just heard. "I'll accept that to be your resignation as deacon, you heartless, drug-addled demon, and I expect you to drop off your deacon's jacket immediately," Pastor Jim shouted to Russ.

Russ extended a middle finger behind himself in the general direction of Pastor Jim, without ever turning to acknowledge him.

Russ looked down beside him at the kid playing first and noticed that the kid had a bad set of buckteeth. "Holy shit, son, have you ever thought about seeing an orthodontist?"

The boy frowned, trying to ignore him.

"I bet you can mow through some serious fucking corn on the cob with those goddamn gopher choppers, Bucky. Jesus, you may be the ugliest kid I've ever seen."

The boy tried to hold up against Russ, but he couldn't. His lip quivered. He was about to cry.

"By the way, that's my boy Jackson at the plate," Russ continued. "If you try to get him out after he smashes the ball in a minute, I'll be using those fucked up teeth on your decapitated head to open my beers tonight."

The kid took a few steps away from Russ, watching him out of the corner of his eye. Noah went into his windup. He delivered a screaming pitch right down the pipeline before Jackson was ready. It was a cheap play to send a pitch that quickly after someone entered the batter's box, but it was technically fair.

"STRIKE!" Dave the umpire called out.

Russ glared at Pastor Jim. Pastor Jim returned a smug grin. The crowd booed.

Noah watched the catcher for his pitch sign. He nodded when he received it, and went into his windup again. It was an inside changeup, easily half the speed of the first pitch.

Jackson waited on it, made a split-second adjustment, and drilled the ball down the first baseline. The ball caught a bad hop at the last second, hitting the first baseman directly in the eye. He dropped to his knees, clutching his face, with the ball lying just a few feet away on the ground. Jackson came barreling by, reaching his hand out to high-five his dad as he turned and headed to second. Noah ran and grabbed the ball, then whipped it over to third to hold Jackson to a double.

Noah was pissed, and he screamed down at the injured first baseman until he rose to his feet.

Russ leaned over to the kid. "Wow, kid, that sucks," he said. "A little bit lower and you could've gotten new teeth. That would've been awesome for you. But now you have a big swollen eye *and* really fucked up teeth. You might as well cut your pecker off. You're never getting laid."

The kid wiped the tears from his face and dropped into the ready position. His eye was swelling quickly. He focused as much as he could, watching TJ step into the box.

Dwayne made eye contact with Jackson. He touched his hat and then his earlobe. It was the "steal" signal. Jackson stepped out and began to gather a healthy lead off the base.

Noah watched Jackson closely. He didn't think he'd go for it, so he went to work on the batter. As soon as the fastball was released from his hand, TJ dropped down and tapped a perfect bunt. Jackson slid into third, avoiding the tag, and TJ easily crossed first base.

Noah paced. He needed some outs. He saw that Jonathan was

coming up to bat. Noah knew he had it this time. Before he could put his strategy together, TJ took off for second base. It was bait he wouldn't take. He knew that if he tried to get TJ out at second, Jackson would take off for home and score. He just grunted and took it.

Jonathan couldn't help but crack a smile. He knew what was about to happen. He just hoped they could pull it off.

Noah went into his windup. He always led with the fastball. Jonathan knew this. He stepped in front of it, dropped down, and laid out another perfect bunt. Jackson and TJ both pretended they were going to run just long enough for Jonathan to make it to first.

Nobody bunted twice in a row. It worked exactly the way Dwayne had hoped. The crowd went nuts as Alex walked out of the dugout with his dream scenario . . . loaded bases, no outs. A large banner that read "BATKID" unrolled behind the backstop.

Noah put his hands on his hips and pretended to size up Alex as he made his way to the batter's box. Noah glared at him and spat. Alex gave him a big smile as he assumed the position and raised his bat.

Noah sent Alex a fastball, painting the outside corner of the plate. Alex didn't budge.

"STRIKE!"

Noah spat again and grinned.

"What are you grinning at?" Alex called out to him. "Is that all you've got? That sucked!"

Everyone in the stands behind Alex began to laugh at Noah. They loved it. These kids were serious.

Noah wound up and sent an even faster fastball to the exact same spot. He strained to throw it as fast as he did. It was a perfect pitch with gruesome speed. Alex simply watched it go by and laughed. Noah frowned.

"I don't understand why everyone's so scared of you, man!" Alex yelled out to him. "Come on, sissy! Put some *pepper* on it for me!"

And so he did. Noah gave it everything he had. He used every muscle in his body to throw the fastest ball he'd ever thrown. Alex sent a thundering, level swing right back at him.

And then that amazing sound echoed throughout the ballpark . . .
TINK!

Noah's arms dropped to his sides and his head tilted upward. His eyes followed the arc of the ball through the atmosphere until it disappeared far beyond the center field wall. Alex took off, jogging through the thick screams from fans, which didn't let up until well after the bases had cleared.

The yelling and whistling from the stands thankfully masked Pastor Jim's voice as he walked out to the mound and castigated Noah. Noah got right back in his dad's face, poking him in the chest as he screamed back. Pastor Jim stormed off the field and into the dugout, kicking over a bucket of practice balls.

Whatever the pastor had said to Noah apparently worked, however. He struck the next three batters out with ease, attempting to get his swagger back. And he knew the game was far from over.

63.

The expression on Alex's face when he took the pitcher's mound left no questions about his confidence. His warm-up pitches commanded respect. He paid no attention to the craziness and commotion occurring all around. He was unaffected by it.

Alex worked his magic on the first two batters, striking them out. He wasn't so lucky with the third. The third batter got a decent read on the pitch and hit a solid double. That wasn't what Alex wanted.

When Noah walked from his dugout to the batter's box, you could have heard a fly fart. There was total silence. Alex and Noah stared each other down the entire way.

"You gonna throw the ball, or just stare at me like a dumbass?" Noah yelled to Alex.

Alex didn't respond. He was waiting for his sign from the catcher, Jackson. Jackson dropped a middle finger down, the universal sign for "fuck this guy, throw it so fast he can't see it." And that's exactly what Alex did.

"STRIKE!"

The crowd went nuts. Alex didn't smile, flinch, or respond. He just caught the ball as Jackson threw it back and waited for his sign again.

He got it. Middle finger down.

"STRIKE TWO!"

Noah kicked at the dirt, and then raised a hand to step out of the batter's box. The people in the stands behind him began to taunt him.

Alex stood ready, checking his shoulder for the steal. He knew they wouldn't dare steal against him or Jackson, but he continued to check just in case. Noah stepped back in, looking ready.

Jackson dropped another middle finger. Alex nodded.

Alex only loved that sound when it came from his bat . . . but this time, it came from Noah's. Noah got ahold of it. The ball cleared the fence behind the right fielder. Noah grinned at Alex all the way around the bases. Alex simply smiled back at him.

The game was 4–2. It stayed 4–2 for the next four innings. No one scored. There were a few singles here and there, but the defense on both sides was outstanding.

Going into the sixth and final inning, both pitchers had reached their maximums. The second strings came in. The backup pitchers were almost as solid as the starters.

The only ones who weren't playing their A game by that point were the Tigers assistant coaching staff and the police officers seated beside them. They had consumed several cases of beer and two ounces of weed. And that didn't include the flask refills that took place under the bench.

Russ walked out of the dugout, pointed to the stands, and ripped his shirt wide open like a superhero. Everyone in the stands went nuts. He slammed the beer he was holding, crushed the can on his forehead, lit a cigarette, and made his way across the field to his first-base coach position. Halfway there, Russ tripped and fell flat on his face, not moving for several seconds after. A large roar erupted from the stands moments later as he jumped to his feet and threw his arms in the air.

The buck-toothed Mariner, who now also had a swollen black eye, was again on first base. "Jesus. All that beer, and you're not a damn bit prettier," Russ told him. "Can't you file those fucking teeth down or something? Do you have any idea how distracting those things are? It looks like you're trying to eat a couple of diving boards or something. Fuck. I feel like I could do a gainer off of your face."

"You know, mister, if you can't say something nice, you're not supposed to say anything at all," the boy said.

"That's a stupid fucking rule, kid. Almost as stupid as your goddamn face. I'll tell you right now, you need to get really good at fighting and really good at masturbating. Your future will be filled with a shitload of both."

Russ turned and looked back at Pastor Jim.

"Hey, Pastor," he called over to him.

"Yes, Russ?"

"Go fuck yourself."

Russ dropped down into a baseball ready stance, and looked across at TJ, who was coming out to bat.

"COME ON, DARKY JUNIOR!" Russ yelled. "KNOCK THE SHIT OUTTA THAT BALL!"

TJ gave Russ an uncomfortable thumbs-up, then cracked a solid double off the first pitch. Then out came Jonathan, who cracked a perfect single that advanced TJ to third base.

A deeply profound look of concern swept over everyone in a Mariners jersey when Alex walked out of the dugout. It was the last inning. The Tigers were up 4—2 with no outs, two men on base, and arguably the most talented little league batter in all of Texas stepping up to the plate.

Suddenly, the sound of Metallica's "For Whom the Bell Tolls" filled the air at a deafening level. Alex glanced back toward the dugout and saw Detective Loffland holding a speaker box over his head, smiling at Alex, with sunglasses on and a cigarette dangling from his lip. Alex couldn't help but grin and throw him the international hand gesture for "rock on."

Then, Alex did something that no one, including Dwayne, expected. He walked to the left side of the plate. He decided to switch hit . . . batting lefty. It was the ultimate middle finger to the Mariners, as if to say, "You're so bad, I can beat you from both sides of the plate."

Alex raised the stakes further by raising his right arm and pointing to the center field wall. The crowd leapt to their feet, yelling as loudly as they could, cheering, going crazy . . .

The backup pitcher for the Mariners was visibly shaken. He looked over at his coach, Pastor Jim, for direction. Alex could see Pastor Jim mouth the words, "walk him." This pissed Alex off.

Alex watched out of the corner of his eye for the catcher, who moved a couple of feet to his right to throw the ball out of reach. The crowd booed, knowing full well what this meant. They didn't have an opportunity to get too terribly upset, because as the pitcher went into his windup, Alex took two steps forward and drilled the ball, sending it precisely where he'd pointed . . . over the center field wall . . . left-handed.

And just like *that*, it was 7–2.

The Tigers weren't done there, though. The entire team wanted to leave their mark that day, and so they did. The Tigers went on to score twelve more runs that inning. Their bats were on fire. The crowd stayed on their feet the entire time, jumping and yelling.

The score was 19–2 going into the bottom of the last inning. The Mariners had given up. You could see it in the way they swung their bats. They just wanted to go home. The first two batters went down immediately.

Noah was the third at bat. Alex was playing first base, and could tell that Noah still had some spark left in him. He knew that the last thing they needed was for the Mariners to get a new burst of energy and make this a game again. Noah had to go down.

But he didn't. He drilled a beautiful line drive halfway up the outfield wall. It made a thundering *POP!* as it hit. Ace Dale was playing center field and dashed to get the ball. Noah had already rounded first by the time Ace got to it. Ace threw the ball to his cutoff man, Jackson, as Noah made his way around third base.

Alex sprinted to cover home, moving the catcher out of the way. Everyone knew this was something Alex had to handle. Jackson threw the ball as fast as he could to Alex at home. He grabbed it from the air and dropped his shoulder a split second before Noah arrived. They both braced for impact. Noah and Alex collided in a spectacular fashion, disappearing into a massive cloud of dust.

Dave the umpire hovered over them until the dust cloud dissipated and he had a clear line of sight, at which point he could see that Alex's body had completely shielded Noah from making any contact whatsoever with the base.

"YOU'RE OUT!" Dave yelled.

The crowd went wild.

"What are you, high, ump?" Pastor Jim came charging out of the dugout, screaming at Dave. "I could see it from here! HE WAS SAFE!"

"Well as a matter of fact, I am high, Pastor," Dave the umpire responded. "But your little douchebag kid never touched the plate."

The crowd had quieted, and many were waiting against the fence in anticipation. They were waiting for the word "ballgame" to be yelled, marking the finish.

Dwayne, Russ, Tommy, Steve, Detective Loffland, and two police officers staggered out onto the field. Pastor Jim's two assistant coaches came out as well. Everyone was screaming at one another. Noah stood beside his dad, and Alex stood beside Dwayne while they all carried on.

"He wasn't safe, Pastor," Dave grunted in a frustrated tone. "I was right there."

"Face it, Pastor," Dwayne said firmly. "Your time is over in this town. You need to accept it. Your kid is out. You're on the losing side now. People are tired of taking shit from arrogant, out-of-touch, social-climbing assholes like you. That's what this crowd represents. This is an uprising. Suck my balls. We're in charge now."

"You listen to me, you son of a bitch," Pastor Jim lunged forward, poking his finger into Dwayne's chest.

And that was all it took. No sooner had his finger pushed against Dwayne's shirt, than the barbs from a Taser gun shot forward at several hundred MPH, hitting Pastor Jim right in the lips. Thousands of volts of electricity sent his body into convulsions, causing him to fall over onto home plate and flop around like a fish.

Dwayne was amused to see it was Detective Loffland standing behind him holding the Taser gun, smiling. "Well, I'm sure we all saw that assault take place," the detective said. "Thank God I was here to step in with nonlethal force."

"Oh my God, are you kidding me?" Noah cried out. "He didn't do anything! You guys are assholes! Somebody call an ambulance!" Noah unleashed a long line of impressively descriptive profanities at Dwayne and Detective Loffland.

"How do those things work?" Alex asked one of the officers.

The officer pulled out his Taser gun. "You just push this little safety button, which activates the charge," he said as he demonstrated to Alex. "Then you pull the trigger, just like a gun. Here, try it out."

Alex clicked the safety button on the Taser, pointed it at Noah, and pulled the trigger. The Taser barbs stuck into Noah's ankle—the high-voltage shock sending him to flop around next to his dad.

One of the Mariners' assistant coaches stepped forward.

"Hey! You can't—"

WHAP! Taser barbs, right on the cheek.

Dave the umpire looked around, waiting to see if anyone else cared to step forward and object to his ruling on the field. No one did. "BALLGAME!" he shouted, throwing his arms into the air.

The Tigers poured out of the dugout and ran to embrace their coaches. The fences along the baselines were incapable of holding back the crowd, collapsing as thousands of fans came stampeding onto the field. TJ and Jackson hoisted a large cooler full of water and dumped it over Dwayne's back. He laughed it off, grabbing them, squeezing them, and giving them high fives. Media cameras surrounded the team, shouting questions and congratulating the boys. Beers went flying through the air everywhere, cutting through the fog of pot smoke that was quickly forming.

Dwayne blew his whistle and called the Tigers in for a final post-game speech. The boys gathered round, hugging each other with ear-to-ear grins.

"Well, soldiers," he announced to his team as they all took to their knees around him, "you accomplished something out here today that you'll carry with you for the rest of your lives. Everyone said you couldn't win, and you metaphorically grabbed them by the ears and smashed their faces into a steaming pile of dog shit . . . and I couldn't be more proud."

The boys fist-bumped each other. The parents were arm in arm, feeling joy for their children's hard work paying off so fully, but also secretly happy that they wouldn't be subjected to the abhorrent language of the coaches any longer.

"I want you men to learn a lesson from this season. I want you to know that, throughout your life, people will pretend to be better than you. They're just insecure assholes. Don't believe them. Throughout life, people will try to give you overwhelming amounts of shit. Don't take it. Throughout life, people will lie to you, cheat you, do wrong to you, try and fit you into a box that you know, deep down, you don't belong in. Be who you're supposed to be . . . and bring the baseball bat of justice down upon them."

One last time, Dwayne looked each player in the eye. "I want to thank you boys for bringing honor back to the game. At the end of the day, honor is what it's all about. So, one last time, warriors. WHAT DO TIGERS DO?"

You could hear the response for miles.

When the team returned to the dugout to pack up their things, Dwayne told his assistant coaches to get babysitters; it was time for a five-star dinner.

Russ and Tommy, with their families, signed hundreds of autographs along the way to the parking lot. Steve and Dwayne hung back, taking it all in, signing posters, newspapers, napkins, and breasts. Their wives and kids had gone ahead of them with a police escort.

They stood at their cars, parked beside each other, and shared a couple of beers while answering questions for the media and fans. Finally, it was time to go. Steve was fading fast from the day's overwhelming excitement and ongoing police company. In an effort to help his weary friend, Dwayne carried Steve's son's baseball bag to the parking lot and tossed it into the backseat of Steve's Prius. When he did, the bag accidentally knocked a jacket down that had been hanging in the rear.

Three envelopes full of pictures fell out of the jacket onto the seat. They were the same kind of pictures as before, but more graphic . . . and this time, it was clear who the two guys with Estelle were.

Dwayne froze. It was like he'd been kicked in the chest. He looked across at Steve.

"Jesus, Dwayne . . . I tried to warn you. I'm sorry. Fuck . . . it's just that . . . I . . . Jesus, Dwayne, they were boning her for months, man . . . I just didn't want you to get hurt."

Dwayne closed his eyes, holding in the screams. He knew that there were still dozens of cameras pointed at him, unaware of what he'd just seen. He couldn't let the world know. He simply tapped on the roof of the Prius and smiled.

"I'll see you tonight," he told Steve.

64.

Dwayne fiddled with the MP3 in his Audi before leaving Jenny Field. He finally found what he was looking for: "Civil War" by Guns N' Roses. The intro to the song was a scene from *Cool Hand Luke* starring the great Paul Newman. He loved that movie. He loved this song. He turned it up loud.

Dust and gravel shot out from behind his car as he fishtailed out of the parking lot. He headed straight for his office warehouse. It was time to execute the "just in case" plan.

Dwayne pulled into the warehouse, which was closed for the weekend. He needed to get his head together before he did anything else. The car came to a screeching stop once inside the large metal building. The light disappeared as the massive garage door closed behind him.

He whipped out his phone and texted Uzi.

DWAYNE: Time to put the plan in place.

UZI: No shit, brah? I thought things seemed fine.

DWAYNE: That's the problem with this town, homie. Just when you think things are going fine, your friends are fucking you over.

UZI: Damn, brah . . . That shit is cold. I hope it works out for you.

DWAYNE: It will. I'm a fucking Jedi knight. It's everyone else you should be worried about. You get my new passports, IDs, and credit cards?

UZI: Damn straight, brah, just got 'em back. I'll drop 'em in your mailbox.

DWAYNE: Cool. Also, I bought an RV at Westside RV a few days back. I need you to pick it up for me ASAP and park it in my backyard, then hang out inside it until I say otherwise. Just bring the ID stuff then. You'll be well compensated.

UZI: I'm on it, boss. You cool?

DWAYNE: I'm cool.

UZI: Cool.

DWAYNE: Oh, one more thing . . . Put a pound of good weed in the RV.

UZI: What kind of good, brah? The knock you down and drool shit, or the semifunctional wicked body-buzz shit?

DWAYNE: I'll take the shit for when your awesome and talented kid gets fucked over in baseball, so you kill the coaching staff and take over the team, then you take revenge on society snobs and financial bullies by killing a half dozen or so of them, then you lead two metro police forces on a massive car chase dressed as Batman, go to jail, become a national hero, become buddies with the same cops who are trying to catch you, win a baseball championship that's covered on every major media outlet in the world, then find out your wife was fucking two of your best friends, before killing a few more people, changing your identity, and abandoning everything you know to start a new life in an RV. So, whatever weed that is, I'll take it.

UZI: That's the drool shit.

DWAYNE: I'm in.

UZI: On it.

DWAYNE: See you tonight.

Dwayne cranked up "Folsom Prison Blues," and assembled the necessary tools in his trunk. Johnny Cash sang about shooting a man just to watch him die. Dwayne understood.

Once finished at the rear of his car, Dwayne went up the stairs to his office, moving the credenza by his desk to the side, exposing his wall safe. This was where he kept his rainy day fund. It was about to start pouring.

Over the years, he'd managed to stash $247,000 into the safe, just a few thousand at a time. Dwayne stuffed all of the money into an old baseball bag, then made a small cut on his finger and wiped his blood on the wall beside the safe. He pushed the desk over and left the door to the safe open before leaping down the stairs and jumping back inside his Audi.

He picked up his phone and texted the guys.

DWAYNE: You guys ready to start the celebration?

RUSS: Ready to start? Are you serious? I started two weeks ago. I'm on 3 hits of acid, 2 hits of ecstasy, and a couple of 8-balls right now. I'm wearing nipple clamps and hanging from a trapeze bar over my bed while Jade electrocutes my balls.

TOMMY: No doubt, D! The party is rolling at my joint too! Glad you didn't call, cuz I've got a ball-gag in my mouth! Kelly just poured a whole jar of honey on me and she's spanking my big black ass with a ping-pong paddle.

DWAYNE: Jesus . . . Steve? What's up with you?

STEVE: Judith and I are drinking wine coolers, listening to NPR, and playing Strip Scrabble . . . She's already naked. So yeah, we're partying too.

RUSS: There goes my boner.

TOMMY: Dammit. Mine too.

STEVE: Mine is flying high.

RUSS: I'll need steel wool to wash that image off my brain.

DWAYNE: Great. Anyhow, I had an idea. Let's meet up at the ballpark before dinner to make one last memory. Just the guys. We'll meet up with the wives afterward. 8 tonight sound good?

RUSS: Yup.

TOMMY: Yup.

STEVE: Yup.

DAVE: Can I com two/

DAVE: Damit. Why wont qwestion mark work/

STEVE: You have to push the shift key.

DAVE: /

STEVE: No, push them at the same time.

DAVE: //????????????????

STEVE: You need to let go sooner.

RUSS: What the fuck? Why is this retard on our thread again? And how old is your goddamn phone that it has a shift key?

DAVE: yu guys kepe textin me.

DWAYNE: Shit. My bad. I just texted the old text chain again. Fine, Dave. You can come too. See you guys there at 8.

DAVE: ?

RUSS: Idiot.

DAVE: Fcuk you.

Dwayne set his phone down in the passenger seat. It continued to quack, but he didn't have time to keep texting. He hauled ass to his house to get showered and ready.

Dozens of media vans and hundreds of reporters and fans were camped out on Dwayne's lawn when he pulled into his driveway. He drove through the gate to his backyard, closing it behind him. He needed to hurry.

The RV was already out back, waiting for him. Uzi slid the back window open.

"Wassup, Big D?" Uzi whispered. "Yo, dog, this thing is *sweet!* I stashed the weed in the overhead storage by the driver's seat."

"Thanks, dude," Dwayne replied, "Here's what I need you to do…"

Dwayne proceeded to tell Uzi about his plan for the next few days. Uzi listened intently and agreed to his role.

Dwayne and Uzi shook hands, and Dwayne went inside his house. Alex was watching ESPN with the babysitter in the living room. He was deeply proud of his son. He knew that the young Jedi in training was going to be fine with the changes that were coming.

"*Pssssst!*" Estelle called out from behind him. She stood in the doorway to their bedroom, wearing nothing but a Catwoman mask and a sinister grin.

Dwayne had forgiven Estelle before he'd ever even seen the pictures of her having wild orgy sex with people he thought were his friends. The pictures were from another life, as far as he was concerned. It was a nonissue for the two of them. But a reckoning of sorts was coming for his so-called friends.

With or without clothes, Estelle still gave him butterflies every time he saw her. She was the love of his life. He knew that would never change, especially now that they had a baby Jedi on the way.

Dwayne glanced down at his watch. It was 7:03. *Fuck it*, he thought. He had plenty of time.

65.

The ballpark was pitch black when the guys pulled into the vacant parking lot. Beer cans and Batman masks littered the ground as far as the eye could see. The assistant coaches and Dave parked next to Dwayne's black Audi. They peered inside. It was empty.

"Come on in, boys!" a voice called out from inside Jenny Field. "The Temple of the Baseball Gods awaits you!"

The guys all looked around. They could barely see a thing. Russ pulled his coke contraption from his pocket and snorted, then cracked a beer and lit a cigarette.

"I had no idea that my nipples were such an erogenous zone," Russ said as he tried to focus in the darkness. "But Jesus . . . if they weren't just two bloody little nubs right now, I'd be rubbing the shit out of them."

"I hear ya, bro!" Tommy laughed. "I have honey solidifying in my crack right now. I swear, every time I take a step, I rip a handful of ass hair out! But it feels so good, bro! So good!"

"Don't get me started, guys!" Steve joined in awkwardly. "I mean . . . Judith kept trying to spell words that she *knew* weren't really words in Scrabble, and then she would steal a handful of my letter tiles and hide them in the fold of her stomach by her belly button, while we're both sitting there totally naked, and it was just like . . . *so sexy!* I mean, seriously! It was getting crazy at my place!"

"That's fucking toxic, bro," Russ said as he winced. "The thought of your wife naked makes me want to stick a hot bayonet in my eyes, then cut my dick off."

Steve looked at Tommy for support. Tommy just shook his head.

Dave sparked up a joint and passed it to Steve in sympathy.

"Meet me at the pitcher's mound!" the impatient voice yelled again. "Stop fucking around!"

The four of them made their way inside. The wind had picked up, and the sound of blowing trash added an eerie Eastern European feeling to things. Russ fidgeted with the gate on the chain-link fence until it gave way, and the members of the Jedi Alliance walked toward the mound.

"Where you at, Big D?" Tommy shouted. His question echoed throughout the ballpark. "This shit is freaky, man!"

There was no response.

The men could see nothing in the imposing darkness. The wind was howling, blowing dirt from the baselines into their eyes. They stood at the pitcher's mound, confused and unsettled.

And still there was silence.

"Real funny, Dwayne!" Russ piped up. "Let's get rolling, bro! We've got reservations!"

A shadowy figure carrying a baseball bat emerged from behind home plate and began to walk briskly toward the guys at the pitcher's mound. The dim moonlight bounced off the jet-black costume. The long dark cape blew out several feet to the side in the gusts.

"Dwayne?" Tommy asked, half scared and half joking. "Is that you, bro?"

Dwayne approached the pitcher's mound slowly and then stopped between Russ and Tommy, pulling two envelopes from inside his costume. He handed one to each of them. "I come bearing gifts," Dwayne he said in a gruff, ominous tone.

"Thanks, man! You scared the shit outta me for a second there." Russ ripped open his envelope. "I didn't know we were exchanging gifts! I didn't . . . I . . . oh, fuck."

Russ never had another thought flow through his mind. Dwayne put all of his batting knowledge into play on that first lightning-quick swing. He stepped forward and drove the bat with his hips on a level plane, swinging mightily, hitting Russ squarely on the tip of his nose, pushing it into his skull. The others could literally *feel* the sound of the crunch. A massive spray of blood shot from Russ's face and onto Steve's as Russ staggered backward before his knees collapsed. That one swing had caved his entire face in, shattering every bone above his neck.

The men stood silently, listening to the blood spurt from Russ's head as he twitched and convulsed on the ground. Tommy raised his eyes to Dwayne. "Jesus, Dwayne," Tommy pleaded. "Come on, man . . . You know I'd never . . . I mean, you know, things were different then! Come on, man! Please! I . . ."

Tommy stopped midsentence, turned, and took off running for the gate. Dwayne angled himself sideways, reared back the baseball bat, and hurled it at Tommy as he ran. The bat looked like a medieval axe thrown in battle, turning end over end as it flew threw the air, seeking out its target. It found it perfectly.

The bat struck Tommy directly in the temple, just as he had turned to glance back and see if Dwayne had given chase. Tommy fell to the ground and rolled. He was unable to pull himself to his feet before Dwayne reached him.

"Stand up and accept your fate like a man," Dwayne growled. "I'll give you a chance to die with honor."

Tommy remained on his knees, pleading with Dwayne to spare him. Dwayne wasn't going to ask twice. He walked around behind Tommy and delivered his second brilliant swing of the evening. He swung the bat so hard that the top of Tommy's head actually came off, landing deep in the outfield. His body remained upright for a few moments, with his brain partially exposed, and then finally fell forward with blood pouring out like a teapot.

Steve bent over and threw up.

"Holy shit, Dwayne!" Dave chuckled. "That was *awesome!*"

Dwayne's chest was heaving in and out. The mask covered most of his face, but you couldn't mistake the raw and visceral anger in his eyes. He walked briskly over to Russ's collapsed body. "What's that, you mother*fucker?*" Dwayne was fierce. "Do you really think you can fuck over the world with your bullshit hedge fund operation, then come to my house and *fuck my wife?* You hairy little piece of shit!"

He raised the bat up over his head, then swung it down with full force into the cavity that once was Russ's face. He repeated the action, until everything that once existed above Russ's neckline was obliterated into tiny chunks of blood, bone, and brain matter.

The mask of the Batman costume dripped red in the moonlight, as Dwayne then turned to Tommy's body again. He proceeded to destroy Tommy's face even worse than he'd done to Russ. "Goddammit, Tommy!" Dwayne growled, bringing the bat down time and time again. "I thought you were different, you superficial fuck!"

Dwayne paused, and then staggered around the infield for several minutes as Steve and Dave the umpire looked on in disbelief. He was snarling incoherently, gripping the blood-soaked bat tightly, leaving a crimson trail everywhere he paced.

He finally walked over to home plate and ripped his mask off, then stared up at the sky angrily while shaking his bat.

"YOU THINK YOU CAN DESTROY ME?!" he screamed until veins on his forehead popped out. *"I'M A MOTHERFUCKING SABERTOOTH CAPED CRUSADER JEDI GRANDMASTER NINJA WARRIOR MOTHERFUCKER, YOU SON OF A BITCH!"*

Just then, as if right on cue, all of the lights on the baseball field lit up. Dwayne's scream toward the skies didn't even have a chance to echo. His eyes went wide. He looked all around. Everything seemed to be spinning. The green of the grass was almost electric, offset only by the brightness of the blood that flowed from Russ and Tommy and was splashed all over Steve's face. It had all been so dark just seconds before.

BANG! The door to the refreshment stand was suddenly kicked open. From deep in the shadows, the figure of Detective Loffland emerged.

The detective began clapping slowly as he walked along the fence line to the gate, and made his way out onto the field.

"Well done, Dwayne," he said. "Well done."

66.

Dwayne was panicking inside. His heart raced wildly, nearly beating out of his chest. He was still breathing heavily. He was drenched in blood and holding a murder weapon. He wanted to run.

He had a baby on the way . . . and what would Alex think?

Suddenly, calmness overtook him. He took a deep breath, and then slowly exhaled. Something inside told him that this wasn't the end for him. He was a dark knight. He was a Jedi. He was still in control.

"That was quite a performance there, Dwayne," Detective Loffland said. "I was wondering how long it would take before you took a bat to Russ's skull. I have to admit that I was a little bit surprised to see you take out Tommy, though. And with such savagery! Damn! I kept thinking that Steve would be next . . . but maybe you're not done, huh? Did I interrupt?"

"Whoa, whoa, whoa," Steve jumped in. "I've always been a faithful friend to Dwayne. Don't lump me in with those guys."

"It's true," Dwayne added. "Steve has always been a—wait, how in the hell did you know it was me, Detective? How did you know to come here?"

"The NSA, Homeland Security, the Patriot Act. You pick," Detective Loffland smirked. "I've been reading your texts from the beginning. You guys fucking party, bro. No doubt about it. You see . . . at first I was just reading Dave's texts, because he's been dealing drugs forever, and he's such a blistering dumbass. Then I was tipped off about Russ's massive cocaine intake, so I started reading his texts too. And then, BOOM. You guys start killing people left and right, and I'm reading the whole thing as it's happening. It was pretty sweet. The thing is, though . . . these guys were all major assholes. Most of them had screwed over the police department at one point or another. I never felt the need to tell anyone what I knew. I know it sounds strange coming from a guy in a police uniform, but I didn't give a shit.

It was vigilante justice. I wanted to see how far you'd take it. And holy fuck, you didn't disappoint."

Dwayne looked over at Russ's dead body and yelled. "I told you, dumbass! *Stop texting!*"

"He's done texting now, Dwayne," the detective pointed out. "But back to your buddy Steve here. Do you ever get the feeling he'll have a hard time keeping his mouth shut about all of this? I mean, you're onto something *huge* here, man! Think of the *good* that you could do if you *never got caught!*"

Dwayne paused and cocked his head sideways. He had no idea where the detective was going with things.

"Have you really thought this through, Big D?" Loffland continued. "I mean, what's your next move here, chief?"

"Well, I have to admit," Dwayne said. "You showing up here makes me a tad unsure of my future, but I do have a plan."

"Let's hear it."

"Okay, well, I was going to bash in Russ and Tommy's skulls and bury the bodies where they'd never be found, then load up Estelle and Alex into an RV I just bought, and disappear forever. I faked a break-in at my office earlier today and stole all of the cash from my safe. I left some of my own blood on the wall to make it look like I was killed in the robbery. Also, I know that Russ has a few million bucks stashed in a safe in his closet, so I figured I'd text his wife to get her out of the house in a few minutes. Then, I'd wipe some of his blood around his closet, take his loot, and haul ass with a sizable fortune. With all of the people that have gone missing recently, I figured no one would ever find out."

"Wow," Detective Loffland nodded. "That's not bad. Let me ask you, all those people that went missing—where are they? Are they really buried here like the texts implied?"

"Yup. Under every base. Except Pete Rearden. I ground him up and spread him around. It turns out that pieces of shit in the hands of a lawn artist really can make a ballpark look better. You can't tell me this place doesn't look amazing."

Detective Loffland chuckled and nodded.

"But seriously, Dwayne. What the fuck happened inside your head?" the detective asked. "You went completely primal in a way I've never seen."

Dwayne gathered his thoughts for a moment.

"In the words of the great H. L. Mencken, sir, 'Every normal man must be tempted, at times, to spit on his hands, hoist the black flag, and begin slitting throats.' Well, I was tempted, and I acted on it. These were awful people, Detective. They pushed people around. They destroyed their lives to make themselves feel better. No one was ever going to stop them. And *baseball*, man . . . the things they were doing to the game I loved, it just wasn't fair. Someone had to bring some balance to the universe . . . some justice."

"You decided to spit on your hands and start slitting throats."

"Yes. Well, kind of. I preferred a bat."

The detective spun around and looked over at Steve and Dave the umpire again. They were dumbfounded. He scratched his head before turning to address Dwayne again.

"I like you, Dwayne," the detective said sternly to Dwayne. "I'm normally not too big on serial killers, but you're a pretty good mother fucker, bro. I like the way you take out the trash. We could do big things together. We just need to tie up a couple of loose ends first."

"Like what?" Dwayne asked.

Detective Loffland whipped around, pulled his .40 caliber police-issue pistol from his holster, and put a bullet between Steve's eyebrows. Steve flew backward, his feet flipping over his head, doing a complete reverse somersault. He was killed instantly.

"That was awesome!" Dave yelled. "I had no idea that people could do so many cool things when they died! I mean, shit, the top of Tommy's head—it went all the way to right field like a damn Frisbee! And that was totally sweet, but it wasn't near as cool as Ricky Dale! Man, you guys shoulda seen that one! And Steve! Oh, man, Steve just did a backflip! At least tell me to get my camera out next time so I can record this shit!"

"Get your camera out, Dave," Detective Loffland smiled.

"Nice! Thank you!" Dave the umpire said with joy before watching Detective Loffland's gun raise toward him. "Aw, man—"

The detective put three bullets in the middle of Dave's chest. Dave stumbled backward a few feet but remained upright. He had a confused look on his face.

"This sucks, bro," Dave muttered. "Everyone else got to do cool shit before they died. I just—"

"Give it a second, Dave," the detective interrupted. "Your body is too stupid to realize it's been shot. It'll figure it out in a second."

"Whatever, man," Dave shrugged.

He frowned at Detective Loffland, then fell forward, landing flat on his face.

"There we go," the detective continued. "Okay, so, the loose ends are now tied up."

The detective reached into his pocket and handed Dwayne a cell phone.

"Here," he said. "Take this. Keep it with you always. If I ever need you to help me hoist that black flag, I'll call you. And you'd better answer."

"Are you sure?" Dwayne asked, completely in awe of the detective.

"Yes. I like your style, man. I can't lie. Your methods may be unorthodox, to say the least, but you get results. And at the end of the day, I'm in the results business. So go text Jade, go get that money, and get the fuck out of town. I'll take care of the bodies. And watch the news. I've got a pretty good way to bring some closure for the community. It's goddamn hilarious. I think you'll appreciate it."

Dwayne extended his hand to the detective. He enjoyed their handshakes. He appreciated shaking hands with a good guy who didn't take shit from anyone. He had a feeling he'd see the detective again someday.

As Dwayne turned to walk toward his vehicle after pulling Russ's cell phone from his pocket and soaking some blood up into his shirt, the detective called out to him.

"Dwayne. One last thing. Get a new costume, okay? You're not Batman. You're not a Jedi. You're something bigger . . . something real. The people need someone like you, whether they know it or not. I look forward to seeing what you've come up with when we meet again."

Dwayne nodded and grinned.

"Yes, sir."

67

Russ had often bragged to Dwayne and the others about all of the cash he kept in an unlocked safe in his closet. They never knew whether or not to believe him, though. Dwayne was thrilled to see that he'd been telling the truth.

In a massive steel walk-in safe, behind an impressive collection of multicolored dildos, varying sizes of buttplugs, a pair of solid gold handcuffs, a mountain of cocaine, a large Tupperware container of weed, and several bottles of pills, stood stack after stack of $100 bills. There had to be $15 million. Maybe more. Dwayne grabbed a couple of Jade's designer suitcases, packed the money in, wiped some of Russ's blood around, and headed to the Audi.

He texted Estelle once he was on his way.

DWAYNE: Hi honeybuns.

ESTELLE: Hey there, sugarweenie.

DWAYNE: Remember when I said to be thinking about what you would take with you if we had to haul ass in a flash, cupcake nipples?

ESTELLE: I sure do, babynuts.

DWAYNE: Great, I . . . Wait. Babynuts? What the fuck are babynuts? I have normal-sized nuts.

ESTELLE: Sorry, sweetie. You have great nuts. I was trying to think of something that sounded sexy and delicious about your balls. That was more of a reference to them being shaved . . . hairless, like a baby's nuts.

DWAYNE: Yeah, let's not bring infants into the sex talk, okay, honey? That's just creepy.

ESTELLE: Okay, candysack. Anyhow, yes, I remember you telling me to think about what I'd bring with me. Why?

DWAYNE: Get it all together. Throw Alex's stuff together, too. We leave in 30 minutes.

The media and fans were still camped out in Dwayne's front yard when he whipped back into the driveway. He smiled and waved as he maneuvered the car through them, down his driveway, and into his gated backyard again.

Dwayne jumped out of the Audi, clutched the suitcases full of cash, and knocked on the side door of the RV. Uzi popped out and unlocked the luggage compartments beneath the passenger cabin. Dwayne loaded up the suitcases, and he and Uzi headed inside the house.

For the next several minutes, Dwayne, Estelle, and Uzi loaded the RV with boxes and duffel bags containing only the absolute *most* important items that Dwayne's family had accumulated over a lifetime. It was mostly photo albums, family heirlooms, and clothes.

Shortly after, the gate to the driveway opened, and the black Audi pulled out, stopping in the middle of the crowd. The window rolled halfway down to reveal a smiling Batman. The crowd went crazy.

"You guys remember that little drive I took a few days ago?" Batman yelled from the car, revving his engine.

Everyone screamed and cheered.

"Let's do it again!" he shouted. "Who's coming with me?"

All of the media and fans ran to their vehicles and started their engines. Dwayne's front yard was emptied out in less than a minute.

Dwayne and Estelle watched from their window as Uzi (with a duffel bag full of cash) led more than a hundred cars down the road, out of the neighborhood, and onto the freeway. They ran upstairs and grabbed Alex, who'd fallen asleep watching *SportsCenter* in his bed, and made their way to the RV.

Dwayne, Estelle, and Alex pulled out of the driveway completely undetected in the dark of night, leaving the west side of Fort Worth in their rearview mirror.

68.

"This is Gretchen Lopez with a breaking news flash here on GNN, the Global News Network.

"Dwayne Devero, the everyman hero seen in recent days leading the Dallas and Fort Worth police departments on a high-speed chase while wearing a Batman costume and cursing about the many shortcomings of Dallas Cowboys owner Jerry Jones, the same Dwayne Devero who was then seen coaching his little league baseball team into the history books, is missing and presumed dead, along with his wife, Estelle, and their son, rising baseball sensation Alex Devero."

Dwayne rustled from his sleep as Estelle nudged him. She was pointing at the large HD flat screen that hung in the massive mobile bedroom suite. Dwayne looked and listened intently.

"It appears as though the death toll now sits at thirteen, and is likely to reach sixteen if the fate of Devero and his family turns out as feared. That number includes the other three coaches from Devero's little league baseball team and the head umpire of the league, whose bodies were discovered early this morning beaten, shot, and hacked up in the trunk of the local pastor's new Porsche. Also among the list of the dead in this murder spree is an as-of-yet unidentified elderly woman whose remains were found in a burned out van several days ago, which is believed to be linked to the case, as well as several prominent local citizens that had great impact on the local economy, and one Walmart employee who had zero impact on the economy . . . or life in general. Police are still searching for Chewie, a young orangutan last seen with Devero and his friends. We'll take you now to Todd Beenis, who's live on the scene with the Fort Worth Police Department."

Estelle nibbled on Dwayne's ear, then put her index finger on his chin. She slid her finger down his neck, dragged it softly down his chest, under the covers, and inside his underwear. "Just so you know, my smoldering-hot sex machine," she whispered, "the door is locked, and I'm *reeeally* horny."

God, he loved her.

She climbed on top of him and rode him like an arcade motorcycle game, biting his lip, trying in vain to keep her moans inaudible so as not to alert Alex to the debauchery occurring at the rear of the RV.

"Thanks, Gretchen! Todd Beenis here. I'm live in Fort Worth, Texas, with Fort Worth Police Detective Rick Loffland. Detective, walk us through what's going on here."

"Hi, Todd Penis, well, here's what's——"

"Beenis."

"What?"

"Beenis, not Penis."

"Beenis?"

"Beenis."

"Are you fucking kidding me?"

"No, sir. And we're live."

"Fucking Beenis?"

"Beenis."

"What the fuck kind of name is Beenis?"

"It's Lithuanian. And we're live."

"Like it fucking matters, bro. Anyhow, any second now, you'll be seeing Pastor Jim Harper from the Westside Church of Jesus being led to the courthouse to be arraigned on sixteen counts of murder and one count of animal abduction. A blood-soaked baseball bat and four bodies were found in his vehicle early this morning after police received an anonymous tip. That tip also led us to Jenny Field, a local little league baseball complex, where crime scene investigators are in the process of exhuming several bodies that Pastor Jim Harper is alleged to have killed. We're not sure exactly what his motivation was in any of the killings, except with the Walmart guy, where we're pretty sure the motive was customer service. We've been unable to locate the bodies of Dwayne Devero and his family, but I can tell you that blood was found near an emptied out safe at his office. We fear the worst. He was a good dude."

Detective Loffland took off his hat, showing respect for his fallen friend. He hung his head and closed his eyes.

Estelle and Dwayne stopped in the middle of their booty session and turned to watch the television. They couldn't believe what they were witnessing on the screen. Pastor Jim was being led to a waiting police cruiser in handcuffs, screaming at the police.

Dwayne grinned and rolled Estelle over, climbing on top of her.

"I love you, sugartitties," Dwayne said.

"I love you too, honeyballs," Estelle replied.

Just then, there was a knock on the bedroom door.

"Mom? Dad? Where am I? Or . . . where are we?" Alex called from the other room.

Dwayne turned the television off. A faint sound of cheering came from outside the RV.

"Yeah, babe," Estelle said, turning to Dwayne. "Where the hell are we?"

"Throw some clothes on. I'll show you."

Dwayne, Estelle, and Alex piled out of the RV. They shielded their faces from the sunlight while their eyes adjusted. There was a little league baseball game going on not a hundred feet from them. It had just started.

"I drove all night," Dwayne said. "We're somewhere near El Paso, maybe an hour from the Mexican border. We had to get out of town for our safety, Alex."

Dwayne didn't know how he was going to explain their new life to Alex. He knew he was a good kid, though, and he knew that everything would eventually work out for the best.

"You see, buddy . . . that life we lived . . . it wasn't real," he continued. "It wasn't good for our souls. Everything revolved around the wrong things. I wanted something better for you and the little baby caped crusader your mom has in her belly. I figured we should just start over and do it right this time.

"So, long story short, I bought us an RV. And last night, we just started driving. Right when I started getting too tired to drive anymore, I saw this ballpark here . . . out in the middle of nowhere. It was all lit up, like someone was trying to give me a sign. I just knew right away that this was the spot for us, so I stopped."

Dwayne put an arm around each of them and smiled. They watched one of the young batters make a beautiful swing and drive the ball to the outfield fence. It was an inside-the-park home run. Shortly after, the coach placed that same kid in right field.

A group of dads standing along the fence cursed under their breath.

Dwayne frowned, raised an eyebrow, and then looked down at Alex. Alex smiled up at his dad. Estelle gripped the back of Dwayne's shirt, holding him back from charging the field.

"You folks new in town?" a friendly thirty-something lady asked with a deep Southern drawl. "We've got a great baseball program for kids here."

"My dad's a great coach," Alex told the lady.

"Well, now, that's an amazing coincidence, because as you might have noticed, we could sure use some help with coaching."

A warm smile washed over Dwayne's face.

"Where do I sign up?"

ABOUT THE AUTHOR

Baseball Dads is Matthew S. Hiley's third novel. His first, 2010's *Hubris Falls*, met with much critical acclaim and dealt, in very raw language, with the taboo realities of race, religion, and politics. His second novel, 2011's *The Candidates: Based on a True Country*, is a dark and absurd comedy in which the author takes swipes at the hypocrisy and self-serving nature of those leading the country, as well as the fame whores in reality television.

Hiley's books always contain a strong message. Sure, you may have to wade through some harsh language, crazy sex, and a plethora of drugs to find it. . . . But it's there, and it might just slap you in the face when you're least expecting it.

Hiley was born and raised in Fort Worth, Texas. He and his wife have four children together, along with five dogs, six cats, and two lizards. A terrible musician, a reprehensible fisherman, a less-than-mediocre golfer, and a talentless children's baseball coach, Hiley has found his place in life as a writer whose voice is sharp, witty, and unafraid.